Courting the Dragon Widow

Cloudburst Colorado series, Book 6

Siobhan Muir

ISBN: 1-947221-12-4
ISBN-13: 978-1-947221-12-3

DEDICATION

Dedicated to time and persistence. This story started in 2009 and now sees the light of day in 2019 when there are series to connect to it and characters to support it. Thanks, Universe.

ACKNOWLEDGMENTS

There are many people who have helped me develop this story and I'm so grateful for their help. To the RWA Golden Heart contest readers – thanks so much for telling me my story sucked. You were right and I had a lot of work ahead of me, but it definitely needed that tough love. Cara Michaels, Silver James, and Tina Glasneck, helped me make the blurb really stand out. Thank you to Emily Drew for editing such old and somewhat mismatched writing to make a coherent story. And of course, thank you to my husband George for his help when I got stuck and his patience when I had to edit for hours at a time. I love you, HB! Great thanks to Kris Norris for creating this amazing new cover that truly captures the characters. And thanks to my readers Chris Jones and Jennifer Johnson who really wanted to read a new dragon story. You lit a fire under my butt to get it done.

CHAPTER ONE

"I'm going on a blind date. Across the country."

A month ago it hadn't sounded like such a bad idea. Now Lissandra wondered if she needed to check her sanity.

Moonlight decorated the tops of the trees awakening in the late spring weather and a balmy breeze brought the scents of new grass and flowers. Upstate New York smelled wetter than her home of Cloudburst, Colorado, and despite her misgivings, she enjoyed the flavored humidity.

Lissandra tucked her wings and dropped closer to the ground. According to the coordinates she'd been given, she approached the location of her rendezvous. A rendezvous she'd asked her mother to set up for her with an eligible dragon bachelor.

Solenarra had been skeptical, but Lissandra had stood her ground. *I've mourned my mate for thirty years, and I'm not getting any younger.* She didn't want to spend her life alone and her two daughters needed a male to give them perspective.

"Think of it this way, Mom. Dragons are few and far between these days, and this would give me a chance to have another baby."

Solenarra had narrowed her eyes. "Are you trying to

bribe me with another grandchild, m'dear?"

"Did it work?" Lissandra had winked before she grew sober. "Please, Mom. You know the dragon community better than I do and I'm finally ready to move on. I loved Mikelorrion, but he's gone. I want to find someone new."

Slicing through the air in a sharp turn, Lissandra spiraled down toward the ground, weaving through a small flock of bats enjoying the insects of the eastern forest. The scents of loamy soil, fresh water dripping off the deciduous trees, and the crickets calling bravely in the night tickled her senses. She opened her wings enough to slow until her talons dug into the soft forest floor.

Taking a deep breath, she concentrated on shifting into her human disguise, pulling the magical energy in to complete the transformation. Holding her human shape always felt a little like being stuffed into too-tight jeans, and taking her true form became a joyous release. Her face flattened and she wriggled her nose as everything settled into the disguise. She stretched her face muscles and shoulders, trying to get the fit right despite the initial discomfort.

When she'd settled, she concentrated on the little fold of magical space each dragon carried with them. It was a way to hide their hoard, a small worm-hole to another dimension that allowed them to store things beyond this world. She concentrated on the materialization of her small overnight bag holding clothes for her human body. A thump at her feet made her smile and she hefted the bag before she dug into her pants pocket for the directions to her meeting.

She angled the paper into the moonlight to read the words scrawled across the surface.

"Find the lightning twinned stump in the honeysuckle clearing." She closed her eyes and shook her head. "Yeah, that's specific." She dug through her bag for her cell phone and powered it on as she stuffed it in her pocket. *Worse*

2

comes to worst, I can always text Sole for more specifics.

According to her mother, she'd be meeting Charlorrion Ravenwing, the foster son to honored dragon hero Waltarrion Goldencoat. Everyone in the dragon community had heard of Waltarrion and his great battle with a demon back a hundred and fifty years earlier. It had set off the Great Chicago Fire, but he'd saved the world.

And now I'm attempting a blind-date courtship with Waltarrion's blood son, Denarrion.

At least she could back out if she didn't like him.

A sound intruded on her thoughts and she froze, scanning the forest around her. The crickets had stilled with the presence of something or someone. Lissandra gripped her bag and darted out of the clearing to the darkness of the trees. Her eyes adjusted as she crouched, waiting for the new intruder to arrive.

The sounds of something moving through the underbrush caught her ears and she inhaled slowly, testing the air for different scents. Her dragon senses reacted slower in her human guise, but she could still taste the flavors of the night. Musky scents of white-tailed deer hit her nose just before the unconcerned creatures entered the clearing. The lead male raised an impressive rack for so early in the season as he scanned his domain.

Lissandra snorted. *If I hadn't eaten earlier, you'd make a lovely meal, bucko.*

The sound of her response sent the deer into flight and they disappeared across the clearing as she gathered her things to leave. *Now I just have to figure out where to go.*

She closed her eyes and took another deep breath, sampling the air for the hot, fiery scent of a large predator. Dragons could easily hide amongst the humans because humanity had forgotten the use of its nose. But even in their human guise, dragons gave off the scent of fire, particularly with the flavor of their native rocks or wood.

The scent of a young adult male with the spice of

mahogany and oak wafted out of the woods to her left. She grasped her bag and headed in that direction, hoping she wouldn't have to do some elaborate threat display. *I'm too damn old and too damn tired.*

She stepped to the edge of a new clearing and inhaled. Along with the scent of young male dragon came the fragrance of honeysuckle perfuming the warm evening air. *The honeysuckle clearing, I presume.* A great burned stump split in half by lightning stood beside a glacial boulder, and a man leaned against the boulder, his gaze fixed on her under the light of the crescent moon.

She paused, standing her ground, but refusing to come closer until she could assess who he was or what he wanted. He rose to his feet and stood with his hands loose at his sides, but she smelled his excitement and curiosity.

"May the Mother's Heart always be open to your footsteps." Lissandra spoke in the Old Language of their people, hoping he wasn't too young to know it.

"And may it cradle you in its warm and comforting Halls." Deep, warm compassion filled his voice, encouraging her to feel protected and comfortable immediately.

"Thank you." Despite the urge to believe in him, she approached with caution. Appearances could be deceiving. "Are you Charlorrion Ravenwing?"

"I am. And you must be Lissandra Charforest."

Solenarra had promised Lissandra that Charlorrion and the Goldencoats were on the up-and-up, but Lissandra had endured too many years of training and three demon attacks to trust hearsay. She let her eyes unfocus until her inner Sight showed the world in brilliant Technicolor. Demons often hid within plain view, but her Sight allowed her to discern the hideousness beneath benign exteriors.

And it sucks to be wrong.

She stretched her rusty skills now, filling the glade with her awareness. The male standing in front of the boulder glowed like a brilliant copper penny in the sunlight. His aura swelled upward until the long skull and twisted horns of his true form hung in the air above his human body. Healthy fire magic swirled within him and she breathed a sigh of relief. She pulled her senses back, satisfied, and his ghostly self disappeared.

"I am. It's very nice to meet you, Mr. Ravenwing." She extended her hand to shake with him.

Charlorrion flowed to meet her with fluid grace, his long ponytail brushing his shoulders. "And you. Welcome to Redfield. I'm so glad you agreed to come." His scent filled with relief as he took her hand. "Was the trip rough? It can be kind of tricky traveling at this time of year with the increase in summer travelers."

She shuddered theatrically. "Yeah, tell me about it. I've had a few run-ins with American Airlines." She shook her head. "Some of those pilots think they're Maverick out of Top Gun, I swear."

Charlorrion raised an eyebrow. "Are you serious?"

"Oh, yeah, I've got scars."

"That can't be true." He grinned. "It would've been all over the news."

"You need to pay closer attention to the tabloids. The stories were there, all right, but no one takes them seriously."

He laughed and motioned ahead of him through the trees behind the boulder. She suspected he didn't believe her, but then, neither had the general public except the UFO "kooks". Those people were sharper than most folks believed.

"Come, my wife Torriandra is waiting and will be happy to get you settled for the night." He gestured toward the trees to his left.

"It's very kind of you to put me up while I'm here. I seriously can stay in a hotel or bed & breakfast." Lissandra stretched her legs to keep up with him. While she'd spent a lot of time hiking around the Colorado Rockies, Charlorrion's height made her work a little harder to keep up. His stride equaled two of hers.

"We wouldn't hear of it. Solenarra knew my foster mother and she spoke very highly of you." Again, the relief she'd sensed before came through Charlorrion's scent.

What the hell's that about?

"Well, thanks, I appreciate it. Have you and your wife been married long?"

"Oh, we're just starting out. We've been together for only a couple of centuries." He waved a hand in the air with a warm smile.

"Do you have plans for children?"

"Yes. Sometime in the next fifty years or so we're going to start trying. Torriandra finds it hard to be patient until she reaches maturity. She says she's going to tackle me the night of her first millennium." He laughed. "I told her she can try."

She laughed with him, happy to know she wasn't the only one who enjoyed children. "So you want to have kids?"

"Very much. Torriandra became a local school teacher to spend as much time with them as possible." He glanced down at her over one broad shoulder. "I understand from Solenarra that you had two kids with your mate before he died. How old are they?"

"Yes, two daughters. One's one hundred and the other two hundred." She sighed with a proud smile. "They grow up so quick. Pretty soon they'll be able to shift shape before we know it."

The nighttime noises flowed around them like a river and Lissandra tried to settle herself into their rhythms. Frogs croaked in the wet darkness and the crickets added their lowland songs to the late spring cacophony. Compared to the alpine environment of her Colorado home, the night in Redfield seemed filled with lush life. The humid darkness wrapped around her, stirring memories of her dead husband.

Aw, Mike, you would've loved it here. She still missed him, but the sharpness of his loss had faded.

"Here we are. Welcome to the Ravenwing household."

A house with green shutters and a white picket fence appeared out of the woods. *White picket fence? Really?* They passed through a gate and Charlorrion led her to the back porch. The outside light illuminated a flower garden with tulips and snapdragons blooming gently in the warm evening.

"Torriandra, we're here."

A woman appeared with a big smile and sparkling eyes as Lissandra followed Charlorrion into the mudroom. She stood almost as tall as her husband with her black hair woven into a single braid down the center of her back. A red *bindi* marked the *third eye* between her black brows and her eyes glowed silver-black, like hematite beads.

"Welcome to our home, Ms. Charforest." Torriandra nodded her head. "Did your trip go well?"

"It did, thank you." Lissandra hitched her back a little higher on her shoulder. "And thanks for offering me a place to stay for this…event."

Torriandra shot her husband a quick look before she returned her gaze to Lissandra. "You are very welcome. Come in. Are you hungry?" She led them into the kitchen of the house.

"No, thank you. I grabbed a bite on the way."

"Buffalo burger?" Charlorrion grinned.

"Venison."

"Nice." He gestured toward the stairs, the feathers of a dream-catcher tattoo appearing from under his short sleeve. "Your room is upstairs. Let me show you where to put your things."

"Thanks." She followed him, wondering about the tattoo. "I like your ink. Does it have a special meaning?"

Charlorrion nodded as he led her down the hallway. "Yes, it's to honor the Iroquois Shaman I've known since he was a child. I've worked with his family to keep things in balance."

A curious tension mantled his shoulders and Lissandra bit her lip. *What's he not telling me?* He'd chosen the appearance of the Iroquois, complete with stoicism, but his body language spoke to his apprehension. He showed her the guest room housing a futon frame with a regular mattress on it and brightly colored bedclothes. Lissandra set her bag down on the futon and rolled her shoulders to loosen them.

"Solenarra never mentioned what you do for a living."

Some of the tension faded from his body. "I'm a firefighter." He winked and she laughed. "Works out pretty well. I keep the community safe and don't have trouble with smoke inhalation or burns."

"Nice." She nodded, but some of her misgivings returned. "Thanks again for the place to stay."

"You're welcome. The bathroom is down the hall and there are towels and extra toiletries if you need them. Can I get you anything else? Tea? Coffee?"

"No, thank you. That's enough for now. I'm just going to get into bed and rest before, well, tomorrow." She rubbed her arms to dispel the feeling that she'd missed something important.

"Don't worry. Everything will be fine. And I think you'll really like Denarrion." Charlorrion hesitated like he wanted to say more.

"I hope so. I mean, this seemed like a good idea a month ago, when I finally felt ready to face the world again." She shrugged. "I wanted to see if I could find someone to love again." She shot a look around the unfamiliar room. "But now I'm having a few second thoughts. Think I'm crazy?"

He tilted his head. "Perhaps, but that doesn't mean

taking this chance isn't a good idea. Sometimes making a simple change in your routine helps everyone heal from losses."

She couldn't help but feel like he meant something other than her widow status. "I can see that. I loved my husband and for a while, I couldn't imagine loving anyone else. But ultimately, I don't want to be alone and I want my children to have a father-figure in their lives."

He nodded. "Give Denarrion a chance and see how it goes. He's a good guy once you get to know him."

Once I get to know him? Why wouldn't I like him first off?

She didn't voice the questions as she nodded. "One day at a time, right? As if I could choose to skip days." She snorted. "Thanks again for the room. I'm going to call home and get some rest. See you all in the morning."

Charlorrion nodded with a smile. "Good night, Lissandra."

"Night."

Lissandra closed the door behind him and slowly relaxed, letting her breath flow out with her tension. They'd welcomed her and she had a safe place to stay, but these dragons were essentially strangers. She'd never been shy about meeting new people, but there was something off about this whole event. She couldn't put her finger on what seemed so wrong, though.

No use worrying until I have the whole story. Tomorrow would be soon enough to figure things out.

She nodded sharply and got undressed before fishing out her cell phone to call home.

"Charforest residence."

"Hey, Luce. How was your day?"

"Mom!" The joy in her oldest daughter's voice warmed Lissandra's heart. "It was an okay day. I missed you. Even more now that you're not here to read us a story."

"I know, but Solenarra should be able to do that."

"Yeah, but she's not as good at the voices as you are."

Lissandra laughed. "It's a gift."

Lucenarra giggled. "That's a good one, Mom. How are you doing? Did you meet the guy yet?"

Lissandra sighed. "Not yet. I just got here. I'll see him tomorrow."

"Will you send us a picture on the phone so we can see what he looks like?" Luce's voice rose in excitement. "Or you could put it on Facebook. Then we could see him."

"Since when do you have a Facebook account, Luce?"

"Oh, I don't, but I see the things you post in Sole's feed." Her daughter sounded smug.

"Sweet Goddess. I hope she's there with you when you're looking at her stuff. You know, to explain it." Lissandra rubbed a hand over her face.

"I don't think anyone can explain humans, Mom."

Lissandra sighed. "There is that."

"The good news is we could Skype with you and your new beau, and then we could hear his voice."

"Luce, he's not my beau yet." Lissandra shook her head. "But I wanted to call and tell you I love you. Will you please hand the phone to Kressendra? I want to tell her goodnight, too."

"Okay, Mom. I love you and I hope the guy's really cute."

Lissandra laughed again. "I'll let you know. I love you, too, Luce."

"Night, Mom."

"Night."

There was some squabbling and a few odd sounds while the dragonets passed the phone between each other, but in the end Lissandra's youngest came on the line.

"Hello?"

"Hey, Kress."

"Hi, Mom. I miss you."

"Aw, I miss you too, *sa garren*. How was your day?" Lissandra couldn't help but smile.

"It was okay. We made a bunch of crocheted blankets for the homeless shelter and gave them out. Everyone said they were so impressed that I could crochet, but you taught me that like twenty years ago. It's not that big a deal, right?"

Lissandra snorted. "It is for most humans who look as young as you do. But for dragons? Not so much."

"Huh. Okay. How was your trip out east? Did you see a lot of cool migratory birds on the way?"

"Not this time, and it was dark when I got here. I just wanted to tell you I made it okay and I love you."

"I love you, too, Mom. When are you gonna meet your new guy?"

Despite the premise of her trip, the idea of a new man in her kids' life made her heart clench. "Let's not get ahead of ourselves. I'll meet Denarrion tomorrow."

"I know he's the right one, Mom. Dad told me so."

Lissandra's eyebrows went up even though her daughter couldn't see them. "He did? When?"

"Today during my nap. He said you would find a new dad for us and he'd make everything better."

Goddess, I hope that's true. Lissandra didn't believe in fairytales. Even if she was a dragon.

"We'll see. But you need to get to bed. It's late. So I love you. Good night, sleep tight, don't let the bedbugs bite."

"Eww! I let the cat eat bedbugs." She paused for a giggle before her voice grew serious. "But you are gonna meet him tomorrow, right, Mom?"

"Yep. A deal's a deal, and I said I'd be there."

"Promise?"

Lissandra frowned, wondering why her daughter seemed so intent on assuring her agreement. "Promise."

"Good. I love you, Mom."

"I love you, too, Kress. Good night."

Lissandra ended the call and lay back in the bed, her mind going over her daughter's words. The closer this trip had come, the more both her kids had said stuff like this, even citing their deceased father. She'd like to discount it all, but she understood the Goddess too well to ignore it. *Why is he sending me messages now, almost thirty years late?*

Something buzzed a warning outside her awareness and she couldn't shake the feeling she might have stepped into a bigger mess than she was capable of straightening out. *At least the girls are safe.* Thank the Goddess for small favors. Now she just had to face whatever came on this extended blind date.

CHAPTER TWO

"Mudfucker, sonuvaprick!"

Denarrion Goldencoat snarled at the chair slowly emerging out of oak and tried not to break the tools he held in his hands. His frustration made him particularly clumsy today and he didn't need to add to it by breaking his favorite equipment.

A fucking blind date. He took a deep breath and closed his eyes. *Essentially an arranged marriage.* Well, not yet, but close enough.

The breathing lessened some of his fury and he returned to the chair. When he damn near snapped one of the back-support rods, he set the tools aside with exaggerated gentleness and took a step back. Destroying the chair would only piss him off more, no matter how cathartic the destruction might be.

He retreated to the work sink to wash his hands and the water soothed some of his angst. He dried his hands and pulled his glasses off to rub his eyes. He didn't really need them, but he'd been told they made him look educated and scholarly. They certainly brought him plenty of women. The ladies couldn't seem to resist the geeky charm of a bespectacled man with a Brooklyn accent, even out here in

Redfield.

The neatly trimmed mustache and goatee doesn't hurt either. He snorted, laughing at himself as he grabbed a broom to sweep up the chips of wood he carved that morning.

Denarrion enjoyed his fair share of women. At just over a thousand years old, he'd cultivated the skill for attracting a willing partner whenever the urge came. And still managed to have no love-children out there.

And thank the Mother for that.

He had no interest in a family or marriage. His parents' relationship illustrated everything wrong with having a long-term mate, and he had no desire to follow their example.

Which is why this blind date is such a stupid idea.

Denarrion loved carving furniture, skiing in some of the gnarliest resorts around the world, shark diving, and jazz music. His interests didn't include blind dates with dragon widows so he could make little dragons with her. *Or living forever in a loveless marriage like Mom and Walter.* Ever since his father destroyed the last demon in a near fatal assault as Chicago burned around them—ever hear of the Great Chicago Fire?—his parents had been uncomfortable roommates.

Fuck that! I'm not gonna mate with someone just because it's my duty.

Sawdust wafted around him in lazy plumes, making him sneeze as he stared out the window. His father insisted it was time he found a mate. *Yeah, so I can bring more dragons into the world to defend against the Underworld demons.* Waltarrion Goldencoat used to be a highly respected and decorated warrior of the dragon race.

Heavy on the used to *part.*

Walter's highest priority had always been protection of the planet and he reminded his son of this, sometimes monthly. According to him, finding a mate and making more dragons equated the utmost importance. But the rigid beliefs on mating for the good of the species turned Denarrion's stomach.

Too bad he'd learned why he shouldn't defy his father the hard way. So, he avoided Waltarrion instead.

I'm not running, I've a found a peaceful solution.

Denarrion shook his head, ignoring the stink of the lie even when he hadn't uttered it aloud. He pushed away from the sink and took his time cleaning up the floor, allowing the scents of the wood to cool some of his anxiety. Working with wood and creating something beautiful from it gave him his greatest satisfaction. He'd structured his life around that kind of pleasure.

But that's all over now, isn't it? He swept up and dumped the sawdust into the large compost bin before going back for more. *What if this Widow from Colorado doesn't like furniture? What if she's just as rigid as Walter?*

Given his father's approval, there was a better than even chance the Widow from Colorado agreed with Walter's views on how dragons needed to behave. Denarrion didn't mind staying in his camouflaged shape. He enjoyed the pleasures to be had in human form, but he resented being told how he should or shouldn't act as a dragon amongst humans. No woman, no matter how beautiful or sexually attractive would influence him.

He'd just finished packing up his tools when his cell phone rang with the distinctive "buh-buh, buh-buuuuh...buh-buh-buh-buuuuh" of Beethoven's Fifth Symphony. Charlorrion's ringtone.

The Widow from Colorado must've arrived.

Had she brought her brats with her? Mother of All, he hoped she wasn't all about having more children to "further the great dragon race among humans." He didn't care what his parents said about the wonderful gift of children. He wanted nothing to do with little kids when he was supposed to be thinking about mating. With sex involved, his mind definitely *wasn't* on children. How did one keep a hard-on when thinking about diapers and cleaning up baby vomit?

"Hey, Charlie. What's goin' on?"

"Hey, Denny. You got a minute to talk?"

"Sure. What's up?" Denarrion sat down on the carved bench inside the door.

"Lissandra Charforest is here. We thought we'd invite you over for brunch."

He scowled, but tried to keep his voice light. "Thanks, but I already had breakfast this morning and I got a lot to do today."

Charlorrion snorted. "Come on, Denny. I know you. You haven't had a decent meal in three weeks, and Torri's making her Italian sausage quiche."

Denarrion's mouth watered, but he shook his head. "Really, thanks, but no. I gotta get these chairs out of here before the shop starts harassing me about 'em." He sold furniture at a local shop in downtown Redfield, fetching good prices to keep him solvent. *And out of my parents' place.*

An exasperated sigh gusted into his hear from the other end of the phone. "Seriously? You're gonna hand me that excuse? I'm pretty sure you're just avoiding Ms. Charforest."

"Hey, we're not scheduled to get together until tonight. It's not my fault she got in early." He paused as he narrowed his eyes. "Is she hot?"

"You're a real dick, you know that?" He could hear Charlorrion's scowl. "It's a wonder you're still single."

"It's a gift."

"Whatever, jackass. If you want to know what she looks like, you'll have to come over to see her. Like tomorrow. If you say yes and are a no-show, Torri will string you up by your entrails."

Denarrion laughed. He could imagine Torriandra

following through with her threat, despite her delicate looks. "Yeah, yeah, promises, promises. All right, I'll be there tomorrow. I should have most of my work done."

"You better. Or I'm gonna introduce her to one of my firefighter buddies. You know Hollis Lupinsky. He's a werewolf and loves playing with fire."

Despite his less than enthusiastic interest in the Widow from Colorado, Denarrion scowled. "Good luck with that. I hear she's all about having more baby dragons. Can't do that with a werewolf."

"How would you know what she wants? You haven't even met her. You have no idea what her kinks or preferences are." Charlorrion gave a theatrical sigh. "I guess you'll just have to wait until tomorrow to find out. Have a good one."

"Charlie—"

But the line had gone dead. He stared at the phone in his hand, debating if he should head over to Charlorrion's place right now, or make the self-righteous bastard wait a bit. But his curiosity ate at him. What were the Widow-from-Colorado's kinks?

He let his gaze rest on the half-finished chair. *There's no way I'm gonna get this done now.* Sighing, he shoved the phone in his pocket, grabbed his keys, and left the workshop, locking the door behind him.

His life was perfect. When he needed sex, he got it from any number of sources. Human diseases couldn't touch him, so selection of partners became easy. What the hell did he need to mate and get married for? He liked his simple life and his solitude. No woman in creation could change that.

****

Lissandra woke to the scent of something savory cooking and warm sunshine streaming in the windows of her room. Despite her daughters' messages the night before, she'd slept soundly and woke with a sense of calm she hadn't felt in years. *Today's the day.* She'd meet Denarrion Goldencoat and see if they were compatible.

Hopefully more than that.

She rose and headed for the shower, shaking her head. She never expected to love anyone after Mikelorrion's death, and she wasn't sure she could. But she wanted to find a friend and companion to share the long centuries with her. She'd mourned her husband and wanted another chance at happiness. Maybe not delirious-head-over-heels bliss, but comfort and support for sure.

She hoped Denarrion would be that kind of guy.

She dressed in jean capris and a V-necked T-shirt with a smiley face on it along with the words, "Crazy is relative." Definitely relative. She hadn't decided if coming this far to have blind date was adventurous or insane, but she didn't mind finding out.

She stared at herself in the mirror, noting a few silver hairs and the lines around her eyes. *It's been too long since I've been on a real adventure.* She thought having dragonets would be enough. But now that Kress and Luce had matured beyond toddlerhood, Lissandra was ready for more.

Checking the mirror one last time, she nodded sharply and descended the stairs into the kitchen. Torri stood at the counter making toast while fending off her husband, Charlorrion. He teased her with little kisses and touches, and Lissandra's throat closed. She missed those little intimate exchanges between mates, the special moments when children or guests didn't intrude.

Which is what you're doing.

She hesitated at the doorway, wondering if she should return to her room when Charlorrion looked up.

"Morning, Lissandra." He stepped away from his wife and leaned against the counter with a smirk. "Sleep well?"

"Yeah, actually, I did." She narrowed her eyes in mock-suspicion. "Did you pump something into the air of my room?"

Charlorrion looked startled and Torri snagged a mug hanging from a hook below the cupboards before she filled it with coffee.

She offered a warm smile. "Glad you slept well. Would you like some coffee?"

"Uh, yeah, coffee would be great." Lissandra sank into a chair at the table, wondering at Charlorrion's new silence.

Torri handed her the mug of steaming black gold. "So, what are your plans for the day? Charlorrion starts his shift at the fire station this afternoon, and won't be back until tomorrow afternoon. And I have to help set up for the Memorial Day Craft Festival this weekend."

"Oh, uhm, I guess I was planning to get together with Denarrion, but other than that, I hadn't thought." She sipped her coffee as Torri pulled a quiche out of the oven. "Oh, and if you have Skype, I'd like to call my kids and see how they are."

"Oh, sure. I can set that up on the computer right now." Charlorrion ducked out of the kitchen

Lissandra raised her eyebrows. "Did you pump something into my room last night?"

Torri had the grace to blush. "Not exactly. I said some mantras to the Goddess to bring you peace and calm, and She often grants my prayers. You weren't drugged or anything."

"Wow."

Lissandra ignored the stab of jealousy. The Goddess hadn't answered her in a long time. *That could be because I've hid from Her, too.* Yeah, Mikelorrion's death had driven her to hide from a lot of things, including her calling as a Warrior Seer. *No, I'm done with that.* Seeking out the evil energy of demons and destroying them had tainted her spirit until she could barely care for her children. She took a deep breath. *That's behind me now.*

"I'm sorry. Your energy seemed erratic so I thought it would help. I should've asked." Torri gave her an apologetic smile. "Let me get you some quiche."

Lissandra grimaced. "You know, if my energy is too all over the place, I can always stay at a hotel in town. I don't want to mess up your sanctuary."

"Nonsense." Torri waved her objections away as she served the quiche. "We're honored to have such a warrior in our home."

Lissandra paused. "Warrior?"

"Oh, yes." Torri tilted her head. "We've heard about your history in seeking out demons and sending them back to the Underworld. Your exploits are well known in this house."

"Oh. Good." She wished her people would forget about her past. The events of her youth and hunting demons were some of her worst memories, and led to horrific nightmares if she dwelled on them. "Thank you for the compliments, but that's in my past. I'm not that dragon anymore."

"Ah, it's like getting on a bicycle after many years, yes?" Torri dipped her head with a smile. "It'll come back when it's time."

What if I don't want to go back to it?

Lissandra nodded and tucked into her breakfast to avoid answering. Charlorrion returned to the kitchen, but his lips tightened and his brows lowered as he settled into the chair beside her.

"You're all set to meet with Denarrion today, yes? And after, I thought we could all get together for dinner." Torri laid a plate of quiche and toast in front of Charlorrion.

"Yes, that sounds good." The savory quiche turned to dust in her mouth with the thought of encountering Denarrion Goldencoat so soon. *He's the whole reason I came to Redfield.* True, but something felt off, like she hadn't gotten the full story. *We're going to start a courtship, right?*

"Good glory, Charlorrion. You look like you've eaten too much cabbage. What has brought on such a sour visage?" Torri poked her husband with a flirtatious smile.

"Denarrion."

Lissandra stilled as Torri frowned. "What about him?"

"He's, uh, a little busy with work today. He said he'll be by tomorrow."

Torri lifted her chin and stared her husband down. "What about tonight? Did he not say he'd meet with Lissandra tonight?"

Charlorrion hunched his shoulders in the face of his wife's anger. "Yeah, I thought that was the deal, but he said he's too busy."

Relief and disappointment hit Lissandra simultaneously. On the one hand, she was glad she could have a little more time to get used to the idea of a dragon courtship. On the other hand, what kind of a guy couldn't uphold his end of the deal to meet?

"You call him back right now, Charlorrion Ravenwing." Torri brandished her finger in his face. "You tell him Lissandra Charforest might not be the high and mighty Goldencoat warriors, but her name is spoken with honor and reverence in other circles, and he'd do well to treat her with the respect she deserves. Call him, Charlorrion."

"It's okay, Torriandra." Lissandra finished her coffee and took her plate to the sink. "Really. Blind dates aren't easy to get your mind around in the best of times. It's fine if I don't see him until tomorrow. That'll give me time to get to know Redfield." She gave them a smile. "I think I'll take a walk." She held up her phone. "I'll have my phone if anything changes."

"Are you sure? Charlorrion can call Denarrion back." Torri scowled.

"No, no, it's all right. I shouldn't be more than a couple of hours." She headed for the mud room to put on her shoes.

"I might call him anyway, but as long as you're exploring, try the hiking trails overlooking the reservoir." Charlorrion followed her. "It's beautiful up there with all the wildflowers and new growth."

She nodded as she opened the door. "I'll check them out. Thanks."

"I'm really sorry about Denarrion. He's usually more friendly."

She shrugged with a rueful smile. "It's okay. Since this blind date wasn't his idea, I can understand his reluctance. I'll see you all later."

She closed the door on his distressed expression, trying to shove her misgivings aside. *I'd be hesitant, too, if someone arranged a blind date without my say-so.* She took a deep breath and let the tension flow out of her.

The morning sounds enclosed her in simple joy. Bees and crickets competed with the rattle of the deciduous trees in the wind. The sun already topped the trees and the heat rolled through the open spaces, but the shadows beneath the trunks held the cool air.

Best stick to the shaded areas.

She set off down the street of old houses straight out of a Norman Rockwell painting. She'd arrived in Redfield in time for Memorial Day Weekend, and the residents had decorated with buntings and flags. Her internet research of the town had listed the festivities starting the next afternoon. The annual Memorial Day Craft Festival promised live music and outdoor movies.

Maybe I can catch a movie this weekend. Her steps faltered a little as she recalled the times she'd gone with her husband. *It won't be the same without Mike.*

No, it wouldn't, but it had been three decades since he'd died. While it was a drop in the bucket in the life of a dragon, she was ready for a new chapter. She didn't want to be alone for the rest of her life. She wanted more than just friends to see her through the tough times. *And back me up with the kids.*

The houses gave way to forest and a game trail pierced underbrush to her left. She followed it, winding northward into the woods along a steep stream valley. The shade of the trees enveloped her and she breathed a sigh of relief. The humid heat of the east coast took her breath away.

Give me a Rocky Mountain summer any day.

The trail rose gently along the embankment of the stream and she enjoyed the sounds of the birds chattering away in the canopy. The stream sparkled in the dappled light, chuckling to itself as it tumbled happily over the rocks in its bed. Lissandra eased her strides to keep the heat from clobbering her energy reserves. Though accustomed to hiking around 9,000 feet of elevation, she didn't want to become dehydrated on a minor incline.

Nothing like a badass Warrior Seer keeling over on a little hill. Yeah, that wouldn't do much for her reputation.

The trail flattened out and left the trees ahead, and a distinct hum rattled in her ears. She frowned and shook her head, pausing just inside the tree line.

The land opened up to a fire burn scar on either side of the stream valley. She'd encountered hundreds of burn scars over the years, often caused by lightning strikes and wild fires. But something about this one didn't feel right, as if the fire had unsettled the land and it had never recovered.

What in hellwinds happened here?

She scanned the land for life, but only some sickly-looking shrubs struggled out of the scorched earth. Where were the fireweed, thistles, and Indian Paintbrush? *Maybe the fire scar isn't that old.* But it was spring and there were no new shoots or grasses. Even the birds seemed to avoid the open space. The stream disappeared there, sinking into the earth as if to hide itself from unclean eyes.

The urge to use her Sight rose in her chest with insistent warning. Something was very wrong and she'd only be able to fix it if she could See. Taking a deep breath, she allowed herself to fall back into her Goddess-given gift.

The immediacy of the wrongness hit her the moment she stared at the burn scar. Everything flickered a drab gray-green, as if covered in mold. The edges of the shrubs and grasses appeared fuzzy and she almost stepped out to touch them. But a warning screamed through her head and she held still.

A thick silence pressed on her as if cotton had been stuffed in her ears. Sticky heat and sickness filled her nose and she panted to bring in fresh air. *What is going on?* Panic built in her chest as the scents of rot and decay suffused her nostrils. She gagged and clutched her throat as she struggled to breathe.

The hum rose in pitch, reminding her of screams from damned souls left in the care of demons. A vision of creatures being burned alive by something blackened and monstrous filled her sight and she clenched her fists to beat it away. Snarling evil turned her way, daring her to step into its stronghold. Evil laughter echoed in the screams.

Dear Mother of all, help me fight this tainted place!

Inhaling despite the cloying decay, Lissandra closed her eyes and reached for the element of fire, buried deep within her soul. Her inner flames roared, burning through her awareness, and cleansing her nose of the rotting stench. The evil laughter cut off, only to be replaced with a high-pitched scream of frustration. She fanned her inner flames, burning away the last vestiges of the encroaching decay.

The pressure abruptly released her, making her stagger backwards into the shade. Lissandra braced her hands on her thighs as she gulped great breaths of clean air.

Holy Mother of all. That was demon trace.

She recognized the stench, both real and psychic anywhere. A demon had been here and torched the place with its evil, denying the land's recovery. *It's been here a while.* She stood up, but kept her eyes closed as she allowed her breathing to come back to normal.

If the burn scar had been caused by a demon, why hadn't the Ravenwings mentioned it to her? *Uh, maybe because you've given up being a Warrior Seer?* Maybe, but any dragon visiting would need to know about the danger. While dragons could withstand a demon's influence, even they could be killed if caught unaware. She'd have to speak to them about it.

Lissandra opened her eyes and scanned the fire scar with her Sight. The moldy appearance was gone, though the land still appeared blackened and dead. But here and there, she caught the sparkle of iridescent light pushing up through the dirt. The lines of energy pulsing through the land slowly cleared of the black taint infecting their muted colors.

She allowed her vision to return to normal and everything appeared calm. The usual forest sounds intruded and the wind rustled the leaves overhead. After a moment, she caught the furtive movement of a bird flitting across the open space.

Much better. She patted a nearby trunk and continued along the trail skirting the open land. It wasn't lost on her that people had avoided the scar. *With demon taint, I'd avoid it, too.* It had been decades since she'd last used her gift, and she was a little rusty, but she still recognized the signs. She'd have to talk to Charlorrion about it and see if a local *Morukai* Shaman could help with the healing she'd initiated.

Misgivings flickered through her as her feet carried her toward a break in the woods. *What if I've been brought here for more than just a blind date?* She stopped under the cool trees and considered the thought. *Solenarra wouldn't be that underhanded to get me back into the trade of demon killing, would she?*

Her mother had been adamant about Lissandra returning to her calling. But with Mikelorrion's death, and the need to raise two young dragonets, she'd retired from the Order of Scales, the Warrior Seers of the dragons. She hadn't felt the need or the inclination to return to the Order, despite Sole's insistence.

Lissandra shook her head. She'd have to get a straight answer from the older dragon when the kids had gone to bed. Anger fired her blood, but she took a deep breath and told herself to relax. *I'm supposed to be on vacation. Sort of.*

The trail ended abruptly at a large granite outcrop and a vista opened up in front of her. A large reservoir filled a glacial depression between the forested hills, sparkling in the sunshine. *Ah, the Salmon Creek reservoir.* The scent of lake water and rich foliage baking in the eastern heat reached her nose as she sat down on rock outcrop in the shade. A red-tailed hawk, disturbed by her appearance, took wing across the shining waters to find an alternate perch on one of the small islands rising from the lake.

Lissandra sighed and tried to enjoy the natural sounds of the forest around her as the remnants of her anger ebbed. She closed her eyes and tipped her head back, enjoying the gentle breeze sifting through the branches behind her. She'd take her time, enjoy this trip, and deal with Sole's motivations later. The soft sounds and tantalizing scents of the early summer forest soothed her concerns. Her mind drifted to thoughts of the girls and her late husband again.

Oh, sa cherro, *I miss you, but I know it's time to move on.* She missed his smile and devil-may-care confidence. Mikelorrion had never seemed afraid of anything. She wished she had a fraction of his assurance.

She sighed and rolled her head forward, studying the sparkling flecks of mica in the granite as she mulled over her situation. *Am I really doing the best thing for me and the girls by going on a blind date with some stranger?*

That was the real question. And Denarrion's apparent disinterest wasn't helping. She bit her bottom lip thoughtfully. She wasn't ready to give her heart to anyone, but having a male around to share the days might be okay.

Pretty callous, Lissandra, and it isn't fair to Mr. Goldencoat Jr. She grimaced and flicked a loose piece of rock off the edge. She did want a friend, a movie-buddy. Hellwinds, even a fuck-buddy would be nice.

"At least then I'd get laid once in a while."

A surprised gasp and the scuff of shoes against rock startled Lissandra. She whipped her head around to stare at the intruder of her thoughts, her heart pounding. She braced for action and defense.

Until she got a good look at him.

The man stood about six feet tall with short, sandy blond hair. He had a slender build, but the arms below the hems of his t-shirt carried toned muscles.

Wiry. The humorous thought trickled through her awareness and she fought a smile.

He tilted his head, his sensuous mouth quirking in a lopsided smile beneath his neatly trimmed goatee and mustache. Icy blue eyes scanned her with casual interest behind wire rimmed glasses, his gaze warming her body.

She resisted the urge to preen, but still straightened her back as she thrust out her breasts.

What is wrong with me? Lissandra tried to rein in her attraction, but her dragon self pushed to the forefront of her awareness.

He's a dragon. A growl of appreciation slipped out.

The male hummed with untapped power as if he hadn't completely discovered his abilities yet, but his aura's energy glowed with the quality of maturity. *At least a thousand years.* His unusual beauty excited her and her breasts tingled as her nipples tightened with awareness. His smile widened and he inhaled as if appreciating the change in her scent.

"Sorry, I didn't mean to startle you. I didn't think anyone would be up here."

Pleasure sizzled down her back at his sultry Brooklyn accent. Lissandra imagined it could be infused with either bitter sarcasm or dry humor, depending on his mood.

She gave him a one-shouldered shrug. "I followed a path up here. I never could resist the mystery of a good game trail."

"Yeah, I totally get that." His lips curled into a boyish smile and she damn near melted.

It's got to be his handsome, Puckish smile. I'm a sucker for Shakespeare.

"You know what they say about curiosity."

"It killed the cat, but won the prize?"

He laughed and stepped onto the granite outcrop with the natural grace of a hunting predator. He cocked his head, a half-smile on his lips, as his gaze ran over her body. She shivered with the impact of it.

Oh, Goddess, yes please. Now she just needed Her to listen.

CHAPTER THREE

Denarrion couldn't believe his luck. He'd chanced upon this glorious woman on his favorite rock perch. She'd pulled her dark brown, wavy hair into ponytail, and the tail hung down her back in a silken fall. Arching brows over sparkling lavender eyes captured his attention and utterly stopped his breath. And her scent. She filled his nose with tantalizing vanilla and lilacs.

This is the kind of woman I want. Why did he have to agree to the blind date with the Widow from Colorado?

He smiled down at her. "I don't remember seeing you in town before. Are you here for the holiday?"

She tilted her head and shrugged with one shoulder. "Something like that."

"It's a good time to visit this place. Mind if I sit with you?"

"Uh, no. I guess that'd be okay." She gestured to the rock and he settled beside her.

"I used to come here all the time. You know, every time I wanted to get away from my dad. It wasn't always a lake, but it was always peaceful."

"It *is* nice here." She turned to look out at the lake. "It's like the world hasn't tainted this place with its fears

29

and pollution. It's beautiful."

He didn't see the lake, just her glorious profile. "Yeah, beautiful."

She glanced at him, meeting his gaze with raised eyebrows and a dip of her chin. He grinned as she snorted.

"Does that line usually work for you?"

"Eh, you know, it's about fifty-fifty." He shrugged ruefully, but his heart warmed with her catch. This wasn't a woman who'd preen and simper for his attention. She'd make him earn every step into her good graces. Usually, that would frustrate him and he'd head for greener pastures. But something about the lavender-eyed beauty kept him willing to try.

"My name is Denny." He gave her his best lopsided smile and her lips curled in response.

"Lissa." She held out her hand to shake his in the traditional human greeting. "Do you live in Redfield, or one of the other towns nearby?"

"Yeah, I'm from Redfield." Close enough in human terms. "My family came here when this was still a river valley instead of a reservoir."

"So it's been a little while at least." She nodded.

He frowned. A little while? In human terms it would be something close to a hundred and fifty years. *Maybe she's referring to the settlers who arrived in the late fifteenth century.* He nodded and tried to figure out how to move the conversation along after her strange response.

"So if you're here visiting, where are you from?"

"Colorado. I live in the Rocky Mountains." She waved at the vista. "It's lush here."

Colorado? "What brought you out here?"

She hesitated just a beat. "I'm visiting extended family."

"Ah. How long will you be staying then?"

"I don't really know. As long as it takes, I guess." She looked away and her shoulders tightened as she drew her knees up to her chest.

He raised his eyebrows at her defensive posture. "That sounds kinda ominous."

Lissa laughed, but it didn't sound happy. "I'm trying to start over. My husband died a few years ago, and while I'm done mourning, I'm realizing it's not as easy as I thought to just get back out there and find someone."

His gut sank. *She was married.* He tried to recapture his lightheartedness. "Why? What's the problem? You're a beautiful woman. I'd think it would be easy."

She snorted. "Thank you for the compliment, but I'm a picky person. And most dating sites are full of trolls and misogynistic "nice guys" who feel entitled to my affection because they're "nice." It's been so long since I've dated, that I didn't even know where to look. So I'm here visiting family in hopes a change of scene will help."

"You couldn't find a guy near your home in Colorado?"

She grimaced and shrugged. "Like I said. Picky."

Denarrion blinked as some of the details she'd mentioned came together. *Colorado. Widow. Picky. Holy shit, she's the Widow from Colorado!*

He nodded but turned his gaze to the reservoir as he swallowed hard. *Dammit, I'm not ready to face her.* But maybe he had it wrong. There were lots of women who lived in Colorado, and he had to assume that more than one had lost her husband.

"Yeah, me, too." He nodded, but he'd lost some of the excitement of meeting her. "You wouldn't be out here to go on a blind date, would you?"

She blinked, losing her smile. Her chin lifted in understanding and her expression turned polite.

"Yes, that's exactly why I'm in Redfield." Her eyes widened with surprise. "You must be Denarrion Goldencoat."

A lopsided smile curled his lips with mocking

amusement. "In the flesh. And you must be Lissandra Charforest, the widow from Colorado."

Her eyes narrowed and her chin came up with challenge. "That's me. I'm pretty sure Charlorrion said you were too busy to meet with me today."

Oh, shit, I did say that. He tried to keep his smile easy, but the chagrin made it turn brittle. "Uh, yeah. I'm taking a break."

The corners of her mouth pulled down enough to show her disdain of his lame-ass excuse. "I'm sorry to intrude on your peace and home. I'll leave you to it."

She made to rise and he panicked. He didn't know why, but he needed more time with her.

"Whoa, whoa, whoa." He jumped up and caught her arm. "You don't have to go. I didn't mind sharing the rock with—"

He stopped mid-sentence as the jolt of power ran between them and crashed through his senses like a juggernaut. His breath froze in his lungs as brilliant fire shot through every synapse in his brain and the muscles of his body. Yet the sensation included no pain.

Radiant light blew open all the secret doors in his life, offering him glimpses of what the rooms held on the other side. *Treasure!*

His eyes widened as he took in Lissa's human face, but his gaze focused on the long graceful neck and elegant horned head of the iridescent dragon aura around her. *Life, Mate!* The words came out of nowhere, and he tried to understand their meaning. Lissa's beauty astounded him, entrancing him like a siren's song. *Must have more.* He understood she could show him these things, offer him the peace he'd been searching for over the centuries. In that moment, he refused to be parted from her. Ever.

Desire and passion for the dragon woman he held roared through him. The powerful emotions overshadowed all his previous sexual urges like a forest fire to a candle flame. He'd found *her* and letting her go wasn't an option

"Holy Mother!" He tried to pull her closer.

She came to him without resistance and planted a hungry and passionate kiss on his lips, setting his mind ablaze. His cock hardened to the consistency of granite and his balls tightened up against his body. Her reaction surprised him and he staggered backwards under her weight, stepping off the edge of the granite outcrop.

With a whoop, they both toppled backwards over the edge and down into the reservoir.

CHAPTER FOUR

Denarrion always loved swimming in the lake in summer, but he usually did it alone and without clothes. Now he found himself hitting the water fully clothed, with his arms full of woman.

The cold water shocked the breath out of him and he immediately let go of Lissandra to scramble back up to the surface. As his head broke through, he gasped for breath and scanned the water for her. She laughed and a grin spread across his lips. She gulped breaths as she treaded water, but her laughter ruffled the liquid around her, sending ripples toward the shore.

"You really know…how to show…a girl a good time." She swam to the nearest shoreline and hauled herself out of the water. She shook the wet hair out of her eyes. "I've heard east coast guys can make you breathless, but this is completely beyond my expectations."

Denarrion laughed a little breathlessly himself. "I always strive to make an impression. I *have* impressed you, right?"

Lissandra laughed as she squeezed her hair. "You've definitely left an impression, but I'm not sure it was the one you were going for."

He liked knowing the fall hadn't dampened her humor as he crawled onto the small rocky beach to rest, dripping and panting. Her t-shirt molded to her body, revealing tantalizing curves and large nipples pushing against the wet fabric. He suddenly wanted to suck on them and run his hands over every inch of her body to warm her up. His own clothes restricted his movement and uncomfortable pressure built in the crotch of his jeans.

Whoa up there, son. Take it slow. You just threw her in the lake.

"Thank you for the unique introduction." She smiled at his attempts to squeeze the water out of his t-shirt. "Hopefully, I'll see you again under better circumstances."

"Wait. Where're you goin'?" Denarrion forced his body to block her path. "I can't let you walk back to Charlie's place like that. It'd be rude. My place is closer and I'll even throw in a meal. Whadiya say?"

He didn't want Lissandra to go so soon. He wanted to finish what they'd started with their aborted kiss, and he'd be damned if he didn't try a little persuasion. He took his glasses off his face and wiped them with his fingers as he tried to give her a seductive look.

"I thought you had to work, and I don't want to impose on your busy schedule." She bunched her t-shirt in her hands, revealing a tantalizing midriff.

"Aw, well, work will always be there, and I did promise to meet with you this afternoon." He shrugged with his best enticing smile. "So we started a little early. Besides, he's gonna think I'm a real asshole if I let you walk back soaked like that."

"It's not going to be better at your place. All my things are at the Ravenwings'. I won't have anything to wear."

That sounds good to me. Probably best not said aloud.

"I think I have a few things you could borrow while we dry our clothes. I know we're back east, but we actually have dryers in the houses these days, and a more recent addition of a cordless telephone." Then he pulled his dripping cell out of his pocket. "But not this one. I don't think even rice will save it."

She gasped and patted herself down, searching for her own cell. He envied her hands.

"Dammit. I seem to have lost mine in the reservoir." She looked back toward the lake as if she could spot where the little phone fell.

"Yeah, it's gone for good, then. Let's head to my place and call Charlie from there."

Lissandra bit her bottom lip as she considered then turned her head toward the granite outcropping from which they fell. He suspected she weighed the virtues of returning to the Ravenwings' or staying with this attractive and intriguing—*Oh, and modest and self-effacing*—stranger who'd dragged her into the lake.

His mind raced. What could he say to convince her to come with him? What would put her at ease?

Other than a good tongue-fucking?

She'd been chagrined when she'd found out who he was. Wasn't she looking forward to their blind date? *You mean, like you?* Yeah, okay, so he hadn't been thrilled, but that was before he met her. Touched her. Hell, smelled her.

Dismay flickered in the back of his mind. *What if she's having second thoughts? Will she leave Redfield?* He didn't want her to go anywhere.

"We were supposed to get together today anyway, right?" He gave an amiable shrug, though his guts churned with unease.

She nodded. "I know, but you told Charlorrion you had too much to do." She bit her bottom lip. "What's changed your mind now?"

"A good dunking?" He grinned as she laughed. "I dunno. I just thought from that kiss up on the rock that maybe it wasn't such a bad thing to spend time with you." He rubbed the back of his neck. "Yeah, I know, I'm an idiot, but how 'bout we start over and take it from there?"

She tilted her head and narrowed her eyes. "It was a damn good kiss, at least on my end."

"Yeah?" A grin stretched his lips. "I thought it was pretty fantastic myself. And, y'know, we are supposed to be on a blind date. Doesn't get more blind than falling off a cliff."

She laughed and it turned his world into brilliant rainbows. *Glory, I gotta get her to do that more often.*

"That's very true." She squared her shoulders. "Okay, Denarrion. Do you at least have coffee?"

"Are you kidding? Hellwinds yeah, I got coffee." He nodded. "We can get to know each other a little better over a cuppa joe while we wait for your clothes to dry."

Lissandra shook her hands to get rid of the excess water. "That sounds great. Lead on."

Triumph surged through him. *Yes!*

She raised her gaze back to him. "I take it you weren't thrilled with this blind date thing?"

Chagrin made him grimace. "Yeah, I wasn't really sure it would work out, y'know? And it seemed weird to do somethin' like this when social media is this rampant thing." He gestured toward the trail leading into the trees. "And my dad set it up. We don't exactly have the same taste in women, if you know what I mean."

Lissaandra wrinkled her nose. "Eww, yeah, that might squick me out, too."

"Yeah, he's stuffy and all about duty, and I was pretty sure any woman he approved would be the same." He shuddered as he followed, enjoying her ass in her wet jeans. "Not exactly traits I look for in a potential mate."

She grimaced. "No, that would turn me off, too. But if it makes you feel any better, I've never met your dad, so I don't know if we'd get along." She smirked at him as she scrambled up the trail. "Best not to judge a book by its promoter, yeah?"

Denarrion laughed. "Not to self: make my own decisions from now on."

"Good call."

He laughed again, enjoying her snark. She wasn't stuffy or boring at all. *And I would've known that if I wasn't a jackass, and visited earlier.* It didn't matter. He'd enjoy the time with her because he'd be damned before he let her out of his sight now.

She waved at the trail through the trees. "So, how far is your place from here?"

"Not far if you're dry." He grinned. "A little longer when you're squelching along in wet shoes."

"If I'd known I was going to take a bath as a first date, I would've brought my sandals and a towel. I guess I'll just have to squelch."

"If it makes you feel any better, I'll be squelching along with you."

"Oh yeah, that makes me feel *so* much better." She grinned to take the sting out of her words.

It made *him* feel better. Lissandra called to him on a level deeper than he'd ever experienced with any other woman. In the moment they'd touched, the understanding of her perfection as his life partner whispered through him. How had he gone from being a determined bachelor to desperate to court the dragon widow?

He had no idea, but it didn't matter. He'd win her regard if it took all his time and effort. Nothing and no one would stop him from claiming her as his own.

Denarrion cleared his throat. "What do you think of the northeast?"

"It's a lot wetter here than in Colorado." She winked. "Though I'm not used to this kind of humidity." She gestured to her wet clothes.

He laughed. "Yeah, it's a lot to get used to. I'm still not really used to it myself." He stomped harder, punctuating his statements with the wet sounds of his shoes.

Her laugh tightened the jeans at his groin.

"I mean all the water in the air. I can smell it." The breeze shifted and he caught her scent, lilacs in the sun. "But grass in every front yard and lots of leafy trees makes it really nice. You know, lush."

Lush was a good word for it, but it wasn't vegetation filling his thoughts.

He kept stealing glances at her as she walked beside him, watching her shirt tighten on her large breasts when she swung her arms. Her nipples strained against the wet cloth each time it grew taut, and his cock stood up in salute.

Cursing to himself, he tried to think of something else to distract his body from the overwhelming urge to tackle her and have his way with her. His eyes drifted to her wet hair when she walked through the sunlight. Red highlights blazed in the flashes of light and tempted him to run his fingers through their shining brilliance.

He inwardly groaned. *Doesn't help!* He tried to imagine washing the dishes or vacuuming his bedroom, but his mind refused to be deterred from the image of her on his black cotton sheets, naked and relaxed.

"I bet your winters are bitter cold."

It took his mind a few moments to remember where he was.

"What?"

"The winters here." She waved at the forest around them. "With all this humidity, I bet they're really bitter."

"Oh, yeah, they can be." He cleared his throat. "But it's not as bad as in Buffalo. Here it's fairly mild 'cause we are so close to Lake Ontario. There was a time, though, when you could skate on the reservoir."

"Really? That must be fun."

"Yeah, it used to freeze solid, but not for about fifty years now. Do you like to ice skate?"

"I've never been."

His jaw dropped. "Never been ice skating? Not even in an indoor arena?"

She shook her head and he tsked.

"If you're here in the winter, I'll take you ice skating on one of the smaller ponds."

Denarrion sincerely hoped she'd be around next winter so he could keep her warm by the fire and entice her with other winter activities. *Like skiing, snow fort building, sex in my oversized bathtub…*

"Have you ever been snowshoeing?"

He grinned. "Not unless you count getting caught in a blizzard with just your sneakers."

She shook her head. "Definitely not. I'll have to show you when you come to Colorado."

Go to Colorado? A pang of disquiet hit him. He hadn't thought of ever leaving New York. This was his home where he knew everyone and how the game was played. Leaving never crossed his mind.

I don't think I could ever live anywhere else. He'd just have to convince her to move here.

"Yeah, that'd be great."

Lissa laughed. "Your enthusiasm is overwhelming."

He ducked his head before he gestured through the trees to a clearing on the other side.

"Here we are. Home sweet home, and a place where hot coffee is always on."

CHAPTER FIVE

Lissandra scanned the space in front of her. A simple, large, A-frame house stood in the center of a mowed lawn with a separate garage behind it. Wooden slats stained black gently overlapped to allow any precipitation to slough off the sides, and a wood pile sat neatly stacked under a horizontal extension of the roof on the west side. Holly and lilac hedges made a natural fence between his and his neighbor's yards.

"Wow, this is your place?"

Usually she didn't like A-frame houses, but Denarrion's home filled her with a sense of quaint coziness combined with practicality. The structure stood larger than most, and appeared to be a real house rather than a winter retreat.

"It's lovely. It feels like a mountain cabin. It must be pretty relaxing to live here."

"It is. The neighbors are far enough away to give me privacy." He led the way to the back door, fishing in his pockets for his keys. She was glad he still had them after their impromptu swim. "But my parents live just ten minutes from here so it's not as relaxing as it could be."

"What do you have against your parents?"

"Remember the stuffy, duty-bound asshole part?"
Lissandra laughed. "Oh, that. Right."

"Come on in. I'll make sure the coffee's on."
Denarrion held the door open so she could step inside.

Golden wood floors glowed in the sunlight from
skylights in the roof and a set of wrought iron spiral stairs
rose to the upper story on the left. She followed it upwards
with her gaze until it straightened into an iron railing
covered with a brightly colored wool blanket. Denarrion
led her past a comfortable set of couch and chairs with an
oak coffee table crouched in the center on a stylish Indian
rug.

"Wow, did you do all the woodwork yourself?"

"Yeah." He shrugged with self-deprecation. "It was a
good way to take my mind off my dad. Let me show you
the laundry room."

"Now there's a sexy place." She grinned as he laughed.

"Oh yeah. It's a good place for our shoes."

The laundry room sat off the kitchen at the back of the
house, but Lissandra stopped in wonder. The open space
contained brushed steel appliances, flagstone tiled floor,
and black and tan granite countertops. A large island with
the stove in it stood in the middle of the room, overhung by
a copper exhaust hood. Stained oak cupboards filled with
copper pots and utensils lined the walls, and the whole
kitchen glowed in warm earthy colors. Track lighting gave
the place a stylish air like a Manhattan loft apartment.

"Please tell me you like to cook."

"Yeah, it's one of the things that relaxes me. Why?"
He tilted his head.

"Because a kitchen this magnificent shouldn't be left
sterile." She ran her hands over the granite countertops.
"It's beautiful. I'm not a fan of cooking, but I could be
coaxed to spend time here just because of how spectacular
it is."

"Oh yeah? I'll remember that. What I like is no one

complains if the recipes don't come out exactly as I planned. Everything tastes good even if the presentation isn't what I hoped." Denarrion gave her his sexy grin again and she shivered with its impact.

"I only like cooking if I can do it with someone else. When it becomes a chore, I run for the hills and depend on Gianni's Pizza."

He smirked. "What did you do before Gianni's?"

"I had a husband."

She'd meant the response to be flippant, but thinking about Mike when she stood in another male's home killed the humor. Denarrion's expression closed down and she wished she'd kept her mouth shut. *Nice going, idiot. Nothing like bringing up his dead competition.*

She grimaced. "Sorry. That sounded better in my head."

"No problem. I haven't exactly been the smoothest today."

"Oh, come on. Pulling your blind date into the reservoir had to score high in originality points." She winked, hoping to coax out his smile again. "I'm pretty sure no one else would think to do it."

He barked a laugh. "Yeah, that's because it only works on special people. Not everyone can pull off those kind of suave moves."

She laughed, relieved. Maybe they could just ignore Mike from now on. She'd certainly try to keep him where he belonged, in the past.

"Come on. Let's leave our shoes in the laundry before we head upstairs."

Lissandra raised an eyebrow. "We're going upstairs?"

"You want dry clothes, don't you? I'm afraid I don't have any in the guest room."

They deposited their wet shoes on the flagstone floor of the laundry, then retreated through the house to the stairs.

"Your house is lovely."

"Yeah?" Denarrion leveled an amused look at her.

"What's wrong with 'lovely'? Too girlie for you?" She raised her chin in challenge. "Would you prefer 'manly' or 'handsome'?"

He laughed and the richness of his voice warmed her heart under her wet clothes.

"I'd be okay with 'welcoming', actually."

His simple answer deflated her sarcasm. "It is welcoming. It feels like a good place to live."

"Thanks. I worked hard to make it that way."

They stood staring at each other for a few moments and Lissandra studied his face. Denarrion's eyes blazed with pale blue fire, his expression intense, and she wondered what thoughts chased through his mind. When his lips curled into a seductive smile, excitement slammed into her and she stifled a shiver.

"You look cold. Dry clothes are up there."

"Yeah, good. Okay."

He gestured for her to precede him up to the second floor. She gave him a smile and climbed the stairs with one hand on the railing to keep herself steady.

Goddess knows I need it.

From the moment Denarrion touched her at the reservoir, all the barriers she'd erected around her heart fractured into nothingness. Burning energy and light scoured all the little dark places where sadness lurked, corroding its jagged edges. She'd never experienced such a connection before with anyone, even Mikelorrion.

Recognition of something rare and precious had followed, and certainty slammed into her like a sledgehammer. Denarrion Goldencoat would be the only one to understand and fit her best. The cracks in her heart knitted together with Denarrion's energy, and she'd thrown herself into their kiss in a desperate attempt to get closer to him.

And that worked out beautifully, didn't it?

She sensed his gaze on her body all the way up the stairs and her breath hitched in excitement. It was odd to be so attuned to a male after being alone for decades.

It has to be from when I touched him at the reservoir.

A loft space opened at the top of the stairs and Denarrion slid past her, shifting his hips oddly as if his pants had suddenly become uncomfortable.

"There's a bathroom right through there." He pointed to a doorway across the loft. "Just drop your wet things on the floor. I'll find you something to wear while they dry." He disappeared into a walk-in closet.

Lissandra trailed her fingers over the golden oak footboard on the large bed. A muted multicolored comforter in a stylish geometric pattern covered the space and several pillows lay piled against the headboard. An ornate oak hope chest crouched at the foot of the bed. The whole bedroom looked like a promotional set from a catalog for Domestications or JC Penney Home. The only thing missing was the dust ruffle.

"You like the room?"

"Huh?" She turned, blinking.

Denarrion motioned to the bedroom as he held some clothing in his hands.

"Yeah, it's fancy, like it belongs in a catalog."

He laughed. "To be fair, it came from a catalog. I liked the pattern and colors."

"It definitely fits the house." She nodded at the hope chest. "What hopes do you keep in that chest?"

He frowned in confusion. "What are you talkin' about?"

"The hope chest. It's where people keep their most sentimental valuables. Do you have some hopes in your chest?"

His expression settled into pensiveness. "Not at the moment, but that might be changing."

"Speaking of changing, I'd like to get out of these wet clothes."

"Oh, right." He laid the clothing out on the bed. "I figured you could wear a t-shirt and sweats. They're clean. And I'll get some towels, too."

"Towels?" She raised her eyebrows.

"Yeah, I thought you might want to grab a shower. The reservoir isn't as clean as it used to be and it would warm you up." He gestured to her body.

"Do I look cold?"

Instead of answering, his eyes dropped to her chest. She followed his gaze to where her nipples pushed against her wet shirt.

"Oh." She laughed. "I guess I might be a little chilled."

Lissandra crossed her arms over her chest self-consciously, but stole a look at the front of his wet jeans. *Hellwinds, if he can stare, so can I.* And she enjoyed his body's response against the tight, wet cloth.

"See something you like, Lissa?"

She'd seen a lot she liked in the last hour, but his voice held enough cockiness to yank her back to the present.

"Not yet, but I'm patient." She lifted her chin with her own cocky smile. "Maybe I will take a shower after all."

"It's right through there." He gestured toward the ornate glass door beyond the bed and she took the hint to investigate.

Lissandra stepped into luxury and gaped. The bathroom held an oversized bathtub encased in more of the black and tan granite from the kitchen downstairs. She shuffled across the black marble floor to lean against the glass door of a separate shower. Two showerheads hung from opposite walls and a black and tan granite bench had been built below one so the bather could sit and still wash or shave.

"Wow." Her breath fogged the glass. "It's just like a fancy five-star hotel."

Denarrion appeared at the bathroom door and laughed. "Oh, good, just the image I was going for."

His laugh sent tingles over her damp skin, heating her in places long forgotten. He held two fluffy towels in his arms and she wanted to throw herself into them. Both the towels and his arms. *Man, I got it bad if I just want to hear him laugh again.*

"You should do that more often."

He raised his eyebrows. "What?"

"Laugh. It takes years off your face and makes the room sparkle."

He shrugged, a little grimace twisting his lips. "I haven't had much to laugh about. Until now." He met her gaze and heat zinged through the room between them.

She cleared her throat again. "After my shower, would you mind if I used your computer to Skype with my kids? I'd use my cellphone, but…"

"It's at the bottom of the reservoir."

"Yeah."

He handed her the towels and retreated, pausing at the door. "I'll get it set up and make some coffee." He closed the door behind him and she let all the breath out of her chest.

Damn, he's hot stuff.

She shook her head and shucked her clothes off as she turned the shower on. She only used one of the heads, not wanting to take too long to figure out the rest. *I just need to get clean, not get a massage.*

She started her shower, hoping to get done soon, but the hot water settled her nerves and made her think about Denarrion again. She snorted. *As if I stopped thinking about him.*

She'd scanned him with her Sight when she first met him, and his dragon essence glowed blue-silver like a glacial mist. But a curious darkness floated at the edges of his aura. Lissandra frowned into the water as she washed

47

her hair.

The darkness didn't represent taint, exactly, more like a geas set by something very strong and powerful, keeping him from using his own abilities. Even stranger, the geas seemed to be of his own making.

Why would anyone put a geas on themselves and their abilities?

Who hid himself *from* himself? *That's like shooting yourself in the foot.* Was he even aware of the geas? Probably not if he hadn't shaken it off. Or maybe he'd gotten so used to feeling subdued, he didn't remember being any other way.

Do I want to get involved with a guy like that?

The question followed her through the completion of her shower and as she dressed in Denarrion's loaned clothes. She allowed herself to close her eyes and inhale his scent, a mixture of freshly baked bread and rosemary, and thought back to the moment they touched.

But I know he's meant to be mine. Did that mean she didn't have a choice?

She hadn't reached an answer when she returned to the kitchen downstairs. Denarrion puttered around the large room while his laptop sat on the counter, cued up to Skype.

"Hey, how was the shower?" He poured a cup of coffee and set it on the counter next to the computer.

"Good." She settled into the chair at the counter. "I didn't use more than one head, but it's spacious."

"Yeah, I built it that way so it's more comfortable for two." He gave her a smoldering smile and she swallowed hard.

Maybe they could take a shower together. *You need to call your kids, remember?*

"Oh, I bet that would be fun." *What am I saying?* "Maybe we could try it out after I talk to my family?"

His smirk widened despite the mention of her kids. "Yeah, maybe we could. Should I give you some privacy?"

"No, that's fine, though you might want to stay out of the camera's eye. Once they see you, they'll want to talk to you." She reached for the coffee and sipped while she logged into Skype.

He snorted. "That scary, are they?"

Lissandra merely met his gaze and raised her eyebrows. "Not scary. Direct and assertive. Like their mother."

Uncertainty flashed through his expression before he covered it with another smirk. "Yeah, I can see that. It's good to have strong women in the family, right?"

"Count on it." She grinned as she made her Skype call, waiting for it to connect. After a click or two, Solenarra's face filled the screen. "Hey, Sole. How's it going at home?"

"Lissandra! I didn't expect you to call today. It's going well. How are you?"

"Hey, Mom, we're making kitty cookies." Kressendra appeared behind Solenarra and lifted the cookie sheet precariously. "See? They're all rainbow kitties."

"They're not rainbow kitties, Kress. They're kitties with *rainbow sprinkles.*" Lucenarra stepped to Solenarra's other side, drawn up with elder-sister disdain.

"Rainbow *kitties.*" Kress rolled her eyes. "Right, Mom?"

"I think they're beautiful, no matter if they're rainbow kitties or kitties with rainbow sprinkles," Lissandra said diplomatically. "Did you ladies sleep well last night?"

"Not as good as when you're here, but good enough." Luce nodded. "Have you met the guy dragon yet?"

Lissandra shot a look at Denarrion over the rim of the laptop. He raised his eyebrows and grinned as he prepared some sort of meal. He mouthed, *Guy dragon?*

"Yes, I've met Denarrion." She smiled but left her tone neutral.

"And what did you think of him?" Solenarra's

expression showed wariness.

Lissandra shot another look at Denarrion. This time he raised only one eyebrow and dropped his chin as if waiting to hear her report.

"I think he has a lot of potential. Of course, the first moment we met, he toppled me into the reservoir." She smirked.

"What?"

"Oh yeah, this guy really knows how to show a woman a good time. First, he dunks her, then he makes her coffee and a meal."

Denarrion rolled his eyes, but his smirk returned.

"He's there, listening, isn't he?" Solenarra's voice had grown dry.

"Yup." Lissandra grinned. "But I want to let you know my cell phone is now at the bottom of the lake, so don't try calling it. I'll get a new one here in town."

"That's crazy, Mom." Lucenarra shook her head. "I dreamt about Dad last night."

Lissandra's chest squeezed, but she smiled as she mixed the cream into her coffee. "You did?"

"Yes, he was working on a really big project in his workshop, and told me it was a special gift for you." Luce winked and went back to the cookies.

Why is Lucenarra dreaming about him now? It had been years since their father's death. Lissandra was ready to find a new mate. She didn't need her old one making another appearance.

"Are things truly going well, Lissandra?" Solenarra searched her expression, her own body language tense on screen.

"They are. It's early yet, but there's nothing screaming a warning, or anything." *Even if he did attempt to avoid me today.*

"Oh good." Sole sighed and her face relaxed into a smile. "Well, we should let you get back to it. This is your time and we don't want to take up too much of it. Thanks so much for calling."

"You're welcome, Sole." She raised her voice a little. "Bye, Kress and Luce! I love you and I'll talk to you again soon."

"Bye, Mom!" Their sweet voices chorused just before Sole ended the video call.

Lissandra picked up her coffee and frowned as she sipped, her gut telling her Sole had been jittery about something. *What in hellwinds was that about?*

"Everything okay?" Denarrion appeared over the top of the laptop's screen.

She frowned, but nodded. "Yeah, I think so. The kids are at least happy."

"I'd say so. Who wouldn't be happy with cookie baking?" He grinned and winked. "All that dough to eat before it even makes into the oven."

She laughed at his boyish grin. "Oh, I see, you don't want the cookies. You just want the dough."

"Well, yeah." He leaned on the counter in front of her. "It's all about the dough."

She laughed again and he tilted his head with a pensive smile. "You should do that more often, too."

She blinked. "What?"

"Laugh. It lights up your whole face, and makes you even more beautiful."

Despite the line-like quality, his compliment warmed her heart. He appeared sincere and the heat in his eyes promised he meant his words about her beauty.

"Thank you, Denarrion." She wanted to let herself go and fall into his glorious ice blue eyes, but she pulled back as she remembered the darkness around his aura. *I don't know him well enough to let go.* "Let me give a call to Torri and Charlie to let them know about my cell phone, and maybe we can go into town to get a new one for me?"

"Yeah, sure. I think we can do that. I'll even give you a

ride." He winked as he straightened. "The phone's on the table next to the pantry."

"Thanks." She slid of the chair and turned away, but she felt his gaze on her ass as she retrieved the handset. "Can you give me the Ravenwings' number?"

She turned and caught him staring. His polite smile had deteriorated into avid intensity as his gaze dropped to her ass. She hid her grin as he blinked and cleared his throat.

"Yeah. Uh, yeah." He swallowed hard and licked his lips before he rattled off the numbers.

She punched them into the phone and smiled coyly. "Thanks."

"Yeah. Uh, okay." He nodded and shot his gaze around the kitchen. "So, I'm gonna just check on the furniture orders for the weekend while you make your call."

Not so cool and collected now, are you, big boy?

He settled at the computer and typed something into the keyboard, despite his wet clothes molding to his body. *Damn, he does have find shoulders and arms.* The soaked t-shirt left nothing to her imagination, and she was good with that.

The scents of mint and cedar returned, and she shivered against the arousal they sent zinging through her. They made her want to forget everything and spend all her waking moments with this man.

Focus! I've never let a male distract me from my responsibilities and I'm not about to start now.

She made herself punch the numbers on the phone. Damn, how was she supposed to talk to anyone when a handsome male watched her with those mesmerizing eyes? Her awareness of Denarrion reached a new sensitivity, and she'd only kissed him once.

When Torriandra answered, Lissandra filled her in on their impromptu adventures in the reservoir and arranged to get her things. Torriandra told her they'd decided to have dinner at Denarrion's place to make sure he met her.

"Fortunately, you beat us to the punch, but we're still coming for dinner. Tell him to be ready."

Lissandra laughed. "Will do."

"Did you want us to bring your things with us?"

"Yeah, that would be great."

"Very good. We'll be there around six." Torriandra's voice softened. "Have a good time with him. He's a good guy, no matter what you might see or hear."

"What will I see or hear, Torri?"

"Nothing that can't be fixed with a little communication. See you tonight."

Apprehension slid through Lissandra as the line went dead. She hung up the phone, puzzled over what sorts of things she'd see or hear about Denarrion. What hadn't they all told her?

"Everything okay?"

"Yeah, I think so…" She replaced the handset and crossed her arms over her chest. "Something Torri said caught me off-guard."

"Oh yeah? What'd she say?" He rose from his seat and the wet t-shirt pulled against his chest, showing off hard sculpted muscles and a tiny ring through his left nipple.

Who knew a nipple ring could be so sexy?

"She said you're a good guy, no matter what I might see or hear. What is she talking about?"

Denarrion sighed and ran his hands over his face. "I suspect she means the shit my father says about me. He hasn't been thrilled with me or my life since I moved away from him."

"So, he spreads rumors about you?"

Denarrion shook his head. "Not rumors, exactly, just casual disdain. He's a well-respected member of the community, so if he mentions I'm not what he'd like me to be, the listeners run that through their own filters, and voila! Bad boy of Redfield."

She snorted, a smile curling her lips. "Parents aren't always thrilled with our choices." She waggled her eyebrows. "But I think I'd like to meet the bad boy of Redfield."

"Oh yeah?" His own sultry grin warmed her from the inside out. "You like bad boys?"

I'm starting to. With his wet clothes molded to his body, her nipples hardened in anticipation. *What's wrong with me? I barely know him.*

But that was why she was here, wasn't it? To get to know him. They were both adults and her children were safe with their grandmother. She could fool around with this guy, try his paces. Because it wouldn't harm her life if it didn't work out.

"I do kinda like bad boys." She took a few steps to him and ran her hands over his chest, wrinkling her nose. "But I don't like cold, wet clothing. How about we get you out of your clothes?"

He stepped back and whipped his wet shirt off his body. Lissandra's thoughts splintered as her gaze fell on his naked torso. A small patch of golden hair grew between his pectorals and trailed in a line down his belly, leading to his groin. She yanked her gaze up to his chest again before she started to drool. *And the nipple ring is damn sexy.* It matched the ring in his left ear.

"This is sexy." She flicked it with gentle fingers. "Do you have any other piercings?"

"How about we go upstairs and I let you discover for yourself?"

He grinned as he unbuttoned his jeans and worked them off his hips. The wet denim made his actions more comical than sexy, but she didn't miss the size of his cock, even three-quarters erect, as it popped out of his clothes.

"I think that's a great idea."

He stepped out of his jeans and left them in a wet heap on the floor of the kitchen as he took her hand, unconcerned with his nakedness. She enjoyed the play of his muscles as he drew her toward the stairs, his cock bobbing as he walked. He was large enough to send a ripple of excitement up her spine.

Arousal shot through her veins, flooding her pussy with cream as she watched his ass flex with each step. She forgot about the Ravenwings, dinner that night, or her missing cell phone, and followed his sexy ass up to his room.

CHAPTER SIX

Denarrion led Lissandra straight to the bed, but turned her back to it. "I think you're wearin' too many clothes."

"You think so?" She raked him with her gaze, licking her lips as she imagined pressing her face against his ripped belly and inhaling his musky scent while curling her hands around his tight ass.

"Oh yeah." A seductive smile curled his lips as his cock jerked. "Let me help you out of them."

He gently grasped the edges of the shirt and trailed his fingers over the skin of her belly. She whimpered and shivered, the sensual touches lighting up forgotten pleasure centers in her body. Glory, it felt so good to have a man's hands on her again.

It's been too damn long.

Her heart thundered in her chest. It had been decades and she was out of practice. But she was ready to enjoy the hell out of what he was doing. She dropped her gaze toward the floor and ended up getting an eyeful of his straining cock. Denarrion wasn't the largest male she'd ever had, but he was certainly large enough. *Bigger than my toys at least.*

She felt the heat of her thoughts bloom across her cheeks and swallowed hard before she raised her gaze again.

"Oh, glory, that feels awesome."

His lips curled into a delighted grin and he rose, pulling her close. "You smell wonderful, Lissandra. Like all the best things in the world." He nuzzled her neck.

"That's the shampoo." She groaned as he chuckled.

"Yeah, I don't think so." His ice blue eyes sparkled with mischief. "I think I'm gonna have to taste your entire body. Starting here."

He crouched in front of her and kissed her belly when it became exposed. A tingle of electricity zinged through her where his lips touched, and she whimpered in surprise. His smirk widened and he pulled his shirt over her head.

"Sweet Goddess, your breasts are beautiful." The reverence in his voice made her smile.

"So is your cock."

He grinned as he trailed his fingers over her sensitive skin. "You think so? It's pretty much like every other cock out there."

"Ah, but this is a dragon's cock." She wrapped one hand around his smooth shaft and shivered with the hot skin against her palm. "That makes it very special."

He chuckled, the dark, sultry sound revving up her arousal. "Yeah, well, today it's yours as soon as we get you out of my clothes. Damn, they've never looked that good on me."

"It all depends on how you wear them." She winked and he grinned.

"I think I'd prefer you out of them."

Denarrion laid gentle kisses on her collar bones and breasts. The brush of his lips and mustache tickled the tension out of her body, and tightened her nipples. She closed her eyes and gave into the sensations swamping her.

"You taste so sweet, Lissa." He peppered her skin with kisses. "Like fire and spices. Better than anything I've ever tasted."

"Come on. In your whole life?" She used a finger to tip his head up and leveled him with skepticism.

He met her stare with intense arousal. "In all my years."

The sincerity in his voice shook her to her core and cream coated her nether lips. His nostrils flared as he inhaled her scent and the corners of his mouth curled upwards.

"You're pretty smooth with the comebacks, but I'm not looking for flattery."

His eyes widened as he dropped to his knees in front of her. "What would you prefer?"

"Honesty." She tilted her head. "I'm pretty sure you've had a lot of experience with women in the centuries you've been alive, and while I like knowing you think I'm pleasing, I'd rather you didn't fluff my feathers with hot air and bullshit."

He lost his smile as he peeled the sweats off her hips and dropped them to the floor. But his gaze remained on hers. "I give my word I'll never bullshit you, Lissa. I will always tell you the truth. And you are the sweetest woman I've ever been with."

She held his gaze for a few moments before she smiled and nodded. "I can deal with no bullshit. And for the record, I think you're pretty hot stuff, yourself. No pun intended."

He chuckled and his hot breath warmed her mound. Heat seared her thighs as his hands slid over her ass. He stretched upwards, nuzzling her breasts with his cool nose. Denarrion opened his mouth and suckled the nearest nipple, making her moan. When he switched to her other nipple, the thumb of his opposing hand took over where his tongue had left off, flicking the hard nub gently to keep her aroused.

"Damn, woman, you smell good."

He dropped his nose to the curled hairs of her mound

and inhaled.

Lissandra jerked as the cool air flowed over her pussy lips and whimpered. Arousal roared through her, demanding she get closer to the heat he provided. She swayed forward into him.

"Easy there, cowgirl. I gotcha." The broad Brooklyn accent washed over her, liquefying her legs until she wobbled in his embrace. "Whoa. Let's get you into the shower before you collapse."

Denarrion rose to his feet and pulled her close to him, her breasts brushing his chest. She gave into the urge to study the contrast between his golden skin and her pale hand.

"Hey." He used one hand to tip her head up. "What's up? Are you afraid of me, Lissa?"

Those silver-blue eyes mesmerized her, and she took her time to answer.

"No. I just can't believe I get this opportunity for intimacy. It's been a long time."

He shot her a rueful smirk. "No pressure, right?"

"For whom? You or me?"

"Me." He tilted his head. "To make it damn good for you."

She let her gaze slide over his body. She followed the trail of hair down from his pectoral muscles in a tapered light brown line across his belly to his navel. She couldn't see where it flared at his groin, but she could feel it pressed against her mound.

Electric arousal shot through her body when he shifted his hips, grinding his hard cock against her. He smelled like a breeze off a glacier, cool, fresh, and ancient, evoking images of rainy afternoons spent in the comfort of a lover's arms.

The way he held her close and gazed at her suggested he could show her. He pushed her gently down on his bed and worked his legs between hers then settled his body over her.

"I thought we were getting into the shower."

"Eh, you already took one and I'm more interested in exploring your body right here."

Lissandra sighed, a twinge of uncertainty slithering through her as Denarrion kissed her neck and shoulders. She didn't know what to do with her hands and she bit her lip and dropped them on bed.

He paused and met her gaze. "Are you okay, Lissa?"

She groaned and shook her head. "Yeah, I'm fine. I'm just out of practice at mating."

She felt his laugh all the up way up her body and he grinned down at her.

"I think you're doing all right." Tenderness filled his eyes and he kissed the tip of her nose. "Besides, we aren't mating. This is what the humans call 'recreational sex'." He gave her a sly look. "And since we can control our fertility, this is purely for enjoyment." He cocked his head. "You *are* controlling it, right?"

She raised an eyebrow. "Yes. Are you?"

"Oh yeah." He smirked. "So, let me show you how good it can be."

He dropped his head and trailed kisses down her chest, pausing only to lick the undersides of her breasts. She gasped and fell into the sensations, arching her back to get closer to his wicked tongue. She hadn't remembered the skin on different parts of her body could be more sensitive than others.

"Oh, Goddess, Denarrion!"

"You're a goddess, Lissa."

He retreated slowly down her body, skimming her skin with feather-light touches. Sparks of excitement flared with each brush of his lips, teasing and tantalizing until he paused at her mound. He looked back up her body as he rested between her knees.

"Have you enjoyed what I've done so far?"

Lissandra sobbed out a laugh. "I don't think the word 'enjoy' could possibly encompass what I'm feeling. Let me put it to you this way, I'll bite you if you stop."

"Promises, promises."

His deep chuckle sent her arousal surging, and all conscious thought stopped as he lowered his head, brushing lightly over the sensitive hairs on her nether lips. His breath tickled her even more and she gasped, squirming. His weight on her thighs held her within his grasp and he growled, sending heat shooting through her. His dominance excited her as much as the exquisite sensation of his tongue swiping the sensitive skin under the hairs.

Oh, Goddess, yes! More.

She let out a low moan and arched her back as his warm, wet tongue caressed her inner labia. He didn't look up this time, sliding his tongue along the skin in one long, slow stroke. Electricity zinged through her when he reached the end of his stroke and sucked on her clit. She damn near melted off the bed.

Dear Goddess, how does he know where to touch me?

"Sweet glory, you taste better than anyone I've had before."

His choice of words jarred her a little, but the brush of his lips and tongue pushed the disquiet away. He licked and nuzzled the sensitive skin between her legs while his hands traced imaginary lines on her inner thighs, building her pleasure and frustration.

"Oh, Goddess, Denarrion. Please."

"Please, what, Lissa?"

His hands slid over her hips while his tongue concentrated on her clit. Each time his tongue slipped over it, bliss swamped her brain and a moan escaped from her throat. Power and emotions pressed into her mind with each touch, and her orgasm swelled.

"Please, what?" he repeated, pulling his head away.

"Please, more." She wriggled her hips before his face.

"More what? This?"

He dipped his head and pressed his tongue into her entrance. She wailed her bliss as pleasure inundated her awareness.

"Or this?"

He sucked at her sweet spot and slid two fingers between her nether lips, massaging her flesh as he coated them with her juices. She damn near tipped over the edge of ecstasy. Each pull against her clit ramped her arousal up higher in time with his finger caresses.

"Lissa?"

Had he asked her a question? She struggled to bring her mind back to coherency.

"All of it. More sucking, licking…Just more."

He rumbled in approval and wiggled his tongue against her clit. "More sucking your clit?"

"Yes!"

Denarrion chuckled at her vehemence and pulled her clit into his mouth just as he thrust one finger into her. She shrieked her pleasure and arched her back as he continued his onslaught of her senses. His hand moved gently in and out as he lapped at her with his tongue, but she squirmed to encourage him faster, harder.

It wasn't enough. Each time he pushed into her, her body seemed to shout triumph through her brain, only to wail with frustration when he withdrew. She panted with each withdrawal, rocking her hips to increase the pleasure, and her body tightened like a bow string. *Just a little more…*

"Come for me, Lissa."

He sucked her into his mouth hard and drove a second finger into her. Lissandra lost all control, riding his tongue and his fingers as she toppled over the precipice into ecstasy. She shot into the stars of bliss, roaring her joy and delight. He kept up his ministration until the orgasm dwindled and her body relaxed from its taut lines.

"Holy Mother." She looked back down at him. "I had no idea it could be like that."

He grinned his Puckish smile at her as he licked his lips.

"I'm glad you approve, Miz Charforest." He pushed back from her, his cock standing out rigidly from his body as he offered her his hand. "But come on. I promised you a shower and what kind of a host would I be if I didn't make sure you were all cleaned up after that tongue-lashing?"

Lissandra laughed and wondered if she could convince him to give her more 'tongue-lashings.' *Glory, I hope so.* His pale blue eyes gleamed as he drew her into the bathroom, lighting more fires within her belly and lower. Each muscle in his backside captured her attention as he leaned in to start the shower water.

Um-hmm, I like his human form.

Pleasure still hummed through her as he drew her under the spray. He adjusted the shower heads before he sat her down between his legs with her back to his chest. She relaxed against him as his hands slid over her thighs to caress her mound. A ridge of heated steel pressed against her spine, and she ached to help him find his release.

"But what about you? I'd like some of that special dragon's cock." She shifted to smirk at him.

His chuckle rumbled through her back. "Don't worry about me. This is about you today. I get pleasure from reminding you how wonderful this can be. It's for you to enjoy."

He gently pushed her head forward and down, allowing the spray to soak her hair. She hung there, closing her eyes. She soaked in the sensations of the water on her back and his cock pressed against her ass. A little thrill of pleasure zinged through her and she resisted the urge to wriggle against him.

It had been so long since someone had taken care of her, in any capacity, and she reveled in it. Denarrion filled his palm with shampoo and scrubbed it into her scalp with expert fingers. Comfort and relaxation followed, and she closed her eyes, nestling into his chest. The hard press of his cock against her tail bone added a level of eroticism to an otherwise ordinary event.

"Rinse for me, now."

His Brooklyn accent wrapped pleasure and delight around her as she leaned forward to submerge her head under the spray. How could his voice be so sexy? She scrubbed her hair, the scent of his sandalwood shampoo filling the space. A bubble of joy welled up at the thought of smelling like him.

He squeezed some body wash onto a puff, working it into lather before he met her gaze and gave her his Puckish smile.

"Ready for the rest?"

She nodded, too relaxed to use her voice.

He slid the puff over her skin, smoothing the lather across her body. It felt delightfully scratchy with the rough material gently abrading. She groaned with pleasure. When his other hand slid up her other side, the familiar electricity she'd experienced at the reservoir zinged through her again, making her grunt in surprise.

"Did I hurt you?" He paused.

"No. Just didn't expect your hand…there."

They both looked down where his fingers brushed her hip.

"Would you rather I put it here?" His free hand dipped into the gap between her legs, stroking her nether lips.

"Oh yes, there is perfect." She rocked her hips to increase the pressure.

"Yeah, I think there is great."

He growled as he washed her slowly, taking time to pleasure her body with nothing more than touches. Each one excited her until her breath quickened, her heartbeat hammering in her ears. She arched, pushing out her chest and he raised his hands to soap her breasts with careful motions.

She gasped as the puff snagged her nipple and he rumbled at her back, dropping the puff to pluck the hardening nubs with his fingers. Each squeeze sent fire to her pussy and she soaked the bench with her own juices. She shoved her breasts into his soapy hands and moaned as he massaged them. The nipples tightened with arousal and she wondered where her body had gotten so much stamina. *Probably from lack of use.*

"Ah, Lissa, you're a dream."

Before she could answer, Denarrion dropped light kisses to the back of her neck and all the stiffness drained out of her bones. The kisses rebuilt her arousal from the ashes of her afterglow. He slid his hands over her belly and between her thighs until his deft fingers stroked her pussy, pulling a gasp from her chest.

To her surprise, he only let his fingers feather over her with soothing caresses. She stifled a groan of frustration as his hands descended over her thighs and down her legs, smoothing on the soap. *There are other parts of your body besides your tits and pussy.* Yes, but she didn't want his hands anywhere else at the moment. She sighed and tried to enjoy his touches, banking back her arousal.

"Stand up for me."

"Why?"

"So I can wash that sexy ass."

Lissandra's limbs felt like Jell-O, but she forced strength back into them and stood with his help.

"You all right?"

"Yeah, I think so."

She hissed when his hands hit her back and butt as the erotic energy surged through her again. Why did his touches affect her this way? She'd never felt anything like it before, but she didn't want it to stop.

"Oh, that feels great, Denarrion."

"Yeah? Just let me finish off here and I can show you some other great things."

She turned under the spray to rinse and watched him lather his body in efficient motions. Her hands itched to do it, but she contented herself with the hot water and a personal peep show. She'd always appreciated the male human form, but Denarrion had redefined the standard. She particularly liked the way his penis stood out from his torso, jutting proudly upward with a slight curve when hard.

He caught her watching as he cleaned himself and slowed his hands over his cock and balls, making it more of an exhibition. His shaft hardened under her gaze. She couldn't take her eyes off his hands as they slid seductively over his scrotum and lifted the sac. She licked her lips as he rubbed his hand up his shaft and over the engorged head of his cock.

She swallowed hard, the urge to kneel before him and wrap her lips around it making her tremble. She'd had plenty of sex over the years without Mikelorrion, but they'd been quick one-night-stands without much intimacy, and no blowjobs. She'd never craved a male's cock in her mouth before, but Denarrion's veined shaft tempted her. Excitement and need flooded between her legs as she watched him caress his flesh.

"You like what you see?"

She raised her gaze and found him smiling lazily at her, pleasure and arousal in his eyes. The challenge she read lit her on fire.

"More than just like."

She grinned as she dropped to her knees between his legs and threw her arms around him, lavishing kisses on his chest and belly. She pushed him to the wall and flattened her body against him, rubbing her aching nipples against his hardening cock.

He groaned and tipped his head back, closing his eyes.

"Oh, fuck yeah, Lissa. That's damn hot."

His slick, hot flesh slid between her breasts and more of her juices dripped from her nether lips. She kissed his chin and his Adam's apple, pulling another groan from him. He dropped his head forward, the fire in his icy eyes warming her more than the cascading water as he wrapped his arm around her shoulder blades. She wriggled her belly against his hard shaft.

"What do you think you're doing?"

She offered him a wicked grin. "Washing you."

Desire flared in his eyes and he leaned forward, capturing her mouth as he drew her face up to his. Lissandra hadn't kissed much using her human camouflage. It had seemed superfluous, but Denarrion's attentions ramped up her arousal with each brush of his tongue. He opened his mouth and licked the seam of her lips. She opened her mouth in surprise, moaning as his tongue wrapped around hers and stoked her arousal up to "blazing" from "insistent". While their tongues tangled, she dropped her hands to his groin and grasped the hardness between them, pulling on the hot skin.

He moaned and pushed her back a little.

"Stop, Lissa, I don't think I can hold back much longer if you keep doing that."

"I don't want you to hold back." She reveled in the burning arousal firing her blood.

"But this is for your pleasure and I want to make sure of it." He caught her wrist and held her hand still, though his cock flexed within her grip.

"If this is for my pleasure then I want all I can get, and part of it is pleasuring you." She squeezed her hand and licked her lips, daring him to stop her ministrations.

"But—"

"No butts. That would hurt. Just in my pussy." She ground said anatomy against his right leg.

He growled in return and lifted her up. She yelped in

surprise as he shoved his knees between her thighs, one hand reaching up to cup her sex.

"Oh, you're wet for me here."

She wriggled her hips against his fingers as she eyed his straining shaft with need. "Wet and ready."

"You want to give me pleasure?"

"Yes."

"Then ride me hard, my dragon lady."

He grasped her hip with one hand and his raging cock with the other, urging her down. She didn't wait for a second invitation. She rocked her hips back until his hot tip brushed her nether lips then she slid down onto his cock.

The intrusion seared her with its glorious pleasure, her pussy clamping down as she wailed her delight. The electricity so much a part of their connection shot through her, making her tremble. Denarrion rumbled a groan full of relief and satisfaction, his eyes blazing with his desire.

"Oh, yeah."

Bracing her hands against his shoulders, she lifted her hips, dragging her pussy off his shaft. The electricity teased her core and her clit, making her squeal. Then she dropped, his cock filling her completely. She rose and dropped again, his hands steadying her as the pleasure built. Each time her clit rubbed along his hard shaft, her arousal surged stronger.

Her need built as she kept rocking, harder and faster, until he reached between them and rubbed his thumb on her clit.

She screamed as her ecstasy seared her mind. The pleasure of the water beating against her back and the hard, hot flesh between her legs drove her harder against his cock and hand.

"Lissandra, I'm going to come!" He ground out the words through clenched teeth. "You have to slow down."

She couldn't slow down even had the desire existed. Her only response to his imperative was a very dragon-like growl and she ground her hips down onto him harder. He growled right back in response and slammed his cock up into her as his arms wrapped around her back, holding her to him.

Their orgasms broke over them at the same time. She let out a roar as she bore down, her inner muscles clamping around his hard shaft with all their strength. He snarled and sank his teeth into her shoulder, holding her still as his cock pumped his release deep into her slick channel.

Lissandra dimly realized he'd marked her as True Bonded dragon mates. *Mikelorrion never did that.* Her mind wanted to analyze, but another wave of bliss from both his cock and his teeth swamped her cognitive abilities. She dove in head-first and allowed herself to revel in it.

Sweet Goddess, I'm Denarrion's True Bonded mate.

CHAPTER SEVEN

Denarrion came back to himself with his cock buried in Lissandra's pussy and his teeth locked on her shoulder. Pleasure still zinged through him each time her core spasmed and his cock responded in kind. The scent of sex and satisfaction filled the shower stall along with the steam.

He'd never had sex like it. It blew all his other encounters out of the water.

Not to mention best fucking orgasm ever.

She sighed and laid her forehead against his shoulder, jerking him back to the present. He slowly released her shoulder, gently licking the bite marks with his tongue as he savored the flavor of her essence. She shivered, and chagrin slid through him. How could he have bitten her? He'd never done anything so vicious before.

"Thank you."

"I'm sorry." They sighed at the same time.

Lissandra stiffened and raised her head to look down at him, her eyes wary.

"Wasn't it good for you? Did I do something wrong?" Alarm filled her expression.

"No. No, no, you didn't do anything wrong." He forced a smile. "And yes, it was amazing. I've never felt anything like it." He ran his hands over her arms in an effort to comfort her. "No, I'm sorry for biting you. I have never done that before. I don't know what came over me."

She frowned. "Don't you know what the Mating Mark is?"

"No, I've never heard of it. What is it?"

She raised her eyebrows. "Your parents didn't teach you about it?"

Denarrion clenched his jaw as disgust swelled to the forefront of his mind. The only things his family had ever taught him was how to hide himself and to live in misery. He refused to let them sully this moment and merely shook his head.

"The Mating Mark usually only happens between True Bonded partners—"

"True Bonded partners?"

"Didn't your parents teach you *anything* about being a dragon?"

Amazement filled her voice and he shifted with his mortification. What could he tell her? That he had lousy parents? *Hellwinds, every kid has that story.*

He had the odd feeling she was disappointed in him as she pulled her body off his lap and sat down on the bench beside him. He stood to turn off the water then returned to his seat.

A short silence filled the shower, interrupted only by the drops from the taps. Dread hit his gut with every little splash and he struggled not to shiver.

"Okay." Her voice sounded hesitant as if she regretted screwing him for the last hour. He swallowed his worry and stared at his toes in the water. "True Bonded partners are pairs of dragons who are mated for life."

"Isn't that the same thing as marriage?"

"No. True Bonding is deeper than marriage. It's more like the connection between souls rather than just an agreement to stay together for mating purposes." She leaned on her hands and looked down at her own feet, sweeping the water toward the drain. "It's like finding a part of yourself you didn't even know was missing and recognizing it in the form of another."

"Humans have something like that," he said after a moment. "They call them 'Soul Mates.'"

"That's an accurate term." Lissandra nodded. "When these True Bonded partners find each other and mate, the male has the urge to mark the female with the Mating Mark. Not only to warn other males away from his mate, but also to begin solidifying the bond between the partners."

He'd certainly felt the urge to bite her, but concern slid through him. What would his father say? *Shit! Why am I worried about what the bastard thinks?* The anger couldn't burn away all the fear. Had Lissandra's husband marked her? Had he lost this game before he'd even started playing?

"I felt it and I marked you."

He tried to keep his voice level, but his revelations worried him. What if she condemned him? He grimaced as he looked her in the eyes. All he found was solemn agreement.

"Yes, you did."

Dear Goddess, does that mean she's my True Bonded Mate? And what in hellwinds am I supposed to do with one?

Another sweep of her foot made him blink back into the present. Goose pimples pebbled her skin. *Damn, she's cold and I'm an idiot.* He rose and headed for the towels, chagrin nipping at his heels. Some host he'd turned out to be. He wanted to wrap the fluffy towel around her, but her expression said she had her mind on other things.

He caught the scent of her uncertainty and his stomach clenched. According to her, he'd marked her with the Mating Mark, but he didn't know if it was a good thing.

The way she held herself away from him now suggested the opposite.

Lissandra dried herself off, her expression closed, and his soul quailed. He wished he could bring back the sweet intimacy they'd shared in the bedroom and shower, but it had drained away.

The hairs on the back of his neck prickled and he caught her staring at him with an unfocused look, as if she saw deeper than his surface disguise. Fear rose up and he tried to shrug it away, but her gaze unnerved him. A little frown creased her brow. It occurred to him he might have hurt her with his bite.

Goddess, I'm so stupid!

"Did it hurt?" he blurted.

"Did what hurt?" She blinked.

"That mark I gave you."

"Oh, no, it didn't." She blushed. "In fact, it felt rather…erotic."

Denarrion couldn't stop his grin. "Erotic?"

"Erm, yes."

Hot damn! But another thought wormed its way to the forefront of his mind. "I suppose your husband marked you before?"

"No." She sounded more thoughtful than sad.

"He didn't?" Surprise and elation surged through him and his smile broadened. "I'm the first to mark you that way?"

"Yes." Again, the thoughtful response drained some of his elation.

"That's very good news." He wanted to puff out his chest and strut, but he settled for a smug smile. *I'm a badass dragon, uh-huh!* "Isn't it?"

"It's definitely a surprise."

Okay, not the response he'd been hoping for, but better than disgust or disdain. He wondered if his parents had ever experienced the Mating Mark. *I can't imagine them ever being happy enough to do it.* And imagining them having sex? Fo-git-about-it.

"I wanna know more about it, but right now I think we better get going."

She raised her eyebrows. "Get going where?"

"Grocery shopping." He shrugged. "I think your clothes should be dry by now."

"Shopping?"

"Yeah. For dinner." He wrapped the towel around his waist and chuckled. "You know, how the Ravenwings volunteered me to make dinner tonight? Besides, you said you needed to get a new cell phone."

Lissandra blinked. "Oh, my glory. That's right. I'd totally forgotten."

"Yeah, well, that's what I'm here for. To remember stuff." He headed to the closet. "Here, wear this to the laundry room." He tossed her a terrycloth robe. "Go ahead and grab your dry clothes. I'll meet you downstairs after I'm dressed."

Denarrion resisted the urge to watch her head out of the loft. *Just get dressed, jackass, then you can watch her all you want.*

He dressed as quickly as possible and headed down the stairs. He'd planned for Lissandra to stay in the extra bedroom while they courted, but now that he'd met her—and marked her—he had no intention of letting her sleep, much less sleep in a different bed.

Hellwinds, I don't think I could survive her sleeping anywhere else.

Now that he'd had her, tasted her, and touched her, he couldn't get enough of her. He thought he'd enjoyed sex before, but nothing compared to making love with Lissandra. He grinned. He'd do it as often as she'd let him from now on.

He found her sitting on his couch pulling her socks on as he came down the stairs. Damn, she was hot. Her grace and sexiness put all the other women he'd had to shame. He'd never experienced the sacred connection provided by the Mating Mark, but it intoxicated him.

Her emotions brushed his mind like a soft breeze, and he reveled in her satisfaction and pleasure. But nervousness intruded, shadowing the brighter, happier emotions, and his gut clenched. *Keep your shirt on.* They hadn't been together longer than a couple of hours. *She'll relax the more we hang out.* He hoped.

She had to be the sexiest woman he'd ever met and he looked forward to spending more time with her. The squeak of his couch as she sat back and extended her feet made him look up. She grinned as she watched him put on his own shoes.

"What?"

She shrugged. "I'm enjoying the show."

"Aw." He gave her a mock-frown. "I didn't get to watch you. You call that fair?"

She offered a mischievous smile. "I'll do a strip tease for you later. You didn't let me undress myself earlier, remember?"

Her playful offer sent the blood rushing to his cock and he had to restrain himself from grabbing her. Dear Goddess, he wanted to throw his shoulder and take her to bed again. Maybe he'd even bite her a second time.

The thought of biting took the edge off his lust and his smile faded as he tied his sneakers. What was that about? He'd never bitten anyone before. He'd never had the urge. With Lissandra, it had been a primal demand he'd been helpless to resist. It scared the hellwinds out of him, but she seemed to accept it as normal.

If biting during sex was normal for dragons, why hadn't his parents said anything about it? Given their intent to have him mated, it seemed a rather pertinent piece of information. *Maybe Mom will tell me.* To ask his father something about dragons was to invite his scorn and fury.

Denarrion had sworn off that kind of suffering decades ago.

He rose and headed for the kitchen to grab his keys, phone, and a baseball cap. Lissandra had turned to watch him, her gaze openly admiring. When he raised an eyebrow, she winked.

"Like I said. Enjoying the view."

Pride swelled in his chest, but he pretended take her compliment in stride. He reveled in her undivided attention. He'd never felt so virile, sexy, or handsome as he did with Lissandra's gaze fixed upon him.

Damn, the woman is like crack.

"You're quite handsome, you know that?" She followed him toward the front door.

"So I've been told." He offered her his best smile while pleasure flooded through his system.

"Great, so I'm just one in a long line of admirers?"

Her sarcasm hurt his pride a little and he held the door open to hide his expression. "I've been told it before, but it means a hell of a lot more coming from you."

"Oh yeah? Why?"

"Because you're a dragon."

She laughed. "I am definitely a dragon. Maybe after dinner we can go for a sunset flight. They're pretty romantic."

Fear and panic shot through him, and his gut cramped. He grabbed his canvas bags and locked the door as he fought to keep his voice steady. *I can't reveal my true nature to humans.* His father's admonition had been drilled into him since he'd reached his first millennium.

"Uh, yeah, probably not."

She raised her eyebrows. "Why not?"

"Too many people. I don't know what it's like in Colorado, but around here, the humans would definitely notice dragon silhouettes in the sky." That sounded plausible, right?

She frowned. "Then how do you spend time in your

natural form?"

We don't. Ever.

"We have to drive out of town. It's a trick, though. Lot of people live out here."

"Oh."

Her voice held reservation and disappointment, and his gut clenched again. *Way to go, jackass.* He wasn't winning points with her. Scrambling to recover, he changed the subject.

"So, you got any ideas of what I should make for dinner tonight?"

She coughed a laugh. "You don't know what you're planning on making tonight?"

"Nope. I'm hoping the grocery will give me some inspiration."

"I've done that kind of shopping." Lissandra followed him as he trotted down the stairs to his truck. "Sometimes it works out great, sometimes is just makes me buy crap."

"That's why I'm taking you with me. We'll tag-team it and see if we can hold each other back from buying crap."

She laughed and the sweet, amused sound sent his blood shooting to his groin. His memory served up the image of her in the throes of passion, and he dropped his keys.

"Having trouble?" Amusement filled both her face and voice.

"Yeah, apparently the keys wanted to escape. Can't you hear them screaming 'run away, run away!'?" He grinned as she laughed again and they climbed in the truck. "Now if I can just find the ignition."

"It's right there on the steering column. You know, if you need the reminder." She winked.

Jeez, you'd think I could be suave for this woman. He consoled himself that she hadn't been dating, so she couldn't compare him to someone else. *Except her dead husband. Fuck.*

"Thanks for the pointers."

"You're welcome." She said it in a sing-songy voice from a recent kids' movie. "This is a nice truck. Does it get good gas mileage?" She ran her hands over the butter-soft navy-blue leather seat.

"Ah, you know, it's not the best, but it's great for hauling furniture to the store downtown."

Denarrion smiled as his baby started up with a muted roar. He loved his truck and it always seemed to be a hit with the human females. It also made him feel normal, as if he was as human as the rest of the community.

"Are you some sort of dragon moving company?"

"What?" He shot her a startled glance. "Oh, no, I carve furniture for a living. I haul the finished products to one of the stores downtown." He laughed. "Dragon moving company. That's great. I'd have to have some sort of slogan like 'I treat your hoard as if it was my own.'"

Lissandra grinned. "That's pretty good. You should get a website and a mobile app."

"It'll be my backup career." He loved her laugh. It turned him on so much he had to divert his thoughts elsewhere to keep his shorts fitting comfortably.

The market was only a couple miles from his house in a shopping center with smaller shops around it. He remembered the cell phone provider had a place next to the market.

"How about we head to the cell phone shop to get you a new phone before we go into the market?"

"Sounds good. I feel naked without it."

He almost closed his eyes to remember how she had looked naked in his bed, but reined in the impulse before they hit oncoming traffic.

Focus, dammit! You don't need an accident to impress her.

They made it to the shopping center without killing anyone, but the parking lot sat fuller than usual with all the holiday tourists. He parked the truck toward the end of the lot and they got out. He remembered to grab the canvas bags out of the back before they headed for the stores, and he reached out to take Lissandra's hand.

She raised her eyebrows as he wrapped her hand in his, but the action seemed natural. He liked the way her hand fit and the softness of her palm. The memory of her hands on his body diverted some of the blood from his brain again.

"Can I hold your hand? I want to."

She tilted her head with a warm smile. "Yeah, I'd like that."

As sense of pride and pleasure puffed up his chest as they strolled into the cell phone store. He'd never experienced joy in showing off the woman with him, but Lissandra made him feel like a stud. He released her while she perused the phones, and soon they had a replacement. Lissandra took his hand again as they headed to the market, warming his heart.

"Wow, they really went all out in décor, didn't they?" She pointed at the forest murals, complete with wolves, moose, elk, cougar, and deer, painted on the walls.

"Yeah, it's like stepping into an alpine market. That's their tagline."

She snorted. "It works better when there are real mountains around."

"You don't think we have real mountains?"

She shook her head. "The Appalachians were high, but they've been worn down over time. I don't think you have anything over seven thousand feet in elevation."

"Yeah, no. That's really high." He widened his eyes in theatrical amazement.

"My house sits at ten thousand six hundred feet in Colorado." She gave him a bright smile.

"Damn. You must get a lot of snow." He could imagine her standing in nothing more than a thick fleece robe in fluffy drifts among the aspens, her lavender eyes sparkling in the sunlight. His cock seconded that idea with a standing ovation.

"We do. But the sunsets are to die for."

"Sounds great up there. I'd like to see it some time, but preferably in the summer first." He winked and she laughed.

As they picked a shopping cart, several people waved and called out to him.

"I take it you're a regular." She inclined her head at another woman waving.

"Yeah, I come here a lot." He responded with a smile and a wave, but kept his attention on Lissandra. He wasn't interested in the human women anymore.

"I can see that." She raised an eyebrow at yet another woman waving and winking suggestively behind the deli counter. "So, what are you thinking of making for the Ravenwings?"

"I've got this great chicken recipe." His mouth watered with the idea of feeding it to her, but he reminded his libido they'd have company. "It makes enough to feed an army."

"Oh good. Maybe I'll learn it so I can feed the kids when they go through another growth spurt." She shook her head ruefully. "There was a while there we had a helluva time keeping them fed with the deer around our house."

"Your kids eat the deer?" Surprise hit his system. It had been a long time since he'd had venison.

"Oh yes, true carnivores, both of them." Her shoulders straightened with pride. The love she had for her children flowed over him like a physical wave. *Whoa, that's weird.* "Luce often fishes in the river near our home for trout and she's great at it. Kress doesn't like to impale worms on the hook, but she can snare rabbits in her homemade traps. It's impressive to watch her hunt. She reminds me of a cougar, all silent and intense."

"You let them hunt and fish on their own? Wow." He thought they were pretty young.

"Yeah, I'd show you pictures of them, but they're on the cloud and I can't get to them yet on my new phone." She shrugged with a grimace.

"They're a little young to do it on their own, aren't they?"

"No, I don't think so." She shook her head , the feeling of love dissipating. "I was hunting at Kress's age, although I think she's better at it than I was. She has more patience. Didn't you go hunting by your first century?"

The word "century" set off warning bells in the back of Denarrion's mind and he gave her cautionary look. His father insisted that dragons must fit in with the general population, and talking in terms of centuries or millennia would give them away.

"What?" Surprise flickered across her face, followed quickly by a deeper frown. The warmth of her energy withdrew a little and uncertainty took its place.

"Well, you know I don't have kids, so I have no idea when you start teaching them to do stuff." He shrugged and smiled, trying to diffuse the tension. "I guess I'll have a chance to learn with your kids."

She eyed him, but her shoulders relaxed a little. "If the courtship works, yes."

"I think it's going okay so far, don't you?" He squeezed her hand again.

"Yeah, sure." She nodded, but her brows remained down as another store employee sauntered past, her hips swaying. He waved to her and smiled.

Lissandra cleared her throat. "So, dinner. What's it to be?"

Her sharp question made him wonder what he'd done. Had he pissed her off somehow? He made his mind focus on food.

"Chicken Yakitori is one of my favorites, with Fennel and Orange Salad, and Smoked Salmon Potato Bites."

"Doesn't that seem a bit fancy for just a family

dinner?"

He shrugged. "It makes a lot of food and there will be four adults." He grinned. "It'll be fun to show off my gourmet abilities to you." Then he winked. "Besides, it's actually really easy."

She laughed and some of her tension fled. "Sure it is."

"You'll see." He picked up a large package of chicken breasts and tried not to think of how much he preferred to be fondling hers.

"So, what do we need for these recipes?" She scanned the meats displayed in front of them.

"Let's start in the produce section and grab some fresh herbs."

"Sounds good…" Her eyes narrowed and her lips tightened as she glanced over his shoulder.

He glanced behind him and caught another female shopper walking by. The woman smiled, eyed him from head to foot and back with a hungry smile, then winked and murmured, "Hi, Denny."

"Hey." Denarrion grabbed a package of smoked salmon and smiled at Lissandra, but she shook her head and retreated, her shoulders stiff once more.

Shit, now what? Are all female dragons this prickly?

Shrugging it off, he followed her and tried to decide how he could help her relax. Perhaps she needed a little wine and chocolate. Women loved those sorts of treats, and they had all night. *Thank the Goddess she didn't bring the kids with her.*

Usually, he did his shopping alone before the female arrived so he could impress her with being prepared. Each date had been calculated and engineered, but he preferred to just wing it with Lissandra. He liked her easy energy. *Yeah, when she's not prickly.* He didn't know her very well, but hopefully it wouldn't take him long to figure her out. He covertly watched her as she selected some oranges.

"How many do we need?" She raised her gaze to his

and smiled flirtatiously.

His body reacted to her smile and he had to swallow a couple times before he could focus on her words. "Uh, three. Oh, and ten pounds of potatoes."

"Red or white?"

"Red."

"'Kay." She turned away and Denarrion let his gaze slide over her backside, enjoying the way the denim hugged her ass. He remembered the feeling of those muscles in his hands, and his cock hardened again.

"Hi, Denny. How are you?"

Denarrion blinked as Carrie from the bakery walked into his line of sight and paused, offering him a coy smile and a wave.

"Good, Carrie, thanks." He gave her a quick smile, but shifted away, unaccountably annoyed with the use of his common name.

"I haven't seen you in a while. You doin' good?"

"Yeah, yeah. Things are going great. Thanks for asking." He turned away before she could ask another question. He'd had her just a few days before Lissandra arrived, but she'd scratched his itch and he'd moved on.

Lissandra's shoulders tensed as he approached and she gave him a tight smile. "So, what else?"

"Uh, soy sauce, and sour cream, I think." *What's going on? What happened to the happy woman I fucked earlier?*

"What about bread? Is this a good bakery?"

He caught her curt tone and raised an eyebrow. "It's not bad. They make some good bagels here. Are you okay?"

"I'm fine, just hungry. I take it you have sampled most of the breads here?"

"Yeah…" Anger and disgust filled the air around her and he tried to gauge the cause. Did she hate bread? "Most of them. Their Italian bread is good with meals."

"Maybe we should pick some up, then." She dropped

soy sauce into the basket. "Sour cream, you said?"

"Yeah..."

She strode off and he followed her, wary for a landmine. Why was she so angry? Had he done something to piss her off? He nodded to some of the local women who passed him in the aisle, but didn't respond to their appreciative smiles. His mind replayed the last few minutes in an attempt to decipher what had gone wrong.

Before he had cleared the aisle, Lissandra tossed the sour cream into the basket and whirled away again, her head up. *Dear Goddess, what did I do?* Denarrion ran through the conversation of the last few minutes, but nothing came to mind to explain her demeanor.

By the time he strode to the bakery, Lissandra wore a curiously bland expression as she examined the breads while Carrie watched her with open hostility. Carrie offered him a brilliant smile and shifted so her ample chest plumped up as she rested her arms on the counter.

"Hey, Denny. What can I do you for?" Her voice had sweetened and she tilted her head coyly.

"Uh..." He glanced at Lissandra, but Carrie pointedly ignored her. "Just getting some bread." Lissandra straightened and met his gaze with icy lavender eyes.

"This one looks good enough." She dropped a loaf of Italian bread into the basket. Then she turned to Carrie. "Thanks *so* much for your help."

"Anytime," Carrie replied with a malicious smile.

Whoa, was Carrie trying to stake her claim to him? Denarrion thought of all the women in the store, those he'd slept with and those who hoped he would. Had all of them reacted the same way with Lissandra? *Oh shit.* If every female had acted like she owned a piece of him, not only would there be very little of him left, but he suspected Lissandra would feel like she'd inherited the dregs.

She strode away with her back stiff and her face impassive.

"Have a great day," Carrie called after her then smiled at him. "Sure I can't get you anything, Denny?"

"Uh, no. I think I'm good. Thanks."

"Oh, I know you're good." She winked and his gut sank.

Hellwinds. Irritation combined with distress slithered through his gut. He was more than a good lay, dammit. Except, he hadn't been looking for more than that with them. Now, he'd have to do damage control when he got home or the courtship would be over. He nodded to Carrie and strode after Lissandra, dread filling his chest.

They reached the checkout stand and his heart dropped into his stomach. Carrie's best friend stood behind the check stand with her elegantly made up face pinched with disdain. She hung up the store phone next to the register and glared daggers at Lissandra as she approached.

Oh, hellwinds.

"Hey, Denny, this all for you today?" the cashier asked in her best bedroom voice. Jeez, were they all going to hit on him? Lissandra arched a brow at him, but maintained her icy silence.

"Yep, that's it." His guts clenched with chagrin and anger swelled. What the fuck was wrong with these humans? He put the canvas bags up on the counter.

"How is your summer going? Carrie mentioned you haven't called her in a while." The woman eyed Lissandra, her lip curling as if to suggest he'd been fooling around on Carrie.

"Yeah, well, I've been pretty busy with my work. How much do I owe you?"

"Twenty-eight, forty-four." Her bedroom voice grated on him. It always had, each time he'd taken her home, but it seemed worse now.

He handed her thirty dollars and glanced at Lissandra. The dragon widow still had a smooth expression on her face, but her lilac eyes flashed fire. *Bloody fucking hellwinds*. He nodded to Carrie's BFF when she gave him his change and took a deep breath as he watched Lissandra head for the door. *I'm so screwed.* Thank the Goddess dragons didn't eat their partners when angry, although Lissandra might. He didn't know her well enough.

"Thanks," he muttered.

Lissandra strode ahead as if she'd already washed her hands of him and his stomach sank. *Shit, fuck, dammit all.* Her anger seethed beneath her calm façade, but when he unlocked the truck's doors, the mask cracked and her fury bled through. He swallowed hard as he set the bags in the extended cab and settled into the driver's seat.

His dalliances with the women in town had never been a problem before. But it didn't take a genius to realize he'd messed up. Bad. He just hoped he'd make it home alive.

CHAPTER EIGHT

Holy shit. He's a fucking man-whore.

"It seems I've been stepping on a few people's toes." Tightly coiled anger washed through Lissandra and she gritted her teeth to keep from roaring. "Apparently, there are a few females in that store who feel you belong to them. Is there a girlfriend I should apologize to?"

She met his gaze as she crossed her arms over her chest, her hands tightening into fists.

"I don't have a girlfriend, Lissa."

"No? Hellwinds, Denarrion, how many of those human females did you fuck?" She clamped her mouth shut and shook her head. "Sorry. It's none of my business who you slept with before you met me." She lapsed into a tense silence, not sure where to go from there.

What a clusterfuck. She might have been a widow for thirty years, but she hadn't fucked her way through Cloudburst to relieve the grief. All those women had stared at Denarrion like they owned him. *Or wanted to.* And he hadn't done anything but flirt and smile back at them.

As he took a breath to say something, she snarled and slammed her fist into the seat.

"You fucking *marked* me, Denarrion, and despite your

distressing lack of knowledge of things dragon, *I* don't take it lightly." She jabbed a finger toward the store's entrance. "If there are women in this town who feel you belong to them, I need to know what kind of shit-storm I'm in for. Will I have to fight off the entire town, or only the ones who work at the store?"

His lips tightened and his eyes flashed anger, but he shook his head. "Not the whole town."

"Well, that's good." Sarcasm writhed in her voice. "Dammit, Denarrion, you had the one in the bakery just a few days ago."

"How do you know that?" His eyes widened.

"I'm a Goddess-blessed dragon. I could smell you on her." Lissandra punched her thigh and he winced. "She obviously feels like you're hers and I'm hoeing in her garden. Did you lie to me? Aren't you eligible for mating? Or are you just sowing wild oats? Because if you're still playing the human love field, I'm gone, Mating Mark or no."

Denarrion raised his chin, anger starting to kindle. She didn't care. If he was planning to fuck around while mated to her, she'd find a better partner. She didn't give a shit if he was her Goddess-blessed True Mate. She wouldn't stand for this kind of slovenly behavior. *Not for me and not for my kids*.

"I'm not playing the field." He growled and gritted his teeth. "None of them own me."

"Really? They seem to think they do."

He shook his head and tightened his hands on the steering wheel. "I have no interest in any of them."

"Bullshit."

"What?"

"That's a load of shit, Denarrion. The one you slept with just a couple days ago is apparently not done with you. If you weren't interested, you wouldn't have plowed her."

"You make it sound so crass—"

"It *is* crass. It's disgusting. You've had more women than a Chippendales show. I'm surprised the bakery wench didn't throw her panties at you."

"I'm done with it, Lissandra. I promise." His voice came out as little more than a growl.

"Oh yeah? Why should I believe you? I'd hate to cramp your style."

"I'm serious. You came here to begin a courtship with me and I'm fully committed to it. I have no interest in mating with a human female. I may sleep with them, but that's recreation, not commitment." He floundered to a stop and shut his mouth in a tight line.

"Recreation?" She widened her eyes as her fury boiled over. "Glory, you really are just a man-whore, aren't you?" She threw the truck's door open. "That's it. Take your 'recreation' and shove it. I'm outta here."

"What? Wait!"

But she was done listening. She had a new cell phone and could call Solenarra to let Charlorrion know she was heading home. What a waste of time. She should've figured out Denarrion wasn't serious when he tried to avoid her this morning. What the hell had she been thinking? He was a confirmed bachelor and too set in his ways.

She headed for the main road through the parking lot, her strides fast. To hellwinds with cocky males with Puckish smiles. He probably used that damn smile to charm them between his legs. She bared her teeth and growled, and another shopper skittered out of her way with a startled gasp.

"Lissandra, wait." Denarrion caught her arm and swung her around.

She snarled and used her momentum to pivot and slam him up against the nearest vehicle. "Don't fucking touch me."

He released her and held his hands up. She gritted her teeth to keep from biting him, but she didn't want the possibility of bonding to him. He'd bitten her, not the other way around.

"I'm sorry, Lissa. I'm sorry. Please hear me out." He begged her, his expression contrite.

Dammit, he's not lying.

"What do you want, Denarrion?"

"Just to talk. Please. Don't leave until I explain. Please."

She glared at him, torn between getting away before he dragged her through the muck of his past and trying to salvage the burgeoning relationship. *He fucking marked me today.* She closed her eyes and shook her head.

"Why should I?"

"Because I need to explain. I need to tell you how my life has been here." He shrugged, his eyes resigned. "If you don't like the explanation, you can go. I won't fight you. Just give me a chance to tell my side."

"I can *smell* your side."

"I know." He nodded, dropping his hands to his sides as she backed away from him. "But that was yesterday. Today everything changed."

She snorted, her lips pulling down in a scowl. "Really? You're going to go with that?"

He spread his hands in helplessness. "It's the truth." He lurched off the vehicle and straightened his shirt. "Come back to the truck where we can talk. Please."

She stared at him, trying to see if he played games with her, but he only smelled of regret and desperation. *At least he's not lying.* She narrowed her eyes and gave him a short nod. His shoulders slumped in relief and he gestured to the truck.

"Thanks."

"Don't thank me yet. I'm just coming for the explanation. Then I'm gone."

****

Denarrion damn near crumpled to the heated asphalt when she agreed to go back to the truck. She'd given him the chance to explain, but he knew he was on borrowed time. If he didn't get this right, she'd disappear like smoke in the wind.

They returned to the truck and he opened the door for her, not certain she wouldn't have kept on walking. She climbed in and he took a moment to catch his breath before sliding behind the wheel. He needed to tell her things had changed, but she sat with her arms crossed over her lovely breasts and anger wafted off of her like a rancid perfume.

"Okay, talk."

He swallowed hard and nodded.

"I've been kinda prolific with the women around here."

If possible, her expression grew even flatter. He cleared his throat and hurried on.

"I think they see it as sort of a prize if they've "had me." I won't give you any excuses for my previous behavior, but I will say I've enjoyed the women for recreation and to gain sexual experience."

"You planning on more human 'recreation' if we mate?"

"No, I'm done with all that." He paused and the silence stretched. "Lissandra, I'm committed to this courtship and I want to be with you, only you."

She raised her chin. "That's a good line, Denarrion."

What more could he tell her to convince her he wanted something different?

"Ah, shit." He shook his head and tried to find words that didn't sound cliché. "It's not meant to be a line, but everything I want to say sounds like it came from a movie or something. I've never met anyone like you, no matter how many women I've been with, and I really want to give this courtship a try."

"Why, because you fucked me already?"

"No. Because after meeting you, all those women seem like junk food snacks when what I really want is a full, rich meal." He shrugged with one shoulder. "I'm done eating junk food."

Lissandra shook her head. "What guarantee do I have that you won't go find yourself a willing human female when you get tired of me?"

"I'll never get tired of you—"

"Don't hand me that bullshit. You don't know me well enough to say that. We're both here on a trial basis, and I'm starting to wonder if we have different priorities." Her voice was quiet, but edge of anger had disappeared. "I came here for a courtship, but there's some other reason you agreed to this, isn't there?"

His gut sank and he turned his head to look out the window toward the cars gleaming in the sunlight. "Yeah. My father said I needed to start looking for a mate."

She sighed and nodded. "And you aren't close with your dad." She ran her hands over her face. "Look, I get it. I wouldn't want to go on a blind date set up by someone I didn't trust for the sole reason of mating, either. Hellwinds, I wouldn't have bothered to come. It sounds like you had a good life with as many women as were willing to put out for you. But I get the impression you aren't planning to quit that life anytime soon, and I'm not going to be your mate while you fuck a string of mistresses."

"I wouldn't do that." The idea made him sick.

"Wouldn't you? How would I know? You didn't choose to go on the blind date, your father put you up to it. That's not a recipe for success."

He nodded. "Normally, you'd be right. And when I learned about the blind date, I was pretty dead-set against it." He met her gaze and straightened his shoulders. "But then I met you and my perspective changed. I've never committed to anyone before."

"You think a commitment will make a difference to you?" Lissandra stared at him with a hard expression, her arms crossed over her chest. She assessed him with those lilac eyes and he suspected she waited for him to prove himself to her.

How in hellwinds am I going to do that?

"The only way I can prove I'm serious is with time." He held her gaze, hoping his honesty filled his expression. "Commitment is a big deal to me and I've never made one to anyone." He took a deep breath. "If we make this an official pairing, I won't need anyone else, human or otherwise."

"Are you sure, Denarrion?"

"Yeah, I am." He realized the words were true. Lissandra's fire and passion electrified him the way none of the human females ever could. The long line of women stretching into the shadows of his past seemed like cardboard dummies with no defining characteristics. She eclipsed them all. "I never thought anyone would have a problem with me seeing someone else, but I guess Carrie figured she'd finally gotten a taste and wasn't about to let it go."

"She wasn't the only one."

"Yeah, I realize that now." He nodded with a grimace. "But I promise, I'm done with human women, and I'll make efforts to prove it as our courtship goes. You're important to me, Lissandra. Important enough to show you I'm serious about this."

They sat for a few minutes in silence and Denarrion wondered if she'd believe him. Would she get up and leave? *Shit.* His guts cramped into a tight knot when he thought of all the human women he'd taken to bed over the decades. Maybe he should consider moving out of Redfield. *Yeah, only if I can go with Lissandra.*

She rubbed her chin with one finger. "If we do get through this courtship and decide to mate, would you be open to leaving this town?"

"In a heartbeat." Again, the words rang with truth, even to his own ears. He'd never considered leaving his family, but the need to be with Lissandra superseded their familiarity.

"Hmm." She nodded, but he couldn't read her expression. "We'd best get back to the house before the heat ruins the vegetables."

"Yeah. Yeah, good idea."

He started the truck and they rolled down the windows to let out the heat, but the tension in the cab still made him sweat. She kept her face turned away out her window, the breeze ruffling her hair. He wished he could see her expression, but wondered if it was a blessing that she hid it from him. *How in hellwinds do I prove to her I'm done sleeping around?*

When they arrived at his house, she slid out of the truck without saying a word, her expression impassive. Denarrion wanted to punch something, but he gathered the groceries and followed her. Lissandra's silence hung heavily on him and he tried to think of something he could say to reassure her.

He trudged up the steps to the door and shoved the key in the lock. "I'm sorry, Lissandra. I never thought I'd meet someone like you, you know, a dragon female, so I didn't see anything wrong with using the humans for pleasure." He shrugged awkwardly. "I knew humans could be possessive, but you know, I've been here a long time and my moving on has always been part of the arrangement with them. I should have told the women to back off. I'm sorry I didn't hold up my end of the deal."

He begged her with his eyes, hoping he hadn't screwed up so badly she'd walk away. His fear ramped up as the silence stretched. *Shit, what do I do now? Beg out loud?*

"Please, just give me a chance."

"What will you do with this chance? I'm not willing to

come second to your previous lovers."

He set down the bags and grasped one of her hands. "You won't. After meeting you, I can honestly say my life actually sucks, and I'd be a jackass to walk away from you. No one has affected me the way you do. I'll do better when we're in public together, I promise."

Lissandra bit her lip as she considered his words, her lilac eyes unreadable. *Oh, please, Goddess. Let her believe me.*

She took a deep breath and nodded. "Okay, Denarrion. But you have to warn me if I'm going to run into anymore of your previous lovers. And you have to show them, *and me,* that you're serious about this courtship. Prove you're off limits."

Relief flooded through him and the tension bled away from his shoulders.

"I can do that. I *will* do it. Thanks for giving me a chance."

She shook her head with a grimace. "Hellwinds, none of us are perfect. And really, it's none of my business who you've been with. Even if it's the whole town." She gave him a dry grin. "Just promise me, at least for our courtship, you'll focus on me rather than them."

"Definitely." *No fucking contest.*

"Good." Her smile relaxed.

"Come on inside and let's get this meal cooking." He shoved the door open and gestured for her to enter before him as he picked up the grocery bags.

She stepped inside and Denarrion breathed an inner sigh of relief. He'd dodged a bullet, and he'd make damn sure he didn't fuck up again.

CHAPTER NINE

Curling her hand tightly around the paring knife, Lissandra tried to diffuse her anger over Denarrion's harem of human females. *It's none of my business.* She knew her condemnation was unfair. In terms of finding sexual gratification and experience, humans were plentiful and dragons scarce. Hellwinds, she'd had a few hookups since Mike died. *Emphasis on few.*

Deep breaths. He apologized and says he's done.

Surreptitiously, she glanced over at him with her Sight as he washed dishes. Dark hazing still edged his aura, but it appeared to be fading in places. *Where is the darkness coming from?* Could she trust him to keep his word? Had the smudges on his soul caused his excessive need to screw humans? She hadn't scented any deceit in him in the truck.

"There, done." He wiped his hands on a dish towel and reached for the open bottle of wine to pour two glasses.

"I think you're the first male I have ever seen who does the dishes of the meal he had just prepared."

"Yeah, well, you can't cook if you don't have dishes or space, right? So I clean it up." He shrugged good-naturedly and the muscles under his t-shirt rippled. She tried to ignore the shot of arousal swamping her system with the memory of his body between her legs.

"I wish I could get my daughters to feel that way."

He laughed. "Not much for cleaning up?"

"No, especially their rooms. It's like they meticulously ransack their personal spaces, but when it comes to cleaning up, there's a lot of bellyaching and stuff gets thrown into whatever container is closest." Lissandra shook her head. "It gives me fits."

"Have you thought of making it a game?"

"A game? To clean up their rooms?"

"Yeah, you know, offer them bribery. If you clean up your room, I'll take you to the park, or whatever." He grinned and winked. "Works on me all the time."

"You bribe yourself?" She laughed.

"Yep. If I finish my work, I can sit back and watch the games on TV."

She paused, eyeing him in surprise. "You watch sports?"

"Hell yeah. Don't you?"

"Not really. What sports do you like to watch?"

"Baseball and hockey, though baseball is more fun live than on the boob tube." He hung the dishtowel up to dry and gestured toward the back of the house. "You want to see what I consider work?"

"Sure. You mean your dragon moving company?"

"Ha ha, very funny." He grinned. "Let me show you around."

"What? There's more to see than this kitchen and your bedroom?"

"You're just full of those little remarks, aren't you?" He swatted her ass as he led her out the back door toward the separate garage. "Out, woman. Prepare to be amazed."

It looked more like a barn than a garage, but the wide doors opened to allow large vehicles inside for easy loading. Denarrion opened a human-sized door and ushered her through.

Scents of wood and stain and paint thinner washed over her as sawdust cushioned her steps. A thin layer of saw dust covered the floor while wood working tools lined the walls. Peace and contentment settled around her. *This is his sanctuary.*

Furniture in various states of completion stood in a gaggle off to one side. Rocking chairs with elegant scrolling along the headboards and armrests lay between straight back chairs with gently undulating seats and claw foot tables with hidden drawers just beneath their tops. Some end tables had intricate wood inlays that created different colored designs and pictures on the top surface.

"Wow." Lissandra trailed her fingers over the headboard of an unfinished chair. "These are gorgeous. Did you make them yourself?"

"Yeah. Do you like them?"

"Oh, yes, they're beautiful." She paused at an inlaid table. "You have a real gift with wood. What do you do with them?"

"I sell them at a shop in town, and at the local craft festivals."

"Wow," she said again, admiring a finely carved dining room table.

The top split down the middle so leaves could be added to enlarge it. He'd carved lion's claw feet at the base and scrollwork on the trim underneath the tabletop.

"These are really amazing. Do you do all the mechanical work on the tables as well?"

"Yeah."

"Just spectacular."

Lissandra touched the items of furniture and sensed Denarrion's joy and satisfaction in each piece. She felt the positive energy suffusing the whole workshop. She scanned the room with her Sight and caught him glowing brilliantly as if a high-powered spotlight shone inside him. Even the tarnish faded from his aura in this place.

"I can see why you like it here. It smells really good."

"Yeah? You like the smells of wood and varnish?" He smirked.

"They kind of remind me of home. It smells like you work with a lot of pine."

"It's a fragrant, soft wood, that's for sure."

She crouched on the floor to inspect the wood inlay of a chest of drawers, but paused when she heard him step up behind her. Her back tingled and she suppressed an aroused shiver as he gently closed his hands around her arms. She stood up slowly and turned her head to look at him with raised eyebrows. He stared back at her with flames leaping in his ice blue eyes and her nipples hardened in response to his intense gaze.

"You really like my furniture?" He pulled her closer until her back pressed up against his chest. Then he laid a very soft kiss at the base of her neck.

"Yes."

"Good."

His kisses slid across her back and shoulders, lighting fires in her belly and beyond. She moaned deep in her throat and gave herself to the pleasure of his touches as she leaned into him.

"Let me show you more of my work."

He pulled away from her and led her by hand to an unfinished table in a sunny corner of the barn. The golden wood glowed in the dusty sunlight and the scent of maple rose from its unvarnished surface.

"This is one of my favorites, you know?"

"Why?" She'd never heard her voice so breathy, but she couldn't seem to catch her wind.

"'Cause it's big and perfect for doing this."

He tugged her t-shirt out of her capris and pulled it over her head before unhooking her bra to expose her breasts.

"Has anyone ever mentioned you have perfect

breasts?" He slid his hands up her arms to her shoulders and turned her gently until she faced the warm tabletop.

"Is this why you're turning them away from you?" Laughter bubbled up from her chest as he nipped the nape of her neck with a short growl.

"Nah, I just wanted to get a good understanding of their textures. I tend to see with my hands." He dragged his palms down the slope of her chest to her nipples. She gasped with surprised pleasure as he massaged the peaks and areolas until they tightened.

"Ah, Holy Mother, I love the feeling of your breasts in my hands." He moaned with delight. "I love how they fit in my palms and the way the nipples tease me." He gently pinched them between his fingers and she echoed his moan. "Ah, so you like that, eh? Me too. Now, lie flat so I can take care of you."

Denarrion pressed a hand to the center of her back until she draped over the tabletop. The scents of pine and sawdust filled her nose as he stretched each arm out until she gripped the opposite edges.

"How is this taking care of me?" Despite the hard surface pressing against her breasts and belly, her arousal surged when he flashed her a lustful smile.

"Don't worry. Just don't let go of the table, yeah?"

She nodded then shivered as he trailed his fingers along her bare arms to her shoulders, pausing there to massage them lightly. She lost sight of him, but she heard him shift behind her before he pushed the large bulge in the front of his shorts against her ass. He groaned in pleasure as she wriggled back at him with her hips.

"Oh, sweet Goddess, your ass is so damn sexy."

"That's not all that's sexy."

His laugh almost covered the rustle of clothing behind her, then he stroked her back with feather-light touches and kisses. She squirmed in delight and her juices coated her nether lips as excitement built. *Oh, Goddess, he's merciless.* His work-roughened hands chafed her skin and shots of electric desire pulsed through her, followed by erotic swipes of his warm tongue and lips.

As she bucked upwards with pleasure, he unbuttoned the clasp to her capris and slid them off her hips until they pooled around her ankles. His hands roamed over her exposed flesh, trailing fiery hot touches that swamped her mind with pleasure.

"Oh, Goddess, Denarrion. Don't stop."

"I don't plan to."

The rumble of his voice combined with his ticklish caresses sent arousal flooding through her. He knelt in the sawdust, the warm wetness of his tongue teasing her tailbone. She shifted to look over her shoulder, but his hand shot up to her middle back and pushed her back down.

"Just wait, my dragon lady. You won't be disappointed." She whimpered as he pushed her feet apart on the floor, her aroused scent filling the air between them.

What is he going—Oh my glory!

His hot mouth hit the flesh on inside of her thigh and his tongue skimmed close to her throbbing core, obliterating all her thoughts.

Denarrion slid his tongue over the curve of her left cheek, kissing where he stopped then repeating the same motion on her right cheek. She shivered at the warm wet sensations while his hands coasted over her skin until they tangled themselves in the hair on her mound. She gave a gasp of surprise as he gently pulled on the strands, sending prickles of sensation straight to her brain, and her pussy flooded with cream.

"Ah, Lissandra, I can smell your sweet musk." He pushed her legs wider apart. "Let me taste you again." Then he licked her down the length of her slit.

She wailed in delight as her hands tightened on the edge of the table. He held her cheeks apart as he feasted on her sensitive tissues smothered in her own juices. He hummed as he held her firmly against his hot mouth, the vibrations electrifying her whole body. She writhed in his grip as his tongue slid in and out of her.

Pushing backwards, she ground her hips against his face until she felt his tongue flicking her clitoris and the tip of his nose pressed into her opening. Pleasure swirled up her spine and she shivered again, drowning in hot lust.

"Holy Mother, Denarrion, I can't take much more of this."

She panted as he licked and played with her pussy while his fingers gently massaged the skin of her inner thighs. Each touch built her arousal higher until she had to have more, harder, deeper. She let out an involuntary squeal-moan and jerked against his grip.

"Easy, dragon lady, easy." Denarrion pulled away from her pussy with one last swipe of his tongue and stood. "Your taste is like sipping electric brandy with a smoky finish. You're sweetness and fire all rolled into one. I've never enjoyed this as much as I am with you."

Then he thrust his hardened cock into her slick opening and she shrieked in delighted surprise, rising on her hands.

She'd never felt so full. The ecstasy swirling through her body topped all the other times she'd made love. Denarrion fit her so well, better than anyone before him.

"Fuck, you are so hot and tight."

His dirty words set her arousal ablaze and she flexed her inner muscles around him He groaned through clenched teeth, holding himself still as her pussy caressed his hard shaft.

"Goddess, I want you hard."

"Oh, you want to play rough, do ya?" He growled and excitement rose in her as he pressed against her until his lips caressed her ear while his hands held her hips still. "I can do that." He pulled his hips back and slammed into her again.

"Ahhhh!" She writhed in his grip and threw her head

back. "More. Oh glory. Please, more."

"Harder?" Amusement colored his voice. "Or slower and deeper?" He pulled back again, but returned with exaggerated slowness.

Lissandra's senses exploded and a tortured moan broke through her lips. Sweet fire licked over her skin. Even the soles of her feet prickled with sensual needles. She rose up onto her toes, trying to work herself backward to make him thrust faster. But he chuckled and held her still as he continued to thrust with agonizing slowness.

"Please, Denarrion, harder. Harder," she begged, writhing around his cock.

"How much harder, Lissandra?" He seated himself balls-deep in her tight cleft.

The sensations of pleasure ripped through her, tearing away any coherent thought other than *more, harder, now!*

"Yes, harder, Denarrion. Harder, harder now!" She thrust backwards while tightening the muscles of her pussy around his shaft.

He roared and slammed into her in a pounding rhythm that stole her breath. He held her hips tightly as he plowed inside, increasing his rhythm until the unfinished table beneath her rocked on its sturdy braces.

Her arousal surged closer and closer to orgasm and she clutched the table, her knuckles flashing white. He grunted and snarled as he pounded her pussy until they shrieked out their release with wild abandon.

Dust motes swirled in the warm air like paisley fractals and Lissandra flew with them on a flood of bliss. When he sank his teeth into her shoulder again, she tripped into another orgasm as her spine arched and her claws gouged the undersides of the tabletop.

Stars cascaded behind her eyelids and she fell with them, joy and contentment warring for superiority. Denarrion's teeth remained clamped to her shoulder and the long canines stabbed into the muscle sent tingles through her. She shivered and the pleasure shot from her shoulder down to her pussy, making it clench. He moaned and his cock flexed within her, sending ricochets of bliss back through her body.

"You are amazing, Denarrion."

He growled at her shoulder and slid his hands up to caress her breasts. She hissed and wriggled her hips, reveling in the pull of his teeth in her shoulder. She loved him holding her there and the vibration of his growls through her body. She wanted more, more touches, caresses, and bites.

When he finally released her, he licked the bite marks tenderly, sending puffs of air over her punctured skin. She shivered again.

"I didn't hurt you, did I?" He pulled out and eased her off the edge of the table, cradling her body against his. She laid her head against his chest and listened to his heartbeat.

"No, I enjoyed everything you did. Particularly this." She pointed to the bite mark on her shoulder and offered him a dreamy smile.

He actually blushed. "I couldn't resist biting you. I just lose my head and want to latch on. It has never happened to me before, with anyone."

She smiled and patted his chest lovingly. "Thank you. That means a lot."

"It does?" His eyebrows rose.

"Yes."

He pulled her into his arms and kissed her neck above the bite mark while his hands slid down her back to cup her ass.

"I guess you're teaching me a few things about being dragon while I teach you a few things about loving in human form."

Foreboding stabbed into her chest with his words, but she shoved it deep. He was her True Mate, and the Goddess would never set her up to take a fall. *It's going to be fine.*

I've never had a True Mate before. I'm probably just nervous from being single so long. But the disquiet settled into her gut. She hid it behind a smile as she grabbed her bra and capris, and shook out the wood shavings.

"I had no idea there were so many ways to make love in this form."

"Oh, yeah, humans are nothing if not pleasure-seekers. You should see some of the toys they use."

"Toys?"

"Yeah, you know, vibrators, cock rings, fuzzy handcuffs. Stuff like that."

Lissandra grinned. "Your cock needs a ring? Is that some sort of weird marriage symbol?"

He laughed. "No, well, I guess it could be." He winked. "But it's meant to keep a guy harder longer."

"Oh, Goddess, I don't know if I could handle you harder longer." She gave him her best coquettish smile. "I might turn into a flaming pile of dragon goo."

"I'm sure on you it would be sexy."

They finished dressing and headed back to the house. She paused on the threshold of the workshop and looked it over. She understood why he found happiness there. It would always hold a warm place in her memories. *Actually, more of a hot, wet, sexy place, but whatever.*

"What are you thinking?"

"I like your workshop. I like it a lot." She winked and he grinned.

"Oh, good. Me, too. Now more than ever."

They returned to the house just as the buzzer on the oven sounded off. Denarrion grabbed some oven mitts and pulled out the potatoes before they got too crispy.

"Good timing."

"I'm good like that." He smirked as he set the pan on the stove to cool.

"Oh, you're more than good." She let her satisfaction show in her smile. The memories of his hard cock buried inside her sent shivers up her spine. "I think I need a nap."

"A nap? Did I wear you out?" His eyes widened.

"You better believe it." She snorted. "I haven't had this much sex in…well, decades. I don't have that kind of stamina yet."

"We'll have to work on that, then." He leaned over and brushed his lips against the mark on her shoulder.

"Breaks your heart, doesn't it?"

"Absolutely. It's a dirty job, but I'm willing to take it on."

"I'm sure you are."

He led her up the stairs and into the master bath again. He adjusted the shower and he undressed her with rapt attention. His touches remained tender and attentive, though hot arousal burned in his eyes. Her body tightened in reaction, but she didn't have the energy to keep it up for long.

"In you go. Take your time, okay?"

"Thanks."

She stepped in, letting the water soak the remnants of sex and wood shavings away from her skin. *Jeez, I've been taking a lot of showers lately.* The idea made her giggle. If this was how Denarrion rolled, she could probably get used to it. She washed herself down carefully, treating her over stimulated flesh with extra care.

When she'd finished, he held up a large fluffy towel for her. She stepped out with a grin and he wrapped it around her, drying her skin with long gentle strokes. He peppered the few patches of exposed skin with light kisses before he led her into the bedroom and lifted the covers without a word.

"Get some rest. I'll be back in a few minutes." He kissed her lips and threw the sheets over her.

Oh, yeah, I could definitely get used to this. Her eyes slid closed and sleep enclosed her in a soft cocoon.

****

Denarrion stood beneath the spray and thought about the beautiful woman asleep in his bed. Lissandra had to be the best thing he'd ever experienced. But some unnamed fear kept creeping in when he thought of what she'd said about true mating. It felt right, yet his mind kept issuing a warning.

Fuck it. He wanted her and he'd make the best of this courtship, scary new dragon issues or not. He'd never been as satisfied after sex as he was with her, and even now his cock rose with the memories of being inside her.

Down, boy. She's resting. He settled onto the bench in his shower and let the water pound against his body. One woman who'd visited him had loved to shave while sitting there. She had also enjoyed his more personal attentions between her legs. He wondered if Lissandra would like that kind of attention. *I know I would.*

He finished his shower and threw a robe over his shoulders. She lay in his bed, completely out, and she'd never looked so beautiful to him. While he would've liked to snuggle with her, he headed downstairs to check on the meal. No point in burning dinner when trying to make an impression.

The other thing worrying him was the biting. She said it was the mark of true mates. *But she hasn't bitten me.* Maybe it was only a male reaction. *Or maybe she doesn't feel the same.*

The insidious voice dampened some of his contentment. She hadn't mentioned her own feelings, but she certainly hadn't turned him down for sex. The times he'd bitten her blazed in his memories with more emotion than he'd ever experienced.

He checked on the food then poured himself a glass of water. If the courtship worked like he hoped, they'd have plenty of time to learn about each other in private.

Except she has kids. His gut sank a little. What did he know about being a father? Hellwinds, he didn't even have a role model to use as a template. Granted, she hadn't spent all her time with him talking about them, but he suspected she was a package-deal. Surely, they weren't her whole world and he wouldn't lose her entirely to them once they mated.

Nah, it'll be fine. Family was important, although he'd never seen it in his own, but Lissandra seemed fully committed to the courtship. But the disquiet remained and the little voice warned he'd lose her in the end.

CHAPTER TEN

The late afternoon sun painted a moving pattern across the windows overlooking the backyard when Lissandra opened her eyes. Pleasant aches accompanied her return to her body and she stretched slowly. Another body shifted with her and she froze.

A moment of disorientation hit her. Was it her husband? *Mikelorrion is dead, has been for decades.* Then who in hellwinds lay in bed with her?

Denarrion's scent filled her nose as his arm settled over her belly, and her tension melted slowly away. True Mate, her mind said, but the distress remained.

While the connection with him was instant and strong, the darkness she'd Seen in his aura made her stomach clench. Add to that his unusual ignorance of dragonlore, and her tension returned. Why was he so ignorant, and where was the darkness coming from?

And do I want that anywhere near my kids?

Lissandra turned over and looked at Denarrion. Asleep, he appeared content and relaxed, handsome and happy. She'd seen evidence of his happiness in his ice blue eyes, cocky grin, and his hard cock. *Especially his cock.* She snorted softly. *Hard to miss that.*

But she sensed a well of darker emotion, especially now that he'd bonded with her. It lurked beneath his happy-go-lucky façade. Not quite anger, but more than simple irritation. It would have been stronger if she'd bitten him in return, but something held her back.

She tried to follow the energy to its source, but the origination kept slipping away from her questing mind as if it had a consciousness of its own. She frowned in concentration as she shifted into her Sight, but the source remained elusive.

Sighing, she closed her eyes and rolled onto her back, letting her mind drift in hopes her feigned inattention would give her a clue. Nothing. Grumbling, she tried to fathom where it could stem from. Thinking back to their conversations, she suspected it had something do to with his family. He'd avoided talking about them whenever she'd asked, which seemed strange. Most dragon families loved to be together. What was so wrong with his?

Maybe it's me. Maybe he doesn't want me to meet them.

The idea unsettled her as much as his obvious interest in human females. While his "research" into human sexual relations had paid off, she didn't like their obvious possessiveness. He said he would commit to her if they made the courtship official, and they were True Mates. Did he regret the pairing already? And what could she do if he did?

You're overthinking this too much. Relax. There's plenty of time to decide.

She opened her eyes and studied Denarrion again, trailing her fingers over his cheek as he slept. *What is this darkness riding you?*

His ice blue eyes opened and focused on her with amusement and lust. "Hey."

"Sleep well?"

"Yeah, very. Best I've slept in years." He rolled and

stretched like a cat. "What time is it?"

She twisted around to look for a clock. "I don't know. Late afternoon, I think."

He groaned. "I guess we better get up then. Charlie and Torri will be here soon."

"Yes, they will." Unease tugged at her attention. "Why do you call your brother and his wife by their common names?"

"It's just easier than saying all the extra syllables," he replied flippantly, but she sensed his stress settle back onto him, and the darker energy surged in response. "I don't mind calling you Lissandra, though. Your name just rolls of the tongue. Come on, let's get up so we can meet everyone clothed."

Denarrion rose quickly as if the thought of the Ravenwings finding them in bed together had unsettled him. Her earlier disquiet flared at his nervousness.

Sex between the courting partners had never been taboo in the dragon community. That was a human trait. But she caught his discomfort and rose to dress, determined to keep her own energy serene despite her mate's disquiet.

"It'll be fine, Denarrion. Didn't Charlorrion suggest this blind date to you?"

He paused and gave her a perplexed smile. "Yeah. Why?"

"I'm pretty sure they'll know we've had sex." She winked.

He laughed, but it sounded strained. "Yeah, well, after this afternoon, I'd rather not make it a major conversation." He grimaced. "It's obviously no secret I've been a player in town."

Lissandra wanted to calm his anxiety, but Denarrion's focus turned to dinner and she let it go. *It's not really my job to make him feel better.* No, but she could let him know she'd forgiven him. *Mostly.* The past couldn't be changed, but she expected the present to be different.

They'd finished setting the food out when someone knocked on the door.

"Ready for this?" Denarrion set the last bowl on the table as he headed for the front.

"Sure." Except anxiety wafted from his shoulders like a new fragrance. "It's going to be fine. They're your family."

"Yeah, that's what worries me." He shook his head and opened the door. "Hey, Charlie, Torri, come in."

The Ravenwings entered, Charlorrion carrying Lissandra's bag. "Hey, Denarrion. How's it going? You look pretty good today. You feelin' okay?"

"Shut up." Denarrion swiped at his foster brother. "I'm fine. Come in, jackass. You want something to drink?"

"Just water for me tonight. I'm on shift at eight." Charlorrion shook his head. "Here's your stuff, Lissandra. How are you doing? He treating you okay?"

"Hey." Denarrion scowled, but Lissandra nodded.

"Yeah, the day has gone pretty well, all things considered." She took the bag. "Thanks for bringing my things. I'm going to take this upstairs."

Torriandra raised her eyebrows. "Upstairs already? I guess things are going well, then."

"Better than expected, eh, Denarrion?" Charlorrion raised a sardonic eyebrow.

"Yeah, yeah, I know. Don't rub it in."

Lissandra shook her head and shoved away any lingering concerns as she took her bag up to the loft. She dropped it on the hope chest at the foot of the bed but paused before she returned to the people downstairs.

Something felt off. They'd gone at this courtship thing a little fast, though she didn't mind the hot sex. But she wondered if she'd come into this with only half the information. Solenarra and Charlorrion had put the blind date together, and on the surface, everything seemed fine. But Lissandra sensed some tension in both Torri and

Charlie with regard to Denarrion. *What the hellwinds is that about?*

She shook her head. *Won't figure it out if you stay up here.* Squaring her shoulders, she descended the stairs, smoothing out her expression to be friendly and polite.

"So what are you drinking tonight, Lissa?" Denarrion gave her a wide smile and she let her lips return it.

"Just water for me tonight. I'm a little dehydrated."

"Are you sure? I have some dragon fruit wine if you'd like some." He held up a crystal decanter with the pale green liquid inside.

"No, thank you. That stuff's too much for me. I'll just stick with ice water." She shook her head to hide her grimace. The last thing she needed was to be distressed and drunk.

"All right. It's here if you want it." He gave her his Puckish grin and set it on the counter.

"Hey we brought over beef and veggie kababs. You got a little grill we can use?" Charlorrion held up the pan full of skewers.

"Oh yeah, let me light one. You shoulda told me you were bringing that over. I would've had the grill going." Denarrion led the way out to the front porch.

"What's the fun in that? We have to show Lissandra how on the ball you are."

"You suck."

Charlorrion's laugh faded as they stepped out the door and Lissandra filled her glass with water and ice from the fridge. She sighed as she settled onto one of the chairs around the table. Torri grabbed her own glass and sat across from her.

"Can you tell they're brothers?" Torri grinned as she shook her head. "They harp on each other every chance they get."

"It's good to see Denarrion has one good familial relationship." Lissandra nodded and hoped her smile was natural.

Torri blinked. "He told you about his parents, yes?"

Lissandra shook her head. "No, not really. But from the things he's said, I can guess they don't get along well."

"No." Torri's expression grew sad. "Charlorrion moved out when he met me and it was probably the best thing for him. But he was a foster brother and could leave anytime he liked. Denarrion and his sister weren't as free to leave."

"Is Denarrion close with his sister?"

Torri shook her head. "Not as much as they used to be. Denarrion and his father Waltarrion don't see eye to eye on much of anything." She closed her lips tight. "I'm sorry. I shouldn't be talking about this as it's not my story to tell. You should ask Denarrion more about it."

Lissandra nodded. "I will. It seems like a sore subject, though."

"Yes, it can be." Torri forced a smile and waved her hand. "But this is good that you're here. Hopefully it'll get him to open up and let go of some of his past issues."

Lissandra snorted. "You mean like sleeping his way through the entire town of Redfield?"

"Oh." Torri's smile faded. "You heard about that?"

"I didn't have to hear. I experienced his former lovers' animosity. Apparently, several of them thought of him as taken."

"Sweet glory." Torri grew pale. "What happened?"

Lissandra grimaced but related the story of their shopping trip. The more she spoke, the paler Torri became.

"Oh, holy Mother, I knew that would come back to haunt him someday." She drank some of her water. "I'm so sorry you experienced that. Denarrion went through a rebellious phase against his father, and being a dragon, that lasted decades rather than just years. He really is a good guy under all the anger."

"Anger?"

"Good glory, I can't seem to keep my mouth shut today." Torri ran her hands over her face. "Let's talk about Charlorrion. You know he's a firefighter?"

Torri's bald attempt to change the subject made Lissandra's narrow her eyes. *They're not telling me something here.* But she let the subject drop and allowed Torri to lead her away from Denarrion's troubled past.

Torri bloomed with joy talking about her husband working with humans in a profession he seemed completely suited to do. True, he had to keep his true nature hidden and he couldn't do more than the strongest human, but the other firefighters seemed to have accepted him as a little stronger and faster than them at a high adrenaline job.

"His favorite part of the job, though, is going to schools and festivals to interact with children about fire safety." Torri beamed. "He's really just a big kid himself. He loves children and can play with them for hours."

"Charlorrion said you really want children."

"Oh yes, very much. I try to get my fix by teaching first grade at the school here in Redfield, but summers are hard." Torri shook her head. "I don't really want to wait to have my own, but I don't have a choice for the next fifty years."

"I know it's hard to be patient. I'm glad you both do things that help you 'get your fix.'" Lissandra nodded, smiling at Torri's wistfulness. "I know both Kressendra and Lucenarra have kept me sane through the grief process after losing my husband. They both gave me someone to focus on."

"Oh, I bet they did. How long has it been?"

"Three decades next year. It goes by in a blink." Lissandra let the last of her grief drift away. "But I realized it was time for me to find a new partner. To be honest, I caught my oldest daughter Lucenarra soothing my emotional upheaval with a deft touch. I don't know how long she's had the ability, but if she's showing it this early,

I'll need to find her a teacher soon." She paused. "My mom and I don't have that ability."

"Oh, that's wonderful. You know, that's my specialty, the emotional Healing gift."

"Really?" Relief and excitement flooded through Lissandra. "I've been thinking about Lucenarra's apprenticeship now that she's over two hundred. It's so important to find the right mentor."

"It is. It can make all the difference in the world." Torri nodded with a knowing smile.

"If I introduce you to her, would you be willing to take her as an apprentice in the future?"

Torri paused, studying Lissandra for a long moment before she said anything.

"Yes, I think that's a wonderful idea." But her exuberance faded as an odd mixture of emotions slid across her face. "I would have to meet her first, of course, and we couldn't make any concrete plans until…"

"Until?" Lissandra's guts tightened as her apprehension returned in a rush.

Torri's gaze darted toward the front door as Denarrion entered the house with the empty pan. He noticed their looks and raised his eyebrows.

"Until you and Denarrion solidify your plans, of course." Torri pasted a bright, false smile on her lips. "I'm sure we could take the kids on some field trips if you and Denarrion want some time alone. You know, if the courtship works out."

"Are you okay, ladies? Did something happen?" Denarrion came back to the table with lettuce and other vegetables for a salad.

"No, no. We were talking about her kids." Torri waved his curiosity away. "Here, can I help with that? You want a fresh salad, right?"

"Yeah, that's what I was thinking." He shot a look at Lissandra. "Are you sure everything's okay?"

"Yes, everything's fine. Do you need help with anything outside?"

She rose and rolled her shoulders to loosen them as the tension returned. She wanted to ask Torri why she stopped, but she didn't think the other woman would answer while Denarrion stood within earshot.

"Nah, but I wouldn't mind the company." He winked and she laughed, hoping to shake off her disquiet.

It's going to be okay. Everything will work out. She took a deep breath and watched Charlorrion and Denarrion tease each other over grilling the kababs. Cautious contentment rose as their easy camaraderie settled over the yard. *Maybe this is Denarrion's true family.*

The tension eased and laughter seemed to be the order of the day. Charlorrion shared stories about growing up with Denarrion as a brother. Denarrion chimed in with his own teasing comments and they all ended up laughing. Lissandra enjoyed hearing the connection between these dragons and she told stories of what it had been like to live in Colorado with Solenarra.

They all retired to the house to eat. Lissandra's concerns drifted to the back of her mind and she relaxed enough to enjoy the conversation. It had been a long time since she'd enjoyed the company of adult dragons. While she loved being with her kids, it was nice to have conversations about things other than Disney movies and kids' books. *I could get used to this.*

"Well, I hate to take off, but I gotta get to my shift at the fire station." Charlorrion rose with Torri and helped her take the dishes to the kitchen. "Denarrion, you knocked it out of the park with that meal. Good stuff."

Lissandra found herself reluctant to say goodbye. Odd misgivings about being alone with Denarrion crowded to the front of her mind. *Don't be ridiculous. You've been with him, naked, twice. What are you afraid of?* But the pep talk didn't erase the concerns Torri had hinted at earlier.

Denarrion rose as Torri came back to the table and Lissandra pulled her aside. "What were you going to say earlier before Denarrion came in the house?"

Torri's eyes widened. "What do you mean? When?"

"Earlier while you were making the salad. We were talking about my daughter Lucenarra."

Understanding flashed in Torri's eyes, but she gave a perplexed smile and shook her head. "I don't remember." She shot a look at Denarrion and her husband before she shrugged. "I'm sure it was nothing." She gave another strained smile as she waved at her husband. "Charlorrion, I'm going to use the bathroom before we go."

Lissandra swallowed her growl. There was definitely something important the Ravenwings held back. Something to do with Denarrion. *And if they knew this before I came here, why wouldn't they have told me up front?*

"Before you go, Charlorrion, would you give me your cell phone number? My old phone is in the bottom of the reservoir." She waved her new phone.

"Yeah, sure."

"Hey Charlie, give me a minute and you can take your pan with you." Denarrion headed back to the kitchen while they waited for Torri to come back.

Lissandra raised her chin and met Charlorrion's gaze. "Level with me, here. Tell me what's wrong with Denarrion."

"What?" Startled panic flashed through his eyes. "What do you mean?"

Bingo. "Come on, I'm not stupid. You and Torri have been giving me subtle clues all night. Is there something I should know about Denarrion and his family? Something you haven't told me?"

Charlorrion opened his mouth to answer, the scent of guilt overriding his usual fragrance, but before he could say anything, Torri rejoined them and took his arm.

"Come on, Charlorrion. You're going to be late if we

don't get going. It was great to see you both again." Torri manhandled her husband out onto the porch.

"Don't forget your pan." Denarrion trotted past her to hand Torri the pan. "Thanks for bringing the kababs."

Lissandra scowled at Charlorrion, but he grimaced and followed his wife out the door. *What in hellwinds are they trying to hide?* Was it just that Denarrion had trouble with his family and slept with the whole town? Or was it more than that? Charlorrion looked back before they climbed into this truck and his expression conveyed regret and guilt.

Dammit, I know there's something wrong.

She stepped out onto the porch and pulled out her phone, intent on calling Solenarra. The warm evening wrapped around her with its crickets and frog songs as the phone rang in her ear. Unfortunately, it went to voicemail and she tucked the phone away without leaving a message. The evening sky turned a rosy pink against the silhouetted trees and she let her mind drift, hoping the snarls and tangles of her worries would straighten out.

Denarrion returned to the porch and wrapped his arms around her waist from behind. He kissed the nape of her neck. Despite her worries, it felt so good to be in his arms. *Because he's my true mate.* But she hadn't bitten him yet. Why was that?

"I think it's bedtime for you, young lady."

She laughed and turned in his arms. "I had a nap today. I'm not tired. Are you?"

"Nah, I just like the idea of tucking you in to make sure you sleep well." He grinned.

"Of course you do." She chuckled as she pulled away, but her smile died as soon as she had her back to him. "Why don't we get some tea and sit out here for a while? It's nice."

His brows came down a little. "Yeah, okay. Everything all right?"

Lissandra nodded. "Yeah, I'm fine."

"Okay, I'll go start the kettle and I'll be back." He ducked back inside and she sighed.

She settled into the lounge chairs on his deck with the intent to relax, but the disquiet bounced around inside, breaking apart her contentment. Something was wrong and Charlorrion had avoided the issue. *Time to go to the source.* She needed to know more before she let this relationship continue.

CHAPTER ELEVEN

Denarrion sensed Lissandra's withdrawal the moment the Ravenwings left. She'd been talking to Charlie, but his foster brother had been uncharacteristically fidgety and taciturn. He had no idea what had set her off. *Did Charlie or Torri say something to her?* He'd rehashed all the conversations in his head, but nothing seemed out of place.

When he'd wrapped his arms around Lissandra, she'd been stiff and reserved. He wanted to give her more pleasure tonight, but when she suggested sitting outside, he sensed she wanted to talk. *What the hell is wrong?* He put the kettle on to boil and pulled out matching mugs before heading back outside.

She'd settled into one of the plush outdoor chairs he had on his porch, her expression distant. Ignoring his foreboding, he turned on the outdoor lights inset at the corners of the porch and sat in the other chair. In his extensive experience with women, pensiveness rarely boded well. Swallowing his dread, he reached for her hand. She let him take it with a distracted smile.

"A penny for your thoughts."

"I think we need to talk."

His gut sank. He'd heard the 'we need to talk' line, and

in his long experience, it meant the relationship was ending. Unreasoning panic rose in his chest and he gritted his teeth against the anguished moan surging from his gut. *Don't panic. She hasn't said anything yet.*

"Okay. What about?" Did it have anything to do with the look Torri had shot him earlier in the evening?

"I want to talk about some things before I decide if I'm going to go forward with this courtship."

He froze and his gut sank as the kettle whistled from inside the house. He barely heard it over the thundering of his heart. *Oh, no. What did I do?*

"You don't want to continue this courtship?"

"No, I said want to *talk* about things before we continue." She crossed her arms over her chest. "I know it seems a little late, but I need to know some things before we do anything more."

"All right." He nodded though he felt like throwing up. "Let me get the tea and we can talk."

She nodded and turned her gaze back to the darkening night. He swallowed hard and forced himself to walk into the house to prepare the tea. His home had seemed perfect with her in it, sharing the meal and conversation with the Ravenwings. But ever since their shopping trip that afternoon, the courtship had shot into uncharted territory with a shit-ton of obstacles and speed bumps.

He took the kettle off the stove and poured the water over the tea bags in two mugs. The warm peppermint scent drifted up off the mugs, but it didn't settle him like usual. *Maybe that's because I'm going to lose at this game before I get a real chance to play.*

He returned to the deck and handed Lissandra her mug. She thanked him, but didn't smile, and he tried to make himself comfortable on the other chair. Too bad it felt as if they sat a million miles apart. He told himself to relax, to go with the flow, but anxiety pinged through his mind as she cradled her mug in her hands.

"Now, what do you want to talk about?" He settled against his chair.

He watched her frown in concentration, a little crease forming between her eyes. She stared sightlessly at the sky and foreboding slithered through him. A vision of her lying on her back filled his mind, her eyes wide open and her features slack. He crouched beside her, shouting, but she didn't respond to his voice.

Fear and rage flooded his system and he inhaled a deep breath to roar with the emotion building within him. *No, she can't be gone. Lissandra, don't leave me!* Then he was back on his deck, staring at her lively face, and he let out his breath with a surprised sigh.

"Are you okay?" She raised her eyebrows.

He tried to catch his breath and decipher what he'd seen. It had seemed so real, as if he'd really been there, his throat raw from screaming.

"Yeah." He swallowed against the rawness and shrugged nonchalantly. "So, you figured out what you want to talk about yet?"

"I want to ask you about your family."

His insides chilled until he shivered despite the early summer heat. Just like when he'd seen Lissandra dead in his arms. *Wait, she was dead?* He cleared his throat.

"Why do you want to know about my family?"

"I want to know why you seem to avoid them and why you spend so much...*time* with humans." Her inflection held a wealth of meaning.

"Ah, you know, I'm a guy." He waved flippantly, offering his usual grin. But he felt like she'd sucker-punched him. "I wanted experience with sex in this form and I'm heterosexual, so I found as many females willing to "teach" me as I could." He shrugged. "Besides, dragons are few and far between. I have to fit in with the humans. Better camouflage. Can you imagine what the Department of Homeland Security would do if they figured out I'm not human?" He shuddered for effect.

Lissandra gave him a half smile in response to his joke, but her eyes remained serious. "What about your family?"

He sighed and sipped his tea. "That's more complicated."

"How so?"

"My parents are in a loveless marriage. If they were true mates before, it definitely ain't the case now. They basically tolerate each other and my sister and me. Being in their house—shit, in their company—is like taking some sort of exam. You're always stressed, worried about doing well, or well enough, and everyone's miserable." He picked at a splinter in the arm of his chair. "I got out when I could, but my sister has to live there, and as much as I want to protect her, I can't put myself into that pain and suffering."

"How old is your sister?"

He frowned for a moment. "I think she's about Torri's age. She isn't sexually mature yet."

"What's her name?"

"Suriana."

"As in sunshine?"

"Yeah." He grinned. "We call her Suri."

"It seems strange that your family is so miserable." Lissandra rubbed her tea mug with her thumbs.

He shrugged. "When I was younger, I remember them being happier, but not anymore."

"What changed between then and now?"

He sat up and draped his arms over his knees. "You've heard of the Great Chicago Fire, right?"

"Sure. It not only made news in the human world, but the dragon world as well. Your father took down a demon there, right?"

"Oh, yeah. Waltarrion Goldencoat, the savior of Chicago." His voice sounded bitter even to himself. "Afterwards, he became a surly sonuvaprick, rigid in his belief we had to hide our true nature and act as human as possible to blend in." Denarrion shook his head again. "It just seemed easier to play along with his demands than get my head bitten off."

"It seems odd your mom would tolerate that behavior. Didn't she say anything?" Lissandra shook her head, puzzled.

"I think she just wanted to keep the peace, and it was easier to say nothing than fight him. She was pretty worried about him." He waved his hand as if he could dismiss the past. "Tell me more about True Bonded partners. What does that mean?"

She studied him for a few moments. "I'm not done asking about your family, Denarrion."

He nodded. "I figured, but if you answer my questions, maybe you'll get a better idea of why I don't seem to know stuff."

"Your parents didn't teach you anything about being a dragon?" Alarm filled her eyes.

He grimaced. "I don't remember if they did before Walter got sick, but they sure as hell didn't afterwards."

"Your father got sick?"

"Yeah, after the fire." Denarrion ignored the urge to hide his family's shame. "It was a long time ago, but it took him forever to get better. When he did, he was pretty bitter."

"That's strange. I've never heard of a dragon getting sick."

"Yeah, no one had. He was an anomaly. Do you think if my folks were True Bonded partners he would've gotten better?"

Lissandra shook her head with a frown. "Yeah, I do. True Bonding in dragons is when the yin-yang of the soul comes together and reconnects. I think it also occurs in werewolves and the *Morukai*, and maybe even in vampires. In dragons, the partners feel the urge to bite their mates while mating."

"Recreational sex," he murmured automatically.

"Whatever." She tightened her lips. "But that's how we get increased strength, vitality, longevity, health, et cetera." She frowned. "You really don't know this? I mean, you've bitten me twice. Haven't you noticed the increase in our connection?"

"Yeah, I guess." He frowned. "I hadn't really paid attention."

She nodded though the corners of her mouth turned down. "The longer we're together, the better you'll be able to sense when I'm in danger and vice versa."

"Whoa, that's kinda wild." He rubbed his chin as a memory surfaced. "But you haven't bitten me."

She was silent a few moments. "No."

"Why not? Haven't you had the urge?" *Oh sweet Goddess, maybe she doesn't feel the same about me.*

She inclined her head but didn't say yes or no. "Tell me why you always refer to things in decades rather than in centuries. And why the idea of shifting into our natural form freaks you out."

"I never said it freaked me out." He tried to appear casual but his heartrate jumped at the idea of shifting.

"You didn't have to. Your body language told me."

He couldn't read her expression and the uncomfortable feeling settled back into his gut. How did she read him so well after so little time together?

She bit her bottom lip. "You're old enough to mate, right?"

"Yeah, of course I am." He growled. "Chronologically, I'm one thousand and forty-eight years old."

"So why do you get nervous every time I use the word 'centuries' when referring to age?"

Denarrion resisted the urge to squirm like a dragonet. "Aaah, I guess it just goes back to fitting in with the humans, you know? *They* don't say their five decades old when they turn fifty. Besides, it always sets my old man off when we talk like that. He jumps down our throats."

The description didn't begin to cover Waltarrion's reaction whenever they talked 'like dragons.' He'd rage and fume, spittle flying from his mouth, and his skin would take on a gray pallor lasting for days afterwards. It was creepy and Denarrion had found it easier to refrain from making any mention of dragon-related things.

"But you moved out and now live on your own away from his influence. You haven't made your own choices about it?" Lissandra tilted her head, her brows lowered.

He held his tea in his hands as he realized he'd just been going along with his father's edicts even after he walked away. It had never occurred to him to change until he'd met Lissandra.

And that was a long fucking time to go along.

Talking about dragon-related things with her felt good, natural, and his curiosity poked its head out of the ashes of his life. *Too bad I didn't notice how locked up I've been without help.* And now she was thinking of walking away from their courtship. Because he was fucked up about being a dragon. He mentally shook his head. How in hellwinds could he be scared of being a dragon? He was one. Anger rose in his chest, but whether it stemmed from his father or himself, he didn't know.

"Isn't your father in favor of this courtship?" Lissandra hugged herself, her expression troubled.

"Yeah." Denarrion nodded. "That's why I wasn't thrilled with meeting you at first."

"Ahh." She sipped her tea, her body language reserved. "You don't trust his motives since you're at loggerheads with him."

"Pretty much."

"Strange that he'd want you to find a mate when he requires you to hide your true self." She frowned and turned to stare at him. "Has he ever told you why he wants you to hide so much?"

He shrugged, the old fear rising again. "Because he knows how dangerous humans can be when they put their minds to it." He sighed and rubbed his arms against a sudden chill. "Humans damn near killed him."

"I though you said it was the fight with a demon that almost killed him."

"Yeah, well, the demon possessed a human host, and riled up the crowd to take him down before he managed to kill the host." Denarrion grunted. "I didn't see the ending of the fight, but Waltarrion was lucky to survive. Ever since then he's been adamant about keeping our heads down and blending in to the community."

"That doesn't sound like the warrior we've all been taught about." She shook her head.

"Yeah, well, you don't really know someone until you have to live with them. Great heroes are usually just guys in the right place at the right time who get lucky. And the rest of us have to put up with the 'greatness.'"

"Is that why you prefer to use your nickname, even around me?"

Denarrion frowned. *That isn't it, is it?* When he'd touched Lissandra for the first time at the reservoir, he felt like she'd shined a light into the darkness in his heart. Like a box of precious things pulled out of the closet, things he'd been missing. Her touch had banished some of the old anger and bitterness dogging his thoughts.

But he sensed her touch wouldn't have worked at all if she hadn't arrived when she did. What the hell did that mean?

"Nah, it's more like habit." He shook his head and shot her a smile. "But I like it when you say my full name."

"I'm sorry for your family, Denarrion." Lissandra reached for his hand and he grasped it like a lifeline. More of the dark anger fled the heat of her touch.

"Yeah, well, he survived, so I guess it worked out okay."

"That's not what I meant." She waited until he met her gaze. "I meant what you experienced at home. I can't fathom why your mother didn't stand up for you and your sister." She smiled at him and it damn near stopped his heart. "I would've stood up for you."

"Hey, thanks." Goddess, he'd never met anyone like Lissandra and he'd be damned before he lost her. "Have I answered all your questions about my family?"

She tilted her head. "For now, I guess. Why?"

"'Cause I don't really want to talk about them anymore. They're not a happy subject. Tell me about your family and where you grew up." Anything to escape the gloom the Goldencoats had brought to their evening.

"My first two and half centuries I spent in what would become Oregon before Solenarra moved us to what's now Colorado."

The mention of centuries pinged inside him, but not enough to kill the pleasure of listening to Lissandra describe her home. Her voice lulled him into relaxation, chasing away the stresses and concerns.

"Why did you move there?"

"At the time, it was still an empty place where humans didn't venture as much. We were just another animal among the mammals." She smiled in memory. "The native peoples were there, of course, but for the most part it was just us animals. But with the increase in human population over the centuries, came an increase in demon activity, and we were called on to seek and fight them more often."

The word 'demon' made his gut clench and an irrational fear of discovery rose in his chest. *Where is this shit coming from?* He shivered and tried to calm the panic by taking deep breaths. *We're dragons. We fight demons.* But the fear only intensified and he struggled to keep calm.

"Denarrion, are you all right?"

Lissandra laid her hand on his arm and the haze of fear dissipated from his eyesight. The panic receded and his breathing evened out with the weight of her hand.

"Yeah, yeah. I'm good. Thanks." He dredged up a smile, hoping she wouldn't take her hand back before the fear had completely drained away.

"Let's go inside." She took her hand away and rose.

He braced himself for the return of his panic, but it only came trickling back instead of the flood he expected, and he was able to fight it off.

"Come on. I'll tuck you into bed." She held her hand out to him and he grasped it, the return of her touch soothing his mind.

They didn't say anything as she led him upstairs to his room and moved her bag out of the way. He headed for the bathroom to get ready for bed and undress, but when he came back out, he found her seated on the bed still in her clothes.

"Are you going to go to bed?" He raised his eyebrows as he settled under the covers.

Lissandra nodded. "Yes, but I'm going to sleep in the guest room tonight."

He froze. "What? Why?"

"Because it's been a long day and I have a lot to think about." She gave him a friendly but firm smile. "I need some time to think over what you've told me and make my decision about continuing the courtship."

"You haven't made your decision?" Ice shot through his veins. What could he do to convince her?

She shook her head. "There's a lot to think over and I have my children to consider as well. You've thrown a lot at me today, and while I've enjoyed much of it, I need to take some time to listen to my heart. The Goddess's wisdom resides there, but I can't always hear it."

"Don't leave me yet, Lissandra." He resisted the urge to grab her hand.

"I'm not leaving, Denarrion. I'm just taking time for myself to think this through." She rose and smiled at him.

"Get some rest. I'll see you in the morning."

"Promise?" He hated to sound so damn needy.

"I promise. Good night."

She switched off the light and took her mug back with her as she retreated down the stairs. He forced himself to relax in bed, but he didn't want to be alone. How could he have fucked up so much she still wasn't sure she wanted to be courted? He'd apologized for his promiscuity, and he meant it when he told her he was done with human women.

Is my damn father fucking this up for me?

Fury surged. Was the dysfunctionality of his family pushing Lissandra away? *Sonuvaprick!* Everything Waltarrion touched withered and died. And even though he'd set up the blind date, his presence infected the one good thing Denarrion had found in centuries. *Centuries! You hear that, you sanctimonious prick?* Lissandra purified him with her gentle voice, scouring away the anger and bitterness accumulated over decades. If he lost her now, he'd have to go back to his life before her arrival.

I think I'd rather die. That cheerful thought followed him down into restless sleep.

****

Lissandra stood outside on the porch and stared up at the night sky. The stars blazed clear, though given the light pollution from the many homes nearby, she couldn't see as many as she could at home.

Home. She missed Cloudburst, Colorado, her children, and the calming presence of the Elder Races in her town.

Instead, she stood here in upstate New York, on a blind date. *With my true mate.*

She nodded to herself. But she suspected the disease affecting him ran deep. Given his aversion to all things dragon and his fury with his family, it had to from them. Why else would he reject all that he was?

She groaned as she ran her hands over her face. The question became, was she willing to make the effort to help him heal from whatever ailed him? Did she want to take the time to see him through the healing process when she'd only known him a day? For dragons, eighteen hours didn't even get on the scale, much less register in memory.

He's my true mate.

True, but was she willing to be a martyr, to slog through the muck with him, always at the mercy of his disease, like the spouses of alcoholics? She'd seen those men and women at the Al-Anon meetings when she was younger, with their hollow eyes and bleak outlooks. They couldn't walk away because they loved the addict too much. Would she become the same way?

Lissandra shook her head. She wouldn't give herself to such a lifestyle. Not with her children hanging in the balance. They certainly didn't deserve it, and neither did she.

But is he irredeemable?

It was what kept her from biting him during mating. *Recreational sex.* Denarrion's voice made her smile, but it quickly faded. He'd bitten her, but she'd held back, sensing the darkness riding his spirit. Would he find his way back to the light, away from the darkness that seemed to be crippling him?

The problem is he has to want to change.

She couldn't make the change for him, and she couldn't ask him to change for her. It wouldn't stick and he'd go back to what he knew best.

"Oh, Goddess." She threw her hands away from her body and jumped off the porch, running into the middle of the backyard. "Give me the wisdom to see the right path."

Gathering the magic around her, Lissandra let it seep into her bones and stretch her true self out of the confines of her disguise. Relief shading toward joy filled her body as her bones lengthened and her tail unfurled. She moaned in delight as her wings spread, catching the soft summer breeze floating close to the ground.

Sweet glory, I needed this.

The world turned luminescent in her dragon's Sight, and she shook herself to settle into her true form. Sounds and scents became sharper, a symphony of sensations as compared to the dulled-out version she received in her human form. She rumbled in relief and launched into the cool night air. The downstroke of her outstretched wings shot her into the sky and freed her from the earthly worries plaguing her mind.

She climbed high enough to be invisible to human eyes, but marked where Denarrion's house sat in relationship to the reservoir to find her way back. Wearing her true form settled her mind and gave her the ability to see the points of light on the ground. Her Sight automatically took over while in her dragon form, and she picked out both the holy places and those in need of care.

The island in the reservoir sparkled with healthy, warm, living energy. She circled the place, listening to the wind in the trees. Someone had blessed this place and made it a sanctuary. Scanning the town of Redfield, she found black spots pulsing with puce-colored tendrils and wondered how the residents of town didn't feel sickened and miserable.

As she wheeled around through the sky, she looked for the source of the insidious rot poisoning the town. Her warrior's instincts screamed that a demon ran loose in Redfield, and perhaps she'd been brought to this little town to find and destroy it.

The black and puce spots grew together in a spreading stain around a small, dark house on the east side of town. She circled around in the air above it, but the stench drove her higher.

Sweet Goddess, this place stinks.

She hovered over the center of putrescence and

snarled. She should burn it to the ground, but she didn't know how many humans lived over the spreading muck, and she couldn't hurt them indiscriminately. Gritting her teeth, she inhaled the stench and fought back a roar.

Demon!

A demon had infiltrated the town and its decay would destroy it if left unchecked. Lissandra's fire churned in her belly. She thought back to the cloying decay she'd smelled at the burn scar on her short hike. *It had to be from the demon.* Dear Goddess, how long had this festering abomination been here?

It's a good thing I've come.

Except she'd given up that part of her life. She no longer hunted demons, choosing instead to take care of her children and living quietly.

Her wing beats faltered and she slid away from the squalid marks of the demon's presence. She glided back toward Denarrion's house, her mind whirling. Could she continue to ignore the presence of a demon harming this community? What if the other dragons here didn't know of its existence? Could she pretend like it wasn't here and let them suffer its destruction without knowledge?

No.

She landed on the ground beyond the porch and shifted back into her human disguise. She wanted to be normal, ordinary, live a quiet life with her children and a mate. But she couldn't ignore the danger and disease infecting Redfield. Though she'd come to enter a courtship with Denarrion, she'd have to make an effort to scour the town of the demon's taint.

Maybe the taint is what's discoloring Denarrion's aura.

She shot a look at the top part of the house where he slept, and anger kindled. A demon had harmed her true mate. She growled as she shot a look east. She'd be damned before she allowed such a creature to survive.

Nodding, she let herself back into the house and locked the door behind her. She'd have to talk to Charlorrion and Torri in the morning to find out what they knew about the demon in Redfield.

CHAPTER TWELVE

Sunlight brightened the room around Lissandra and she opened her eyes to study the elegant scrolling designs on the head and foot boards of the guest bed. Despite her concerns experienced the night before, she'd slept well. Better than she had in months.

That's because you remembered your calling.

She inhaled the air of Denarrion's home, enjoying the emotional scents of comfort, contentment, and satisfaction.

Mine or his?

Her concerns from the previous night returned with more insistence. Some of his ignorance had been explained. Denarrion's family hadn't behaved in a dragon-like fashion, leaving him without all necessary knowledge of their people. But more than that, the presence of a demon in Redfield may have precipitated that behavior. She'd already seen the darkness tarnishing his aura. But despite his ignorance, she sensed the strength and goodness at his core.

He could be a magnificent dragon.

She sat up and rested her arms on her knees. To be honest, she liked him for his sarcastic humor, his Puckish grin, and his handsome male body. What wasn't to like?

Her nipples hardened at the thought of his mouth on them.

Whoa back. It's not all about sex.

No, and while she'd enjoyed it, sex wouldn't mean shit in the long run. She still had time to decide if she'd officially mate with him. *Everyone has faults. All he's missing is some knowledge, which he can learn.* The connection was real, though a little unsteady.

The question remained what to do about the darkness she'd Seen in Denarrion's aura. It appeared to be fading the more time she spent with him, but she worried about the source of it. Did it have something to do with his family? Or only the demon in town?

She shook her head. She needed to talk to Charlorrion, but he was still on call at the fire station. *But I can call Solenarra.* She'd set up this blind date with Charlorrion's help.

Lissandra swung her feet to the floor and pulled on her light sleep pants before heading out the door to the kitchen. The clock on the stove read 8:30 a.m. Taking time zones into account, she estimated Solenarra and the kids would be awake.

I deserve coffee for this conversation.

She set up the coffee maker and dug through the cabinets for something robust. She'd need it for what she knew was coming. She took her time setting up the coffee and logging into Skype on Denarrion's laptop. Once the coffee sat in her mug, she settled into the stool at the kitchen counter and started her call.

"Hey, Mom." Lucenarra's face filled the screen. "How are you doing?"

"Hey, my beautiful girl." Lissandra let her sweet joy flow over her. "How was your day with Solenarra alone?"

"It was great." Luce's face glowed with radiant joy. "She took us into town to visit the music store and we met a street artist who makes mandalas."

"What's a mandala?"

"They're pretty sand paintings, Mom." Kressendra ran up behind her sister. "Kinshalla—that's the artist—she says they're for healing and balance. I can see them shining in the air, too."

Lissandra raised her eyebrows. "What did they look like?"

"Like big columns of swirly colored light. You know, like when you can see the dust in a sunbeam?" Kress opened her arms as if hugging a tree.

"The Tindal Effect?"

"Yeah, just like that. I could see it."

"That's wonderful, Kress." Lissandra let her excitement show in her voice. "You'll have to show me when I come home."

"When are you going to come home?" Luce tilted her head. "Do you like that guy dragon, Denarrion?"

"I do like him." Lissandra nodded. "He's got a wonderful Brooklyn accent and a wicked sense of humor."

"The wicked sense of humor is an East Coast thing." Denarrion padded into the kitchen wearing only a robe and his Puckish grin.

"Is that him? I can hear his funny accent." Kress giggled.

"Hey." Denarrion came around into the view of the camera. "I don't have a funny accent. Out here, this one is normal."

"Kressendra, meet Denarrion Goldencoat." Lissandra leaned out of the way. "Denarrion, I would like you to meet Kressendra, my youngest daughter."

Kress looked up at Denarrion for a long moment, her face growing pensive. Lissandra's gut clenched. She'd never been so nervous as now. *Denarrion is my True Mate. Please, Goddess, let my daughters approve.*

At last, Kress waved slowly. "Very nice to meet you, Denarrion. Why are you so mad?"

A startled silence hit the room. Lissandra's heart

lurched. Kress often spoke bluntly, but this brought Lissandra's worries to the forefront of her mind again. *Holy Mother, is there more wrong with Denarrion than I thought?*

"Mad?" Denarrion face creased with a confused smile. "I'm not mad."

"Mom uses a different word." Kress thought for a moment. "Angry. You're angry."

"Do I seem angry?" He cocked his head, his eyebrows up. "I don't feel angry."

"In here." She pointed a finger to her own chest. "In your heart. You're angry in your heart."

Another silence fell as Denarrion glanced at Lissandra, but she gazed at her daughter.

"What makes you think he's angry, Kress?"

"He's all growly inside." Kress finally looked at her, her expression guileless. "I can see it like the mandalas."

Lissandra didn't know what to say. How did she fix 'growliness'? The tension escalated until Solenarra stepped up behind Kress and pulled her into a hug.

"You know who else is growly?" Sole teased in a raspy voice. "Me. I get growly when I haven't had my coffee yet. Grrrrrrr!"

Kressendra shrieked in delight and writhed in Sole's grip before she let the dragonet go. Lissandra laughed, but Denarrion's smile became strained, and her disquiet spiked again. If Denarrion was angry and ignorant, how would she be able to help him? *First, find out what Sole knows about the courtship and demon.*

Lucenarra tilted her head and narrowed her eyes as her sister and grandmother puttered around the kitchen behind her. She switched her gaze between Denarrion and Lissandra, then nodded slowly.

"Don't worry, Mom. It will be okay, you'll see."

Lissandra stared into her daughter's peacock-green eyes and felt a warm sensation flow over her like a comforting bath. It took her a moment to realize Luce had used a strong Healing gift to ease her sorrow and worry, powerful enough to be felt nearly two thousand miles away. *Sweet Goddess, how long has she been doing that?*

She smiled. "Thank you, Luce. I appreciate it."

Luce offered a wise smile spiced with her pleasure and nodded. *If Lucenarra has this gift, I should definitely consider apprenticing her to Torriandra.* None of the dragons Lissandra knew in Colorado had a well-developed Healing gift.

"I miss you, Mom. When do you think you'll be coming home?"

Lissandra shrugged. "I don't know, sweetheart. I've only been here a day and there's lots more to figure out. Denarrion and I have been getting to know each other."

"That's good, right?"

Lissandra nodded. "Yes, very good. Do you want to talk to him?"

Luce hesitated. "Okay."

Lissandra leaned out of the way. "Lucenarra, this is Denarrion Goldencoat. Denarrion, my oldest, Lucenarra Charforest."

"Very nice to meet you," Lucenarra said gravely, nodding.

"And you." He gave her a friendly smile. "You can call me Denny."

"Why?" Luce frowned. "That isn't your name."

Denarrion stilled as his eyebrows lifted in surprise. "Well, it's my common name."

"Don't you like your real name?"

"Yeah, but it's easier to use the common name around here. That way the humans don't know we're dragons."

"Yes, but you're not with humans right now and it's always better to be who you truly are…Right, Mom?"

"I think so." Lissandra nodded as she shot a look at him.

Lucenarra returned her gaze to Denarrion and cocked her head a little. "You don't have to be afraid to be yourself around us."

Denarrion stood nonplussed as she turned and spied Solenarra handing Kressendra a plate of fruit. "Hey, I want some of that." She left the computer and slid into her seat at the kitchen table.

"Sometimes I think they're tapped into the Goddess more than I am." Lissandra's heart filled with pride for her daughters. "They see truths the rest of us often ignore."

She returned her gaze to Denarrion. "She's right, you know."

He raised an eyebrow, his expression wary.

"I do like you as you are, and I'd rather call you 'Denarrion' than 'Denny.'"

"Oh." He sounded relieved, but a frown creased his face. "I just thought it would be easier for her to remember."

"She is two hundred, Denarrion. She's not a baby." Irritation bloomed at his dismissal of Luce's abilities. "She knows when to call you by your common name and when to call you by your True name."

"I'm sorry, Lissa." He squeezed her arm, his face contrite. "I guess I'm not used to kids. I haven't been around any for years."

"If you're going to be with me, you better get used to them." She didn't like the surge of dark energy she sensed from within him. "They're my family and if you want in, you're going to have to treat them with the same respect you want for yourself."

He nodded. "I can see that. Both your kids seem great." He gestured to the three dragons in the background of the camera view. "Is that your mom?"

"Yes. She's watching the girls while I'm away."

"Why don't I let you talk for a bit while I drink my coffee out on the front porch? It'll give you a chance to catch up."

"All right. I'll join you after."

"Sounds good." Denarrion sauntered away with a full cup of coffee. He closed the door behind him and she sighed with a mixture of disquiet and relief.

What's wrong with me? She rubbed the back of her neck to relieve sudden tension. *It must be that creepy energy I sense within him.* She needed answers from Solenarra.

"Okay, *sa garren*, y'all need to keep your voices down while I have a chat with your mother."

"Okay, Grandmama." The girls focused on eating as Solenarra settled herself in front of the computer.

"So, what makes you call at the crack of dawn this morning?" Her mother sipped her coffee, her golden eyes wary.

"I want to talk to you about this courtship, Mom." Lissandra tilted her head. "How did you find out about Denarrion, anyway?"

Sole shrugged. "I do have friends beyond you and the girls. I put the word out and Charlorrion Ravenwing was the first to reply."

"Charlorrion. Not Denarrion."

Sole shook her head. "No, it was Charlorrion. He said his brother was single and seemed to be floundering in his personal life."

"What about Waltarrion Goldencoat? He approved of this blind date move?"

Sole shrugged again. "I only talked to Charlorrion, but he said he had Waltarrion's blessing and permission to offer a courtship." She sipped her coffee a moment with a frown. "To be honest, I was surprised when he used the word "courtship." It's an old custom, like back when I was a girl. But it hasn't been something more recent dragon generations have done. I chalked it up to the unusual situation—you being a widow."

"Hmm." Lissandra sipped her own coffee, trying to find the best way to bring up what she'd learned. "And what about the demon trace here in Redfield? Was that part of the courtship parameters or just an unhappy coincidence?"

Lissandra watched the screen closely, waiting for a change in Solenarra's expression. The older dragon woman tried to hide it, but her shoulders tensed and her face blanched before she resumed her placid mask.

"There's a demon in Redfield?"

Damn, she sounds almost normal.

"Stop, Mom. I smelled it yesterday and last night I found its spreading decay. Was that the real reason I was supposed to hook up with Denarrion?"

Before Sole could answer, Kress and Luce broke into a loud argument about who had the most fruit on their plates, and it wasn't fair.

"Take the fighting outside, you hooligans. Go catch a deer or something." Sole rolled her eyes. "I have to go head this off at the pass. I'll talk to you again soon, Lissandra."

Before she could say anything, Solenarra had terminated the call. Lissandra stared at the dark screen with narrowed eyes. Sole usually didn't let the kids distract her. *She's hiding something.* The problem was she couldn't corner Sole to get answers. Lissandra grabbed her coffee and headed for the porch. She'd have to talk to Charlorrion and Torri.

****

Denarrion rested against one of the deck chairs and tried to shove away his anxiety. Why was Lissandra on Skype to her family so early in the morning? Had she changed her mind about the courtship after all? She'd insisted on sleeping alone, which worried him after all their intimacies, and now she was calling home.

Fuck, I've lost her.

That didn't take long. Granted, usually it was him trying to cut a relationship short, but this time he wanted to stick it out with Lissandra. Just having her around made him feel better in ways he hadn't known he'd been missing. She made the world richer and fuller, bringing him out of the dreary brain-fog in which he'd been existing. He didn't want to go back.

A few minutes later, she came out and settled on the other deck chair, her hands wrapped around a steaming mug of coffee. He glanced over and swallowed hard. She bit her bottom lip and frowned.

"Do you think someone set us up?"

Denarrion raised his eyebrows. "Set us up? It was a blind date, Lissandra. Of course they set us up."

"Yeah, but I mean more than that." She nodded, tapping her mug with her fingers. "Do you think they had ulterior motives in getting us together?"

"Who?"

"Solenarra, Charlorrion, even your dad."

He shook his head. "What kind of ulterior motives?"

"I don't know. It seems like they wanted me to come out here for more than just the courtship." She glanced at him. "You don't get that impression?"

He blinked. "I don't know. I guess I never really thought to ask. I mean, Charlie and Walter suggested I was getting on in years and I should think about settling down." He shrugged. "Why?"

She shook her head. "Just some things Charlorrion and Torri have said in passing. And now Solenarra has taken to avoiding answering questions." She sighed and sipped her coffee. "I really need to talk to Charlorrion, but he's still on his shift until eight tonight." She rested her head against the back of the chair.

Denarrion thought back over the conversations he and Charlie had had about the courtship, and he tried to remember anything that seemed out of place or context. At first, the only thing that came to mind was his father's insistence on starting a courtship with any dragon female. But after a moment, other conversations with Charlie came into focus, and his foster brother had been pushing Lissandra in particular for months before she arrived.

"You know, Charlie did seem to think you were the best candidate after I agreed to go for a blind courtship."

She raised her eyebrows. "There were other dragon women looking for courtship dates?"

He nodded slowly. "Yeah, one or two. But once Charlie found out more about you, he really thought you were the best choice." He let a smile curl his lips. "I can't say he was wrong."

She laughed and the world brightened around her. "Thanks. It's nice to have his vote of confidence." But her smile faded and she shook her head. "I'd like to ask him why he thought I was such a great choice. Something tells me it's more than just the usual dating site drivel." She sighed and sipped some more coffee. "But I'll have to wait until tonight."

He tilted his head and let a smirk curl his lips. "I bet I know something we could do to distract you until then."

She gave him a look out of the corner of her eyes. "Oh yeah? What's that?"

He set his mug aside and rolled to his feet to stand in front of her. The robe tented in front of him as his cock reacted to the thought of her naked in his bed. *I didn't get any last night. Best make up for it today.*

"How 'bout we go upstairs and start this morning off right?" He held out his hand to her.

She raised an eyebrow and lifted her mug. "I thought coffee was starting the morning off right."

"Depends on the morning." He took her mug and set it beside his, before pulling her up. "This morning, I'd like to do a more thorough wake-up exercise."

"Oh? What did you have in mind?"

"Come with me, dragon lady, and let me show you." He grinned. "It's more of a show activity than a tell."

The slow smile on her face made his dick stand up and take notice. "I like show and tell. Just as long as I get to be an active participant."

He laughed as he drew her inside the house and up the stairs. "That's the only way I like it."

He released her hand at the top of the stairs and threw his robe into the closet before he turned to face her. Her eyes filled with desire and she licked her lips as her gaze scrolled up his body from feet to face. *Looks like she likes what she sees.*

"Let's get you undressed." He took a step toward her, but she shook her head.

"Get on the bed just like that, Denarrion." She slid her sleep pants off her hips and his mouth watered.

"You want me on the bed naked?"

"Yup. And on your back." She gestured to the bed and followed him there, her gaze on his cock waving between his legs like a flag. "It's my turn to enjoy some of your charms."

"Whadiya think yer gonna do, huh?" He layered on the Brooklyn accent as he settled on the bed, and she shivered.

"You'll see."

She wriggled her way down his body, the heat of her belly and tits scraping over his hardened cock and balls. *Damn, that's hot.* He groaned and watched her as she smirked up at him.

Lissandra laid soft kisses on his chest and belly as she moved until she settled with his cock between her breasts, the head poking up above their rounded tops. His dick flexed and she moaned. Then she dipped her chin, opened her mouth and licked the tip.

"Oh, Holy Mother!"

Hot, wet pleasure shot straight from his groin to his

head, and he closed his eyes to absorb it. He'd enjoyed blowjobs before, but just the teasing touches of her tongue already put this one above and beyond the others.

She flicked the head with her tongue, caressing the slit where his pre-cum beaded. The electric sensations of her slightly rough tongue sliding over the edges of the head short-circuited his brain. He moaned and hissed his breaths while she dug her fingers gently into his thighs.

"Oh glory, your mouth is amazing." He rocked his hips to encourage her to engulf his whole shaft, but she pulled back to tease him. "Damn, you're killin' me."

She dipped her chin and closed her lips around the top of his cock, sucking lightly while dragging her nails over his sides and belly. Denarrion whimpered, sliding his cock between her breasts and pushing it a little deeper into her mouth. *Need more.* She sucked harder, pressing her chest down against his balls.

"Holy fuck, Lissandra. Suck my cock. Suck it hard."

He rocked his hips again and she released his shaft from her breasts with a lustful grin. Grasping his dick, she slid her mouth over it all the way to the back of her throat. And swallowed.

Sparkles flashed across this vision as the beginnings of his orgasm built in his balls. Lissandra tightened her mouth around his rod and fondled his hot, tight skin with her tongue. He grew harder, the shaft flexing against her lips. He resisted the urge to fuck her mouth, thrusting hard against her tongue.

"Yeah, suck that cock, Lissa."

She hummed against his hard flesh and he increased his thrusts, moving his hands to her head to hold her where he wanted her. The extra vibration had him driving his hips as his arousal surged. *Oh sweet Goddess. She's gonna make me come.*

She tightened her lips again, grabbing the base of his shaft with one hand and digging her nails into his hip with the other. He dropped a glance down his body and met her burning gaze. Damn, it was almost as hot as her tongue around his cock. He grimaced and his breathing turned ragged as he fought to hold back.

"Oh yeah. Oh, fuck, yeah!"

The scents of sex and hot, aroused female hit his nose and ratcheted up his pleasure. She tightened her grip on his cock. Wet sounds of her sucking his flesh sparked more arousal and he tightened his hands in her hair. The scent of her cream coating her netherlips added another layer of delight as he shuttled in and out of her mouth. She rumbled a happy growl and Denarrion lost his grip on his orgasm.

"We have to stop." He groaned but kept thrusting. "Oh, shit, I'm going to…*aaahhh*!"

His release shot through him, scouring away some of the darkness lining his heart. Pleasure and hope mixed with fierce joy as he lost himself in his orgasm. This was home, and something he never wanted to lose.

CHAPTER THIRTEEN

Lissandra savored Denarrion's cum and smiled as he took his pleasure. He tasted like sweet marinara with garlic, warm August evenings, and earthy male musk. His whole body tightened under her and she hummed with satisfaction. She swallowed and swallowed and swallowed, unable to get enough of his ambrosia.

"Oh glory. You're so fuckin' sexy."

He sounded breathless and she smiled up at him as she licked the last of his cream off his shaft. He growled as he reached down and hauled her up his body to plant a kiss on her swollen lips. He thrust his tongue into her mouth, stealing some of the ambrosia from her, and groaned again.

"Damn, but you taste good with my cum in your mouth."

"I'm a big fan of it as well." She grinned as he growled again.

He flipped her over onto her back and settled his mouth over one of her taut nipples, flicking it with the tip of his tongue. Pleasure blazed across all her nerve endings and she arched her back, pressing her breast deeper into his mouth.

Her earlier concerns faded in the heat of her arousal,

and she let herself fall into the knowledge that he was her true bonded mate. She wanted him and wanted to connect. She ignored the warning whispering in the back of her head that it was still too early.

"Sweet Goddess, Denarrion." She moaned and squirmed beneath him as he pushed his knees between her thighs and settled the tip of his cock at her hot, wet entrance.

"My turn." His low growl echoed in her chest as he slowly pushed his cock into her.

Sensual ripples of bliss swamped her mind and she flowed with them, her breath escaping in a drawn-out moan. Her pussy clenched around his shaft as she pushed her hips against his weight.

"That's it." He clamped his hands onto her hips. "You're so damn tight. I'm gonna pleasure you until you scream."

He thrust all the way in then pulled out slowly, electrifying her. She met his gaze and found his expression tight with arousal and desire. His eyes blazed silvery blue and he wore a half smile of predatory determination. Her own arousal responded to his and her pussy flooded with more liquid as she bared her teeth at him.

"Stop teasing and fuck me." Her growl made his eyes flash.

He grinned and slammed deep. She squealed as he reversed direction until only the head of his cock remained, his smile taunting her. She opened her mouth and he covered it with a hot, demanding kiss, his tongue thrusting in and tangling with hers. Her arousal jumped up a notch and she moaned as he thrust in hard.

"Oh, Goddess, Denarrion. Faster."

"Do you know how sexy it is to hear you say my name?" He pounded into her.

"How sexy?"

"Enough to make me want to do this." He slammed his

hips against her and she let out a shriek of delight. "Like that?"

"Oh, yes. Yes! Harder. Faster."

Her arousal built higher and higher until her entire awareness filled with his blazing eyes, aroused grimace, and pounding cock. She thrust back at him, matching his moves.

"You want it faster, dragon lady?"

"Yes, yes. Faster."

"Say my name, Lissandra."

"Denarrion."

"Again." He pounded harder, working her up to a fever pitch.

"Denarrion."

"Again."

"DENARRION!" The word ended in a shriek as she toppled over the precipice of ecstasy, launching herself into erotic oblivion. Then she sank her teeth into his shoulder, sharing her bliss with her True Bonded Mate.

Biting him triggered his release and he threw his head back with a roar, thrusting a few more times until his body stiffened like a strung bow. Ricocheting orgasms built higher and higher until the pleasure detonated and left them both floating back to earth. They collapsed onto the bed, panting like dogs.

"Holy Mother of All, is that what it felt like when I bit your shoulder?" Denarrion raised his head to meet her gaze, his eyes wide in wonder.

"You mean, extraordinary ecstasy and ricocheting orgasms?"

"Yeah."

"Yes, that's it." She ran her hands over his heaving shoulders. "That's what makes the bond so special."

"Dear Goddess. That's fucking unbelievable."

He rolled to the side and gathered her into his arms. Lissandra's contentment settled around her and she snuggled against his hot body, listening to him breathe. He smelled good to her, his masculine scent sliding over her like a second skin and holding her. No question about it, he was her True Mate. She thrust away the small niggle of unease still poking holes in her satisfaction.

"You're incredible, you know that?" he murmured as he squeezed her gently.

"Why do you say that?"

"Because it has *never* felt this good to me. Ever."

She shot him a dry look. "If you're comparing me to humans, that's not much of a compliment."

He had the grace to look chagrinned. "Humans don't even hold a candle. Shit, humans are to you what caterpillars are to pythons. There's no comparison."

She cocked her head to one side, with a half-smile. "Good, because if you're my True Bonded mate, I would hate to think you prefer humans over me."

"Lissandra." He rolled over on top of her and placed both hands on either side of her face. "I will never, *ever* prefer humans over you. You're the only one I want now that I've had a taste."

She Looked at him with her Sight. The truth of his claim burned through his eyes, rippling over his aura. He believed what he said with all his heart. But the stubborn darkness hovering at the edges made her gut clench. It had improved from when she'd first arrived, but its presence frustrated her. The darkness seemed familiar in a primal way. *Where the hell is it coming from?*

"Do you believe me?" His expression tightened.

"Yes." She believed him but worried the darkness might cloud his awareness.

"Good."

"But we should get up and eat. I'm starving."

"Are you? Can't have that." Denarrion rolled off the bed. "Give me a moment and I'll clean you up." He paused with a smirk. "Though I gotta say, I like the idea of you with my cum on your body."

"How about we clean each other?" She slid her feet to the floor and stood. "I promise I'll make sure you're completely clean."

His Puckish smile returned. "What if I don't want to be clean?"

"Into the shower, you dirty little dragon!" She shoved him playfully in the back. "I shall scrub that obnoxiousness out of you."

"Good luck with that." He yelped when she smacked his ass with her hand. "Hey. What was that for?"

"For being a smartass."

"Sweetheart, you're on the east coast. It's a way of life."

****

Denarrion wanted to take his time fondling Lissandra in the shower, but she had other ideas, her motions quick and efficient. He sighed, but he couldn't really complain. She'd certainly made sure he was relaxed after her Skype call. Only the odd feeling he'd screwed up somewhere marred his contentment. She'd been on fire while they made love, but the distance of the night before had returned, and he wondered what had gone wrong.

I answered all her questions about family, didn't I? What more does she want?

She was attentive in the shower but didn't waste time under the water.

"Are you coming?" She smiled at him as she paused at the door.

"Yeah, just gonna finish up here."

"Okay." She ducked out of the shower. "I'm going to get dressed and maybe start breakfast." But she took her time drying herself with a smirk. His cock stood up and saluted.

"Yeah, yeah. I'll be done in a minute."

She laughed and ducked out of the room.

Quiet, you. He thrust his face into the spray to distract himself from his raging dick. He didn't understand why his libido had control. *I'm a thousand years old.* One look at Lissandra and suddenly he was less than three hundred. Usually he had more control over his body.

At least when you bothered to control it. He grimaced.

The constant reminder of all the females he'd screwed over the years left a bad taste in his mouth. *Damn, I might as well be just a dick with legs.* Yeah, he didn't get paid, but that hardly mattered with respect to Lissandra.

It idea of bedding female humans nauseated him now. After being with her for just a day, the humans seemed poisonous, like eating too much junk food. A little wouldn't kill him, but too much would make him sick.

Already has.

He hadn't realized he felt sick until she appeared on his favorite rock at the Reservoir. She made him realize the extent of his illness. A single word couldn't describe the sensation. *Meh? Crappy? Slimy?* More like a combination of all of them plus "achy" and "shitty." The more time he spent with her, the better he felt. Stronger.

I gotta prove to her I'll remain faithful. Any other option disgusted him.

****

Lissandra dressed in denim capris and a plum-colored V-necked T-shirt before she picked up her phone. She nodded to herself. She'd made the right decision to complete the True Bond with Denarrion, even if he needed more work and healing. *That's what partners are for, right?*

True, she could help him more if she understood where the darkness in his aura had come from. *And for that, I need to talk to Torriandra.*

She dialed the number as she returned to the kitchen to make sure they had more coffee.

"Hello?"

"Good morning, Torri. It's Lissandra."

"Oh, good morning. How is everything going?" Torri sounded cautious. "Everything okay?"

"Yeah, it's fine." Lissandra paused as she grabbed the carafe from the coffeemaker. "Why?"

"You're calling us in the morning after spending a day with Denarrion."

Lissandra frowned. "Yeah, about that. You keep making comments like that about him. What's really going on, Torri?"

The other dragon paused. "What do you mean?"

"Why did you and Charlorrion suggest a courtship between me and Denarrion?"

"Isn't a new mate what you wanted?"

"Yeah, it's what *I* wanted, but I suspect you and Charlorrion wanted more than just that for Denarrion. Spit it out, Torri. What's really going on?"

A long sigh drifted over the phone. "You know Charlorrion is a foster son of Waltarrion, right?"

"Yeah. I think that's why my mother approved of this courtship."

"When I met Charlorrion, he'd just moved out of the house into his own place and he was filled with a lot of anger. I didn't know where it came from until he finally introduced me to his foster family." Torri sighed again. "They were all so angry, and Charlorrion fell into that mood every time we visited. We finally had to stop going to their house because I couldn't stand to be there."

"Whoa. Don't you have the Healing gift?"

"Yes, but I can't help heal anger that is freely taken on. After a visit, Charlorrion wouldn't shift into his natural form for days. And I couldn't get him to see how bad it was until he recovered. Then I could work on him and heal the sickly energies surrounding him."

Lissandra's stomach twisted. "What about Denarrion?"

Torri hummed. "Denarrion is worse. He's older than Charlorrion, but he stayed longer. I saw the anger eating away at him for years." She paused. "But he did get out and he is slowly healing. He looks much healthier after spending just a day with you."

Torriandra's words didn't dissolve Lissandra's concerns.

"Why would anyone recommend Denarrion for a courtship if he's this unhealthy?"

"To save him."

Lissandra gritted her teeth. "Save him? From what?"

She could hear Torri shake her head. "Something's wrong, but it's not something that is easily discovered or reversed. From the times I tried to help him, it seems as if he's fighting himself. His heart says one thing, but his head disagrees."

"Why do you think that is?"

"I don't know." But the hesitancy in Torri's voice suggested otherwise.

Lissandra scowled. "Do you think it has anything to do with the demon trace I found last night?"

"What?" Panic came through loud and clear.

Bingo.

"There's a demon in Redfield." Lissandra headed out onto the deck again, not wanting to involve Denarrion in her conversation until she had more facts. "I saw the decay it's spreading last night when I flew over town. And it's getting worse. How long has it been here? How long have you known?"

The silence lasted for several seconds. "Is Denarrion near you?"

"No, he's still upstairs."

"Okay." Torri took a deep breath. "A few decades ago,

Denarrion had a big blow up with his dad. There was a lot of yelling, destruction, and hurt thrown around, but it seemed to be the catalyst to get him out of the house. Charlorrion and I thought it would be an improvement, and he'd start to heal from the anger. And he did, somewhat. But then he stagnated."

"Stagnated how?"

"I wish I could explain. He seemed distracted and unfocused. I thought maybe someone told him the wrong things about being a dragon, insisting on them, and he took them as gospel."

Lissandra gut sank. Made sense given his severe lack of dragon knowledge, but who could have confused a dragon that much?

Demon.

"It's got to be the demon. It would definitely try to destroy any dragons in its path. Do you think his stagnation came from its arrival?"

"Not its arrival, but maybe it finally got strong enough to affect him." She sighed again and lowered her voice as if someone on her side of the call would hear her. "Charlorrion noticed the problem about ten years ago but didn't know anyone who could do anything about it except Waltarrion. But Waltarrion hasn't been well for over a century and doesn't welcome any talk about dragons or dragon kind."

"So, when Solenarra put out the call for a courtship, you jumped on it?"

"No, not at first. We did respond that Denarrion was single, but Charlorrion was hesitant until he found out about your Sight. Then he said you'd be perfect."

"Two birds with one stone."

"Yes, something like that."

"Glory to the Goddess." Lissandra scowled and shook her head. "Why didn't you tell me about this before I came?"

"I think Charlorrion thought you wouldn't come at all and we needed you. Solenarra mentioned you'd retired from demon hunting and you weren't ready to hear about resuming your work."

Thanks, Mom. Way to be underhanded.

"That's low, Torri. Really low to get me out here under false pretenses."

"They weren't entirely false. We do want to see Denarrion mated and happy. But if you can seek out and kill the demon, it's win-win for everyone."

"Except for me or my children if I'm killed."

"I'm sorry, Lissandra. We should've told you."

"Yes, you should've." She shot a look behind her at the house as Denarrion came down the stairs. "Does Denarrion know about the second reason you brought me here?"

"No. We weren't sure he'd even agree to the courtship. And any time we hinted at demon trace, he'd get very agitated and angry."

"Great. Just great. Look, I gotta go. But tell Charlorrion I need to speak with him when he gets off shift tonight."

"All right. I'm very sorry—"

Lissandra ended the call with only a minor twinge at being rude. *Ha. As if failing to mention the demon here wasn't rude.* She shoved the phone in her pocket and took some deep breaths to calm the anger coursing through her.

How in hellwinds was she supposed to just go back to believing this was a simple courtship? Dammit, she'd been brought out here to save Denarrion. Mating with him was just a lucky break, at least from Torri's and Charlorrion's perspectives.

"You know it's gonna get worse before it gets better." Yeah, that's the way it worked when a demon was involved.

Lissandra leaned against the porch railing and closed

her eyes, her mind spinning. Denarrion was her True Bonded mate, but if the demon had targeted him, she might not be able to save him. And if she couldn't save him, she'd either have to let him go, or…

Kill him.

A scream of despair worked its way up her throat, but she swallowed against it. She'd bonded with him, so his hurt and disease would eventually affect her.

Or my strength could help him throw off the taint.

But only if he wanted to be free of it. If he didn't, she'd have to figure out how to break the bond. *Nothing but death breaks that bond. Hellwinds.*

She wanted to blame Solenarra, or Torri, or Charlorrion, but she'd seen the warnings and ignored them. She was up to her eyeballs in this shit. The only way to save anyone now was to kill the demon, whether she wanted to or not.

"Hey, there you are." Denarrion's voice came from behind her. "Everything okay?"

She turned and studied him with her Sight. *Demon taint.* The darkness she'd seen edging his aura came from the demon in town. It had gotten better since she'd arrived, but now that she knew what it was, it'd be hard to believe he was healthy.

The question was, should she tell him?

No, because it'll alert the demon that we're onto it. Dammit. But dragons could smell lies.

Summoning every skill at deflection she had, she sighed and shook her head. "Yeah, I think so."

"What's going on?" He stepped up to the railing beside her.

"You know how I thought maybe we'd been set up for more than the courtship?"

"Yeah."

She nodded. "I was right. Torri and Charlorrion weren't sure I'd come all the way out here if I knew about your relationship with your dad and your habit of sleeping with all the women here."

"Oh." He scowled. "Yeah, well, it's no big secret that Walter and I don't get along well. And you already found out about the women. At least there are no more big secrets between us."

Her gut cramped, but she nodded. "Yeah, I think that's for the best." Except she hadn't told him what else the Ravenwings wanted her to do.

"I know what can take your mind off their manipulations." He brightened and took her hand. "Why don't we go into town today for the craft festival? They're having the big Memorial Day celebration with craft and food vendors. It'll be fun."

"Yeah, okay. That sounds great. But breakfast first." She growled and grinned. "You worked up a big appetite in me this morning."

He laughed. "Yeah, in me, too. Come on."

She followed him inside, hoping everything would be easier from now on. But she didn't count on it.

CHAPTER FOURTEEN

Denarrion noticed the change in Lissandra immediately. She'd grown pensive and quiet as they ate breakfast, and he wondered who she'd been talking to when he came down the stairs.

"Everything okay?" He poured coffee into two to-go mugs and handed her one.

"Yes, everything's fine. Why?"

"I dunno. You're kinda withdrawn and quiet all of a sudden. Did your mom have bad news or something?"

She shook her head. "No, just have a lot on my mind with all she didn't say. And I can't verify Charlorrion's role in it until later. I hate having the wait."

"We'll enjoy the Redfield Craft Fair. It'll be a good way to distract you from your worries until Charlie gets off work."

She sighed. "Yeah, I guess it would."

"It would also give us a good day before we have to have dinner with my parents." He grimaced, wishing the event didn't have to happen.

"We're having dinner with your parents tonight?"

He nodded as he led her toward the front door. "Yeah, my mother called and told me they expected us at six on the dot."

"It should be okay, right? I mean, you're doing what they wanted you to do by having a courtship with me. That should make them happy, right?"

He frowned. "Honestly, I don't know. Nothing I seem to do makes them less pissed off. Will this be that one thing? I have no idea."

Spending time with his parents had become akin to getting a tooth pulled at the dentist, only without the anesthesia. Every time he visited, he felt sick and exhausted, and his restlessness only diminished the farther and longer away he stayed. He shook his head as he opened the doors of the truck.

"I guess it's a good thing for you to meet them, though, so you can decide what they're like for yourself." He shrugged against the urge to get into his truck and drive like hellwinds westward without looking back. "I'd rather we never saw them at all, but since this courtship is partly their idea, it's probably necessary."

"Denarrion, if you don't want to have dinner with them tonight, I'll back your play."

He met her gaze in surprise. "You don't want to meet my parents?"

"No, I said if you don't want to go, I'll stand with you. You're my priority here, not them."

An odd wrenching feeling slashed through his chest as if he'd pulled a muscle, and he grunted in surprised pain. He inhaled to cry out, but it ended as if it had never happened. *What in hellwinds?* He rubbed his chest as the sensations faded, leaving him lighter and more relaxed. *Weird.*

"Thanks, Lissandra. It means a lot, but I think we should just bite the bullet and get it over with." He started the truck and grimaced. "At least we only have to be there for dinner. Afterward, we can duck out quick."

"Sounds like a plan."

It was a great plan. One with a happy ending if he had anything to say about it. His mind gave him images of her riding him, her face suffused with pleasure, her breasts bouncing. He loved it when he made her come. It was almost better than coming himself.

Lissandra shot him a look with a raised eyebrow. "Having some good thoughts over there?"

He looked back at her in guilty surprise. "What?"

"I can feel your arousal and I see its result for myself." She nodded to the tightness of his shorts.

He shifted his body a little. "You can feel it?"

"Oh yeah." She grinned. "I've heard it will be that way for a while. We'll be able to feel strong emotions in particular. Apparently, you feel pretty strongly about something sexual."

He grinned to hide his embarrassment. "Hey, I'm a guy. Guys do that kind of thing."

She snorted. "Guy humans do that kind of thing."

"I've spent a lot of time around humans." He shrugged as he pulled into a parking spot along the street. "But as a male dragon, I'm a big fan of remembering what it's like to be with you." He growled playfully and pulled her close to his chest, wrapping his other arm around her. "This male dragon looks at his female and thinks about how good she smells and how great she looks against my sheets, and how good she tastes…" Then he bent his head and kissed her softly on the lips.

Lissandra opened her mouth to receive his tongue and tickle it with her own. Her willingness to give as good as she got made his arousal ramp up. An answering surge of arousal hit his system and made him gasp. He rumbled his approval as the kiss became hotter and more demanding. Her breasts flattened against his chest and his own nipples tingled with the contact. His cock hardened from maple to oak in that moment and he was sure it would break the zipper on his shorts.

This is my true mate. She's mine.

When they both came up for air, Denarrion realized what it meant to be bound to his soul mate. He'd always want her near him, kissing him, smiling at him. Her smile left him weak in the knees and just holding her hand electrified his whole body like a live wire.

"Damn, Lissandra. You take my breath away."

"Well, don't steal all the oxygen." She panted with her own smirk. "I need some of it after that kiss."

He laughed. "Let's go visit the craft fair before I turn this truck around and take you home for more of that kind of kiss." He hadn't felt this good in a *very* long time. *What the hell was wrong with me?*

They got out of the truck and he locked it before he met her on the sidewalk and took her hand. He tried to keep his mind on their plans rather than what he would prefer to be doing. *Sucking on her clit, licking her pussy.* He took a deep breath. *Focus.*

"So where are we headed?"

"The Redfield Craft Fair held in the city park baseball field, right in the center of town. Everyone puts up these white canvas tents and you can walk around checking out their stuff. It's pretty big."

"Are you selling any of your furniture at the fair?" she asked.

"Kinda. Simple Elegance, the shop where I sell my stuff has a tent this year, so there might be a few chairs and small tables for sale. Who knows? Guess we'll just have to take a look."

He suspected Charlotte Abernathy, the woman who owned Simple Elegance, would have a few of his things on display to entice the out-of-towners into her shop. They both made a killing on the craft fair weekends.

But Charlotte had been one of his first lovers when he'd started his "furniture kick", as his father called it. Charlotte had never given him cause for worry despite his promiscuity, but he'd never been as serious about a woman as he was with Lissandra. He hoped Charlotte wouldn't prove to be possessive.

"This is a cute town." Lissandra nodded to a group of people coming toward them on the sidewalk. "Why do they call it Redfield?"

"Back in the day, this town had its own baseball team, the Redfield Raiders. They were pretty good." He grinned. "Good enough to get the talent scouts from the big leagues to come looking for rookies. The baseball field has this huge fence all the way around it. At the time, they only had red paint on hand, so they used what they had."

"The Redfield."

"Right. The successive mayors have it repainted every few years to keep up the tradition." They paused at a crosswalk, waiting for the light to change. "That's where they hold the craft fairs inside the field. Helps with both containment and security."

They arrived at the baseball field, but it had been transformed into a carnival of sorts. White canvas tents stood in three rows in two half-circles with the park entrance at one end and the temporary stage at the other. The space in the middle had been left for audience and dancing.

"Wow, this is quite the festival." Lissandra's gaze scanned the forest of stalls ahead.

"Yeah. I love to see what all people create to sell. There's some great photographers who come each year."

Denarrion had his favorite vendors, but he held back to watch Lissandra enjoy the offerings. She murmured in approval over the remarkable photography of landscapes and old abandoned buildings in black and white. Another stall sold wind chimes and wind spinners made from copper and marbles.

She stopped at several stalls displaying jewelry of different kinds, and he swallowed a laugh. *Definitely a true dragon. Attracted to precious metals and stones.* One woman sold old glass bottles flattened for kitchen spoon rests, some with funny designs melted into them. Lissandra purchased some small brightly colored bracelets for her daughters and a spoon rest with "Kitchen Dragon Lady" on it for her mother.

"There are some very clever things here. I liked the bone-handled hunting knives."

Denarrion raised his eyebrows. "Really?"

"Yeah, it's always good to carry one if you plan to bring the meat home for more than yourself." She nodded as they passed a booth with laser-cut brass welcome signs in a variety of shapes. "I have a really nice one made from Damascus steel. The swirls on the blade are gorgeous. Oh, that's funny."

"What?" He peered over her shoulder as she pointed at something on the ground.

"See that "Welcome" sign? It has the four Earp brothers walking, each packing a rifle in silhouette." She grinned. "That would he a helluva welcome."

"Yeah, I prefer a different kind of welcome." He wrapped his arms around her waist and pressed his face against her neck, dropping a kiss on the skin below her ear.

She laughed and squeezed his hands before he released her. "I think I'd prefer that kind of welcome, too."

The food stalls perfumed the early summer air with scents of frying bread and popcorn, cotton candy and cooked meat as they browsed. He'd often come to the craft fairs to check out the competition, but he'd never enjoyed it as much as he did now. Lissandra's interest sparked his own and he could enjoy the variety of goods with new perspective.

Charlotte's stall came out of nowhere for him and he gritted his teeth against urge to grab Lissandra and run. *Please, Goddess, don't let it be like yesterday.*

Lissandra stepped into the shade of the Simple

Elegance tent and scanned the furniture intently. She took in the woven wicker chairs and matching table, the small nesting tables, and a couple of rustic bureaus. She nodded to Charlotte in greeting, but kept her attention on the goods.

"Oh, what a beautiful rocking chair." She ran her hand over the scrollwork on the headrest. "And the round table, too. So lovely."

"Those were made by a fabulous local artist." Charlotte smiled with pride as she approached Lissandra. When she spied Denarrion, her smile widened. "In fact, here he is. Denny, this woman was interested in your chair and table."

"Yeah, actually I brought her by to see your tent, Charlotte." He nodded. "Sandy is in town visiting and I wanted to show her some of my finished work."

Lissandra shot him a surprised look at her nickname but smiled for Charlotte. "Denny…said he'd have some pieces here this weekend. Are these all?"

"Oh no, there are several more in inventory I'll bring over the weekend. His work always sells so well." Charlotte's eyes lit with satisfaction before shifting to curiosity. "So you're the new woman in Denny's life, hmm?"

Lissandra's brows rose. "Sorry?"

Charlotte shrugged. "It's a small town and gossip travels fast. Carrie mentioned that Denny had a new lady love."

Denarrion stiffened but tried to laugh. "I'm pretty sure she didn't use those words."

"No, she said something less complimentary, but she's rather possessive." Charlotte shook her head. "I warned you to leave her be years ago. She's a brat and doesn't take rejection well."

"You warned me?" Denarrion raised his eyebrows. "I don't remember that."

"Maybe that's because you were thinking with the

wrong head." Charlotte winked. "Just be ready to deal with any rumors she'll circulate."

Lissandra narrowed her eyes. "Fabulous. Thank you for showing off his work, Charlotte, and for the warning."

"You're welcome. I can see you're better suited for him." She shot Denarrion a smile.

"It was very nice to meet you and good luck this weekend. I hope there's a good turnout."

The air rippled with a subtle motion and a blessing settled over the tent and its proprietor. *Damn, that's cool.* Charlotte would sell almost everything she had brought to display that weekend thanks to Lissandra's blessing.

"So far, so good." Charlotte smiled before she returned to her chair. "Thanks again for stopping by."

Denarrion took Lissandra's hand. "That was nicely done. Charlotte will make a killing this weekend."

"That was my intention, especially if she sells your items." Lissandra winked. "She was very 'proud' of you and your furniture, almost proprietary."

"Well, she did "discover" me when I first started out." They stood to the side as a flood of people gravitated toward the tent to inspect the furniture. "But thanks for doing it anyway. She, uh, she was one of the first women I, uh, well…"

Lissandra nodded, laying a hand on his arm. "It's okay, Denarrion. It's your past and it can't be changed. I'm more interested in your present."

"And future, right?"

"Yeah, that too."

Her response unnerved him, but before he could ask about it, she'd turned away to inspect a booth with silver and beaded jewelry laid out on black velvet.

Necklaces made from lapis, carnelian, abalone shell, turquoise and onyx lay beside silver rings, some with stones and some without, in neat little rows. A plastic rack on a swivel displayed pairs of earring, and long loops of matching silver and stone beaded necklaces and bracelets dangled for the tourists.

A few leather dreamcatchers woven with turquoise, shell and hematite beads threaded within the webs and feathers hanging from the edge loop waved in the breeze through the tent. A young Iroquois woman dressed in a long-sleeved button-down shirt and jeans sat behind the tables working on another necklace/bracelet set. But she wasn't what set Denarrion's teeth on edge.

An older man rested deeper in the shade of the tent. His thick gray hair was held back from his face by a black leather headband and fell in two plaits on either side of his head. He sat back, his dark eyes assessing everyone, but they sharpened on Lissandra before turning to Denarrion. A rush of intense power flooded over him and the craft fair faded into darkness.

What in hellwinds?

Panic clawed at him and he struggled to breathe through it. He swallowed hard until light flickered into his awareness.

Holy shit, did someone start a fire?

A crackling campfire flared in front of him and the old man sat beyond its hypnotic dance. Other figures sat on either side, watching with intense concern. The scents of charred wood and smoke, pine trees and dirt scuffed by boots filled his nose as chanting voices called in the air.

He turned his gaze to Lissandra as she pointed to the fire. Following her lead, he found his hand among the flickering heat. *What the-?*

"Wake up, Denarrion!"

The wind blew a little smoke into his eyes and he blinked, suddenly returning to the sun-warmed tents of the craft fair and the old man watching him with narrowed eyes.

He took a deep breath in surprise, but Lissandra distracted him by tugging him closer to the table. He shot a look at the old man and swallowed hard when he met his gaze. *Not quite human.* The man stared with enigmatic attention before he switched his gaze away toward the young woman.

The young artist stiffened and looked up at Denarrion, her own gaze assessing. "I have something for you."

Lissandra raised her eyebrows. "For me?"

"No, for your beau."

She reached under the table and rooted around in a container filled with her jewelry supplies. She drew out a little black velvet bag and opened it, dumping its contents into her hand. She polished the item to her satisfaction and she held it out to him.

A bracelet made of three heavy, woven strands of copper snaking around five large, raw olive-green stones rested in her palm. He reached for the bracelet with the intent of examining the stones.

The moment his hand closed around it, something wrenched inside him. The world shimmered as if a veil had been pulled away and colors became vibrant. The sounds of people talking morphed into musical background rather than white noise, and the scents of food, sun, trees, and grass became sensual delights on the wind. Denarrion felt renewed, refreshed, happier than he'd been in decades.

"Whoa."

"That's gorgeous." Lissandra tilted her head and narrowed her eyes. "Are you okay?"

"Yeah." He nodded. "Yeah, I think so."

"Let's see what it looks like on you."

She turned the bracelet sideways and slid it over his wrist until the wide part settled just above his hand. It looked fiery green against his tanned brown skin and it felt wonderfully cool in the heat.

"What are the stones?" Lissandra turned her attention to the woman.

"Peridot, raw." She offered a shy smile. "It was made

for you."

He snorted a laugh. "Uh-huh. How much is the bracelet?"

"Eighty-five dollars."

"What?" Denarrion gaped and reached to take the bracelet off his wrist. "That's too—"

"We'll take it." Lissandra laid a hand on his arm. She winked as she purchased the bracelet for him. "Thank you. It's beautiful work."

"Thank you. We're honored by your interest. My grandfather said this bracelet would be for someone special." She gestured to the back where the old man sat.

Lissandra followed her arm with her gaze and stiffened. *She seems spooked.* To his surprise, she nodded reverently, damn near bowing to the old man. Denarrion narrowed his eyes and tried to figure out what would make a dragon bow to a human. They were pretty much all alike. Right?

"Thank you again. We're grateful for your work." Lissandra nodded again.

Denarrion tried to take the bracelet off again, but she shook her head.

"You should wear it. It looks really good on you." She took the velvet bag from the young woman and stuffed it in her pocket.

"You think so? I'm not much of a jewelry kind of guy." Usually.

"Copper bracelets on men are pretty sexy." She grinned as she let her gaze rest on the goods in the booths they passed.

"Really? Sexy?"

She laughed. "Yes, really sexy."

He shot a look at his wrist and he had to admit he liked the feel of the copper against his skin.

"All right, then."

"Oh, look at this." She pulled him over to a booth with

a banner that read Redfield Library System. A sign-up sheet for a Storytelling Contest with prizes for first, second, and third place finishers lay on the table. "That's cool. I'm going to sign up." She wrote her name down on the sheet.

"You're going to tell a story?"

"Sure, why not? I haven't done this since I was a kid. I wish the girls could see me. Maybe you can record me on my phone? I have just the story to tell this time, too."

"You used to tell stories to large audiences?" He raised his eyebrows as she nodded to the librarian.

"Not large audiences, but you know, about thirty or forty people. Back when oral storytelling was their version of the radio show."

Denarrion loved to see her so elated. Her lavender eyes sparkled and her face lit with joy. Her breasts bounced with her enthusiasm and his cock approved. *Down, boy!*

"Come on, it's about to start."

She tugged him into the open area before the stage and they sat in the grass of the infield while the librarian from the table announced the event.

"Welcome to the first annual Redfield Storytelling Competition," she began with a gentle smile. "The stories must be ten minutes or less in length, must be rated PG, including violence." She shot a stern look to the audience. "All stories must follow the theme of beginnings, as we are at the beginning of summer.

"Competitors may tell a traditional story or one of their own making and will be called up in order of the list." She waved the signup list. "So, give a round of applause for our first contestant."

The man who stepped up to the microphone was tall, thin, and looked like an accountant. He adjusted his glasses and began to recite a story in a sonorous voice that lulled his audience into a stupor by the second paragraph. Something about a bunch of bunnies trying to save the forest from some sort of insect. Denarrion hid a yawn.

He recognized he next person as a young woman he'd slept with a few years earlier, and he shot a look at Lissandra. Fortunately, she was too engrossed in the competition to notice.

His erstwhile one-night-stand told a story about fairies that was very good. The audience came alive, swept away with her tale of daring and adventure. It was the beginning of the environmentalist movement in the little town outside the forest. It was a good story and had people laughing at the antics of the fairies. The applause was thunderous.

There were ten people, including Lissandra, who told stories, but most of them blurred together and faded in Denarrion's memory. At last Lissandra was introduced and she winked at Denarrion as she took the microphone. She took a few deep breaths before she settled her shoulders and smiled out at the audience.

"This is called The Tale of Why the Moon Winks. In the beginning, when the world was newly made and its Peoples were just beginning, the Mother of All looked down upon our world and knew that Her Peoples, those of the Wolf, Coyote, Badger, Deer, Moose, and Bobcat, were unprotected from greater, stronger threats. She worried that these Peoples would not be able to evolve, to grow and to prosper without someone to guard them.

"She searched for a protector of Her new world and found a big, black dragon with opalescent eyes. He was an old and wise dragon, first among his kind and kindly like a grandfather, but as fierce as a warrior. His scales were glossy and reflective, yet he blended into the night sky, nearly invisible.

"'Oh Great Grandfather Dragon,' the Mother Goddess beseeched him, 'Please come and watch over my new world and protect it from demons and others who would harm its fragile balance.'

"The Great Grandfather Dragon opened one of his sleepy, opalescent eyes and regarded the Mother Goddess for what seemed an eon or two before saying anything. She had to be very patient." The audience laughed.

"'Great Mother of All,' he replied in a voice so unused it sounded like great granite boulders sliding against one another. 'Why should I wish to watch Your world for You? I have spent millennia watching galaxies form, stars evolve, and the Universe expand in brilliant blazes of color. What could Your world offer to compensate me for taking my eyes away from such wonders?'

Lissandra winked at the crowd. "Dragons are noble creatures, you see, but they are hoarders, and the Great Grandfather Dragon hoarded the delights of the expanding Universe. He hoarded the births and deaths of stars like brilliant diamonds and topazes to be looked upon and admired. He'd seen more worlds come and go in the dance of life than he had scales and he held each memory like a cherished bauble given by a lover.

"'Oh Great Grandfather Dragon, the Universe is a wondrous place, indeed,' the Mother Goddess agreed, 'but this world I wish you to protect holds wonders that the Universe has never seen before. There are Peoples in this world, great and small, two-legged, four-legged, six-legged and more, who are inspiring in their own right. I have coaxed them into being, but these Peoples will create and evolve in their own ways and they will be wondrous to behold.'"

Lissandra dropped her chin with a dry look at the crowd. "The Great Grandfather Dragon did not look convinced." The audience laughed. "'Mother of All, I am a very old Dragon. Perhaps this duty would be best suited to a Dragon who is younger and has seen less. New worlds are not so new to me.'

"'But a younger Dragon, while excited by the newness would not have your vast experience or wisdom, and may be so excited by the Universe that she'd forget her duty to the new world,' the Mother Goddess pointed out reasonably. 'You, Great Grandfather Dragon, are the best, oldest, and wisest of Dragons. I would only ask the greatest to watch over My newest and most wondrous world.'

"Again, the Great Grandfather Dragon eyed Her skeptically, so the Mother Goddess added hastily, 'Please, Great Grandfather Dragon, try it for one month. If My new world does not compete with the wonders you have seen in your millennia of watching the Universe, then I shall release you from your duty and find a new Dragon to protect my world.'

"The Great Grandfather Dragon considered for a while longer and the Mother Goddess worried that he might yet turn Her down once more. But at last, he agreed to watch over Her new world and he carefully curled around the blue marbled ball. He folded his great wings into long lines along his body and made certain that he had one eye always focused on the world within the circle of his form." Lissandra curled her hands as if holding a ball.

"For one month, he watched the world, his one eye glowing down upon our world, shedding its opalescent light upon the ground when the sun hid its face. But though he was a great and mighty Dragon, he, too, needed his rest and his eye would slowly close until it was invisible in the night sky. Once closed, he slept for one solid day, then would jerk awake and his eye would slowly open again until it shone round and glowing once more.

"And in the month he watched our world, the Great Grandfather Dragon became so enamored of the Peoples growing and changing upon its surface that he chose to remain as Guardian of the World as the Mother Goddess had requested.

"So, if you look up into the night sky, you can see him still, watching over us all. His great opalescent eye opens and closes, and he sleeps but one night a month, before his eye opens and shines upon us again. The glittering lights of our world sparkle upon the facets of his reflective scales to make the stars and shine along his wing folds as the Milky Way, and his great eye we call the Moon.

"So when you look up and see him, give him a wave and you might just be lucky enough to see him wink at you. Thank you."

Thunderous applause flooded the small gathering and Denarrion clapped along with the rest though his guts clenched in unreasoning panic. What right did she have to tell *that* story? It was one of the True Stories, of how the Goddess had asked dragons to watch over the Peoples on this world and protect them from demons. Not as the moon, per se, but as protectors, nonetheless.

If humans knew how true the story was, it would frighten them and they would come after him and his family. His father had warned him often enough. The anger and fear rose in his chest and he swallowed against them as Lissandra joined him in the grass.

"So, what did you think? Do I have a chance to win?"

"Yeah, it was good." He smiled at her, but she narrowed her eyes.

"Are you all right?"

"Yeah, I'm good." He nodded.

"Are you sure? You look like you've sucked on a lemon."

"Yeah, no, I'm okay. I—"

His cell phone shrilled with Wagner's *Ride of the Valkyries* the ring tone he'd set for his parents as an early warning system. *They would call now.* He shot a nervous look at the stage as they began to announce the winners of the competition. He almost didn't answer, but that was asking for more trouble than it was worth.

"Give me a minute. I gotta take this."

Lissandra nodded as he reached for his phone.

CHAPTER FIFTEEN

Lissandra watched as Denarrion's whole body stiffened and wariness tightened his expression.

"This is Denny."

Anger, disgust, and reluctance streamed down the bond from him, and she fisted her hands to keep from wrapping her arms around him. *Who the hell can make him that unhappy?*

She waited a little longer, hoping he'd give her an indication of what he heard on the phone, but the librarian for the Redfield Library began the list the winners for the storytelling competition.

"In second place, for her story of Why the Moon Winks, Ms. Sandy Charforest."

What?

Lissandra gasped in surprise and shot a look at Denarrion. Unfortunately, he remained focused on his phone and whatever news he heard. She bit her lip but rose and made her way to the stage. Several people cheered for her and she waved in response.

"Congratulations, Ms. Charforest, you've won an Amazon.com gift card for fifty dollars."

She took the little card from the librarian and nodded.

"Thank you. It was fun."

The applause continued as she made her way back through the crowd toward Denarrion, but some of her elation died at the frustration etched on his face. What had gone so wrong?

She paused a few feet away, trying to give him some privacy. She tucked the gift card into her pocket and let her gaze slide over the bright colors of the craft stalls. The day had been getting steadily better after their morning discussion, but his apprehension had returned the moment they bought the bracelet from the *Morukai* Shaman and his granddaughter. It only intensified after she offered the oral tale.

She shot a look at him and found him still frowning at the ground as he talked on the phone. She'd have to ask him if he understood what a gift they'd been given to receive the bracelet from a Speaker of the Goddess. She was sending them a message, though Lissandra couldn't translate what it meant yet.

"Yeah, okay, we'll be there." Denarrion's voice full of resignation made her turn. He swiped the phone and shook his head.

"Denarrion? Is everything all right?"

"Yeah, it's fine." He shrugged, his mouth tight. "They want us to come over for dinner by five."

"Five?" She pulled her own phone out to check the time. "We have a little over two hours. That's enough time, isn't it?"

"Uh, yeah, I guess." He nodded, but he didn't sound convinced.

"Hey." She tugged on his arm, turning him toward her. "It's going to be fine. And the best part is, if we're there earlier, we can be done earlier. Right?"

A tired smile curled his lips. "Yeah, that's one way to look at it."

"Tell you what. Once we get done with dinner, let's

take my Amazon gift card and do some online shopping." She waved the little gift card as his smile broadened. "I won second place in the storytelling competition." She tilted her head coyly. "Maybe we can find some fun 'toys' online."

"Oh, yeah? What kind of toys did you have in mind?"

Before Lissandra could respond, a body hurled itself into Denarrion's arms, clinging like a starfish. The woman planted a kiss on his mouth that made Lissandra want to snarl. *What the fuck is she doing to my mate?* She recognized the woman as the bitch from the market bakery, the one called Carrie. She smelled like too much alcohol and floral perfume, and she pressed her body tightly against Denarrion as she mauled him.

"Carrie, stop. What are you doing?" He pushed her back and held her at arms' length.

"I just wanted to remind you what you were missing by not answering my calls." She slurred her words as she cocked her hip outward in an attempt to look seductive. Her lack of balance ruined the effect. "Come on, Denny. We were soooo good together, especially in bed, hmmm?"

Lissandra ground her teeth, aware of the pool of silence around them. Nearby shop keepers shot speculative glances at them, while others wore smirks. *Looks like plenty are familiar with Denarrion's habit of sleeping with anything female.*

"It was nice, but I never made you any promises. We agreed it would be no-strings-attached." He shook his head. "We're done, Carrie. I've moved on."

"Oh, please." The woman tried to throw herself at him again, but he side-stepped her, and she tilted to one side, a sneer curling her lips. "It was *way* better than 'nice'. You don't wanna miss out on this." She gestured sloppily to her body.

"Aaahh, you know me." He shrugged though his eyes sparked with anger. "I don't stay with one woman very long."

You better not mean me, mate.

Anger tripped through Lissandra's system, but she let it settle into her gut. She tried to calm herself down with the reminder that Denarrion said he was committed to the courtship. *And we're true mates.* But another voice argued that he didn't know much about dragons. What if he decided that he didn't want to honor the bond after all?

Carrie pouted. "But you gave Suzy Wilkerson almost a month. I want my fair share."

Sweet glory, like he's some sort of time-share treat.

Denarrion shook his head. "It doesn't work like that. And we agreed it would be short-term."

Carrie snorted, woozily shifting her attention to Lissandra. She scowled with disdain. "You're taking up with her? Damn, Denny, she's older than dirt." She swung around and pointed. "You're not from around here, so you don't know. He'll walk when he gets tired of you. And you're old. He'll move on faster because of that." She shrugged and swayed. "Just sayin'."

Anger made Lissandra offer a half-smile. "Maybe, but it's my concern, not yours. Maybe you need to find your own boyfriend rather than hitting on mine."

"Fuck off, bitch." Carrie sneered, crowding against Denarrion a little more. "He's not boyfriend material. You're just a vacation fling."

Lissandra raised her eyebrows and laughed. "Oh, glory, there is so much wrong with that I can't even describe it."

As Carrie snarled and tried to launch herself at Lissandra, her own words penetrated. *So much wrong.* She narrowed her eyes and tilted her head before she allowed her Sight to take over her vision. She swung her gaze back to where Denarrion held Carrie by the arm to keep her from stumbling as she bared her teeth at Lissandra.

Brilliant colors encapsulated the sellers' booths and the

trees around them. The people glowed with varying levels of health, all the myriad parts of life. But on Carrie, the black and puce colored stains marked her as demon-tainted. *By the Goddess, how did the demon get to her?* Worse, the same markings smudged Denarrion as well, though a soft green light glowed on his right wrist where the *Morukai*'s bracelet rested, fighting off the influence.

Demon tainted, both of them. How in hellwinds had it gotten to a dragon?

The answer didn't matter. The path ahead of her lay clear. Lissandra allowed her sight to return to normal and focused on Denarrion holding Carrie back.

"Denarrion, let her go."

He shot her a look of surprise. "Are you serious? She's damn near feral."

Lissandra nodded. "I know. Just do it."

"Sonuvaprick. Okay." He shook his head and released Carrie.

The woman shrieked and lunged at Lissandra, her inebriation making her wobble and stumble in her fury. Lissandra was ready for her, and caught her hands, folding them across her chest before wrapping her in a tight hug until her mouth was next to Carrie's ear.

"Listen to me, Carrie. I don't care about your past, your petty jealousy, or your wants. Denny is off the market as of today, and nothing you say, do, or hope for will change that." She squeezed the woman as she struggled to get free. "Your turn is over and he was never right for you, anyway."

Lissandra pulled back to meet Carrie's furious gaze. "I'm trying to give you a graceful out. Because if you persist in chasing after my partner, especially after he's told you no, you'll really piss me off."

"What're ya gonna do, bitch? You don't scare me." Carrie scowled.

Lissandra released a little of her glamour, allowing her

dragon essence to color her eyes and elongate her teeth. "I should scare you, little girl, but I try not to make a habit of it. But if you continue to come after him, there's a good likelihood they'll never find your body. Got me?"

Sobriety abruptly filled Carrie's expression and she swallowed hard as her gaze focused on Lissandra's altered appearance. Lissandra widened her smile and the other woman whimpered. She'd never actually kill Carrie, but she might be tempted to erase Carrie's memory of both herself and Denarrion. As it was, she used her magic to scour away some of the demon-taint, and Carrie relaxed marginally.

"Are we clear, Carrie?"

"Y-yes ma'am." She nodded, her eyes still wide.

"Good. Do you need help getting home?"

"No, ma'am. I can do that on my own."

"Good to hear. Be safe, now." Lissandra released her and stepped back. Carrie swallowed hard, nodded, and staggered away as fast as her drunk legs could carry her.

"What did you say to her?" Denarrion moved to Lissandra's side as they watched Carrie disappear among the booths.

"I told her you were off the market and she needed to find someone who was better suited for her." Lissandra tilted her head a bit with a smile. "I don't think she'll be hitting on you again."

"Good." He frowned. "I think. Damn, my wrist is killing me."

He lifted his arm and pulled the bracelet off his wrist. A red mark scored the skin above his hand as if he'd sustained a mild burn.

"Good glory, what happened?" She grasped his arm and examined the burn.

"I don't know. It started to heat up when Carrie kissed me." His eyes widened at her growl and he held up his hands. "She threw herself at me, Lissa. I wasn't into it, I swear."

Lissandra sighed, swallowing her frustration. "I know, but it was all I could do not to throw her across the field." She shook her head as she handed him the black velvet bag for the bracelet. "We should get back to the house and put some lavender oil on that so it won't scar."

"Yeah, okay." He caught her arm as they started for the truck. "I'm serious, Lissandra. I wasn't interested in her, I just didn't want to cause a bigger scene. Do you believe me?"

She paused and met his gaze. "Yes."

He grimaced. "I know it's gonna take a while to prove that, especially here in this town, but I'm committed to you. Seriously. I'm done with my past shit."

"I believe you, Denarrion. Now let's get that tended to."

They retreated through the crowds in silence. Many people looked after them with curiosity and a few whispers, but she could handle that. At least the altercation hadn't escalated into an all-out brawl.

When they reached his truck, she rested a hand on his arm. "Do you want me to drive?"

He blinked as if coming a long way back from his thoughts. "Oh, nah, I got this. I'm okay."

They climbed into the truck and settled into their seats. Denarrion pulled out into traffic, but once they were on their way, he reached over and grasped one of her hands. Lissandra shot him a look of surprise, but he didn't say anything and continued to hold her hand until they pulled in to his driveway.

He shut off the truck but didn't get out immediately. She waited with his warm palm against hers, sensing churning emotions coming from him. He took a deep breath as if to say something, but in the end, he shook his head and released her, sliding out of the truck. She frowned and followed.

"Are you okay, Denarrion?" She caught up to him as he unlocked his door.

"Yeah. Kinda." He shook his head as he headed for the kitchen. "I don't know. My gut's tellin' me you still don't trust me because of my past." He raised his pale blue gaze to meet hers. "But one thing became really clear while Carrie was doing her thing. I didn't want to be anywhere near her again."

"I believe you. But that burn's going to get worse. We'll talk about this after we get it treated." Lissandra pulled him to the sink. "Can you wash that while I go find the lavender oil? Or do you need help?'

"Nah, I got this." He turned on the water, hissing as it hit the burns. "It's weird. Most of the time I don't burn. You know, 'cause I'm a dragon and all."

"Yeah, that is odd."

Except she Saw the bracelet holding off the demon-taint. More than likely the wound would scar to remind him of how close he came to being permanently damaged by the demon's magic. Hopefully the lavender would help. She grasped the bottle and some bandages before heading back to the kitchen.

"Found it."

Denarrion sat on one of the stools, drying his wrist with a paper towel. She joined him and set down the bandages before she uncapped the bottle.

"This is probably going to sting." She gave him an apologetic grimace. "Ready?"

"Yeah." He held his arm out to her.

The burn was impressive, already showing the body's efforts to protect the underlying skin. But from what her Sight told her, the bracelet had scoured a lot of the demon-taint out of him already. Taking a deep breath, she smoothed the lavender oil over the damaged skin, hissing in sympathy with his sounds of pain.

"Holy shit, that hurts." The muscles of his jaw bunched

as he clenched his teeth.

"I know. I'm sorry. Let me wrap it up to keep it protected."

She wrapped his arm, trying to keep her thoughts to herself. She didn't want to push him on Carrie's insistence, or why the demon had targeted her to seek him out. Was this part of a greater scheme to manipulate the only archenemy that could take the demon down? *I just don't know enough.* She shook her head with a frown.

"Hey, I want to tell you something." Denarrion grasped her hands when she'd finished. "I want no other mate than you, Lissandra. I mean it." He met her gaze, a vee appearing between his brows. "I won't chase any other female. Not for friendship, pleasure, or sex. You're too important to me. This whole relationship is too important. Tell me you're mine."

She nodded, biting her lip. "I want to, Denarrion. But you said something to Carrie that made me worried."

He swallowed hard. "I did? What did I say?"

"You said you don't stay with any one woman very long, and I wondered if that meant me, too." She shrugged with on shoulder. "It shook me up. After all we've shared, including the True Mating bond, it had me worried that you might not really want this connection."

"Oh." He squeezed her hands gently. "I had to remind her of that or she wouldn't have given up. Plus it was a way to keep my life and decisions private. Everyone here expects me to be a Don Juan, with a new woman each week. It kinda provides me some anonymity. No one really knows who I'm with. And I like that."

He released her hand to rub the back of his neck. "I guess that wasn't the best idea, huh?" He sighed. "Yeah, I was an idiot. The truth is, I only want you and to stay with you until the Goddess sends for us."

"Are you sure, Denarrion?" She couldn't believe she was offering him an out when they'd already bonded. But she didn't want to fight every woman who came near him for his attention.

"Yeah." He nodded, his shoulders straightening. He met her gaze without flinching. "From now on, you're mine, Lissandra, and I'm yours. With all my heart."

A ripple fluttered in the air as if something had washed over them and she recognized the magic of a sworn vow. She stared hard at Denarrion to see if he realized what his words meant, but she couldn't deny that the Goddess had heard and accepted them.

"If you're mine, then I'm yours as well." She raised her chin and gave him a smile. "I commit to this courtship in the name of the Goddess. I mean to see it to the end, and take you, Denarrion Goldencoat, as my mate. Do you accept my commitment?"

"I do." His eyes glowed with his promise. "I also commit to this courtship in the name of the Goddess, and take you, Lissandra Charforest, as my mate. Do you accept my commitment?"

"I do."

The world seemed to fill with light and sound, like a Technicolor hurricane. It wrapped around them, swirling through the room with all the sunlight, then it was gone, as quickly as it had come. They stared at each other with amazement.

"What the hell was that?"

Lissandra blinked. "I think it was the Goddess accepting our vows to each other."

"Holy shit."

She laughed. "No, holy Goddess."

He grinned. "Do you think it's like that between every True Mated pair of dragons?"

She shook her head. "I don't know. I've never asked. It wasn't one of those things that ever came up in polite conversation."

He snorted. "Aw, come on. You never just pulled some

random dragon aside and asked them about their most personal and intimate secrets? I'm surprised."

"Hey, sometimes I actually have manners and don't pry." She raised her chin with a grin as she let her Sight flow over him. The shadows that had dogged his aura had faded. "But next time, I'll definitely ask."

He laughed. "Oh yeah, I'm sure that'll go over well." He shook his head and seemed to come back to himself, losing his humor. "I don't know very much about being a dragon. I think there's something wrong with my family, so I'm probably not much of a catch in terms of a mate."

She trailed her fingers along his arm above the bandage and he shivered as he turned his eyes away. She sensed fear and uncertainty and squeezed his arm to get his attention.

"What's wrong?" She waited for him to look at her. "Talk to me. Tell me what you're thinking."

He frowned hard and shook his head. "I dunno. It's like there's this voice in my head, screaming at me that I'm not good enough for you. That I'll hurt you and let you down. But another part of me knows our connection is right and I've proved to you that you're mine...and—and I'm yours."

"Denarrion, look at me."

He took a deep breath and turned to look at her once more.

She placed one hand on his cheek as she held his gaze. "We're bound together, you and I. By the Goddess, who accepted our vows to each other. That other voice is lying to you. It's not real."

"But my past—"

"Is just your past. We both have them separate from our relationship," she stated firmly. "It's up to us to go forward from here, in whatever way we choose. I've your vow to be my mate, my partner, my protector, and my lover. Don't you want those things?"

"Yeah, I do." He nodded. "But I've been with humans so long, I don't know what's right for dragons. What if I lose control over myself while we have sex? What if it gets so rough, my claws and teeth come out?"

"Oh." She grinned and shivered. "I'd love it."

"You would?"

"Oh yeah. It would be really sexy."

"It would?"

"Good Goddess, yes." She closed her eyes and hissed. "It's a fantasy of mine, one I've never shared with anyone. Not even my late husband."

"It doesn't freak you out at all?"

"No, the idea is exciting." She pulled his shirt away from his shoulder and trailed her fingers over the mating mark on his skin. He shivered. "My sweet dragon mate, I might let you do it the next time we have sex…if you can catch me."

His chuckle rumbled from his chest as he grinned. "Oh, I think I can do that." But he sobered as he looked at his wrapped wrist. "But promise me I don't have to wear that bracelet while we do it."

She shook her head. "Rule one: no jewelry." She grimaced. "Let me see it again."

He dug around in his shorts pocket and drew out the copper and peridot band. She took it gently in her hands and ran her fingers over the metal and stones. The bracelet was warm from his body heat but showed no signs of burn damage.

"Did you know that peridot is the gemstone species of olivine?" She studied the green stones set between the loops of copper.

"How do you know that?"

"I live in Colorado, near the Colorado School of Mines." She winked. "They have a great museum where you can see all sorts of minerals in their rough and gemstone varieties." She frowned and shook her head. "I can't think of why it would burn you, though. Unless…"

"Unless?"

"Unless it has to do with the demon in Redfield."

She hadn't meant to reveal it to him, but she couldn't keep it from him as her mate.

"What?" His eyebrows went up. "What are you talking about?"

"There's a demon in Redfield, Denarrion." She frowned as she rubbed the bracelet. "You didn't know?"

"That's impossible." He shook his head as he stepped back from her. "I would've sensed it."

She nodded, though she didn't think it was true. "Maybe it's been here so long, laying low, that it blended in with the background energy of this place." She held up a hand when he opened his mouth to protest. "I don't know why you didn't know about it, but I sensed it the first day I was here and I saw it the other night."

He closed his mouth. "Wait, you saw the demon?"

"Not the demon itself, but the marks of its decay. It has infected this whole region."

"That can't be. I would've sensed it." He shook his head again. "Seriously. My dad is a warrior and demons were his thing."

"I don't know why you haven't noticed it, but I know it's here."

She almost added the secondary reason behind Charlorrion's support of their courtship, but kept her mouth closed. If the demon had tainted Denarrion, it might have the ability to sense his emotions from the influence it had over him. She checked his aura again, just to be sure.

Remnants of the stain remained, but there were far fewer and his energy appeared stronger. She hadn't seen any outward signs of his healing, but he didn't immediately leap to anger as he had when she first met him.

"Shit. I'm a damn failure as a dragon, aren't I?" He met her gaze, his eyes filled with dismay. "I don't know much about mating or how dragons get along. Hell, I can't even sense a demon in town. Are you sure you want to continue this courtship? I'm pretty sure you're gettin' the short end of the stick."

"Come on, let's go sit out on the deck and relax. I'll make some tea."

"I'm sorry, Lissandra, for being a lousy mate." He grasped her arm before she could move. "I'm gonna try to do better. See where I've been ignoring too many things. Although I don't know if I can wear that bracelet again for a bit." He pointed at the jewelry she still held.

"I can understand that." She nodded as she set the bracelet aside. "But I love seeing it on you. Why don't you hold onto it while we drink our tea? Even if you don't wear it, having it close might be a good idea."

"Oh yeah? Why's that?" His gaze sharpened, as if the fog haze had cleared from his vision.

"Because peridot paired with copper makes a great healing talisman. I think it will help you 'do better,' as you said." She waved him toward the deck. "I'll start the tea and be right out."

"Yeah, okay."

She let her own Sight flood over him as he walked away. The remaining darkness in his aura flaked away under the onslaught of light. The bracelet blazed with the power of healing, burning the tarnish on Denarrion like flames consuming wood. She had to look away from it before she blinded herself. *Thank the Goddess for the* Morukai.

She frowned as she set the kettle to boil. Why hadn't the *Morukai* noticed the demon? She rubbed her chin as her gaze returned to Denarrion settling on the chairs outside. *Maybe he did notice, but like Charlorrion, couldn't do a damn thing about it.*

It made sense. The other dragons in town didn't have the skillset to locate and eradicate a demon in their midst, even if they sensed something wrong. And she'd never heard of a *Morukai* being a warrior.

The kettle whistled and she poured hot water over the teabags in two mugs. *Seems like the Goddess wanted me here as much as Charlorrion and Torriandra.* She shook her head as she strode to the deck.

"Here's your tea." She handed him a mug.

"Thanks." He waited for her to sit beside him before he said more. "How long do you think the demon's been here?"

Lissandra shook her head. "I can't tell you that. How long ago was the fire that burned the hills above the town?"

Denarrion frowned. "Around sixty years ago, I think. It was started by a campfire by some hikers." He shook his head. "My family was lucky not to get caught in it. We were out hiking that day, too."

"Were you?" She raised her eyebrows as she sipped her tea. The demon's taint had been strong at the burn scar. "I'm glad you weren't hurt. You didn't see anyone else that day?"

"Nope." He focused on her face, tension tightening the skin around his eyes. "You think the fire was started by the demon?"

She shrugged. "When I found the scar, there was no vegetation growing there, and the birds wouldn't even fly across it. It reeked of demon-taint until I broke the spell on it. From what I've learned of the bastards, they love to create decay and discord. The land wasn't healing. I'd guess it had a hand in creating the damage."

"Which means it's been here for at least that long." He scowled. "Shit."

"Don't beat yourself up over it." She waved his unhappiness away. "You know now and after we have dinner with your parents tonight, we can work out how to defeat it."

"Oh, glory, dinner." He rubbed his hands over his face.

"Can't we just skip that part? Why ruin a perfectly good evening?"

"Think of it this way. We get it over and done with, and we can move on with our courtship, since this is really all about us." She winked.

He shot her one of his patented Puckish smiles. "I'm good with that. But let's make sure to just eat without lingering. They're damn near toxic."

A warning light blinked in the back of her mind, but she noted it and set it aside to worry about later. The Goldencoats' toxicity would be dealt with in time, but for the moment she wanted to relax with Denarrion and help him heal from the old wounds inflicted on him.

"Let's just relax for a short time." She offered him a warm smile. "I just want to sit here with you and do nothing. We can take on their toxicity when it's time."

He settled back with a nod and his body relaxed as he sipped his tea. He finally seemed happy for the first time since she had met him. He was in no hurry to do anything or go anywhere.

"I'm glad I came here, Denarrion. Even if there have been some rough moments."

"Yeah? Me, too. I've never met anyone like you before. I didn't know what I was missing, but you sure made it obvious." He chuckled ruefully. "It feels good to be with a woman like you."

"Just good?" She raised an eyebrow. "Not 'great' or 'phenomenal'?"

He laughed. "Yeah, you know; all those." He grasped her hand and kissed her knuckles. "Next time I'll get out my thesaurus."

"You do that." She could feel his happiness wrapped around them like a light blanket.

This was the true Denarrion; funny, relaxed, and contented as he watched the shadows dancing across yard. She would happily mate with this version of him for the remainder of her long life.

Now we just have to destroy the demon.

She just hoped it'd be that easy.

CHAPTER SIXTEEN

"Ready?"

Denarrion's jaw clenched and his hands fisted as they stood in front of his truck. Lissandra shot a look at the brick house with a manicured lawn, sculpted bushes, and horseshoe driveway beyond the curb. The energy around the house seemed calm and quiet. Almost dead in comparison to the rest of Redfield.

"Sure. Are your parents really that bad?"

He sighed. "Nah, not bad, but my dad can be overbearing and nobody is really happy here. It's why I moved away and usually avoid them if I can."

"Glory, that sounds terrible." She shook her head. "Do you want to just skip dinner tonight? We can say I got sick or something else innocuous. We don't have to do this."

"Nah, it's okay. You learn to live with it and let it go, you know?" He waved nonchalantly, but pain and anger tightened his shoulders. "Come on, let's get this over with. It's only dinner and then we can take off, right?" He took a deep breath and led her up to the front door.

The tension in his body screamed to her through their bond as they neared the house. She understood his reluctance to visit when he pressed down on the antique door pull and shoved it open. A chill ran down her back despite the heat of the May evening and she shivered, rubbing her arms.

She expected him to announce their arrival, but he remained silent as he closed the door behind her. *Like he's sneaking back home after curfew.* They paused in the entry at the foot of a curved staircase. A mahogany end table stood in the center with a lace doily and a crystal bowl of potpourri that smelled like oranges and cinnamon. Despite the pleasant scent, another fetid odor permeated the air.

What in hellwinds is that stink? She wrinkled her nose and shot a look at Denarrion. He smiled ruefully and shrugged.

"You get used to it."

"Denny?"

A young woman squealed with delight and flew down the stairs, launching herself in to Denarrion's arms. Lissandra hastily moved out of the way and tensed for action until he laughed with surprised pleasure.

"I'm so glad you're here." The young woman hugged him fiercely. "Mother said you would come, but I had my doubts."

"Aah, come on, Suri." He scowled with mock severity. "It hasn't been that long since I last visited."

"No," Suri agreed, "but it *has* been a decade since you agreed to come and stay for dinner. *I'm* glad you're here. It breaks the monotony."

He laughed and released her as he gestured at Lissandra. "Let me introduce Lissandra Charforest from Colorado. Lissandra, this is my little sister, Suriana."

"Very nice to meet you." Suri nodded, but her indigo eyes remained wary and she didn't offer to shake hands.

"And you." Lissandra tried to relax despite the tension.

"How do you like Redfield?" Suriana studied Lissandra intently, her eyes guarded and tired.

Is this guarded exhaustion an East Coast thing, or is it more evidence of the demon's meddling?

"It's nice, but very different from my home in Colorado." She offered a polite smile. "It's a lot more humid. I'm used to a dryer climate with less heat." *And no demon-taint.*

Suriana wrinkled a nose similar to her brother's. "Yeah. In the summer, you might as well not even take a shower. You're wet the moment you step out the door."

"It can get hot in the lowlands of Colorado, but there's no humidity."

"How are the people there?" Suri tucked a lock of milk chocolate-brown hair behind her ear.

Lissandra shrugged. "They are like people everywhere, I guess, but the Elder Races community of Cloudburst is pretty strong. Most of us are refugees from life; just trying to regroup from past events."

Suri shot a look down the hallway behind Lissandra, subtle lines of fatigue and ill health tightening around her eyes as she swallowed hard.

"It sounds nice." She returned her gaze to Lissandra. "Maybe we will all go there sometime after you marry my brother."

"Suri!" Denarrion rubbed the back of his neck.

"What?" She raised her pencil-thin brows. "Isn't that what a courtship is for?"

"Yeah, but nothing's been decided. I've only known her for two days."

She shot him an exasperated look. "You have heard of love-at-first-sight, haven't you?"

He snorted. "You gotta stop reading those trashy romance novels."

Suri raised her chin. "They aren't trashy, and you'd probably have longer, and better, relationships if you stopped to read one once in a while."

"Why would I need to read one when I can just ask

you, right?"

Lissandra grinned as Suri rolled her eyes, enjoying the banter between the siblings. Denarrion relaxed around his sister, though the edginess remained present. She'd True Mated to him, but there were still many things they'd have to work out before she'd allow him to be around her children long-term.

And then there's the demon. That would have to be addressed before any long-term plans were solidified.

"Denny? Is that you?" A short, plump woman with silver gray eyes and the family nose came down the hall, drying her hands on a dish towel. "I'm so glad you could come. And you must be Lissandra. How very nice to meet you. Do you prefer to be called Lissandra or Lisa or Sandy?"

"Lissandra, please." She took the woman's proffered hand. "Very nice to meet you, Mrs. Goldencoat."

The moment they touched, Lissandra's Sight took over her vision and presented her with a view of Denarrion's mother. Horrible streaks of puce and red shot through the black of her aura, and in a few places, it appeared to be completely eroded away. Lissandra yanked her hand back and swallowed against bile, resisting the urge to wipe her hand on her pants.

The dank and rotten stench became stronger and the room appeared shadowed despite the bright chandelier overhead.

"Please, call me Gloria." A curious tightness filled her voice and her lips flattened. "Welcome, welcome. I see you've met my daughter Suri. Come into the kitchen and have some lemonade to cool off." Gloria turned and headed back down the hall, expecting them to follow.

Lissandra glanced at Denarrion. *Can't he smell that?* But he shrugged with a rueful grimace and ushered her deeper into the house and the stench. Something about the scent niggled a memory, but she couldn't quite put her finger on it. She wrinkled her nose as she entered the kitchen.

Her overall impression of the room was yellow. Yellow Formica countertops, pale yellow wallpaper with mustard yellow flowers, and old yellow appliances that looked like they had been around since the 1970s.

Again, her Sight took over and the stench intensified. The room appeared moldy and dank, dark stains covering the cupboards, counters, and walls. *What in hellwinds?*

"Lemonade?" Gloria held out a tumbler full of opaque liquid, jerking Lissandra into her usual sight.

"Oh, thank you." She took the glass but didn't drink.

"So how was your trip here, my dear?"

"Uneventful. No problems traveling." Lissandra braced her weight on her feet, unwilling to lean against anything.

"I understand you have children."

"Yes, two daughters." She was glad she hadn't brought them anywhere near Redfield.

"How wonderful." Gloria nodded with a smile. "Did you bring them with you?"

Lissandra paused. *Odd question.* She shook her head. "No, they're at home with their grandmother. It didn't seem appropriate to bring them all the way out here for my courtship."

An odd grimace of disappointment slid across Gloria's expression before it changed to bland pleasantness. "Of course. Don't want the youngsters honing in on your private time, I suppose. How old are your daughters?" She handed Suri a bowl full of steamed green beans. "Take these to the table, honey."

Lissandra set down the glass of lemonade on the kitchen counter when Gloria's attention was elsewhere. Denarrion raised his eyebrows, but she shook her head, and mouthed, *Not thirsty.* She hesitated to say her daughters' names aloud in this house, her gut warning her against giving too much personal information.

And my gut's kept me alive before.

"My oldest is two hundred and my youngest is just a century."

Everyone in the room stiffened with her words and Denarrion scowled. Suri's shoulders hunched and she clenched her jaw as Gloria's face tightened. The stink increased for a moment, before fading back to the previous noxious level.

"Did I say something wrong?" Lissandra rolled her shoulders to loosen the tension.

"No, no, my dear." Gloria turned away to the stove, speaking over her shoulder. "It's just that we very rarely refer to our ages outside the human concepts of decades. It's a protective measure."

Lissandra tilted her head. "Protection against what?"

"Humans, of course. They're a lot more dangerous than most believe." Gloria shrugged, her gaze flicking away.

Lissandra frowned. "There aren't any humans here now, are there?"

"No, of course not. Why do you ask?" Gloria raised her eyebrows as she loaded a basket with rolls.

"I don't understand why we have to be circumspect in our speech when only dragons are present." She shrugged, rubbing her arms to dispel the disquiet. *This must be why Denarrion was so prickly about dragon terms.* "We are all dragons here, aren't we?"

"Of course." Gloria nodded, but her jaw remained clenched as she turned to hand Denarrion the rolls. "Denny, please take these to the table, and bring me your father's favorite glass."

He took the rolls and ducked past Suri without a word. *What in the name of the Goddess is wrong with him?* She tried to think of a different conversation to go with.

"You must be very proud of Denarrion. Today at the craft festival I saw some of his recent work and I was very impressed. He really has an eye for beauty in woodwork."

"Yes, very proud." The older woman shook her head despite the agreement.

So much for that subject change.

Lissandra turned her attention to Suri with a smile. "So what do you want to do when you grow up, Suri?"

"She has been studying economics at Princeton University."

The deep, baritone voice froze the air in the kitchen and the earlier stench increased until her nose burned with it. Everyone around her shut down and hid behind veils of indifference, fear percolating through their scents. Suri's expression turned to polite blandness and Denarrion's shifted into implacability as a stooped man stepped into the room.

Holy shit, that's *Waltarrion Goldencoat?*

"Isn't that right, Suri?" He shifted his black eyes toward his daughter, a hint of eerie green light flashing as he turned.

Suri nodded but her lips compressed into a flat line and she took a step away from her father. Lissandra wanted to do the same. *Dear Goddess, the rotting smell is coming from him.* It pulsed in waves, and she resisted the urge to cover her nose and mouth.

"You must be Lissandra." He nodded his balding head covered in age spots as the black eyes took her measure. "Welcome to Redfield. I've heard a lot about you from Charlie. Are you all he hoped you'd be?"

She blinked. *What the hell does that mean?* She frowned. "Charlie? I thought I was here for Denarrion."

A low growl sounded in the room and the hair on the back of her neck stood up. She braced for combat as she curled her hands into fists.

"Denarrion, is it?" Malice dripped from his voice. "Is that what she calls you, boy? I thought I made it clear you went by Denny now."

"Yeah, Walter. I got it." Denarrion's voice remained flat and unemotional, but his eyes snapped with anger.

"See that you remember it." Waltarrion returned his gaze to Lissandra and she tightened her fists. "I trust you have availed yourself to some of our...cultural charms." He licked his lips and ran one bony hand over his bald scalp. "Hopefully it exceeded your expectations."

She swallowed a shudder at the sexual implication and nodded. "Yes, I attended the craft fair held in the park where some of Denarrion's furniture is being sold. He's quite talented."

Waltarrion's black eyes snapped back to her face and narrowed with calculation. "Is he now? I'm pleased to hear my son has an admirer. Of course, he's been known to have several, yes?"

He cackled, the tendons in his throat straining to hold up his gaunt head. "Ah well, we all most sow some wild oats before we're shackled. Isn't that right, Gloria?"

Gloria's lips pursed so tight they almost disappeared. "Dinner's almost ready. Would you like some lemonade, Walter?"

"No." He stretched for a moment and licked his lips again before resuming his hunched stature. "But Denny has been focused on you. That's good, I suppose. He's been reluctant in the past to take any advice offered him in regards to his living situation. We are pleased you have come to remedy that."

"Remedy?" Lissandra raised an eyebrow. "Denarrion is his own dragon and more than capable of making decisions. We're courting and getting to know each other better." She offered him a smile, but Denarrion didn't return it, and she swallowed against a trickle of fear. He'd completely shut down and left her to take the brunt of his father's malice.

She cleared her throat. "So far things have gone well, I think."

Waltarrion took a deep breath in through his nose. "Yes, I believe they have." He licked his lips again and his gaze slid down her body pausing at her crotch and her breasts before returning to her face.

Gloria hissed as if she'd burned herself on the stove, breaking the rising tension in the room. "Dinner's ready. Suri, would you please get the wine to go with the meal? Denny, please take a seat and offer one to Lissandra. Here's your tonic, Walter."

He reached for the glass with one of his claw-like hands without taking his eyes off Lissandra. The slither of disgust shot up her back and the smell of rot in the kitchen grew stronger. *I know that smell. Why can't I remember what it is?*

This was the warrior of legend? The honored dragon they were all meant to revere? She clenched her teeth and followed Denarrion's silent gestures into the dining room. An elegant round oak table with claw feet stood with five places set and all the placemats glowed yellow to match the kitchen. Lissandra swallowed against bile as she seated herself.

Waltarrion's gaze never wavered from her, burning into her as she settled to Denarrion's left. *Last time I ever show him my back.*

Suriana brought the wine, the scent of fermented dragonfruit breaking some of the stench coming from Waltarrion. But the odor of fermentation set her on edge, the smell rancid and cloying.

"No wine for me tonight, thanks." She rose with her glass in hand. "I'm pretty dehydrated. Would it be possible to get some ice water?"

"Sure." Suri took the glass with unwarranted relief. "I'll get it for you."

"Thanks." Lissandra resumed her seat, ignoring Waltarrion's stare. *That's just frickin' creepy.*

Waltarrion's leering gaze surveyed her as he sat at the

"head" of the table. He drank the foul-smelling tonic from a crystal glass, the viscous liquid barely moving into his mouth. It had the color of an oil slick and her stomach rolled at its texture.

"You don't like our wine, Lissandra?"

She raised her chin and offered a cold smile. "Not tonight. I want to be clear-headed while I'm here with Denarrion."

Satisfaction sparked through her when Waltarrion flinched each time she said his son's full name. *Petty, Lissandra. Very petty.*

"Perhaps you would prefer an older vintage." He licked his lips with a curiously pale tongue. Lissandra fought to keep her expression bland as revulsion slid into her belly.

Gloria and Suri returned to the table with the food and Lissandra's water, and they all sat. There was a moment of awkwardness as they all stared at the table, except for Waltarrion, who kept his lecherous gaze on Lissandra.

She wondered why Denarrion said nothing about the way his father projected his sexual interest. He sat with his jaw clenched tight and his left fist closed on his leg.

"Denarrion, are you okay?" She laid a hand on his arm.

"What? Yeah, no, I'm fine." He moved his arm away from her touch.

Gloria stood with a loud scrape of her chair to serve everyone. As she placed some green beans and meatloaf on the plate, she met Lissandra's eyes with a look of pure hatred. Why was Gloria angry with her? Lissandra couldn't stop Waltarrion from hitting on her, nor was she interested in his thinly veiled attentions. Good Mother, he insinuated that if Denarrion wasn't to her liking he'd take the younger dragon's place in her bed.

Yeah, fuck no to that.

"Suriana, you were going to tell me what you wanted to be when you grew up. Now that I know you're studying economics at Princeton, did you want to be an economist?"

"Actually, no." The younger woman turned her head and stiffened her shoulders away from her father's pointed gaze. "I changed my major last semester. I'm now taking classes in Environmental Policy and Toxicology. I'm interested in working on ways to detect harmful toxins in water resources and how to clean them up naturally, rather than adding more chemicals into the system for cleaning."

Lissandra nodded, impressed. "That's an admirable goal—"

"We talked about this, Suri." Waltarrion's slimy baritone slid into the conversation. "You will study economics."

"No, Walter, *you* talked about it." Suri shook her head, anger threading her voice. "I told you that I wanted to learn something that had to do with healing the Earth, not filling it with more avarice."

"Humans thrive off of money and greed." Waltarrion shrugged but his voice matched her anger. "You must learn more of their ways to keep yourself hidden among them. To do otherwise invites their notice and their wrath. You will change your major back this fall."

Suriana's jaw clenched but she said nothing to her father's demand.

Again the conversation stalled with an overabundance of tension, anger, pent up frustration, and hatred. Lissandra tried to swallow her food as her head filled with questions.

Did no one gainsay Waltarrion? Would Denarrion do nothing if his father made his attentions to her more physical? What kind of a True Bonded partner did that? What about Gloria? Surely a mother would stand up to her mate when it came to her children. Lissandra's eyes shifted to Gloria's face, but the older woman was stoically ignoring the confrontation between her husband and daughter.

All the problems are coming from Waltarrion.

He was the source of the disharmony. She'd been resisting the urge to slide into her Sight for the last half hour, but she let the world change until she could see the rancid decay on the walls and surfaces. She almost gagged at the rot on the table.

But her heart damn near stopped when she got a full glimpse of Waltarrion.

Sweet Goddess of all.

There was nothing left of the dragon Waltarrion had been. A black and green ooze had completely consumed his aura, with long tendrils sucking the life out of Gloria and Suriana. Smaller tendrils reached out to Denarrion, bleeding the life from him as well. Gloria's aura sat misshapen and sallow. Suriana had erected some barriers to stop the leak, but she wouldn't last much longer.

He's the fucking demon!

That's what the smell was and why it had seemed so familiar. The demon-stench filled the whole home. She had to do something. What could she do? The demon sat in front of her, poisoning an entire family of dragons, and they were letting it happen. *I have to get out of here.*

Making sure her fork sat empty of food, she carefully placed it with the handle overlapping the edge of her plate, took a drink of her water and then dropped her hand on the handle's edge. The fork flew up over Denarrion and clattered to the floor in the tensely silent room like a thunder strike.

"Oh, glory, I'm sorry." She rose to retrieve the fork. Everyone's gaze rested on her, wide with surprise, except for Waltarrion. He shot pure malice. "I didn't expect that. Let me get another one. Where's the silverware drawer?"

Right back atcha, sheddach.

"Next to the sink, Lissandra." Suriana pointed distractedly, as if she'd awoken from a drugged sleep. Gloria shook herself as if she'd been under the same spell. Denarrion frowned tensely and looked away.

Fuck, what do I do? What do I do?

"Thanks."

Lissandra retreated to the kitchen to find cleaner air and clearer thoughts. Her inner senses came alive and raged against the sickness from Waltarrion. *Walter.* The dragon was gone. Her inner fire burned away the suffocating fog of deception coming from the demon.

How the hell had the demon taken over their greatest warrior?

The Great Chicago Fire. It had to have been then that the demon got a foothold. And with Waltarrion being so badly wounded, the other dragons hadn't noticed when the demon possessed him. *No wonder Torri experienced Charlorrion's anger and Denarrion's decline.* The demon had been there the entire time. Poisoning the Goldencoat family from within.

She found the drawer and retrieved a new fork, thumping it against her hand. The demon inside Walter was too powerful and too entrenched for her to take on alone. More than likely it'd get Gloria and Suriana to turn on her if it felt threatened. *And given the way Denarrion's not protesting, probably him as well.* She had to get him out of here and regroup somewhere safe.

She returned to the table, frantically trying to come up with a plan to get away with Denarrion. What could she do to help them escape?

"So what have you done while you have been here?" Gloria poured herself some wine and sent Lissandra a strained smile.

"We have been on a hike and then we visited the craft fair." Lissandra kept her eyes on the others around her, hoping she could get out without causing more tension. "They really make some lovely pottery and textiles around here. I bought some jewelry for my daughters from the local Shaman. He was a very interesting man."

"Was that Wise Heart?" Gloria raised her eyebrows.

"I don't know; he never introduced himself, but he seemed very interested in me." Lissandra shrugged.

"That's because you stood out." Denarrion's mutter fell into the conversation.

Lissandra shot him a surprised glance. Did he just accuse her of standing out? Why would that be a problem? It took her a few moments to remember him telling her about his father's wish to remain hidden among the humans. Standing out, being different, was wrong.

And that's how I'm going to get out of this without the demon knowing I've caught on.

"What did you say, Denarrion?"

"He is very interested in our people, but we've managed to avoid him and keep him at arms' length." Gloria waved her hand to distract Lissandra from her son's comment.

Lissandra narrowed her eyes. "Possibly. But he was particularly interested in me. He seemed to know I was more than human without any effort on my part." Tension rose again as Denarrion scowled.

"I heard you joined the Storytelling Contest." Suriana offered a strained smile, her eyes flitting nervously between her father and brother.

"I did." Lissandra nodded. "It was fun. I told the story about the Moon and how the Great Grandfather dragon watches over the Earth. I actually won second place."

Waltarrion hissed a breath of outraged surprise, while Denarrion swore softly and shook his head.

Gloria actually growled. "That is highly inappropriate."

"I'm sorry?"

Lissandra lifted her chin and narrowed her eyes, allowing her anger to seep through. *Gotta keep them distracted. Make them think I'm unaware of the taint.* She only hoped it would be enough to allow Denarrion to go home alone where she could get him to Torriandra to work some healing on him.

"By telling our stories to the humans, you endanger our very existence." Gloria's voice grew cold, her silver-gray eyes flashing with fear and anger. "We've lived in this community for centuries without the humans' awareness of our kind. The only reason we can stay here in safety is because they *don't know* what we are. You'll bring their fear and hatred upon us if they discover the truth."

Lissandra gaped at them, her gaze switching between all their angry faces. *Holy shit, their delusion is complete.* The townspeople might not know dragons lived among them, but they understood the Goldencoats were more than human. Or at least a few of the more attuned humans knew. *Damn, the demon has done its work well.*

"Are you telling me you think you've hidden your 'otherness' from the humans?" She sat back in her chair, shaking her head. "You haven't. There are several here who already know you're more than human."

"Because you've exposed us!" Gloria snapped.

"I haven't exposed anyone. I told a story. Most humans thought it was a cute tale."

"You were showing off too much. I didn't like it."

Lissandra stared at Denarrion, her eyes widening. "What did you say?"

"I said I didn't like you showing off so much. It was embarrassing." He shook his head, refusing to meet her gaze.

She let her Sight take over, dismayed to see the demon feeding Denarrion with thick, black tendrils. *Oh, Denarrion, I'm so sorry we had to come here tonight.* But she only allowed anger to show on her face.

"Showing off."

He nodded without meeting her eyes.

"How was I showing off, Denarrion?"

"Just showing off. Like when you faced off with Carrie."

Hurt filtered into her awareness despite the need to keep everyone focused on the anger. How could he bring that up when they'd talked it out? She mentally shored up her defenses and raised her chin.

"You mean, defending my mate from an intruder? Being a dragon?"

"Being too dragon. We're supposed to hide our true natures from the humans. If they find out what we really are, there'll be a helluva lot fewer of us in the morning." His jaw bunched but he still wouldn't look at her, as if he fought the words coming out of his mouth.

"How was I 'too dragon?'" Her voice cracked with cold anger, the growl sounding under her breath. This was the opening she needed, but it hurt to deliver.

"Just too dragon." His own anger ignited as he finally met her gaze.

"That's not an answer." She set her fork down before she stabbed him with it. "I can't be 'too dragon.' That's what I am. I'm not human, no matter what camouflage I wear. What in hellwinds do you mean by 'too dragon'?"

Waltarrion's gaze bounced between them, malicious delight widening his eyes. Lissandra resisted the urge to call him on it has she focused on Denarrion's icy blue gaze.

"You showed Carrie your essence, dammit." He snarled, his lips pulling back from his teeth as his fear and fury broke through his control. The surge of energy seemed to strengthen Walter. "Maybe where you're from you can walk around and show off your otherness. But around here, we keep a low profile. We've spent hundreds of years building up our family and reputation as part of the human community, and I can't allow you to jeopardize everything with your actions."

"Is that what this is about?" She raised her chin and clenched her hands into fists on the table. "Your reputation?" She coughed a sarcastic laugh. "Let me fill you in on a not-so-well kept secret. There are those in this community who know you aren't human. I saw them today. They might be the artists and the wise ones, but they're aware, have been for probably longer than you think. And if you haven't been aware of them, then you haven't been paying attention."

And the demon probably banked on that.

"You've slept with nearly all the female humans in town and you think you've kept a low profile? Believe me, people notice when a guy can't keep it in his pants long enough to make a real relationship." She curled her lips into a scowl. "Congratulations. You definitely appear to be just like every other randy, player male human out there. Not that it's an accomplishment."

Lissandra rose and pinned the others at the table with her gaze. Suriana stared down at her plate, picking at her food as her shoulders slumped. Gloria's face turned white with some emotion, but she couldn't tell if it was embarrassment or anger. Walter returned her stare coldly and implacably, his black eyes blazing malice as if she was a bug to be crushed under his heel.

"Is this what you've taught your children, *Waltarrion* Goldencoat?" She pushed her chair away and set her hands on her hips. Walter's expression turned derisive. "To hide who they are? To dampen their abilities? To forget that they're dragons?" Her voice grew colder. "And you, Gloria. You stood by and allowed your children to learn this garbage, this *sheddach*, and hide what they are? What kind of mother are you?" The older female dragon flinched at the ice in Lissandra's voice and looked away.

Now to seal the deal and get out of here.

She narrowed her eyes and scowled. "I will not have my children around you to be defiled by this attitude. I am a dragon. I'll always be a dragon and I'll act as I see fit." Her gaze landed on Denarrion and her lip curled, even while her heart sank. "I won't mate with anyone who suggests they should be untrue to themselves. You're nothing but shams; shadows and husks of the beings you are supposed to be. I can't believe I've stayed as long as I have." Denarrion blanched white under his tan.

This is the only way to get us out of here alive. But his complicity with the demon's views hurt more than she expected. She didn't want to deliver the final blow, but it had to be convincing to give her a chance to save her mate.

She straightened. "The courtship is over. You have sullied the name of Goldencoat. It will be remembered like the humans' Benedict Arnold. Good luck in finding a mate, *Denny.* I wouldn't choose that road if you offered me your hoard, much less your *reputation.*" She paused and her lip curled with ultimate disdain. "Maybe you should find a human woman after all. At least then you'd never have to be a dragon."

She spun on her heel and stalked out. Her heart pounded in her chest, but she hoped they all thought it was her fury rather than fear. She wouldn't be able to take on the demon while it had such tight control of Gloria, Suri, and Denarrion. She'd need help to destroy it, and she needed to get Denarrion clear.

She slammed the front door behind her and strode down the driveway to the street, her back stiff. If Denarrion was paying attention, he'd realize she wasn't as angry as she appeared, but she hoped he was too enthralled to detect the deception. She ripped out her phone and punched Torriandra's number.

"Hello?"

"Torriandra, this is Lissandra. I need you to meet me at Denarrion's place."

"What? Good glory, what's wrong?"

"I need to get out of his house. I've figured out where the demon is hiding and I can't destroy it alone. I'll need your help, and Charlorrion's, too." She sighed as she increased her steps away from the decaying house, ignoring her dismay when Denarrion didn't come after her.

"Denarrion is too enthralled by the demon. I can't help him until I can get him away from it and I need to maintain the illusion that I'm leaving town."

"Oh, holy Goddess. All right. I'll be there in ten minutes. Do you have a key to get in?"

"No."

"I'll bring ours. I'll see you soon."

Lissandra hung up the phone and shoved it into her pocket, her gut churning. She just hoped between the three of them, they'd be able to pull Denarrion out of the demon's darkness.

CHAPTER SEVENTEEN

Torri met Lissandra at Denarrion's house and helped her pack the few things she'd brought with her. She kept shooting worried looks at Lissandra, but didn't ask any more questions as they loaded into her car and drove back to her own house.

"Have you talked to Charlorrion?"

Torri nodded. "Yes. He understands what's going on." She grimaced. "I'm really sorry, Lissandra. We should've told you the demon was here."

Lissandra nodded. "Yeah, well, it doesn't matter. Now we have to figure out a way to get Denarrion away from it and clear its taint from his aura. It was almost completely clear until we went to dinner tonight."

Torri swallowed hard. "The demon is at his parents' house?"

"Worse. It's possessed his father. Waltarrion Goldencoat is dead. The demon's been inside his body all along."

"Oh dear Goddess." Torri parked the car and shuddered. "No wonder Charlorrion and Denarrion were so angry and sick." She gasped. "What about Suriana and Gloriana?"

Lissandra shook her head. "I think Suri is fighting it in her own way, but Gloria…" She sighed. "Was she True Mated to Waltarrion?"

"I don't know. Maybe. Why?"

"If she was, she's already too damaged to be freed of the demon's influence." Lissandra rubbed her hands over her face. "It's too late for her, but we might be able to save Suri and Denarrion."

Torri's shoulders drooped as they exited her car. "We should've looked closer and deeper. We should've done something."

Lissandra gave a one-shouldered shrug. "You didn't know where the demon was, only that it was here. And if you did, what could you have done? It has the Goldencoats wrapped around its claws. They would've been forced to defend it. Dragon against dragon. Only the demon would win."

"So, how is it different now?"

Lissandra followed her inside the house. "The difference is now we know where and who the demon is. And we can come up with a plan to draw it out away from its supporters, especially if we can get Denarrion on our side."

"How will we do that?"

"I don't know yet." She shook her head. "Let's start with making tea. Charlorrion should be home in about an hour or so, right?"

"Yes." Torri set the kettle on to boil.

"Good. And do you have any connection to the *Morukai* Shaman here in town?"

"I don't, but Charlorrion knows him. Why?"

"I saw him at the craft festival today." Lissandra settled into one of the kitchen chairs. "I'm pretty sure he knows there's a demon in town." She rubbed her face with her hands. "Oh, glory. I'm also pretty sure he's why the whole town hasn't festered worse than it has."

"How do you think the *Morukai* can help? Aren't demons a dragon issue?"

"Normally, yes. But this demon has been hiding *within* a dragon, amongst dragons, for years now, and has become more than we can take on ourselves. We're going to need the Goddess's help on this one."

Torri nodded as she poured the water into their mugs. "I just hope it'll be enough."

"Yeah, me too."

They lapsed into silence and Lissandra thought about calling her kids. She missed their cheeriness, and her relatively quiet life in Colorado. The alpine flowers would be blooming now that the weather had turned toward summer, and the little insectivores would be emerging from their burrows. *Goddess, watch over my girls if I don't make it through this.*

Charlorrion finally came home, his expression full of tension as soon as he saw Torri and Lissandra seated in the kitchen.

"What's going on?" He kissed Torri hello and stood beside her, his hands gripping the counter top.

"I found the demon."

Despite his swarthy complexion, he blanched white.

"I'm sorry, Lissandra—"

She held up a hand. "Save it. It's in the past and right now, we have to deal with the immediate future." She met his gaze. "Do you have a way to get in touch with the *Morukai* who lives here?"

"Wise Heart? Yeah, we're part of the Iroquois Nation. He's the one I've known since he was a boy."

"Oh, right. I should've paid closer attention." She didn't scowl, but he stiffened at the mild rebuke. "After spending time with the demon, it's clear we're going to need everyone to defeat it. Including the *Morukai.* Can you arrange for us to meet with him?"

"Yeah." He nodded, his shoulders hunching. "I really

am sorry I didn't tell you about the demon."

"Help me defeat it, and we'll call it square."

"All right. Give me a few." He left the room with a last look at his wife.

"Are you going to be okay?" Torri reached out to touch her arm.

Lissandra nodded. "I will be, but I'm worried about Denarrion. I left him in the demon's lair and I'm concerned it'll be pumping more poison into him to recover lost ground."

"Is it really that powerful?" Torri swallowed hard.

"Yeah."

Charlorrion returned to the kitchen, his shoulders tight. He'd changed from his firefighter uniform into a black t-shirt and jeans.

"Wise Heart said we should meet him in twenty minutes on the island in the middle of the reservoir."

Lissandra nodded. "I should've known. I saw his sanctuary last night while I was scanning the town. That's as good a place as any. Hopefully it's strong enough to entrap a demon and send it home."

He bit his bottom lip. "Yeah, let's hope. What about Denarrion?"

She took a deep breath. "I'm hoping Wise Heart will have a solution for him, too. I suspect it's going to take all of us, including Denarrion, to bring this creature down."

"Hellwinds." Charlorrion rubbed the back of his neck.

"Exactly."

"And if he doesn't?" Torri set down her mug.

"One problem at a time." Lissandra refused to think of what she'd have to do to her True Mate if he was too tainted.

****

Lissandra spread her wings and launched into the air,

the cooling evening caressing them like the hands of a lover. She adored being in her true form. Living amongst the humans necessitated a disguise, but experiencing the night with the smells, textures, and sights available to her senses reminded her she definitely was not human.

A copper dragon of sleek lines and burnished spines caught up with her, and he was joined by a golden dragon, petite and agile. Lissandra tried not to feel heavy, but the others made her look like the good robust Scottish stock she came from.

Charlorrion took the lead and they used the last of the rising warm air to carry them away from the town. The reservoir flowed under their wings like a black carpet against the edge of lights. But another light flickered from the island in the center. *Talk about a beacon.*

She turned on her wingtip and slid down through the air until she back-winged into a stall just above the trees, dropping to the ground with a thump. *Yup, good, hearty Scottish stock.* The others landed far more gracefully as she shifted into her human disguise. Not that it would fool the *Morukai*, but it made conversations easier.

"Let me introduce you." Charlorrion headed toward the fire they could see through the trees.

Lissandra nodded, letting him take the lead. Honoring tradition seemed the wisest course of action if they wanted the *Morukai*'s help.

Torri and Lissandra stopped at the edge of a clearing that held a birch and oak bole house with spruce and pine branches as roofing material. Charlorrion approached the man Lissandra had seen at the craft festival. He sat on a small three-legged stool with chipped red paint beside the fire pit, tending a small blaze.

The *Morukai* raised his gaze from Charlorrion to hers and nodded, the faded colored beads at the end of his braids clacking in gentle agreement. Charlorrion waved them closer to the fire. Lissandra stopped across from him as

Torri settled beside her husband.

"Be welcome, Fire Brother and Sisters." The Shaman nodded meeting Lissandra's gaze again. "You must be here to find ways to destroy the demon that infects this place."

"Yes, sir, and to ask for your help." Lissandra settled onto the ground.

"My help?"

She nodded. "I know where the demon resides, and what form it's taken, and it's too powerful for me to kill alone. I'm not even sure if the three of us can kill it." She took a deep breath. "It has poisoned my mate and his family."

He nodded, poking the fire a bit to allow the sparks to rise. "Do you think there's a way to save them?"

She shot a look at the Ravenwings before returning her gaze to the Shaman. "Not all of them." She hated to admit it, but she could only save the younger Goldencoats. "Is it possible to save my mate and his sister?"

"It is possible, Fire Sister. Your mate has only been corrupted by his own thoughts. Thoughts can be changed. And his sister is a fighter. She's been resistant to the demon's coercion." He let his gaze rest on Torri and Charlorrion. "You will all be needed to complete this task. Your Fire Sister can't do it alone. Are you willing to help her fight for her mate and his sibling?" He held up one hand as Charlorrion opened his mouth. "It will be dangerous, with a real threat of loss. However, it can't be done unless you all help. The Goddess has your back, but the threat is real." The beaded dreamcatcher with a feather in the center around his neck winked in the firelight as if to underscore his words.

"We will fight to save our brother and sister dragons. We were born for it." Torri raised her chin as Charlorrion nodded. "What do we need to do?"

A sad smile curled the *Morukai*'s lips. "You must bring one of the corrupted bloodline here to me. You can only defeat this parasite with a blood member of the family, but you also need a fourth dragon. We'll need to harness the energy of the elements to send this creature away. Earth, Water, Air, Fire, and Ether. But all of you must be in accord. If there is dissention, your efforts will fail."

"I think we can get Denarrion here. We might need to incapacitate him a bit, but it's doable." Charlorrion nodded. "Anything else?"

"When you bring your Fire Brother here, you must recount the story of the demon's coming. Listen carefully because in its telling is the solution to the demon's destruction." The Shaman stirred the fire again. "Torriandra, you will represent Earth, and anchor the five points of our circle with your energy drawings."

"My energy dr—My mandalas?"

"Yes." The Shaman nodded. "Fire Man, you will represent Water, keeping the battle contained within this space so no other part of the world is damaged."

"All right. A bit ironic that a Fire Man represents water." Charlorrion snorted.

"Isn't water what you use at your job?" The *Morukai* raised an eyebrow and Charlorrion grimaced.

"You, Fire Sister, will represent the sacred Fire that burns within all dragons. You were brought here to destroy the demon, and it's your task to make sure it burns." He rested his gaze on Lissandra and she nodded.

A woman's work is rarely done. "I accept my task."

Wise Heart nodded. "Very good. I need you all put your hand in the fire."

"What?"

The *Morukai* gestured to the rising flames. "The Fire Spirits and the Goddess require your acceptance of their task."

Lissandra rolled onto her knees and reached into the fire as Torri and Charlorrion did the same. The heat welcomed her, calling on her inner fire to come out and play. Unconditional love and warmth flowed over her as the flames rose higher.

Someone chanted nearby and she fell into the soothing sounds, focusing her attention on the shapes writhing in the flames. The Fire Spirits recognized her as a creature of fire, offering her their blessing and accepting her commitment to destroy the demon in Redfield. She gave her agreement with a roar that sent sparks flying into the night sky. Charlorrion and Torriandra added their voices to her cry, and the deal was sealed.

CHAPTER EIGHTEEN

Denarrion slouched on the deck chair with a bottle of dragon fruit wine in the dark. *Better to be in the dark where I can't see my own ugliness.*

The disastrous dinner with Lissandra and his parents brought to light just how far he'd fallen as a dragon. He'd retreated to his home only to find it cold and dark. She'd taken her things and left without saying goodbye.

And why should she? She made it pretty clear I'm a useless bag of shit. She hadn't pulled any punches when she reminded him of all the things he'd been ignoring within his family. He loved her and had committed to being her True Mate, but he hadn't lived up to her expectations.

You're making a huge mistake. She embarrassed you by her refusal to hide her true nature behind her camouflage. She endangered you and your family.

The insidious voice sounded suspiciously like his father at his most divisive, and Denarrion hated that voice. But Walter wasn't wrong about the humans and their reaction to finding dragons in their midst.

You can't be with Lissandra unless she *changes. She's the dangerous one.*

If her response at dinner was any indication, she

221

wouldn't change her behavior. Her fury and disgust at him and his parents slammed into him like a bucket of ice water. He'd never seen her so angry or horrified at anything, even when the human women had treated her as an intruder.

"Fuck!"

He raised the bottle to his lips and took a big swig. Sweet fire burned down his throat into his belly and he closed his eyes to appreciate it. Despite his best efforts, the dragon fruit wine didn't bring the usual joy. *That's because it's meant to be sipped.* He scowled at his father's voice intruding again. He'd probably drunk too much, but he didn't have the energy to care.

Without Lissandra, nothing fucking matters.

He'd thrown caution to the wind, but it did nothing to dampen the loss and misery that threatened to overwhelm him after she'd said she was sorry she'd met him. He never thought a female could mean that much to him in such a short time. Her suggestion that he find a human woman to mate crushed and hurt him deeper than he thought possible.

Rage kindled in an effort to stave off the hurt.

"What the fuck does it matter what one Widow from Colorado thinks?" His voice stilled the crickets singing under his porch. "I don't need her. I don't need anyone. I was doin' fine before she came."

Except he hadn't been doing fine. And he couldn't shake the feeling that everything she said about trying to hide his true nature was right on the mark. While he'd been uncomfortable with her actions at the craft festival, he felt right when he was with her.

She'd been real, honest, and beautiful and despite his inebriation, his body responded to the memory of her skin under his hands. She was passionate and tireless. He'd wanted to take this evening to show her his gratitude.

"Goddess, Lissandra, your pussy was so sweet." He shook his head at the sound of his voice. "Shit, you're pissed, my boy. You should go to bed." He laughed sadly, but made no move to get up. *What you should do is apologize and tell her you fucked up.*

That was a new voice, one that sounded more like him when he wasn't drunk.

"Hey, *I* didn't fuck up. *She* was the one who didn't want to be human around the humans!" He growled, shaking a barely pointed finger out at his imaginary conscience.

Yes, but she isn't *human, is she? She's a dragon. You are just a dumbass wannabe.*

"I'm *not* a wannabe." He raised the bottle, only to find it empty. "I'm just as much a dragon as the next guy."

You mean, your father? *He's no more dragon than the deer in your backyard. Maybe Lissandra was right and you should find yourself a human woman to fuck. Then you can definitely pretend you're not a dragon.*

"I donn want a human woman. I want *Lissan'ra*. She's my True Mate."

So what are you going to do about it? She already told you she wants nothing to do with you and your "human" tendencies.

"That's no' fair. I'm only doin' that tuh please my dad. I donn wanna be human!"

Shut up, she had you dead to rights. And you better figure out some way to show her you're gonna dragon-up, because she's gonna be gone back to Cloudburst, Colorado faster than you can spit. And it'll take another millennium to find you a mate, if any dragons will have you.

"There is no other mate for me." He bared his teeth and threw the bottle off the deck. "Just Lissan'ra! Whaddo I have t' do tuh convince you? Lissandra's my mate an' there's no one else!"

Denarrion tried to stand up from the deck chair, but he couldn't find the horizon. He slumped back against the wood, his head lolling.

When the shadows moved, one pinned his arms against his sides with an iron grip while another arm snaked around his neck, cutting off his airway. He struggled, roaring his fury at being attacked at his own home, but the inebriation dampened his efforts.

Whoever held him knew his pressure points and had the leverage to make good on them. *Oh, Goddess, please give me the chance to tell Lissandra I'm sorry.* Then the darkness sucked him down into silence.

****

Lissandra looked at Charlorrion as he eased Denarrion back into the chair.

What in hellwinds was that about? Denarrion's one-sided conversation hadn't made much sense. *Who was he talking to?* She looked for his phone, but she hadn't seen it.

"I didn't think he'd be so easily caught." She shook her head at her mate. "Is he usually this docile?"

"No." Charlorrion tilted his head, narrowing his eyes. He leaned closer to Denarrion and sniffed, jerking away with a disgusted growl. "Dragon fruit wine, and a whole lot of it. He's hammered. No wonder he didn't hear or smell us coming." He grimaced. "Let's get him to the *Morukai* and see if he can help Denny come back to his senses."

"I'm hoping we get Denarrion, not Denny. Denny can stay with the humans."

Charlorrion draped Denarrion over his shoulder in a fireman's carry, his ass in the air. "Glory, I hope the dumbass doesn't throw up on me."

"I should get out my phone and take a picture of him like this, but that would just be mean."

Charlorrion snorted. "I dunno. From the way he's been acting, he might deserve a little karma." He paused and angled Denarrion's limp form toward her. "You sure you don't want to get a shot or two? You could use it for blackmail later."

Despite the seriousness of their situation, Lissandra laughed. "You're definitely his younger brother. Just take him to the truck."

Charlorrion grinned as he stepped off the deck with the older male's hands flapping against his thighs. Lissandra picked up Denarrion's phone and took it inside before grabbing his keys off the counter. His scent made her heart ache. *Please, Goddess, help me heal him. Help me save him from the demon.* She couldn't be with him unless he changed. And if he refused, she might have to kill him. Any connection left to the demon would allow it to survive.

What if he's clear of demon taint, but remains afraid of being a dragon?

She hoped she could convince him otherwise. She was a dragon and would never apologize for it. If he couldn't accept himself, she'd have to go home to Colorado alone, leaving part of her heart with him. Sighing, she locked the doors and followed Charlorrion into the night.

****

The world slowly came back into focus. Denarrion floated in the gray awareness between sleeping and waking, sweet voices singing just beyond comprehension. Heat and comfort wrapped around him, and he relaxed, releasing some of the pent-up tension he'd been carrying. *Damn, it's been decades since I've been this relaxed.* Hellwinds, it had been longer than that. *Since the fire in Chicago.*

More memories surfaced, clarifying against the languid softness of sleep. He didn't remember falling asleep. He'd been on his deck drowning his sorrows in dragon fruit wine, and someone argued with him over what he should've been doing.

I should be loving Lissandra.

The sweet voices burned away some of the sleepy fog

and his memory sharpened. He'd been arguing with his conscience. *Because I've lost my mate.* What had they been talking about? Oh yes, dragon versus human, pleasing Lissandra versus pleasing his father.

He snorted. *No contest.* He'd rather please Lissandra than his father any day and twice on Sundays.

Too late for that. She'd gone, saying she wanted nothing to do with him. But he still wanted her and wanted to convince her he would change. He'd promise anything to bring her back. She was his mate. Being without her equated to living in a world without color.

The sweet voices surged, assuring him everything would be fine once he'd helped destroy the demon.

Demon? There's a demon in Redfield?

The voices insisted there was and that his strengths were needed to defeat it. His abilities as the son of the famous Goldencoat warrior were needed or the battle would be lost. Strength and determination trickled into him. How could he live in a place where a demon festered? It needed to be destroyed. He'd claim his birthright and fight to cleanse the world of this ancient evil.

He roared his claim and determination, shaking the world around him. The power and strength of the fire burned away the drugging fog and steadied his mind. He was meant to fight and kill demons and nothing would keep him from that duty.

Silence hit him like a solid thing, the absence of sound so profound it made him open his eyes. Stars shone through breaks between the trees. Firelight flickered on the branches and trunks around him. When the hell had he gotten into the forest? He turned his head toward the source of the light and yelped. His hand lay swathed in the flames. He yanked his hand away from the campfire and sat up, waiting for the pain to hit him.

But his hand didn't hurt and he dropped his gaze to study the flesh. No blistering, no blackened nails. Nothing but whole skin and healthy flesh. *It's gotta be all the dragon fruit wine.*

Except he didn't feel foggy or dissociated from himself. He felt good, healthy, strong, alive. *Happy for the first time in centuries.*

That wasn't completely true. Lissandra made him happy. *Lissandra.* Sorrow took away some of his joy and he focused on his environment.

The clearing held a longhouse made of birch and pine and the fire pit beside him. The ground showed a light covering of native grasses and wildflowers cut short. The Shaman from the jewelry booth at the craft fair sat on a short stool across the fire, meditatively smoking a pipe and gazing into the flames.

Denarrion frowned and shook his head. How in hellwinds had he gotten here and where was 'here' exactly? Memories of someone holding him down and choking him resurfaced. Fear and anger surged in him and he hissed, his gaze scanning the clearing for assailants.

Charlorrion sat on the ground beside the fire, his expression unreadable. He met Denarrion's gaze but made no other acknowledgment of his presence. Instead, he poked the fire with a stick as if waiting for something.

What's Charlie doing here?

Denarrion opened his mouth to ask when motion struck him silent. Lissandra strode through the clearing with mugs of fragrant tea in her hands. The firelight caressed her features and hair, highlighting her beauty. But instead of welcoming, her expression remained implacable and distant.

Fuck, I did that to my True Mate. He had a lot to answer for.

She crouched beside him and silently held out a mug. He took it, scanning her face for any sign that he hadn't lost her completely, but she showed nothing. She started to rise, but he caught her arm and tugged her back down.

"I'm sorry." He threw his heart and soul into those two words. He'd made a mistake and he knew it.

Her expression softened around her eyes and mouth as she nodded. "Take it slow and drink the tea. Tea makes everything better."

He let her go and sniffed the tea. It smelled like honeysuckle and blueberries, and reminded him of sharing the space with her on his deck. *Damn, I fucked everything up.* He hadn't defended her against his father, both the asshole's sexual advances and his accusations, and he'd even insulted her. *I've definitely won the jackass-of-the-year award.* He hoped she'd forgive him despite his actions.

"I, uh, don't really know what's goin' on, so if you wanna fill me in, that'd be great." He shifted his body so he sat facing the fire.

"There's a demon in Redfield, Denarrion." Lissandra's voice fell into the pool of silence as Torriandra appeared from the longhouse and settled beside Charlie with her own tea. "We're going to kill it and send it back to the Underworld, but we need your help to do it."

"Are you sure there's a demon here?" He squinted, trying to remember what the voices had said.

She nodded. "I'm sure." She shot a look at Charlie and Torri before returning her gaze to him. "It's the reason I'm here."

His stomach dropped as the truth hit him. "For the demon."

"Yes."

"Not for me."

She shook her head. "Not entirely, no. I told you I thought we were being set up."

"Wait, I thought you came for the courtship." He scowled.

"Yeah, I did." She nodded. "But Charlorrion and Solenarra had ulterior motives getting us together." She raised her chin, her expression turning cold. "Solenarra asked for eligible bachelors and Charlorrion was looking for someone who could seek out and destroy demons. Turns out we fit both sides of the equation. I was ready for a new mate, and you…" She trailed off with a grimace. "You needed to be rescued."

Anger and hurt rose in his chest. Denarrion glared at Charlie, who met his gaze with solemn compassion. "You thought I needed to be rescued?"

Charlie snorted. "Man, I didn't need the Fire Spirits to tell me that, though they did."

Denarrion raised an eyebrow. "Come on. Fire Spirits?"

"Yeah. You know you're a child of Fire, right? It comes with being a dragon in case you've forgotten."

He scowled. "Fuck you."

"No thanks, you're not my type and I'm married." Charlie bared his teeth at him as he squeezed Torri to his side. "Look, you dumbass, you were so sick and broken, we're lucky Lissandra came here at all. Goddess knows, no one should've mated with you. But it's a good thing she came when she did, because the Fire Spirits weren't gonna accept you except for her intercession on your behalf."

Denarrion shot a look at Lissandra. "What?"

"The Fire Elementals, guardians of the Earth, thought you were too damaged from the time spent with the demon, Denarrion," Lissandra rubbed her thumbs over her mug. "I asked them to give you a chance."

He scowled at Charlie. "Give me a chance at what?"

Charlie rolled his eyes. "At surviving. Dammit, Denarrion, you needed a mate and we needed help. We were just lucky we found the same person to do both jobs." He shook his head. "I've watched you fold in on yourself for years. Torri and I thought a mate would help bring you out of that. And she did. But she can't save you from yourself. You're drawn straight back into the foulness and you soak it all up until you're tainted."

"Tainted?" Denarrion tightened his hands into fists. "I might not be the dragon you want me to be, but I *am a* dragon. I can't *be* tainted."

Charlie's lip curled. "You can and you are. I have smelled it on you for years."

"What are you *talking* about?" Denarrion rose and brushed himself off as his anger swelled.

"When was the last time you changed into your natural form? Years? Decades? Centuries?" Charlorrion shot to his feet as well. "In public you hide what you are and you aren't much better in private. You call yourself a dragon, but you're more human than anything else. It's disgusting."

"Not all of us want to get married as soon as we're fertile, Charlie." Denarrion set the mug down before he hurled it at someone. "Just because you did and I didn't doesn't mean I'm tainted. Some of us aren't that desperate for company."

Torri gasped, her dark eyes widening as Charlie growled.

"All right, that's enough." Lissandra's voice cracked like a whip into the middle of the argument, and Denarrion cursed under his breath.

Any other insults you want to throw at your True Mate? How 'bout she's not good enough? He scrubbed his face with his hands as he swung away from the fire, trying to recover his composure. Could he be tainted, rotten to the core? And if so, could he be cured?

"None of you have a leg to stand on when it comes to being honest with me." Lissandra pegged each of them with her brilliant violet gaze. "Torriandra, you and Charlorrion brought me her under false pretenses. You lied by omission, putting my life in danger, and potentially robbing my children of their only living parent. I'm pretty sure you wouldn't have entertained the idea of doing that except for your exposure to the demon."

Charlie's expression turned solemn while Torri looked

away, chagrin radiating off of them in waves.

"And you, Denarrion, didn't bother to tell me you'd slept with the entire town of Redfield before I showed up. No, I didn't need to know your past sexual history, but a little warning of how many women I'd have to face off with would've been nice." She swung her gaze between them, her shoulders tight with anger. "None of you have been completely honest with me, but all of you are going to help me destroy this demon for three reasons."

She held up one finger. "One, because you're dragons and it's your job to stamp out a demon's decay when you see it. That you've let it fester here is criminal."

She held up a second finger. "Two, because I'm not powerful enough, even with the help of the *Morukai* Shaman, to kill it. It's gotten too well entrenched and strong for me to take out alone."

She raised her chin and added a third finger. "And three, because you knew it was here and you set me up to face it without disclosing the danger, which could've gotten me killed."

Denarrion shook his head. "I didn't know it was here."

"No, which means it hid right in front of you this whole time." Lissandra sighed. "I need to know how it got to be where it is. Wise Heart says both of you know the story. So why don't we start with that."

"What are you talking about?" Denarrion threw his hands out from his sides. "I didn't know the demon was here. How would I know it's story?"

"Because the demon has corrupted a dragon." Her voice remained implacable.

Ice flowed through his veins with attending panic. Was she referring to him? White hot anger followed. "I *am not corrupted!* I told you before—"

"No, not you." Charlorrion held up his hands.

"It's in your father, Denarrion."

"My...What?" He stiffened, the ice in his veins

solidified and he couldn't move.

"The demon has corrupted Waltarrion. Didn't you sense it when we went to dinner with your family?" Lissandra raised her eyebrows. "Why do you think he acted so inappropriately?"

"Get outta here! No, it can't be." Denarrion found his voice without throwing up. "My father was a great warrior. He fought demons all his life. He'd never let one take him over. He'd die first. You have to be wrong."

"He did die, Denarrion." Lissandra met his gaze, sorrow in her eyes.

"No. No, he's still here in Redfield, living with my mother and sister. You're wrong."

"He's not. Waltarrion is gone. The demon has hidden all this time *inside* a dragon. No one suspected a thing." Her voice remained quiet and firm. "The creature inside your father's body has forbidden you to *be* a dragon. That didn't set of any warning bells for you?" She sighed and shook her head. "I'm sorry, Denarrion. I wish I was wrong, but the *Morukai* only validated what I suspected."

Disgust rolled through him and his lip curled. "You believe an outsider over one of your own kind, Lissandra? I expected more from such a sought-after *warrior*."

"And I expected more from you as a dragon's mate," she snapped. "I expected not only a man, but a male dragon. If I wanted a human wannabe, I would've found one in Colorado."

The venom in her voice rocked him back on his heels. Anger, disappointment and betrayal blazed in her eyes as she stared him down across the fire. *Fuck.* This was *not* how he wanted to speak to her. He was supposed to apologize for being an ass and ask her to give him another chance.

Instead, he found more and more ways to insult her and she fired back with the same. What was wrong with him? Why was he being so combative? He hadn't liked his father since the mess in Chicago. Why in hellwinds was he defending him?

"How long will it take for Denarrion to be stunted for life if he continues to deny his abilities and nature, Wise Heart?" Lissandra turned away.

What the hell was she talking about? Stunted? He wasn't stunted.

"That depends on the dragon and the level of corruption he is exposed to on a consistent basis." The *Morukai* Shaman tapped his chin as he met Denarrion's gaze. "But a rule of thumb is about a hundred and fifty years or so."

Charlie raised an eyebrow. "How long has it been since you lived in that house? How long has it been since you assumed your true form?"

Denarrion clenched his teeth together. "That's none of your business."

"It's *my* business as your True Mate." Lissandra stood with her back to him and his heart froze under her icy voice. "I have to know how weak you've become and whether or not I can depend on you when the time comes to fight the demon."

Denarrion's stomach churned with sickness. How could his father get possessed by a demon? How could that have happened?

"I don't know what you mean by weak." He hadn't felt right for decades, but he hadn't known why.

"When was the last time you took your true form, Denarrion?" Charlie asked again.

"I–I can't remember." Shame and fear writhed in his gut.

Lissandra turned her face away, sorrow pulling the edges of her mouth down. "I need to know the story. I need to know what happened in Chicago all those decades ago. If I know that, I can figure out how to kill the demon."

"Do you want to tell her or should I?" Charlie waved at

him while Torri wrapped her arms around herself.

Denarrion dropped his head and ran his hands through his hair as he stared at the ground near the fire. How the fuck had he been so blind? *Demons are the masters of disguise.* Yeah, but he should've seen. He should've sensed something was off with his father. Waltarrion had completely changed.

"You know, I always thought I was so damn observant about stuff like this, but after the big fight Walter had with the demon in Chicago, I thought we'd seen the last of it." He scrubbed his face with his hands and raised his gaze. "I mean, Waltarrion Goldencoat was the baddest badass of our kind, so of course he won the fight. Right?"

Both the Shaman and Lissandra looked at him with surprise. He grimaced at their disbelief.

"It was cold, clear, and windy that October in Chicago. The city was mostly made of wood because stone was too expensive and there was a lot of forest around the Great Lakes." Denarrion grimaced. "Despite that, it had been really dry with almost no rain. We'd been living outside the city at the time. Waltarrion had heard rumors of odd goings on so he went into town that night to check it out, and took me and Charlie with him."

At the time, Denarrion had thought it a great adventure to visit the famous human city, but he hadn't liked the closeness of the buildings and the overwhelming stench of the slaughter houses and human excrement.

"The story told in human circles was that old lady Catherine O'Leary set a lantern down in a cow byre and the cow knocked it over, starting the fire. But in reality, my father had tracked the demon all over Chicago that evening to a small shed in an alley and in an effort to destroy the bastard, used dragonfyre on the structure."

"Didn't he think about what dragonfyre and wind on dry wood could do to the city?" Lissandra turned back to face him.

"I don't know. He might've thought the risk was worth it." Denarrion shrugged. "He was pretty rabid about destroying the demon that had eluded him all day. The demon had possessed a homeless Irish immigrant. It escaped the shed and ran across town to a church on the west side of the river before my father caught up with it. By then the humans were aware of the fire but the close construction of the buildings and the winds made it impossible to stop. My father fired the church and then dropped into it to fight the demon hand-to-hand."

"Where were you during all this?" Lissandra asked.

"Denarrion and I were trying to get the fire department going in the right direction. The idiot guard had seen the glow and thought it was on the other side of the city, so he sent the fire crews the wrong way." Charlorrion scowled. "We were trying to turn them around and get people out of the burning buildings when the fire jumped to the south side of the river and we heard the roaring in the church. We left the fire crews and headed for the church. I don't even remember the name of it anymore."

"The whole building was burning from the inside out. It was the one structure that had stone walls." Denarrion squatted and stared into the fire as the memories returned. "By the time we got inside, Waltarrion was there alone, lying on the floor next to the body of the homeless guy. It was burning weird green flames."

"We didn't see the fight, but the demon must've shifted enough to use its claws and venom. Waltarrion was damn near disemboweled and he had several severe cuts and scratches all over his body." Charlorrion shuddered. "It was sickening."

"He was a mess and we weren't sure he was gonna make it." Denarrion closed his eyes on the memory of his father sickly gray and bleeding out. "He was so weak. He wasn't the same after that. It was as if his will to live had just disintegrated with the fight. He was pissed from then on and he took a long time to get better. Longer than usual."

Lissandra frowned, her head bowed as she stood with her arms crossed over her chest. Denarrion wished she'd look at him and tell him what she thought, but she kept her head down. He didn't want to think about the night his father had almost died.

Fuck that. If he's possessed by the demon, it must have killed him that night.

"Were there any bite marks on your father's body when you found him?"

Lissandra's voice jerked him out of his memories.

He met her gaze with a frown. "Bite marks?"

"Yeah." Charlie's eyes widened. "At the base of his neck on his left shoulder, just like a vampire makes, except there were four punctures and they were torn."

"Were they putrid when you got close to them?"

"He'd just finished fighting a demon in a burning building. He didn't smell good." Denarrion rolled his eyes.

Charlie shot him a quelling look. "He smelled tainted, like infection had already set in."

Lissandra nodded as her lips thinned. "That's how it did it. The bite wound. The demon possessed Waltarrion before it died, using his body as a host." Lissandra shook her head. "Sonuvaprick. We're going to have to kill him."

"Kill Walter?" Torri covered her mouth with her hand.

Lissandra closed her eyes and nodded.

"Sweet glory." Charlie wrapped his arms around his wife and bowed his head.

"But first we all have to be strong enough to do it." She fixed her lilac gaze on Denarrion. "You need to shift. You've been in this form too long already. You're going to lose yourself."

"What are you talking about?" His head came up and anger surged.

"Take a flight, Denarrion." Her voice hardened. "Go

shift into your true form before it's too late. We'll deal with our plans for "Walter" tomorrow. Go."

Denarrion rose to his feet, his hands fisting at his sides. *How dare she demand you change? Who is she to tell you what to do?* The angry, frightened voice screamed at him from the back of his mind. The same voice he'd heard for over a century.

Damn straight. I make my own decisions and know what's right for me.

He took a breath to tell her to fuck off when the *Morukai* made a complicated motion with his hands. The fire leapt from its bed and engulfed him, burning away his clothes and his anger in a breath of heat and life.

Denarrion yelped and covered his face with his hands as the angry voice wailed in panic. The voices of the Fire Spirits scoured his mind clear of the debilitating corrosion sucking the life from him. The angry voice shrieked and faded away into nothingness, leaving a healing silence behind.

He gasped and dropped his hands.

The fire had returned to its bed, burning placidly on sticks of oak and spruce. Denarrion looked down at his naked body. Wounds and deformities stood out starkly under his skin and he patted himself in horror. But these weren't physical markings. They were spiritual and emotional. The pain of their incomplete healing roared into his awareness and he groaned, sinking to one knee.

The only way to completely heal is to be yourself.

That voice spoke with confidence and strength. He had to shift shape and be a dragon, or he'd sicken and die.

Holy shit. I am stunted.

Avoiding the others' gazes, picked his way out of the clearing to the west. He needed room to breathe air clear of sorrow and recrimination. His strides increased in speed until he was damn near running by the time he hit the shore.

Oh shit! He skidded to a stop before he slid into the water. The shore of the reservoir across the water showed no light and seemed a metaphor of his life. Tilting his head, he gazed into the sky, a few stars peeking through the high clouds. Crickets sang in the darkness, filling the night with their songs.

Can you rise to the challenge?

Denarrion took a deep breath and steeled himself for his shift in form. He suspected it would hurt as bad as the first time he'd shifted at barely five hundred years. He tried to remember the last time he'd taken on his true form, but the memory slipped away.

Sweet Goddess, please don't give me too much pain.

He closed his eyes and squared his shoulders, then made the shift before he could chicken out.

Excruciating pain greeted him, burning and tearing along every limb and down his back. His long keening wail carried across the water as his bones and muscles shifted into his dragon form. Scents, sounds, and textures clarified while his perspective shifted up higher than he was used to. His muscles screamed their protest as they stretched and repaired, and he groaned, twisting his head to identify the locus of the pain.

Dark bruises marred his pale blue body. *Where the fuck did those come from?* Old wounds showed as scars along his scales from the many traumas he'd sustained while pretending to be human. Sadness welled up and tears started in his eyes. He'd been strong and healthy once. But he'd let it all go to shit.

He sat on the shore of the reservoir and wallowed in his disappointment and sorrow for all the time he'd lost. He listened to the sounds of the living world around him and the music on the wind, tempting him to fly. He wanted to answer, but unfurling his wings hurt almost as much as his shift.

Come on, dammit. You can do this.

Spreading his wings, he took a deep breath and launched into the sky. His downstroke wasn't nearly as confident as it should've been and the atrophied muscles strained to push him aloft. He immediately tired, but the delight of flying filled his heart and mind with wind song, and he kept pushing.

He'd only climbed a few tens of feet above the water when his strength failed him. *Fuck!* He desperately tried to turn back toward the land, but his muscles protested the extended use and he floundered in the air. He searched for the clearing with the fire in hopes he could land there, but he dropped too far too fast.

Aw, hellwinds, this is gonna hurt.

His muscles shook with exertion and he tried to slow down, but the last of his strength failed and he slammed into the shallow water with a resounding splash. He folded his wings before they dragged him into the reservoir and scrambled onto the island using the rocks as hand and footholds.

He shook his head clear of water, wishing he could shake off the chagrin. So much for being the magnificent and graceful dragon. *Oh yeah, stories will be told for years about the idiot dragon who damn near drowned.*

He almost shifted back to his human disguise, but he didn't want to. He'd been the biped long enough. He blew the water out of his nostrils and staggered through the trees toward the fire. It was a tight squeeze, the forest not meant for one of his size.

Denarrion reached the clearing faster than he expected, but only his head, neck, and shoulders fit beside the fire. He hadn't realized how big he'd grown. *Fat and heavy is more like it.* He closed his eyes to keep the recriminations at bay. When he opened them, the energy glowing around Charlorrion and Torriandra showed their health and strength. But the *Morukai* and Lissandra radiated brilliant, scintillating waves, offering heat, comfort, and home.

Glory, what I would give to feel that all the time.

Lissandra raised her eyebrows as she took in his sodden state. "Are you all right?"

:Yeah, probably. I guess I needed a bath.: He broadcast his thoughts to everyone in the clearing. *:I forgot how much strength it takes to fly and I'm way out of practice. Hummingbird, I am not.:*

She laughed and stood beside him, resting her hand on the bridge of his snout. The simple contact allowed him to sense her love and attraction for him, especially in his dragon form. She found him beautiful and pleasure slid down his spine.

But she said the courtship was over.

She'd repudiated him, pointing out all the ways he was broken. *Yeah, well, I'm gonna fix those things.* He loved her and she was his True Mate. If he had to remain her knight in dragon armor to keep her in his life, he'd never change back into his human disguise. She was too important.

CHAPTER NINETEEN

Lissandra stared at the ice blue eyes of the pearlescent dragon dripping with lake water and couldn't stop the flutter of her heart. Long graceful horns flowed off the back of his head and a line of broad spines ran down his neck into the trees. The spines and horns glittered blue against the opalescent white of his body. He kept resettling his wings along his sides as if unused to them, the thumb claws flashing their sharp points in the firelight.

He was big, his body disappearing into the darkness beyond the fire. She suspected he had a good couple of meters of length on her in her dragon form and she wasn't small.

Glory, he smells good. Like cedar with a hint of mint.

She hadn't smelled the mint on him before and she shivered as arousal slid through her. She wanted him, particularly in this form, but she reined in her baser instincts to focus.

He still needs to heal and strengthen himself. And

Charlorrion, Torri, and the Morukai *are watching.* She took a deep shuddering breath and straightened her spine, turning her attention back to the fire.

"Are you sure you're okay?"

He wuffled a snort. *:I will be. Is it okay if I stay in this form for a while longer? I know I'm big, but I don't want to shift yet.:*

"You don't have to change on my account. I think you're pretty handsome." She winked and he rumbled in approval.

"It's probably wise you remain as you are for much of the night, Fire Brother. You will need what strength you can gather." The *Morukai* removed the pipe from his mouth and tapped the ashes into the fire.

Denarrion dipped his chin and the sound of a big body settling to the ground came from the trees. She hoped he didn't knock too many over.

Rather than walking away, she settled to the ground beside his head, trying to ignore the urge to shift and wrap her body around his. She scrubbed her face with her hands to shove away the surge of arousal over seeing his dragon form. *Holy glory, he's beautiful.* She took a few deep breaths to regain her equilibrium.

"What are we going to do about Walter?" Torri rested against Charlorrion, shivering in his embrace. "Do you think he's still in there with the demon?"

Lissandra met the Shaman's gaze and sighed. "No, I don't think so. I think Waltarrion was too weak to fight both the infection and the possession. I suspect the reason he took so long to recover and was so irritable while doing it is because it was the demon getting used to his body. That thing living in the Goldencoats' house isn't Waltarrion. He's gone."

A wave of grief washed over her from Denarrion. The father he'd known before the Great Chicago Fire was long gone, but he only now understood it. He closed his eyes and bowed his head while the fire crackled in sympathy for his loss.

She had to hand it to the demon. It couldn't have chosen a better disguise. Possessing its archenemy for a hiding place was a stroke of evil genius. It had almost crippled an entire dragon family, encouraging them to hide what they were and kept them from becoming powerful enough to fight it.

"How in hellwinds did we miss that?" Charlorrion shook his head. "How could we miss the demon within him? Surely his smell changed with the possession."

She nodded. "I could smell it the moment I walked into the house."

:I could smell it, too, but I thought it was Walter fighting the infection.: Denarrion raised his chin. *:I guess I just got used to it and figured it was him as he got older.:*

"Yeah, I did, too." Charlorrion nodded. "But now that we know, we won't mistake that stench again. The only question I have is if we can actually kill it. It possessed the body of a dragon. It's impervious to dragonfyre."

"Not impervious, only resistant."

The *Morukai* met each dragon's gaze, stopping at Lissandra. "Your human disguise is fire-resistant, but it does burn. It's your dragon body that's impervious. The demon resides in the human disguise, but it doesn't have the strength or imperviousness of the dragon body. And if you badly injure the body and it becomes weakened..."

"Are you saying that if we weaken the body, it will be susceptible to dragonfyre?" Charlorrion shared a look with Lissandra before returning his gaze to the *Morukai*.

"Not just weaken, but physically injure it." Wise Heart nodded, his expression grave. "You must ensure the fire can reach the underlying muscle and tissue. After all, when the soul leaves the bodies of your ancients, do you bury your dead or burn them?"

"We burn them, but without the soul, the body no

longer has the charm against fire." Torri drew her knees up to her chest and rested her elbows on them.

:But if Lissandra's right, my father isn't in his body. Only the demon is still there, so it should be susceptible to burning,: Denarrion dipped his chin. *:Right?:*

"Because the soul inside belongs to the demon, the charm remains."

Lissandra growled, crossing her arms over her chest. "We'd have to damn near eviscerate the demon to weaken it enough for the fire to work. But demons are tough. And this one has had nearly 150 years to shore up its defenses. It's not going to be easy."

"That's why all of us will be needed." The Shaman held up a hand with three fingers raised. "There are three islands in the Salmon Creek Reservoir. The smallest of these is a holy place despite its barren appearance. It has been blessed by the Medicine men and women of our nation for generations. You must bring the demon there and each of you must represent one of the five elements. It's the only way to send it to its home place."

"Does it need to be alive?" Charlorrion scowled.

"Yes, but it will be easier to contain the demon if it is…quiet."

"Quiet," Lissandra snorted. "You mean out cold."

The *Morukai* shrugged.

:I guess we'll just whack him on the back of his head and bring him out there.: Denarrion shot a look up at the sky.

"Right. Sounds easy." Sarcasm oozed from Charlorrion's voice. "Which elements will we each represent?"

"You, Charlorrion, will be Water, because it is the element you use every day in your quest to ensure safety to the town." Wise Heart pointed to Torri. "Torriandra, you will represent Earth and all her healing energies. You must make energy mandalas of the Five Elements so we have anchor points."

"I've never done that." Torri's eyes widened.

"It is the same as using chalk or beads, only with energy. Think of the CG effects in modern movie-making, like in Dr. Strange."

Lissandra blinked. "You watch movies?"

The *Morukai* laughed. "Of course. I want to see how close the humans' imaginations come to the truth of magic." He winked. "You, Lissandra, will represent your parent element, Fire. It will be you who must face the demon and channel your element into it. Only you can see it and keep it from possessing others."

She nodded. She'd expected it would be her job to kill the demon. *I have to do this even if it might kill me.* She didn't want to think of that, or the loss her children would experience, but the truth hovered in the back of her mind.

"Denarrion, you'll represent Air, and be the breath that fuels your mate's fire. She'll need your strength and vitality to send the demon away."

The big white dragon nodded, his eyes sad. She understood he mourned for his crippled family and wished she could comfort him. But it would have to wait.

:What element will you represent, Shaman?:

"I will represent the Ether, where the energy of the universe fuels life and the Goddess's voice is loudest."

"When should we be there?" Charlorrion asked.

"Just after the sun sets." The *Morukai* rose and waved them off. "I suggest you get as much rest as possible. This will be neither as simple or easy as we hope, but if you all do your parts, it will be successful."

Lissandra nodded and met Torri's gaze. "Will you be able to make all the mandalas fast enough to contain the demon?"

"I will come to the site a little earlier than sunset and lay the ground work for the anchor points." Torri bit her lip. "I'll use painted posts to show you which element is in which direction. Blue for water, green for earth, red for fire, yellow for air, and white for ether. I'll complete the circle once you arrive with the demon."

Lissandra sighed. "We'll be there." She switched her gaze to the Shaman. "What will we need to do when we arrive?"

"The demon must be thrown into the fire and held there. And the blood relative of the host body must add his own flame to the fire to bind the creature." The *Morukai* met Lissandra's gaze with a raised eyebrow and she grimaced. "Go, get some rest. I will see you tomorrow at sunset on the Sacred Isle."

"Thank you, Wise Heart, for your counsel and help." Charlorrion shook the *Morukai*'s hand before he gestured for them all to return to the western shore of the island.

Lissandra inclined her head to the Shaman before she stepped away from the fire. Before she could take more than a few steps, Denarrion's dragon self shimmered in the flickering light and he shifted into his human disguise.

"Oh, Denarrion. You heard what Wise Heart said. You need to stay in your true form for most of the night."

He nodded, dismay tightening his shoulders. "Yeah, I know. And I will. But, uh, I'm so out of shape, I can't fly very far, and since we're on an island…"

Sorrow and amusement churned inside her and she gave him a half-smile. "Are you saying you need a ride?"

"Yeah, uh. Yeah. Could you give me one back to my house?" He rubbed the back of his neck as he looked at her from under his brows.

She nodded. "Give me a moment to shift and we'll go."

They made it to the shore just as Charlorrion and Torriandra lifted off into the night sky. She understood they had to be careful—Goddess knew the U.S. military would dangerously interested in dragons—but she wished the humans could see the beauty and magnificence of her people taking flight. *And hopefully when this is all over, Denarrion will be back to his proper health.*

She took a deep breath and released her hold on her human disguise. The world shifted and settled into a clearer, brighter, sharper place. Denarrion's human body shrank to the size of a doll and she sealed her lips around a laugh. *He wouldn't care for the comparison.*

:Are you ready?: She tilted her head to meet his gaze, grateful his diaphanous dragon self appeared above him.

"Yeah. Holy shit, Lissandra, you're fuckin' gorgeous as a dragon."

She rumbled a laugh. *:You're pretty handsome yourself. Let's get back to the mainland and you can be the dragon for a while.:* She winked and held out one clawed hand.

"Just be gentle, okay? It's my first time as a passenger." He stepped into her hand and she gently closed her fingers around him.

:Oooh. A virgin. Hold on.: She winked before she leapt into the air and he yelped in her grip.

She couldn't help but laugh, but she made sure her flight was smooth and steady. She didn't want to clean her hand of vomit. The night world spread out beneath her wings and despite the creeping decay, the Salmon Creek Reservoir and the neighboring town were beautiful in their own way. She soared over the rock where they fell into the water before his house came into view.

:Home sweet home.: She touched down with her hind feet first, bracing herself with her other foreleg as she released him.

He rubbed the back of his neck again as he stepped away. "Thanks."

She dipped her head in acknowledgment as he took a deep breath and shifted into his dragon form. Lissandra gasped and staggered as the pain of his shift hit her through their mating bond, and her heart ached for his condition.

:Oh, Denarrion, I'm so sorry it hurts that much.: She met his agonized gaze as he resituated his wings and tail, curling up like a cat.

:Yeah, well, it's pretty much my own damn fault. I'm the dumbass who fell for the demon's shit.: He raised his head and shook it, his horns rattling with his spines. *:Sweet glory. You're even more beautiful than I thought. I–I've never seen a female as impressive as you.:*

:Thank you.: She dipped her head, his words warming her more than she expected. *:I'm going to shift back and get going. You should stay in your true form until at least morning. The more time you stay as the true you, the better off you'll be.:*

She closed her eyes and stuffed her true form down into her human disguise, the loss of clarity in scents, sights, and textures making her heart ache. *I gotta remember to spend more time in my dragon form when I get home.*

Home. Her thoughts turned to her children still in Colorado with their grandmother. What would happen to them if she was gone? They'd already lost their father. *And Denarrion isn't ready for fatherhood, even if he is my True Mate.* Hellwinds, he wasn't even ready to be a dragon again. It was much better for her kids to be orphans in a world cleansed of demons. Lissandra would pay the price of death to make certain her children and the humans were safe. She rubbed her face with her hands and prepared to say goodbye.

:Please don't go, Lissandra.:

She met his glorious ice blue eyes and her heart squeezed at the misery in his expression. He was the male she'd love more than any other for all of her life and beyond her death. He was the connection she had been missing even during her marriage to Mikelorrion. She loved him, but she couldn't sacrifice her well-being and that of her children until he healed from the demon's damage.

She shook her head. "I can't stay. I need some sleep if I'm going to take on the demon tomorrow night."

:Please, Lissandra.: He angled his head and body to keep her from leaving the yard. *:I need to explain a few things. Will you stay long enough so we can talk?:*

She sighed and scrubbed her face. "I'm really tired, Denarrion."

:I know, but give me a chance to…to explain what I figured out about myself.: His thoughts touched her as gentle whispers.

"Yeah, okay. Settle where you're comfortable and I'll sit with you."

:Thank you.: His mind voice held such relief that she smiled as he settled beside his deck.

She realized just how big he was when he dwarfed the house. *Damn, he must be about sixty feet long from nose to tail tip.* The moonlight caressed his opalescent scales in soft rainbows and he glowed with refracted light.

Sleek, smooth, powerful. She admired his lovely body as he curled into a ball. Despite her concerns about the next day, her arousal rose in appreciation of the hot male in front of her. She shivered with lust as he turned and looked back at her.

"You're so beautiful." She gave him a sad smile. "I wish you could stay in your dragon form until I leave."

Denarrion's head jerked up and his eyes widened in surprise. *:Leave?:*

Sorrow pushed its way back into the forefront of her thoughts. "Yes, leave. I'll be going back to Colorado on Monday." *If I survive Sunday night.*

:What about you and me? What about the courtship?:

"The courtship is over, Denarrion," she stated firmly. "We bonded as True Mates, but I can't be with a male who's afraid to be himself, the dragon he's meant to be. My children deserve a better role model. Hellwinds, I deserve better. I need a partner who doesn't look down on me for being my real self. I'm a dragon, Denarrion, and I'll *always* be a dragon, no matter where I am or who I'm with."

Denarrion's eyes widened further, this time with growing anger. *:What about tonight? What about how I am now? I'm in my true shape, now. I'm a dragon.:*

She raised her eyebrows. "What about later, when you're around humans, day in and day out? Won't you just fall into old patterns, renouncing your culture, your species? You're so much more than human. It's good to see you in your natural form, but I need this more than just once every decade."

He hissed. *:Whoa, whoa, whoa! Who says I'm just gonna do this once? I might've been deluded by a demon for 150 years, but that doesn't mean I'm still in the dark. I realized several things that put my life into perspective. You're right, I've been a stupid jackass and afraid, but tonight I learned my father is a demon that has been corrupting me, my sister and my mother for decades.:*

His barbed tail lashed the ground, digging furrows in his agitation, but his voice softened. *:I've been avoiding my natural form a long time, but you brought me back to who I really am. You're the only one who could do this and I thank the Goddess you showed me how far I'd strayed from myself. Changing into my natural form hurt like a sonuvaprick, but it also showed me just how connected I am to you. You are my True Bonded mate, Lissandra, and no one else, not dragon and certainly not human, could ever fill the place you've made in my heart.:*

He paused and shot a look at the house sitting silent and dark. *:I thought I'd be fine alone in my life, staying how I was, but you made me realize just how sick I'd gotten. I don't want to be alone anymore. I don't want to be human and deny what I am. And I don't want to be without you.:*

He returned his gaze to hers, his ice blue eyes beseeching her to reconsider. *:I want to be with you until* *the day I die. I need you to help me remember how amazing being a dragon is. So please, Lissandra, don't tell me the courtship is over. Please.:*

Lissandra stepped closer to his head and grimaced. "Oh Denarrion, I want to continue the courtship. I really do."

:But...?:

"But I don't want to have to train my mate to be a dragon when I already have to do that with my children. I need a male who's my equal, not my student." She sighed and shook her head. "And you have to consider the possibility that I won't live past tomorrow night."

:What do you mean you might not be alive after tomorrow?:

She dropped her chin and her gaze. "You don't know how powerful the demon is, and my skills at killing them are rusty. It's been over thirty years since I did anything like this and there's a good possibility the demon will kill me."

:Yeah, it's powerful, but you won't be alone. Charlie, Torri, and I will be there along with the Morukai. *That should be enough to bring down the demon.:*

"It might not be enough, Denarrion. I have this gut feeling that there will need to be a sacrifice to keep everyone safe. I'm the warrior who was brought here to do this task. I can't ask anyone else to give their lives to kill the demon. It has to be me."

Denarrion's head lifted and his wings drooped. He said nothing for a long time and she raised her gaze to gauge his reaction. The expression in his eyes shifted from disbelief to fear to anger in rapid succession.

:No.: The growl in his thoughts was matched audibly. "No, what?"

:No, I won't let you pay this price, Lissandra.: He lashed his tail and it slammed against his deck. *:The demon's in my family. I should be the one to pay this price*

since I didn't kill it a hundred and fifty years ago. I won't let you sacrifice yourself for my mistake. Your children don't deserve to lose another parent.:

"No, but they'll be taken care of by their grandmother. And they'll know their mother died saving the world by doing her duty." She'd rather find another way to do her duty, but there was no getting out of this one.

:No they won't. They'll only see that their mother never came home.: He raised his wings in agitation. *:You can't do that to them. I won't lose you this way. I can't lose you! You're my mate.:*

"I may not have a choice, Denarrion." She shook her head and rubbed her hands on her thighs. "I don't want to leave you or my children, and I definitely don't want to die. But if anyone has to, I'm willing to pay the price so the rest of you will survive and the demon is destroyed. It's my duty as a Seer."

She turned away from the look of frustrated fury on his face. She understood the emotions and wished she could alleviate them. She wanted to stay with him and smell his white chocolate and mint scent for years to come. But fighting a demon this deeply entrenched wouldn't be easy or simple and there was a very real possibility of casualties.

Denarrion threw his head back and blasted the night with a roar of frustration. *:You have other duties too, you know. You have your duty to your mate, Lissandra.:*

She grimaced and gritted her teeth. "What are you talking about?"

:Me, Lissandra! You're my mate and I'm yours. I need you.:

"Denarrion, I'm too tired to puzzle shit out tonight. What exactly are you saying?"

:I love you, Lissandra, more than anyone else in this world and I don't want to lose you to misunderstanding or death. Please don't leave me here alone to try to remember what I should be. I need you to remind me, to help me, to

love me.:

He looked at her with his ice blue eyes whirling with fear and entreaty. He even trembled as he reached out with a talon and scraped it gently down her back. It sent shivers of pleasure and desire straight to her pussy and she wished she could make love with him. His nostrils flared as he caught the scent of her arousal, but he didn't move.

:Please, Lissandra. I know you gotta fight the demon, but remember we're gonna be there, too. Let the rest of us help you. You don't have to do it alone.:

"Wouldn't you give your life for all that you love?" She gave him a sad smile, while her heart hammered with his declaration of love.

:I would if I had no other choice,: he admitted softly, drawing her closer to his opalescent body. *:But you* have *a choice. Let us help you and take some of the burden. If we work together that sacrifice might not have to be made. We'll do what has to be done, but don't go into this with the intent of dying. Please, Lissandra.:*

By the time he was done speaking, she was leaning against his warm side. He curled his head around to be next to her. She sat surrounded by his scent and his warmth and her fear and anger at him melted away. *Glory, I want to stay here forever.* She slid her way down his shoulder until she sat on the ground between his forelimb and his head. She raised her knees and draped her arms over them, bowing her head. She wished she could stay, but even if she survived the demon, she had to return to Cloudburst. For herself and for him. *Dammit, that's going to hurt.*

He rumbled with pleasure as she relaxed and she couldn't help but smile.

She leaned her head back and closed her eyes. "That was never my intent, Denarrion. But if the decision must be made, I won't hesitate from it, either. Now, just hold me tonight."

He settled her into the crook of his arm and she

snuggled closer to him, savoring the quiet moment and the rich scents of white chocolate and mint. She sighed contentedly, releasing her worries, and let herself enjoy being close to Denarrion, if only for one more night.

CHAPTER TWENTY

Morning arrived only four hours later and banished the quiet relaxation in Denarrion. He opened his eyes to watch the sky turn from indigo to lilac and on to pale silver, with pastel-colored streamers only visible to dragon sight.

Holy shit, I've missed so much.

The surprising sound of early morning traffic along the road grabbed his attention and he took a deep breath before shifting into his human guise. While it didn't hurt as much as the night before, it still felt like stuffing himself into the sack that came with a sleeping bag. *Way too small.*

He waved to whoever drove past before he fished the keys out of Lissandra's pocket and ducked into his house. The air still had a bit of chill to it so he started coffee and returned to the deck with a thick fleece blanket. He threw the blanket over her and crawled in beside her, cradling her in his arms. He listened to her breathing softly next to him and he realized two things.

First, he was more content and happy than he could ever remember being. Lissandra's presence in his arms made the world brighter, even in his human disguise. *How in hellwinds did I ever cuddle with anyone else? Damn, the demon fucked me up.*

Second, he'd no intention of losing his mate, either to death or negligence. He wouldn't hide what he was any longer. He was a dragon and he'd act accordingly. The demon was in this town partly because of him and he wouldn't let Lissandra pay for the mistake.

Charlie, Torri, and the Morukai *better find a way to keep her alive.*

He dozed as the sun rose higher in the sky and Lissandra shifted against him, a deep breath filling her chest as she opened her eyes. He loved her lilac eyes and when they focused on him, he could see so much life in their depths.

"Ugh, is it morning already?" She stretched, arching her back. "I'm so not ready for today."

Denarrion enjoyed how her nipples pushed against the fabric of her shirt. His body slowly hardened and he shifted to make room in his shorts.

"Yeah, already." He buried his nose in her hair. "But I made coffee."

"Oh, coffee." She smiled on the end of her sigh. "Coffee helps a lot." She opened her eyes and met his gaze. "You shifted back."

"Yeah, couldn't have the neighbors noticing a big white dragon in the front yard. It's too late in the year to claim it's a snow sculpture." He winked as she snorted. "Besides, if I didn't, we wouldn't have coffee waiting for us."

"Coffee schmoffee." She growled without heat. Her stomach echoed the sentiment and she smirked. "I guess I'm hungry, though. You didn't happen to make a gourmet meal with that coffee, did you?"

"Nah, but that's not hard to whip up." He didn't bother to move. He'd stay there as long as she did. "That's not all I could whip up."

Lissandra stiffened and the earlier comfort retreated. She pulled away from his embrace and stretched before climbing to her feet.

"I think I'll get some coffee. Do you want some?"

She disappeared into the house and he scrubbed his hands over his face. *Way to go, jackass.* Apparently, sex wasn't what she wanted to do the day of a battle. He couldn't think of anything he'd rather do than sex before a battle, but he rolled to his feet and folded the blanket. He carried it inside and found her doctoring her coffee.

"I just realized none of my things are here. Maybe we should call Torri and see if she's up for breakfast." She rested a hip against the counter and gave him a distant smile.

"Hey, don't shut me out, okay?" Denarrion set the blanket down and stood in front of her, trying to catch her gaze. "I know today's our last day together, but whether we survive the night, I want to be with you—really be with you—all day. Okay?"

She studied him with solemn attention, her gaze sliding over his face as she considered. Eventually, she nodded, but she didn't smile.

"I don't want to die tonight, Denarrion." Her lips tightened and she swallowed hard. His chest contracted at the thought. "I have too much I want to still do with my life. Continuing the courtship is just one aspect. You're my True Bonded mate and I want to spend more of my life with you." She sighed and studied her coffee cup a moment. "I just have to be sure we kill the demon for good this time."

"We will," he promised, feeling it in his heart. "I promise we will. Just let me, Charlorrion, and Torri help you. We'll do it together."

She gave him a sad smile before she leaned forward and brushed her lips across his. The sweetness of her kiss sucked him down and he wanted to drown in it. His gut tightened when she pulled away.

"I promised you last night that I wouldn't go into the

fight trying to get myself killed. I meant it."

"Good, 'cause I'm gonna hold you to that." He held her gaze before he smiled. "We'll do it together because that's what mates do, right?"

"Right." She sighed and rested her head against his for a few moments before pulling back. "Come on. Let's call the Ravenwings. I'm sure Torriandra has made something delicious for breakfast and I don't want to miss it."

Denarrion nodded as she pulled out her phone and tapped the Ravenwings' number. He grimaced at the smell of sweat and wondered if they could take a shower before they headed over, but Lissandra seemed determined to leave.

"Okay, see you soon, Torriandra." Lissandra hung up the phone and shoved it in her pocket. "They're good with us coming to visit this morning. They said I could even Skype with the girls while I'm there."

"Oh, yeah, that's good. You want to take a shower before we head over there? I'm pretty ripe." He tilted his head, trying to entice her upstairs, but she shook her head.

"No, you go ahead. I'll be ready to go when you come downstairs." She stared out the windows, lost in her own thoughts.

Disappointment curdled in his belly at her response, but he nodded. "I won't be long and then we can get going."

She didn't turn as he headed up the stairs and he hoped he could reconnect after his shower. *I can't lose her. Not now.* But he feared he might not have a say in the matter.

****

Lissandra listened to the water start to run and let her shoulders slump as she leaned her forehead against the window. She hadn't told Denarrion why she was so sure the battle tonight would end her life. She couldn't. He didn't deserve to lose again, but that seemed to be the Goddess's plan for him.

Glory, this sucks. The Fire Spirits had spoken to her as much as they'd spoken to Denarrion, but what they'd asked of her was far more costly. They'd asked her if she would complete this task even if it meant the loss of one of her own. Her children were safe in Colorado with Solenarra and Mikelorrion had already returned to the Goddess. That left her.

Or Denarrion.

But she wouldn't do that to him. He wasn't really hers, and she couldn't ask it of him. She could imagine the conversation: *Hey, Denarrion, we need to sacrifice someone to the Fire Spirits to save the world, and I thought, you being my True Bonded mate and all, you could just take on that job. What do you say?* She grimaced and shook her head. Yeah, not gonna happen.

"So it's me or no one." She sighed and stretched her neck from side to side.

There was always the possibility she'd be able to kill the demon. She'd killed demons before, but none of them had been entrenched as long as this one. She'd hope for the best and plan for the worst.

"All right. I'm ready. Let's go." Denarrion grabbed his keys as he stuffed his wallet in his back pocket and gave her a smile. "Everything okay?"

"Yeah, it's all good." She tried to match his smile, but it came out flat.

"It is, you'll see. It's gonna be a great day. Let's live it up so we can both remember it, yeah?"

Some of her tension bled away. "Yeah, okay. Good advice."

He grinned. "We'll take the truck so you don't rip one of my arms off and chow down on it."

She laughed as he locked the door. "Don't tempt me."

They climbed into his truck and made the drive in a

companionable silence. The front door was open when they arrived and Torriandra responded to their greetings from the kitchen. They followed the delightful scents to watch her serve up some of her famous quiche with rosemary rolls and assorted fruit slices.

"See, I told you this was a good idea." Lissandra elbowed Denarrion as she winked at Torri. "I knew we'd get a much better meal here than at his place."

And it's good to eat with friends before the shit hits the fan.

"Oh, struck in the heart." He moaned theatrically and leaned backwards on the counter with one hand to his chest.

Torri laughed. "Karma pays everyone back."

"Man, I'm just gettin' it left and right today." He smirked to show he teased. "See if I ever invite you over for dinner again."

"What's this about not getting dinner again?" Charlorrion stepped into the room and narrowed his eyes.

"No such thing." Torri shook her head, her long braid sliding over her shoulders. "Come on, go sit down. Food's ready."

They all settled at the table in the morning sunshine and chatted about inconsequential items. Lissandra was able to relax a little and enjoy the company of dragons. Even Denarrion appeared to be more comfortable with discussing night flights with maverick airplane pilots, hunting elk in the dead of winter, and attending an Ice Demon Blizzard party. Charlorrion's story of damn near getting outed while trying catch an over-adventurous toddler climbing a tree had them all in stitches, but the elephant remained in the room despite the humor.

As the conversation wound down, Lissandra swallowed the last of her coffee and met Torriandra's gaze.

"The food is fabulous, Torri. Should this be my last day, it's definitely good to eat well."

Everyone lost their smiles as the reason for her trip flared into clarity.

"Would it be possible to set up the computer so I could Skype with my family in Colorado? I want them to remember something sweet from their last day with their mother."

"Oh, Lissandra, it won't—"

She held up a hand to keep Torri from saying more. "We don't know what tonight will bring and I know you all plan on helping me kill it. Frankly, I'm going to need all the help I can get. But just in case, I need to talk to them. It's important to me."

Charlorrion rose. "Let me go get the laptop. We can set it up here."

"It *won't* be your last day, Lissandra. I promise." Denarrion took her hand and squeezed it as Charlorrion left the room.

"You can't promise that, but I appreciate the support." She gave him a sad smile. "I'm definitely counting on your backup."

Charlorrion returned with the computer and set it on the table. "This should be all good to go for you to log in." He tilted his head. "Do you want some privacy?"

"No, I'm just going to talk kid talk, is all. If you want to stay that's okay." She tapped out her login information and listened to the startup sounds of the program. She hoped they were all awake out west and she'd have a chance to really talk to all of them. She suspected Solenarra might still be avoiding her for her subterfuge.

"Hey, Mom. I knew you would call today." Lucenarra proclaimed as she crowded her sister on the chair in front of the camera.

Tears almost started in Lissandra's eyes as she gazed at her daughters and she grinned to hide her heartbreaking sorrow.

"Hello, my little fire-breathers, what are you up to this

morning, hmmm?" She mock-growled at them, making her youngest laugh and her oldest grin mischievously.

"We're making boysenberry pancakes," Kressendra piped up, grinning widely with red staining all over her face.

"I can see that. Did you save any boysenberries for the batter?" She motioned to her own mouth. "Because you kinda have them everywhere."

"I made sure she didn't eat them all." Luce winked. "How are you doing?"

"Things are good here. Are you going to go to the Cloudburst Art Festival this year?"

"Oh, yeah. I like hanging out with the Cloudburst Hot Shot firefighters." Luce grinned.

"And the witch who makes lotions." Kress rubbed her hands together.

The girls rattled off all the things they planned to see at the art festival, but Lissandra could only focus on how beautiful they were and how much she wanted to see them reach their first five hundred years. *Not much chance of that after tonight.*

But she kept her focus on the new dragons who'd take on the world after she was gone, and hoped they'd be stronger than her.

****

Denarrion stood out of the camera's eye behind Lissandra and resisted the urge to sweep her up in his arms and make love to her. Her sorrow and love were killing him. Her emotions flooded through him, mixing with his, and he couldn't quite separate them out. He envied the girls' unconditional love for their mother. Would that he'd felt that sooner. It was a delight to be there to see it. He refused to allow it to be the last time. He and the Ravenwings would figure out a way to keep Lissandra safe.

Charlorrion came up behind him and clapped a hand on his shoulder, making him jump.

"Oh, sorry, Denny. I didn't mean to surprise you." Charlorrion grinned, belying his words. "Did you sleep well? Did you sleep at all?" He winked.

"It's Denarrion, actually, and yeah, we slept damn well." He glared at his foster brother, still pissed at his ulterior motive to bring Lissandra to Redfield. *Even if she is my mate.* "Why the fuck didn't you tell me why you wanted Lissandra in particular?"

Charlorrion raised an eyebrow. "Would you have agreed to go out with her if I had?"

Denarrion opened his mouth, but the words stuck in his throat. He hadn't been thrilled with the actual blind date coming to be, but he suspected his disfigurement from the demon would've made him more reluctant.

"No, probably not. But it's still shifty as hell."

"Yeah. I'm sorry I had to do it." Charlorrion nodded as his smile slowly faded. "Did you tell Lissandra what you needed to?"

Denarrion bit his lip. "Yeah, I did, but I don't know what good it'll do."

"What do you mean?"

Denarrion looked toward the kitchen where Lissandra sat laughing and talking with her daughters through the computer. He wanted to soak up the warmth and comfort coming from them, but Lissandra's belief that this might be her last day made him hesitate.

"You got a minute?"

"Sure. Let's go out to the garden."

He followed Charlorrion out to the back deck and though they'd been quiet, Torriandra poked her head into the mudroom. "Are you going outside?"

"Yeah, Torri. I wanted to show Denarrion something in the back yard. I'll just be a minute."

"Could you bring some fresh rosemary when you come

back in?"

"Sure. Will do."

"Thanks, Love." She blew him a kiss and he shot her a sappy smile.

Denarrion's gut clenched at the love and contentment in Torriandra's voice as she spoke to her husband and his own life appeared as empty as a rain barrel in a drought. He wanted to hear Lissandra speak that way to him. He hoped she would if he could keep her alive after what they planned.

They stepped out the door into the warm air and Denarrion tried to enjoy it, but his mind kept churning over what he needed to ask Charlorrion. He didn't even know if it was possible, but he had to try, and he needed the others to try, too.

Charlorrion led him to the edge of the trees and paused, staring down at the ground. The morning sunshine painted a lacy pattern on the grass, but Denarrion couldn't concentrate on the beauty.

"So what did you want to talk to me about?" Charlorrion met Denarrion's gaze.

"It's about Lissandra. She doesn't think she's going to survive tonight." Denarrion didn't sugar-coat it. He didn't have time.

"What? Why does she think that?" Charlorrion's voice grew hard and tight.

"She said the Fire Spirits asked her to do this even if she might lose one of her own and she isn't gonna make her kids pay that price." Denarrion swallowed against the fear of her loss. "I got her to promise not to *try* to get herself killed, but she won't hold back if someone's life is required to seal this deal." He raised his gaze to meet Charlorrion's. "You have to promise me, if anything happens to me, that you'll make sure Lissandra survives tonight. Promise."

His foster brother raised a dubious eyebrow. "You know I'll do what I can. But why do you think something's gonna happen to you?"

"Because the fucking demon has had me under its sway for almost two centuries. Who knows what it's capable of? I don't want her to die, Charlorrion. She has kids who've already lost a parent. Promise me."

"Why me?"

"Because you fuckin' brought her here under false pretenses. You owe her. Promise me you'll make sure she survives tonight." Denarrion bared his teeth, fury rolling through him. "I get why you didn't tell me. If I'm fucked up because of the demon, that makes sense. But you didn't tell *her*. You lured her here with the offer of a possible future. Now she faces the possibility of an early death. You owe her, Charlorrion."

Charlorrion regarded him solemnly for a few moments. "This coming from the guy who wanted nothing to do with the 'widow from Colorado' a couple days ago?"

Denarrion scowled.

"Ahh, leave me alone, willya? I know it's a change of heart—"

"Change of heart?" Charlorrion echoed doubtfully. "More like a change of personality, lifestyle, whole world—"

"All right, all right. I get it. I'm serious, Charlie."

Charlorrion raised a doubtful eyebrow.

Denarrion shook his head. "You said it yourself that I needed a mate. I'm remembering who I am because of her. I definitely needed her. Please, Charlie, you have to make sure she survives, no matter what happens to me."

Charlorrion considered for a few moments without an expression on his face as his gaze rested on Denarrion like a laser beam. He nodded slowly.

"It's Charlorrion, actually, and yeah, I'll do my best to make sure she comes through this tonight. But you make damn sure you're worthy of her because she doesn't deserve anything less than your fucking best. Got me?"

"Yeah, I got it. Probably better than you, jackass."

"Whatever." Charlorrion snorted but a smile curled his lips. "Come on, better get some rosemary or Torriandra's gonna kick my ass."

Denarrion tried to match his foster brother's smile, but he was still too sick at heart.

Charlorrion clapped him on the shoulder. "Hey, don't worry. It'll all work out. And she's strong and healthy. With the three of us plus the *Morukai* looking out for her, it should be no problem."

Denarrion hoped it would be "no problem", but at least he had Charlorrion's help to keep Lissandra alive. He helped his foster brother gather a small handful of rosemary sprigs, then followed him back into the house.

CHAPTER TWENTY-ONE

Lissandra smiled at her kids, her heart breaking. She didn't want to leave them, but she couldn't allow the demon to remain in Redfield.

When the conversation lulled, she caught Torriandra's eye. "Can I take the laptop into another room? I need some privacy for a bit."

"Of course." Torriandra nodded. "You can use the dining room, through there."

Lissandra nodded as she rose and carried the laptop into the dining room, glowing with morning light. She settled into another chair and took a deep breath.

"Lucenarra, would you please ask your grandmother to come to the computer? I need to talk to her." Lissandra gave her daughter a warm look. "Go ahead outside with your sister and I'll talk to you again after."

"Okay, Mom." Luce paused. "I love you. You're coming home soon, right?"

Lissandra swallowed hard. "Yeah, that's the plan, *sa garra*. I love you, too. Let me talk to Grandmama."

"Okay."

Luce ducked away and Lissandra closed her eyes to hold back her tears. How would she able to tell them she wasn't coming home? *Don't jump the gun quite yet. There's room for change.* She hoped.

Solenarra settled in front of the webcam and gave her a wary smile. "Good to see you, Lissandra. How are things going?"

Lissandra sighed. "Mom, I need you to listen carefully because I don't know how long I have alone and I need to discuss a few things with you." She scrubbed her face with her hands. "First, I'm pissed at your duplicity and your lack of honesty. You should've told me why you wanted me to court Denarrion. You should've given me the chance to decide. You don't know what I would've chosen to do."

Solenarra ran her hand through her short silver hair. "I know you, Lissandra. You'd given up your Seer's lifestyle to stay with your children. You wouldn't have gone to meet with the Goldencoats."

"No, you don't know me that well, nor where I was when I said I wanted a change. Lying to me by omitting details is infuriating and sickening, especially from someone who always told me to tell the truth, no matter how tough or ugly." Lissandra snarled, her fury at her mother's duplicity riding her. "But congratulations, you got your wish. I'm here and I'll be facing the demon tonight. The problem is, this demon is stronger than any I've faced in the past and it's well-entrenched here. It's strong enough that I might not be coming home. Which brings me to the second thing I need to discuss."

"Come now, Lissandra, you can't be serious."

"I'm very serious. Just let me finish. If I die tonight, which is a distinct possibility, I need to know the girls are safe with you. I need to know you'll raise them to be the best at their abilities, no matter what they are." Lissandra's voice cracked as her throat closed. "If I don't make it home, I need to know you're going to help them become the best dragons they can be, and to know their mother did her best despite the lies and deceptions. You have to promise you'll care for them."

"Don't be so dramatic. You'll be fine." Solenarra scowled and waved her hand. "You've done this before."

Lissandra shook her head. "This is different, Mom." She took a deep breath. "It possessed Waltarrion Goldencoat."

"What?" All the color drained from Solenarra's face.

Lissandra nodded. "The demon's inside Waltarrion's body."

"How's that possible? A dragon would die before he or she allowed herself to be possessed."

She shrugged. "I suspect Waltarrion died in his last fight and the demon took over to save itself. What better way to win than to take over a dragon's body and cripple the dragon's family? It's been here almost two centuries."

"That can't be. We would've known. You must be wrong, Lissandra. I knew Waltarrion and Gloriana personally. They'd never let that happen. You must be mistaken."

"I'm mistaken?" Lissandra narrowed her eyes. "You *knew* there was a demon here, but you didn't tell me so I'd come out to see for myself. I've done that. I'm the one who's here, and I'm the one who must face it. And I'm telling you, it's inside Waltarrion. It has corrupted your friend Gloria and possibly her children, Suriana and Denarrion. Someone has to kill the demon inside of Waltarrion, and I'm pretty sure you nominated me for that task."

"But Lissandra—"

"No, look, I don't have much time. I need you to promise you'll take care of the girls for me if I don't come home. Promise me, Mom."

"Of course, but—"

"No buts. This is what you got me into and I'm doing it, but the balance needs to be restored and this is the only way. The price is steep, but I'll pay it."

"You really believe it's too powerful for you to destroy?" Solenarra sounded alarmed for the first time.

"I don't know. I hope not, but the Fire Spirits seemed to think a sacrifice will be required, and I won't let anyone else pay the price for safety." She sighed and rubbed her eyes, willing the tears to remain inside. "You'll know if I'm coming home by tomorrow morning. I'm sure my True Bonded mate will tell you if I don't make it."

"Wait, you have a True Bonded mate?" Solenarra's eyes widened. "That's wonderful. Who is it?"

Lissandra gave a mirthless laugh. "Denarrion Goldencoat."

Sole frowned. "That doesn't make you happy?"

Lissandra raised her eyebrows. "He's been under the sway of the demon lodged in his father for more than a hundred and fifty years and he doesn't know how to be or act dragon. How would you feel?"

"Sweet glory, is he able to be healed from the damage?"

"Maybe, but not if the demon isn't destroyed." She looked over her shoulder as she caught Denarrion's voice in the other room. "I can't talk more about this now. Can you please bring the girls back in? I want as much time with them as possible."

"I still think you're being melodramatic about this. It'll be all right, I'm sure."

"Of course. Send the girls in please."

Solenarra grimaced but nodded and rose to call Luce and Kress in from playing. Lissandra took a deep breath and let it out long, shoving the sorrow and fear aside to be with her daughters on what might be her last day. *Goddess, please let them be strong even if I don't make it.* Her daughters would be greater than her in many ways. *Don't let Sole fashion them into Seers.* She wanted Luce and Kress to develop into their gifts, and neither had shown Seer abilities. *I just hope Mom realizes that, too.*

****

Denarrion found Lissandra talking to her daughters on Skype in the dining room. While her face remained light, the flood of sorrow and despair down their bond damn near choked him. He wanted to gather her up in his arms and hold her tight, protecting her from the fears and dangers. *But I'm the reason she's in danger.* Disappointment and guilt gnawed at him, but he put on a smile and touched her shoulder.

"Hey, everything okay?"

She shot him a smile, but her eyes remained sad. "Yeah. Would you talk to the kids for a moment while I go get some more coffee?" She rose and gestured at the screen.

"Hi, Denarrion." Lissandra's oldest daughter smiled and waved.

"Yeah, sure, I'll do that." He nodded and swallowed against his nervousness. How in hellwinds was he supposed to talk to kids? "Hi, Lucenarra. How you doin'?"

Lissandra left the room as Luce shrugged. "I'm good. Mom seems sad, but she won't say so. Do you know why?"

"I have some idea and I'm trying my best to reassure her, but sometimes our emotions mess us up. You know what I mean?"

Luce nodded. "Yeah, I know. But can I tell you a secret?"

Denarrion raised his eyebrows. "Yeah, of course."

She leaned close to the camera and lowered her voice. "Everyone's looking out for her and they'll help her when she needs it most." She sat back and her lips curved into a serene smile. "We made a Mandala this morning. Do you wanna see it?"

He stared into the peacock green gaze of this little dragon. She had more wisdom and compassion in her gaze than he'd seen from his mother for decades. *How can she be so young and so wise already?* Energy flowed over him from the dragonet on the other side of the screen and his emotions smoothed out until they no longer tore at his insides.

Holy shit, she's a powerful Healer already.

"Yeah, that'd be great, Lucenarra."

"Okay. Grandmama, I'm gonna take the computer outside to show Denarrion the Mandala, okay?" Luce shot a look to the side of the screen as she picked it up.

He heard Solenarra respond the affirmative and his view shifted as she walked outside.

"You know, you look better today, Denarrion."

"Do I?" he asked, amused. "I feel better, too."

She nodded. "I can tell. You're listening to your heart now instead of the wrong ideas in your head."

"Yeah, I'm tryin'. I think your mom had a lot to do with that." He sighed ruefully. "She helped me see I was pretty messed up. I have been for a long time."

"Decades?" Luce asked.

"Longer, I think. Maybe even a century." It felt good to admit it now.

"Are you done being messed up now?"

"Yes, I am. I'm gonna work hard to stay that way, too."

"Good. Mom needs someone to make her happy instead of sad. I knew you would make her happy when you were done being sad yourself." Luce stopped and turned the camera toward the ground. "Here's the Mandala. It's a really good one for today. See the swirly red designs? That's a protective pattern to aid in a battle of wills. And see the metallic gold square around the whole thing? That's so evil can't break into and corrupt the protective design."

Denarrion stared at the chalk painting with wonder and awe. The energy pulsed through the design in waves, and he could feel them through the screen. The Mandala had a circular shape, though it was contained in the golden square. Geometric patterns in blue, purple, green, and varying shades of yellow and orange surrounded the central pattern of swirling red.

The orange and yellow had been fashioned into flames, rising at even intervals to total seven large tongues. They licked through the crenulations of the greens, but remained encapsulated by the wavy lines of blue and the perfectly round circle of purple. The gaps between the purple and the metallic gold square were filled with four white lotus flowers with golden-yellow centers.

"Wow." He took in all the beauty on the ground. "What does it all mean?"

"Purple is for love, which is the foundation for the blue, strength, and strength allows for healing, the green." Lucenarra pointed at the design for him. "From all those, you get the power, the orange and yellow, to protect yourself and those you love, the red. That protection affects everyone in the family and community against evil. The metallic gold keeps that evil from disrupting the pattern."

"Wow." He swallowed hard. "Did you make this for your mom?"

"Yeah." Lucenarra turned the camera back to her face. "And for you."

"For me?"

"Yeah, because you're going to help her tonight." It wasn't a question.

"Yes, I am. I promise we'll do this together."

"Good, 'cause she needs you and your help. Don't let her die, okay, Denarrion?"

The world caved in on him for a moment. "I won't. Charlorrion, Torriandra, and I will help her and keep her from dying. I promise."

"Okay." She bit her lip and nodded again. "I'm gonna give the computer to Kressendra for a few minutes 'cause she wants to talk to you, too. Okay?"

"Yeah, okay. Hey, Lucenarra?"

"Yeah?" She paused to look straight in the camera.

"Thanks for showin' me the Mandala. I appreciate it." He gave her his best smile.

"You're welcome, Denarrion. Just keep your promise, okay?"

He didn't have time to nod before she yelled for Kressendra, and the computer was handed off to a younger girl. He didn't know why Kress would want to talk to him, but he waited patiently for her to settle with the computer on her lap.

"Denarrion, do you like my mom?"

Well, damn, she doesn't pussyfoot around.

"Yeah I do, very much." He raised his eyebrows. "Why? Doesn't it seem like I like her?"

"Yes, it does and you don't feel as 'growly' as you did before," She looked him up and down.

"That's good, right?"

"Yes, that's good." But she still wore a thoughtful frown on her face as she looked at him, tapping one little finger against her lips.

"What?" He hid his smile at how cute she looked.

"I was talking to her before you and she was sad. She'd lost some of her sparkle." She fixed him with her deep purple eyes. "Did you take away her sparkle?"

He grimaced a bit as he rubbed his chin. "I might have. It wasn't my intention, but sometimes we all make mistakes."

"Is she sad because you're too stuck being something you're not?"

He nodded slowly. *Might as well take my lumps.* "Yeah, I wasn't feeling well for a long time before your mom came to Redfield. I didn't know it until she showed up. We've had a few disagreements, but it doesn't mean we don't like each other."

"Disagreements about what?" Kressendra tilted her

head and frowned.

He sighed. "We disagreed about how much we should show the humans. Dragons aren't supposed to show humans we exist because it's dangerous. There're a lot more humans than dragons and we don't want them to try to hurt us."

Kressendra bit her bottom lip. "But Mom and Grandma say some humans are "practicers" of the old ways and they're the ones the dragons must stay connected to. To protect the earth from the Evil Ones." She dipped her chin to meet his gaze. "Dragons can't do it alone. They gotta have the help of the younger people so the protection can be complete. Mom says the dolphins have already agreed and so have a few humans, but the dragons gotta hold up their end of the deal."

The last of his father's beliefs cracked and fell away, defeated by the simple logic of a dragon child. *Damn, this kid's smarter than me.* She wasn't less careful around humans, but she understood the value of their help in the fight against the demons.

"You know, you don't need anything else to be a dragon. You're good just the way you are."

"I don't?" He laughed. "Not even horns on my head, a long tail or wings on my back?"

"You already have those, you just aren't wearing them right now." Kressendra shrugged and grinned. "But I can see them anyway."

Denarrion raised his eyebrows. "You can? Even through the computer?"

"Yes. I think you're a pretty dragon. Just like Mom." She nodded with a big smile. "I'm gonna go outside now. Bye, Denarrion."

He laughed as she darted away from the computer, trying to ignore how much her compliment meant to him. He rose and returned to the kitchen to find Lissandra sipping her coffee with Torriandra.

"I've been dismissed if you'd like to talk to your kids again." He gave her a smirk. "Those ladies are a force to be reckoned with."

"Oh, yeah, they're gonna bleach my scales when they get old enough to shift." Lissandra shook her head and disappeared into the dining room.

"Was it good to talk to her kids?" Torri offered him a full mug of coffee.

"Yeah, actually, it was kinda awesome. I'm looking forward to meeting them in person."

Torri nodded. "I hope that works out."

He raised his eyebrows. "You don't think it's gonna work out?"

She shrugged as she shot a look toward the dining room. "A lot can happen between now and what we have to do tonight. Demons are tricky and it might not go as easily as we hope. If you have anything you need to tell Lissandra, I suggest you do it before tonight."

"Why?" He clenched his jaw.

She shook her head. "I don't know. Just a feeling I have. Like the old tortoise says, 'the future is a mystery, the past is history, but this moment is a gift. That's why it's called the present.' Use it to your advantage before it's gone."

He swallowed hard and nodded. Whatever happened that night, he wanted to be sure to tell Lissandra how he felt about her and her kids and their courtship. She was his True Bonded mate and his place was with her, beside her. *In her.*

He snorted. His attraction to her had grown since the moment he saw her and now he wanted no one else. This would be his family and he'd do his best to uphold his role in it. He was done denying who he was.

The urge to shift into his true form rolled through him as he sipped his coffee. *Thank the Goddess.* It'd been decades since he wanted to shift at all and he planned to do it as often as possible when everything was over. What would it be like to fly with Lissandra, the moonlight shining along her wings and scales?

All they had to do was survive the night. *Yeah, a total walk in the park.*

****

Lissandra ended the Skype call and dropped her head into her hands. *Sweet Goddess, I don't want to die.* She wanted more time with her kids. More time to watch them grow, learn, and shift. And if she was completely honest, she wanted more time with Denarrion.

He'd changed significantly from the angry, lost, and disillusioned man she'd met a few days earlier, and she sensed his shift from human-centered views to dragon-centered. She wanted to be there for him, too.

But has he grown enough?

She closed the computer and sipped her coffee. Not yet, but only time would tell, and she didn't want to miss any of it. She'd told him she wanted a mate who already knew himself, but it wasn't completely true. She wanted to be with him and strengthen their connection as mates, but she'd help him learn all the things she knew about being a dragon.

You were being too dragon.

Denarrion's words echoed in her head and she shifted uneasily. Yes, she wanted more time with him and would help him find his true dragon self, but those words reminded her he needed time. He wasn't ready to be the dragon she needed. Even if they killed the demon—*when we kill the demon*—he needed to grow up and learn himself without her before he could work on their dynamic.

And he hasn't spent any time with the kids.

She'd been thrilled when he willingly spoke to Luce and Kress on Skype. He didn't seem nervous or uncomfortable at all and that made a world of difference to her. She'd promised she wouldn't seek death in the fight ahead, but she meant what she'd said about paying the price if a life was needed.

She sighed. *Only time will tell.* In the meantime, she'd have a nice afternoon with the Ravenwings and Denarrion, and hope the Goddess protected them all when the time came.

****

The rest of the afternoon slipped away from Denarrion like smoke. He tried to hold onto it, being present every moment, but his disquiet ramped up the closer they got to sunset. His concern for Lissandra and the Fire Spirits' warning wouldn't leave him alone.

I have to protect her, no matter what.

He wanted to hold her tight and defend her, but she was here specifically to kill the demon and he couldn't get in her way. *Dammit.* She was a warrior, but that didn't stop him from worrying.

"Hey, I wanted to tell you your daughters are amazing." He caught her around the waist and swung her chest-to-chest with him.

"Yes, they are." A soft, proud smile curled her lips. "They're beautiful and will be excellent dragons. I miss them."

"They already are excellent dragons." He nodded as he squeezed her. "They probably learned it from their beautiful mother." He paused to meet her lavender gaze, need and something else making his smile fade. "I love you, Lissandra."

"After only three days?" She tilted her head, but her voice held only curiosity.

"Yes, after only three days," he admitted. "I can't imagine my life without you in it."

She smiled, but sadness sat on the edges. "Let's see

how tonight goes."

"Seriously, I love you and I need you." He stared into her eyes, trying to put all the sincerity into his gaze. "We all will be there to help you when you take on the demon. Let us help and we'll all make it through this."

"I promised, Denarrion." She squeezed his arms. "I won't try to die. I definitely don't want to, but I also can't allow the demon to escape. It has to die tonight." She grimaced. "We'll take it as it comes, okay?"

"I know, Lissandra, and we won't let it get away. Just know that I love you. We can have a great life together." How could he make her understand? "I've changed. I already feel better after my time in my natural form. I don't want to be anything other than a dragon. Do you believe me?"

"I do, but let's just see how it goes, okay? We still have to make it through tonight."

"Why are you holding back? What more can I say to convince you?"

Lissandra laid her hand on his chest and bit her lip. "You don't have to say or do anything, Denarrion. You're already better than last night."

He narrowed his eyes. "Why do I hear a *but* in there?"

She shook her head. "No buts. You need to heal and there isn't time before we have to fight the demon. I don't want to make any promises beyond what I already have."

Denarrion's fears and worries banged around inside him, but he closed his eyes and tried to let the barbs of panic pass him by. He pulled her into his embrace and held her tightly against his body. She fit perfectly within his arms. He loved her scent and her heat comforted him. He knew he had to let her go, but he couldn't seem to release her.

"Just don't give up on me, okay? I know I've been a blind jackass, but I'm not out of the fight yet." He pushed her back and met her gaze. "I see the truth and am working back to health. Don't give up on me."

She cupped his cheek with a compassionate smile. "I know you are." She patted his cheek and stepped out of his arms. "I'll see you on the island, okay?"

"Yeah." He sighed. "Okay. See you."

She opened the door to the house and stepped inside as Torri came out. She nodded to him before she strode out into the yard and shifted into her golden dragon form. She shot him a look with one amber eye before she launched into the air with a powerful stroke of her wings.

He watched her fly toward the reservoir. She'd set up the energy Mandalas to cage the demon in once they brought it to the island. Denarrion straightened his shoulders and lifted his chin. It was time to take down the demon that had fooled him for decades. *You're gonna die tonight, mudfucker.* He took a deep breath and strode off the porch to his truck.

CHAPTER TWENTY-TWO

Denarrion parked his truck in his parents' driveway and sat for a few moments. He needed to find calm if he had any hope of sneaking up on Walter. His thoughts churned with fury at the thought of the demon in disguise, but he soothed himself with a reminder that they knew it was there now. He just had to get the jump on it.

He took a deep breath and let it out slow. He didn't have much time to get the demon to the island, but he needed a few moments. Fear for Lissandra's loss popped up and turned his guts cold. What if he lost her? How would he make it through the rest of his miserable life? He shook his head. *No, there has to be a way to make the sacrifice without losing her.* He raised his gaze to the little brick house and scowled. *I'll find a way.*

He sealed his emotions behind a mental wall and pushed out of the truck. He wouldn't let the demon know it had riled him. That had been its advantage all these years and he never understood why he felt so empty and drained when he left his parents' home. *The mudfucker was killing us all slowly.* He shook his head as he walked to the door. The reign of destruction had almost reached its end. Denarrion took a deep breath before opening the door and stepping inside.

"Dad, Mom, you home?" He inhaled as the door closed and damn near gagged at the rotting stench. He'd recognized it as part of his father's illness, but it'd never been this bad.

"Denny?" His mother's voice came from the kitchen. "That you? What are you doing here?" She stepped into the hallway, wiping her hands on a dish towel.

"I came to see Dad. Is he around?"

Gloria's face creased with a frown. "I think he's out back. Where's that widow of yours? Did she calm down and come around like I thought she would?"

Denarrion tipped his head, scanning her body. She appeared to be covered with a putrid haze as if she wore a shroud. *Aw, Mom.* Lissandra had been right. The demon had used the bond between Gloriana and Waltarrion to cripple them both. The hackles on the back of his neck rose, but he resisted the urge to blast her with cleansing dragonfyre. How could he have not noticed the taint before?

He cleared his throat and looked away. "No, Mom, she didn't. She's still angry and I don't think she'll ever forgive me for hiding my true nature."

Gloria's nostrils flared and her eyes glowed an eerie green for a moment. Denarrion braced himself for an attack, but she shook her head and shrugged. The threatening energy receded and he breathed a little easier. *When did I start sensing energy?* He swallowed hard and tried to keep his own energy calm and innocuous.

"Give her time. I can tell she really liked you so she might be able to get around that little fact." Gloria set the towel aside.

"I dunno, Mom. She was really mad." He rubbed the back of his neck. "I kinda need to talk to Dad about it."

She narrowed her eyes but nodded. "Sure, sure, honey. Go ahead. I think he's on the back porch."

"Great. Thanks."

Denarrion clenched his teeth together and tried close his nose to the increasing stench as he approached the back door. A headache stabbed at him from the odor and he rubbed his watering eyes as he stepped outside.

The source of the stench sat in a chair on the back porch, drinking overly sweetened lemonade. Denarrion paused on the threshold and studied the husk of his father.

The once healthy head of hair had been reduced to thin wisps over the mottled crown. Age spots showed through it and the scalp appeared gray. Waltarrion had been tall with wiry strength, but the body now sat stooped and hunched as if the demon hadn't been able to fill the space. The hand grasping the glass of lemonade beside the chair was skeletal and clawed, the nails long and discolored.

"Is there something you need, Denny?"

The withered creature in the chair didn't bother to look at him. The voice sounded scratchy and irritated, instead of smooth and calm. *Maybe I never noticed the scratchiness because I was too fucking enthralled.*

"Yeah, Walter, I wanted to talk to you about this blind date you set up." Denarrion made his voice hard and angry. *Not hard to fake.* "Why in hellwinds did you set me up with that widow anyway?"

"Don't you swear in this household, young man." Walter glared at him, malevolence swirling off him like smoke. "You'll speak respectfully toward your elders."

Denarrion clenched his jaw to keep from laughing. *Elder my ass.* His father had died decades earlier and it pissed him off.

"Yes, sir." He bowed his head and the demon relaxed. "I'm serious, though. Why her?"

Walter shrugged, his lips pulling down as he gripped the lemonade. "You needed a mate. Isn't that what dragons do? We mate and beget more dragons. It's our role in the circle of life, or whatnot."

Denarrion nodded, shoving his disgust down deep. "And you thought she'd be the right mate for me?"

Walter smirked as he licked his lips. "It didn't matter what I thought. Pretty much any female is right for you, yeah?" A rusty, derisive laugh rattled from his chest.

Denarrion tightened his hands into fists, allowing some of his anger to fuel his movements. The demon wouldn't go down easy unless he caught it by surprise.

"Is that what you think, old man? That I fuck anything that walks by?"

"Isn't that what you've done? Damn, boy, your scent is all over this godforsaken town. Every woman carries it except your mother and sister. I'm surprised you haven't fucked them, too."

Walter grinned with pure malevolence and reached to set down his glass. Denarrion spun and slammed his fist into Walter's head, just above the left ear. The old neck snapped back and the older man slumped over the side of the chair. Denarrion swallowed hard and reined in his fury as he listened for footsteps. Had anyone heard him?

Precious seconds passed as he held his breath, but no one came to rescue Walter. *Serves you right, you old mudfucker.* He stared at the broken body of his father and saw nothing but the putrid energy wafting around it.

You killed my father, you slimy mudfucker. He couldn't stop his snarl as he grasped the old man's body. Gritting his teeth, he hefted it over his shoulder in a fireman's carry, swallowing hard against the smell.

He stepped off the porch and headed for the back gate of his parents' yard. The alley behind the house remained empty of life and he briefly wondered if even the animals avoided the demon. *Wouldn't surprise me.* He ducked back as a car pulled into the alley from the cross street and moved to the side so its headlights wouldn't catch him.

Fuck, that was close.

How in hellwinds would he get the demon to the

reservoir from here? He bit his lip and carried the stinking body around the side of the house, hoping he met none of the neighbors. This part of town was densely populated and someone would notice him carrying Walter.

The sun sank behind the trees and darkness crept out of its hiding places. He carried the demon to his truck, praying his mother remained in the kitchen and his sister didn't look outside. He'd caught the demon off guard. Hopefully it hadn't been able to send out a distress call to his mother and sister.

He threw the body into the back of his truck and bound the mouth, wrists, and ankles with duct tape. *That should hold it until I get to my place.* He started the truck and backed out of the driveway, fighting against the urgency firing through his body. He had to look at ease or someone would clue into his nefarious actions.

Denarrion was white-knuckled by the time he arrived at his place and parked the truck. He'd almost gotten caught when a cop pulled up behind him at the stoplight before the bridge. But he'd accelerated in a calm manner and drove toward home, only remembering to breathe when the cop turned left off the bridge. Thank the Goddess.

He jumped out of the truck and opened the tailgate. Walter remained unconscious. *Good.* Denarrion took a deep breath and called his true form. Muscles cramped and shifted, bones snapping into place. The transformation didn't hurt as much as the night before, but he had to suppress a groan once he'd reached his natural form.

All right, asshole. Ready to go for a ride? Denarrion plucked the demon's body out of the truck bed and prepared to jump into the air. *Come on, wings. You just gotta hold us up until we get to the island.* He spread his wings and leapt, the downstroke not nearly as strong as Torriandra's had been. But he managed to climb above the trees. He just hoped that he had enough strength to fly with the body's weight to the island without crashing.

****

Lissandra stood beside an iron pole driven into the ground in the center of the smallest island in the Salmon Reservoir. The sun sank below the horizon, spilling pink, orange, and golden light onto the clouds in the sky, and she tried to take comfort in Nature's beauty. But the task ahead stole her pleasure.

This is why I'm here in Redfield. It's what I'm meant to do.

It didn't stop the damn butterflies in her stomach. She shook her head and stepped out of Charlorrion's way as he piled wood around the pole's base. They'd tie Walter to it and split his skin until the dragonfyre could extract the demon. She swallowed hard against the violence she'd be required to do. She didn't do torture, even on the demons she'd faced before. But this was a special case and she'd do whatever she had to to get it done.

Sweet Goddess, give me the strength to do it.

Wise Heart looked up from the lit brazier at the edge of the clearing and nodded once. He threw fragrant herbs onto the coals, encouraging the scented smoke to drift in the evening breeze. She inhaled a purifying breath and hoped it would bring her some much-needed calm. He chanted in a soft voice, the sounds mixing with the scents to create a sacred place for their ritual.

She dropped her chin, closing her eyes. Soon Denarrion would arrive with the demon and she'd have to face it. She gripped the special swords she'd retrieved tightly in each hand, testing their weight and balance. She rubbed her thumbs over the wrapped leather hilts as she studied the clear quartz pommels catching the last light of the day.

She hadn't used them in decades, but the narrow, double-edged blades remained sharp and clean. *They'll run with blood before this is done.* Done. That's where she wished she stood, not waiting for the event to start. *I'd like my fast-forward button now.*

Motion in the darkening sky caught her attention and she raised her gaze. The silhouette of a dragon winging its way toward them blazed against the indigo darkness. The setting sun painted him fire-orange as she stepped back away from the pole to give him space to land.

Glory be, he's beautiful.

His natural form, all sleek muscle and scale, sent arousal shooting through her. Her nipples hardened and her pussy wept when she thought of twining her long dragon's neck with his and feeling that hard, sinuous body wrapped around hers. Tears threatened to fall at the overwhelming desire to be intimate with him one more time.

Not tonight. Maybe not ever.

Denarrion landed hard, his wings fanning the flames of Wise Heart's fire. He kept himself from crushing his burden, but the strain showed in his panting breaths and his shaking limbs.

"Are you okay?" She bit back a smile.

:Give...me...a...minute.: Even his mental voice was out of breath.

All humor fled as the ghastly figure in his talons rolled onto the ground. The demon. It no longer looked like Waltarrion, not that she'd seen the dragon warrior in his prime, but the body had become more hideous since the night before.

The creature's skin was gray and flaky as if peeling from a bad sunburn. Dark age spots dotted the head and hands and the body looked emaciated, the cheeks of the face gaunt enough to see the edges of the humanoid skull beneath the skin. The nails on the hands had grown long and curled as if the creature had not bothered to take care of them, but she distinctly remembered its nails being manicured the night before. What had happened between then and now?

The demon's head lolled to one side and she swallowed against bile.

Holy shit, that thing's hideous.

:Fuck, flying is hard enough. But carrying a load took it outta me.: Denarrion shook his head, his wings slowly folding back up. *:Let me stand this piece of shit up.:*

He shoved the body against the pole, holding it upright while Charlorrion wrapped steel chains around the throat and legs, and tied the wrists behind the back. Lissandra stifled a shiver. She didn't want to touch the putrid thing, but they couldn't take the chance the demon would worm its way out.

"It is time, Fire Sister." Wise Heart threw more herbs into the flames.

Showtime.

She threw her head back and allowed her natural form to come forward. Freedom and relief followed as her body shifted into its proper dimensions, and her perceptions of the world clarified. The demon's putrescence solidified in front of her and she no longer could see anything of Waltarrion. The evil creature inside had disfigured the body too much.

She shook her head to clear her nose of its stench but it suffused the very air.

:Now, Denarrion.:

Her bonded mate exhaled a plume of sacred dragonfyre onto the wood at the base of the pole as Wise Heart chanted in a voice that seemed to come from the rocks of the Earth herself. The unfamiliar words held power and seductive temptation to the Underworld denizen. The power slid past her and wrapped itself around the emaciated body bound to the pole.

Crimson red flames licked at the wood and the body hungrily. She rejoiced in its sacred purity and stepped close, bathing her nose in its heat. She would've stayed longer but the stench of the demon's rot drove her away.

Scowling, she reached forward with a talon and tore through the belly. The demon's eyes opened and it shrieked in fury and pain. She growled and tore another gaping wound in its opposite side. Putrid yellow blood spattered onto the ground, hissing as the dragonfyre consumed it. But the wound closed faster than she expected. Hatred oozed through the air in a gray haze as the demon struggled to free itself from the chains.

"You think you can burn me, maggot? I'm in one of your stinking bodies. It doesn't burn."

Denarrion growled, but Lissandra laughed and swiped her claws across its exposed belly, reopening the wounds.

:We can burn you. You're flammable on the inside.:

The demon raised its head and howled as the fyre caught on its protruding entrails. They briefly smoked in the flames before the wounds closed, again too quickly.

"You can't kill me, you stupid bitch. You can't burn it and it heals fast. Did you think I'd be easy to kill?" The thing laughed but winced as she swiped at its legs. "When I get free of these chains, I'm going to destroy your relations, your whole festering brood. There won't be anyone left to stop me."

It wouldn't get free. She'd make sure of it, but her talons weren't doing lasting damage. *Why can't I wound it enough?* If by chance it did manage to get out of the blessed chains, it still remained caged by Torriandra's Mandala star. *I hope.* She couldn't sense the power, but the *Morukai* didn't appear concerned.

The glowing green eyes fastened on her. "You have daughters." It grinned and wiggled its hips. "Are they ready for mating? Would they enjoy feeling their innocence lost to my fucking? Because I will take them and hold them down, until they scream while I use them for my pleasure."

Black fury rose in her chest. *It can't hurt the girls if I kill it.* She couldn't let it distract her, or all their efforts would be for nothing. She had to weaken it enough to allow the body to die. She gritted her teeth and focused on her rhythm. *Slash, slash, slash, slash*, on her heartbeat.

"More fire, Denarrion."

She struck harder to open larger and wider wounds, but the wounds still closed. He took another deep breath and strengthened the dragonfyre, pouring it over the gray, desiccated body.

The demon turned its attention to Denarrion. "You pathetic whelp." It sneered at him, its wounds closing without burns. "I'm surprised you could find your disgusting form. The sight of it offends me. Do you hear me, boy? Don't you know better than to show off?"

Denarrion continued to blow tongues of flame into the tears in the demon's flesh. When the goads didn't work, it scowled.

"You were so easy to deceive, so gullible! Did you enjoy fucking the entire population of Redfield? Did you use all the females up? Perhaps you even moved on to the animals when you ran out, hmmm?"

Lissandra shook her head. It wasn't working. It had been so long since she'd faced a demon, and she'd always been in human form when killing them. *Yeah, but they were never in a dragon's body.* No, but she'd used blessed swords, much like the chains encircling this demon's body. *Damn, I've been out of the game too long.*

She stepped back away from the pyre and took a deep breath then focused on stuffing herself back into her human disguise. The world grew dull and muted as she opened her eyes to face the glowering creature bound to the post. She concentrated and reached into her little wormhole of space between dimensions, retrieving her blessed Damascus steel swords. They settled into her grip like long lost friends and their blessings hummed along their blades.

Now let's see how well you heal with these babies.

"Swords?" The demon cackled. "How primitive. What

do you think swords are going to do, maggot? Dragon body, remember?"

She didn't bother to answer as she stepped closer and slashed at the demon, falling into the rhythm she hadn't practiced in nearly three decades. Her arms ached immediately but she kept her movements fluid. The demon shrieked as the blessed steel slashed through its skin. The wounds appeared to take a little longer to close, the edges cauterized by her blades. She had to keep going, despite the fatigue growing in her arms.

She threw herself into her moves like a dance, slashing in a constant blur of motion. Her attention centered on damaging the old dragon's body enough to burn the demon out. She heard nothing but the crackle of the fyre, the chanting of the shaman, and the singing of the blades.

You will die and we'll be free.

Charlorrion shouted a warning as someone slammed into her, knocking the breath out of her. She shrieked as she dropped the swords, trying to roll out of the way. *What the fuck?* Her assailant kept beating at her with their hands and she couldn't get a clear view of them to retaliate. *Oh, Goddess, give me strength.* She kicked out with one foot, slamming into her attacker's chest and scrambled to her feet.

Walter's body had started to burn, the flames of the dragonfyre licking at his wounds like a hungry dog. Denarrion kept adding more fyre to the pyre as Charlorrion added wood, but neither could stop. If they didn't keep up the heat and flames, the ritual would fail.

A shadow distracted her and she shot a look toward the other side of the clearing. Another dragon had arrived, a gracile, indigo-colored beast with graceful horns and spines down her back. *Suriana? What is she doing here?*

The person attacking her moved closer to the fire and Lissandra got a good look. *Sweet Goddess, it's Gloria.* The older dragon staggered to her feet, her face a mask of hatred as she stood glaring with green, glowing eyes.

Lissandra's gut sank. *Aw hellwinds, the demon's controlling her.*

"You will pay for this, worm dung." The older woman threw herself at Lissandra again.

Lissandra hissed and dodged, trying to edge closer to the discarded swords.

:Lissandra, shift and she can't hurt you.: Denarrion called to her but kept his head facing the flames eating away at Walter's body.

She shook her head. *:I can't. There isn't enough space with you and your sister here.:*

"What the fuck are you doing, Gloria?" She danced around the pyre as she searched for her blades.

"Protecting my mate!" The older dragon snarled in a hideous voice as she snatched one of the discarded swords. "He must not be harmed and you'll pay for trying to kill him."

Lissandra darted to the second sword and spun to meet Gloria's new attack. She stared into the woman's mad eyes as she parried the swift and vicious blows. Nothing was left of Denarrion's mother and she had to make a decision.

I'm so sorry, Denarrion.

With the demon's added strength, Gloria fought harder than Lissandra expected. *Sweet Goddess, don't let her win.* But this was all her fight. Denarrion had to keep blowing the dragonfyre, and it burned so hot, it constantly needed fuel or it would fizzle out. She spun past Charlorrion who watched with sorrow as he threw more wood on the pyre.

"I'll keep Suri occupied in case she's being held in reserve." He nodded to the indigo dragon as Lissandra stepped past him.

"Thanks."

"Die, dragon bitch." Gloria sneered as she came at Lissandra again.

Holy glory, I might not win this one. She was on her

own.

****

Denarrion's guts clenched as his mother tackled Lissandra. *What the fuck?* He wanted to separate the women but he couldn't stop the stream of fyre without allowing the demon to heal. *This gives a whole new meaning to a sucky blowjob.* He tried to keep his focus on the flames licking at the dying body, but the shrieks and snarls distracted him. He shifted his body to keep one eye on the fight.

Lissandra and Gloria battled with the swords, sparks flying from the blades' contact. Denarrion had never seen his mother so animated before in his life. She attacked like a wild thing, slashing at Lissandra with a hellish scowl. The older woman drove her hard, slashing and stabbing until Lissandra tripped over a root in the ground behind her and fell to her back. Gloria landed on top of her in a second, driving the sword down into her belly and twisting it viciously.

Lissandra shrieked and her pain and shock blazed through Denarrion as if the wound had been given to him. He threw back his head and roared in agony.

:Suriana!: He keened a shrill sound at his little sister. She swung her blue gaze to him in confused fear, shifting her weight to different feet. *:Help Lissandra.:*

Suriana hummed in distress, her wings fluttering as she stared at her mother leaning on the sword through Lissandra's gut. She whined but didn't move, panic tightening her body.

Denarrion snarled with frustration. *:If you're not going to do anything, get your ass over here and blow fyre at this asshole. Now!:*

When Suriana hesitated again, he roared, *:NOW!:*

Suri scuttled to his side and took a deep breath,

exhaling dragonfyre as Denarrion whirled to face his mother. She pressed down on the sword in Lissandra's gut and gloated, her eyes glowing an eerie green. *She's gloating at my dying mate.* Rage nearly blinded him as he rose up on his hind legs.

Gloria whirled to face him, yanking the sword free. She raised it above her head to ward off his strike, but he knocked it aside and slammed his hand across her body, trapping her under his weight.

:*You attacked my mate!*: He snarled and pressed down on her body. :*How could you do that to me, mother? She's a dragon.*:

Gloria's lips pealed back from her teeth. "That's exactly why, you whining whelp. The fewer dragons on this gods-forsaken world the better. We would've gotten rid of a whole nest if not for this troubling maggot. Now she's dying and my mate will heal in her body."

Denarrion reared back in shock and horror. Who the hell was this? What had happened to his mother? The creature under his claws grinned back at him with malice as it struggled to get out from under his grip. He narrowed his eyes. Gloria no longer had control. She'd been corrupted by the demon's influence, and now it seeped into her the same way. *Holy shit, she can't even shift anymore.* Lissandra had been right. His mother was crippled, and the demon would try to save itself by shoving its essence into her while Waltarrion's body deteriorated.

Not on my fuckin' watch.

He struck before he could change his mind. He closed his jaws around her head at the neck and snapped his teeth together. A sickening crunch echoed in his breaking heart as he twisted the head sideways and decapitated his mother's corpse.

Blood fountained from her torn neck as the keening rose from the demon on the pyre. Walter's deteriorating body jerked as the demon returned from its desperate attempt to hide in Gloria. Denarrion spat his mother's head into the same pyre and stepped back off her body, his heart aching like it had been shredded with knives.

Aw, Goddess, Mom. What in hellwinds happened to you?

Grief tore holes in his gut as he turned away from the headless body to focus on Lissandra as she lay in a crumpled heap between the two fires. Suriana kept throwing him looks filled with fear, but she never stopped breathing dragonfyre.

Wise Heart's voice changed and the energy within Torriandra's Mandala star shifted. Instead of holding the demon, the ripples of power moved into an unraveling pattern. He'd never seen energy like this before, but it seemed to be "un-making" the creature within his father's body.

The body on the pyre collapsed in on itself, the flames glowing white as each piece burned to smokeless ash. The energy simply disappeared. *Holy shit, the* Morukai's *actually ripping it from the fabric of the Universe.* The shrieking hit a glass-shattering pitch as the demon unraveled into nothingness, but Denarrion turned away, grief and guilt searing pain in his gut.

That's not my pain.

"Lissandra!"

He needed to get close to her, but his dragon body was too big. Taking a deep breath, he focused on shifting into his human disguise, stuffing his body down into the smaller form. It hurt less and less the more he did it, but that pain was nothing compared to his mate's. He skidded in the dirt at Lissandra's side and checked her body. A large gaping wound marked her belly, oozing blood.

"Sweet glory, why isn't she healing? Come on, Lissandra. You gotta heal, now." He gathered her gently against his chest.

Charlorrion threw the last of the wood on the pyre and

dropped to his knees beside them.

"It's the swords. They're blessed, but the steel makes sure to cauterize the wounds so they can't heal as quickly." He met Denarrion's worried gaze with sorrow. "It's why they're so effective against demons. But it's the same for dragons, too."

Denarrion shook his head. "No. No, she's gonna make it." He angled Lissandra's face toward him. "Lissandra, come on, woman. Don't give up, dammit."

She opened her eyes and looked for him, but her gaze seemed unfocused.

"Denarrion." Her voice came out as a weak whisper. "I'm sorry. I think I got hurt." She grimaced. "I thought we could do it, but the Fire Spirits warned me."

"No, no, we *did* do it. The demon is dead. The Shaman did this crazy thing and unmade the POS. It's gone from every world now. I totally saw it. It's a done deal."

Her head lolled and he shook her gently. "No, no, no. Don't lose consciousness, Lissa. Please."

"I'm sorry about your mother, Denarrion." She closed her eyes. "I'm sorry I couldn't save her."

He shot a look back at the headless body of his mother. In the flickering light of the fires, a sparkling mist rose from the remains. His eyes focused on it despite his grief. The mist coalesced into the body of a dragon with eyes full of darkness and stars. For a brief moment, his dragon's sight overwhelmed his human form and he recognized the energy and spirit of his mother. The ghost rose away from its discarded body and swirled around him, smiling at him in gratitude.

:*Thank you, Denarrion.*: The voice he remembered from decades past tripped across his ears. :*Your actions saved us all. I'm free from the demon's grasp to fly with your father on the Spirit Winds. Your sister is free to grow into her beautiful self. And you, my son, won't be hurt any more. Be the best dragon you can.*:

Denarrion stared, sorrow closing his throat.

His mother smiled at him compassionately. :*Lissandra is dying and she needs you. Only your strength can save her now.*:

"How?"

:*Remind her that she's a dragon.*: The spirit of his mother winked before she soared upward and blinked out with the sparks from the pyre.

Remind her that she's a dragon. How in hellwinds would that help?

Then he knew.

"Lissandra, you gotta shift. Do you hear me? You gotta get into your true form or you're going to die." He moved her to the soft ground. "Come on. You gotta shift. Okay? Do it for your kids. SHIFT, DAMMIT!"

"Can't...Too tired." She shook her head, her breath slowing.

"Oh, Goddess, no. No, no, Lissandra!"

He shouted at her, shaking her to keep her eyes open, but she lay limply in the dirt. Her eyes remained open, but they didn't flicker or move to take in their surroundings.

"Lissandra, please." He moaned and held her face in his hands so her "sightless" eyes faced his. "You gotta shift into your true form to survive this, okay? The sacrifice has been made. Don't let the demon take more than its due. Please, Lissandra, I love you. Don't leave me here to forget again. I need you."

Denarrion stared at her and held his breath, waiting for some sort of response, but nothing came to his ears. The voice of the Shaman chanting and the crackling of the fire as it consumed the body punctuated the awful silence. Dread filled his being. *Please, Lissandra.* But she was too far gone, her eyes staring sightlessly up at the night sky. Tears filled his vision and a high pitched moan escaped from the back of his throat.

"Oh, Lissandra, no..."

The tears slid down his cheeks and he closed his eyes, bowing his head over her as the grief surged. What would he do without her? What would he tell her daughters? How could he face them after his own mother had caused her death?

"Please, Lissandra, don't give up. Don't die. We need you. Just shift for me, please."

Hope deserted him and he dropped his head against hers.

CHAPTER TWENTY-THREE

Agony tore through Denarrion. He'd lost so much. How would he recover from this?

When his forehead touched hers, her body shivered beneath him. He pulled back and stared at her, hoping he hadn't imagined it.

Her eyes had closed, but her breathing moved her chest and her arms pushed against his as if struggling to get free. He sucked a breath and scrambled to the side, using his arms to help her weak body turn onto its hands and knees. *Come on, Lissandra. You can do it.*

Her body rippled, her clothes fading and her skin turning light purple, but the effects wouldn't stay. The clothes reappeared and her skin lost its color. Again, the ripple effect shimmered across her form, but this time it had less power than the last.

It took him a moment to realize what was happening before he shot to his feet.

"Sweet glory." He backed away, waving to the others. "She's gonna shift and she can't move anywhere else."

Charlorrion backed into Suriana who watched with wide eyes. Denarrion waited, praying she'd be able to make the shift. But Lissandra lay on the ground unmoving, her eyes closed.

Please don't say she's done.

He crouched beside her, touching her shoulder. "Come on, Lissa, one more time. I'll do it with you, right? And you can use my energy to shift. Shift with me."

His words and his touch seemed to electrify her. Her body gave one last effort to change. As she pushed, he shifted with her and his energy blended with hers, strengthening the power meant to make the change.

This time, Lissandra's clothes disappeared and her skin turned purple, with scales. Her head lengthened and a tail shot out from above her buttocks. Her hands became talons and a pair of wings grew from her shoulders. The wound in her belly closed as her torso grew and lengthened. A pair of twin horns curled up from the back of her head, giving her a regal look. At last a large, iridescent lavender dragon with deep purple spines running down her back lay on the ground.

Thank the Goddess.

Denarrion admired his mate, her beauty striking him in a primal way. Her eyes remained closed, but her sides moved with her breath and steam rose in the warm air from her nostrils.

:Lissandra?: He brushed his muzzle along her neck and tingles of recognition sparked between them. They'd had a connection in their human disguises, but it was stronger after shifting with her and blending their energies.

:Denarrion? Where are you? I can't see!: Panic infused her voice and her tail lashed in the trees.

:Easy. I'm here, Lissa. Your eyes are closed. Open them and you'll see me.: He blew a breath against her cheek, following up with his muzzle.

:I can't. Oh Mother, why can't I open my eyes? What's wrong with me?: Her anguish stabbed at him like a sword, but he forced himself to stay calm.

He rumbled a soothing hum. *:Go slowly, Lissa.*

Breathe deep and relax. Take your time coming back to your body. You almost left us, ya know? When you remember the feeling of your body, you'll be able to open your eyes.: He hoped.

Her breaths came in bursts as her fear surged but soon she slowed her breathing and her body relaxed. He continued to hum, a sound he vaguely remembered from when he'd been young. It brought him comfort and he shared it with her as he nuzzled her cheek. She took a deep breath and slowly opened her lilac eyes.

:How you doin'?:

Her gaze rolled to meet his. *:I'm...still here. Is it done? Did we kill it?:*

:Yeah, it's gone.: He settled beside her body, lending his warmth to her as he continued his rumble.

Relief and happiness shot through him from their bond as she relaxed more, but confusion remained.

:What about the sacrifice? Who did we lose?:

Wise Heart had stopped chanting, but the drum kept the rhythm like a sacred heartbeat. Charlorrion stood to the side with Torriandra in front of him, wrapped in his arms. They both wore solemn expressions as Suriana's body shimmered and she dropped to her knees beside her mother's headless corpse. Tears cascaded down her cheeks, but she didn't make a sound.

:Oh.:

Lissandra gathered her strength beneath her and pushed up so she could stand on all four limbs. She groaned in exhaustion and braced herself against Denarrion's side.

:I'm very sorry.: She heaved a sigh as she took in the charred remains on the pole. *:Thank you for saving me. If you hadn't killed Gloria, the demon would have lived on in her and it would've killed me for sure. It was trying to siphon its essence into her when you tore her head off.:*

He nodded. *:I know.:* He grimaced at the memory.

:Do you?:

:Yeah, I felt the change in her energy.:

:That's good. Oh, not that your mother died, but that you're using your dragon gifts now. I'm sorry, Denarrion. She was so coated with taint, I couldn't see the dragon part of her anymore.:

He took a deep breath and let it out in long, sad, sigh. *:Yeah, she was too far gone.:*

:I'm sorry. For both of you.:

:Don't be.: He shook his head and rattled his wings. *:It had to be done and it freed her and my sister from the demon. It freed us all. And I still have you.:* He tentatively stretched his neck out so he could nuzzle her cheek with his nose. *:Don't I?:*

She swung her head to look at him with both eyes, her expression thoughtful.

:Please, Lissandra. Tell me that I haven't lost you after all we've been through.:

He felt his heart plummet into his gut as she studied him. *Dear Goddess of All, don't let her turn away from me now.*

She took a deep breath and closed her eyes, shifting back into her human disguise. She staggered a little but caught herself and braced her hands on her knees, breathing hard. He missed the weight of her against his side but forced himself to hold still.

"Damn, I'm tired. That demon packed a serious punch."

Denarrion rumbled his laugh despite the fear coursing through him. *:There's a reason it hid so well for so long.:*

She nodded as she slowly straightened. "Yeah, that's true. I'm just glad it's over and I can go home."

He stiffened. *:Home?:* Was she leaving Redfield without him?

She nodded. "Yeah, home to Cloudburst. I miss my kids and I came close to dying tonight. I want them to know I'm okay. Hug them. Let them tell me about melting crayons in the sun or hunting elk in the lowlands."

:What about us?: He hadn't meant to ask the question, but his heart sank as she gave him a sad smile. *:After tonight, it can't be too late.:*

She laid her human hand on his snout. "You need to heal, and to figure out who you really are, Denarrion. You've been under the demon's influence for so long, you've forgotten to be a dragon."

:But I'm remembering, and I'm growing stronger. Please, don't go.:

She sighed and straightened. "You need time. You're already learning how to be the dragon you can be, but you're not there yet. There's no shame in that, but I have my own healing to do. Take all the time you need, then come find me. You know where I'll be."

:But we're True Mates.: His voice had grown panicked, but he didn't care. *:Please, Lissa. We're meant to be together.:*

She shook her head. "Yes, but you need time to recover, and to help your sister, too. She's just as lost as you were when I arrived, and now she's lost her mother, too. She needs you to be there for her. Help her find her own footing, get your affairs in order, and come find me. I'll see you in Cloudburst when you're ready."

She straightened, took a deep breath, and shuffled over to where the *Morukai* stood with Charlorrion. Denarrion wanted to scream and rail at her not to go, but he couldn't argue with her logic. He *had* been under the influence of the demon, and he'd forgotten all the things that made him a dragon. But her determined retreat tore a hole in his heart deeper than the loss of his mother.

"Denarrion?" Suri's voice came out watery with grief.

He concentrated and stuffed himself back into his human disguise before he crouched beside her, wrapping one arm around her. "Yeah, I'm here."

"Mama's gone." Tears streamed down her face.

"Yeah, I know."

"Why? Why did you have to kill her?" He didn't hear anger, only confusion.

He sighed. "Because the demon would've used her body after we destroyed Walter's. She was bound by her True Bond, and it would've killed her the moment it possessed her." He squeezed Suri gently. "Before she left, Mom thanked me for freeing her to fly on the Spirit Winds with Dad. Our real dad, the dragon who taught us everything we knew before the Great Chicago Fire."

"Really?" She met his gaze, her indigo eyes full of hope.

"Yeah. No foolin'."

She nodded. "What are we gonna do now, Denarrion?"

He bit his bottom lip and shot a look toward Lissandra. "We're gonna finally get a chance to live our lives the way we want to." He met his sister's gaze. "You're gonna go back to Princeton to study environmental toxicology, and I'm gonna finish up my woodworking projects."

"What are we going to do with the house?"

"To be honest, I dunno." He shook his head. "I'm okay with razing it to the ground and selling the land. No one should live there until the demon's shit is removed. I'll stay in Redfield until we get it all squared away."

She frowned. "Are you going to leave Redfield?"

He dropped his chin to his chest, closing his eyes. "Yeah. It's not home anymore." He opened his eyes again. "But that won't be for a little while. I got some stuff to do first."

Suri frowned as she looked toward the others. "What about you and Lissandra? Aren't you going to be together? You're True Bonded mates, right?"

Denarrion nodded. "Yeah, we are. But she's gotta go home to her kids and let them know she's okay. And…"

"And what, Denarrion?" Suri's expression grew sadder.

"And we're pretty fucked up from living with a demon."

"Oh." She nodded and rubbed the back of her neck. "I'm not as fucked up as you might think, you know."

"What?" He raised his eyebrows and stood. "You're not?"

She rose with him and they backed away from the body on the ground. "No. Being away at school really helped. And, well, I met someone there who gave me a better perspective than Walter."

Denarrion narrowed his eyes. "Who's this person you met? Male or female? Is this person a dragon or something else?"

Suri chuckled. "I guess you are the big brother. Don't you worry about me. I might only be eight hundred and fifty years old, but I can take care of myself."

"How do I know this person is good for you?"

She raised an eyebrow. "You don't need to know. *I* know they're good for me." She patted his arm. "We have a lot to take care of here anyway, and I won't be going back to Princeton until August, so that gives us some time." She paused and tilted her head. "Will you be moving to Colorado then?"

He nodded. "We'll see. I definitely hope so. But I gotta fix myself and figure out all the things I've forgotten in the last century and a half.

"Yeah." She glanced down at the body again. "What do we do with that?"

"Burn it." Denarrion nodded sharply. "She's free and doesn't need the husk anymore."

Suri sighed and wrapped her arms around herself. "I didn't realize it had gotten so bad until I came home this summer. I wish I'd figured it out earlier."

"Yeah, me too. But the damn demon was there since the 19th Century. We should've noticed then." He wrapped an arm around his sister. "At least we got free and Mom isn't suffering anymore. We'll figure it out from here. And you can tell me who this friend is." The last came out as a growl.

Suri laughed. "Nice try, big brother. Ain't happenin'."

"Oh, you'll tell me, but I'll let it go for now."

She rolled her eyes before she retreated to stand with Charlorrion and Torriandra. She'd tell him eventually, but he had enough to worry about at the moment. *But her time will come.*

"I'm gonna get going, Denarrion." Lissandra patted him on the shoulder.

"What? You're leaving now?" His jaw dropped. "But you're exhausted. You should at least stay the night before you leave."

She shook her head. "I'm tired, but not so tired that I can't make it home."

"Oh, come on. We both know that's not true. Stay one more night with me, Lissandra." He turned and grasped her hands. "Please."

She tilted her head with a sad smile and cupped his cheek with one hand. "I love you, Denarrion. But I love you enough that I know staying even one more night won't help you. I need to go home, and you need the time to grieve and to regroup." She held up a hand to stop him when he opened his mouth. "I know it's not what you want, but we've only been together for three days. A few months apart will give us all the chance to be fully present in this relationship."

His shoulders slumped and he swallowed hard. "So this is it, then?"

"Not by a long shot, but I think we all need this time. You know where I'll be." She patted his arm. "Take care, Denarrion."

He grasped her arm before she could pull away and dragged her into a close hug, needing to feel her body against his one more time.

"I'll find you in Cloudburst. I love you."

"I love you, too." She squeezed him before she stepped back.

Nodding to the others and the *Morukai*, Lissandra gave him one more smile before she shifted and launched into the sky. He watched her wing away to the west, chasing the sunset.

He rubbed a hand against his chest where his heart ached until Charlorrion slapped his shoulder, making him jump.

"Don't worry. Cloudburst isn't that hard to find."

Denarrion raised an eyebrow. "How would you know that?"

A smug smile curled Charlorrion's lips. "'Cause I got a friend who lives there. His name is Shandor and he's the Captain for the Cloudburst Hot Shots. When you're ready, I'll hook you up with him."

"Hot Shots?" Denarrion snorted. "What, he's got a big ego or something?"

"No, dumbass. He's a Hot Shot, the groundcrew who works the wildfires that burn the living daylights outta the west." Charlorrion shook his head. "Man, you gotta get out of the east and expand your knowledge."

"Yeah." Denarrion lost his humor. "I'm working on that." He looked west, hoping to catch one more glimpse of Lissandra, but the night had swallowed her form. "Definitely working on it."

CHAPTER TWENTY-FOUR

"You okay down there?"

Denarrion raised his head from under the hood of his suffering truck and met the gaze of a blonde woman with steel-gray eyes and the scent of "other" on her. *Human, but...more.*

"Yeah. Kinda." He nodded with a grimace. "I'm not dead, but the truck might be."

Traveling across country from New York to Colorado in August had seemed like a good idea. The weather would be nice and the trailer he hauled wasn't too big. But he hadn't taken the higher and drier conditions of the Rocky Mountains into account. His truck overheated half way up Wolf Creek Pass on Highway 160 with only 35 miles left on his 1950-mile drive.

"Yeah, I'd say your truck is gonna have to sit a bit. Where are you headed?"

He straightened his back and rubbed the sweat off his face with his t-shirt hem. "I'm tryin' to get to Cloudburst, Colorado."

She gave him a brilliant smile. "Today's your lucky day. That's where I'm going. Lock up your truck and I'll give you a ride to town where you can arrange a tow truck."

Denarrion paused. He didn't really need a ride. He could shift and fly the rest of the way to Cloudburst, but not at midday in public.

"Yeah, okay. That'd be great." He grabbed his duffle bag and coat out of the cab, locked his truck, and climbed into the passenger seat of her jeep. "Thanks. Name's Denny."

She shook his hand. "Hey, Denny. I'm Moira. Where you comin' from?" She threw the jeep into gear and pulled back onto the highway.

"New York."

"The city or upstate?"

"Upstate. Little town called Redfield. You know it?"

She shook her head. "Nope, but if you're comin' from a small town, Cloudburst should suit you just fine. What brings you out west?"

"Would it be too cliché to say a woman?"

Moira laughed as they climbed the pass. "Nah. Usually that's the woman's line, comin' west for a man. Good to see it goes both ways." She shot him a grin. "This woman have a name?"

His lips curled into his half-smile. "Yeah."

Moira laughed again. "Ah, keeping that close to your vest, I see. That's fine. Just remember, while we're friendly to strangers, we do take care of our own."

He nodded. "I can appreciate that. She knows me and knows I'm comin'."

He'd never been much of a communicator before, but the events in Redfield had woken him up to a lot of the things he'd been missing. Like the large and varied Elder Races community around his little town. He hadn't realized a small but well-established werewolf pack lived just north of town. Or that the reservoir actually had a guardian. He'd been so blind.

He'd also started calling and Skyping with Lissandra

and her family. He didn't want to lose their connection. She seemed happy to talk to him, but the strain of being away from her took its toll while he dealt with selling his home, getting his sister set up to start her own life, and disposing of his parents' place.

And relearning to be a dragon.

It'd been tricky to shift and fly with so many people living in or around Redfield, but he'd managed to find times and places where he could be himself. The few times he was caught in his natural form, he managed to convince those who saw him that they either had seen a large bird or they were dreaming. He sincerely hoped it would be easier out in Colorado.

"That's good. Long distance surprises aren't always fun." Moira shrugged.

"But you might know another friend. He works as the captain of the Cloudburst Hot Shot team. You know, wildland firefighters?"

She nodded. "Yeah, I know them. They do search & rescue during the winters when the fire threat is lower. How do you know them?"

"My brother is a firefighter and he met Captain Shandor in the fire academy."

"Very cool. I own the Cloudburst Coffee & Spa in town, and we always treat the firefighters to coffee. They keep our town safe when the weather turns dry."

They chatted more about Cloudburst and the people she knew in town until she pulled up in front of an attractive brick building with large glass windows on the first floor. The summer sunshine made the whole place shine, but the coffee shop did a brisk business despite the heat.

"Hey, thanks for the ride into town." Denarrion grabbed his duffle and slid out of the jeep.

"You're welcome. I hope it works out with your lady. Maybe I'll see you around." Moira nodded.

"Yeah, thanks." He closed the door and let her drive on.

From what he'd seen of Cloudburst, he liked the look of it, though the energy was completely different from Redfield. *Must be a western thing.* He pulled out his cell phone, slung the duffle over his shoulder, and dialed his call, hoping Lissandra would be happy to hear from him.

****

Lissandra finished mixing herbs and spices into the burger meat when her cellphone rang. She moved to the sink to wash her hands before picking it up, and her heart leapt at the name on the display.

Denarrion.

Walking away from him back in May had been the hardest thing to do. His pleas to stay had almost changed her mind. How could she walk away from her True Bonded mate? But she knew in her gut he needed time. Time to heal, time to help his sister recover, time to deal with their parents' demise.

But she missed him and his company, and his touches. Sweet glory had she missed his touches. She loved getting his calls and the Skype connections, but she'd played it cool to make sure by the time he came to find her, he'd be totally ready.

"Hey Denarrion. What's going on?"

"Hey, Lissa. I love you."

She grinned even if he couldn't see it. "I love you, too. How are you?"

"Well, not as good as I'd hoped, but not bad." His voice sounded amused despite the words he'd chosen.

"Oh? What's wrong?"

"I kinda need a ride. Do you think you could come pick me up at the Cloudburst Coffee & Spa?"

Time froze and her voice stuck in her throat as the

ramifications of his question settled into her gut.

"Oh my glory! Are you here? Are you really here in Cloudburst?" She shouted the words into the phone, her heart pounding in excitement.

A short silence sounded on the other end of the phone. "You actually sound glad."

"Holy Mother, of course I'm glad. It's been three fuckin' months since I last saw you." She washed her hands before she headed to the front room to get her shoes.

He chuckled. "Yeah, I know. I just wasn't sure you'd be happy to see me after the way you said goodbye."

She shook her head with a grimace. "It was the hardest thing I've ever done, Denarrion. But I think it was the right thing." She paused as she shoved her feet into shoes. "But you're really here in Cloudburst?"

"Yeah, I'm really here and I really need a ride."

"Wait, how did you get here? Did you fly?"

"Nope. I drove, but the truck died on the east side of Wolf Creek Pass. Apparently, it's not used to dry heat and tall mountains." Chagrin and amusement mixed in his voice.

"Oh, no." She chortled into the phone. "I'm so sorry. How'd you get into town, then?"

"A nice woman named Moira Callahan saw me and stopped. She said she owns the Cloudburst Coffee & Spa shop in town."

"Well, aren't you just a lucky duck." She grinned as she grabbed her keys.

"Dragon. I'm a dragon, and yeah, I'm damn lucky."

She laughed as excitement zinged through her. "I'll be there in twenty minutes, dragon mate."

"Oh yeah, I like the sound of that. See you soon."

She hung up and shoved the phone in her pocket before throwing on a baseball cap.

"Mom, I'm gonna run into town for a bit. I'll be back in about an hour!" Lissandra shot out the side door without waiting for an answer. Her True Bonded mate had come home and she wasn't going to wait longer to see him.

She hopped into her Forerunner and turned the key, excited. *He's here. He's here. He's here.* She'd spent the last few months worrying if she'd made the right decision leaving him behind. *What kind of True Bonded mate does that?* But her gut told her he needed the time to find the real Denarrion under the bullshit the demon had propagated. How would he learn who he was alone if she'd stayed?

It didn't mean she'd walked away happily. She'd come home and reconnected with her kids, though she'd remained cool with her mother for a while. The underhanded way she'd arranged the blind date with Denarrion still irked Lissandra and it would take a while to trust the woman had her best interests at heart again. But he'd arrived and she had to force herself to stay at the speed limits on the roads so she didn't miss anything.

She pulled into a parking spot in front of the Cloudburst Coffee & Spa, and scanned the sidewalk. A blond man without glasses rose from one of the outside tables and she squealed as she shoved out of her truck.

"Denarrion."

The Puckish grin curled his lips and her whole body lit up with pleasure and arousal. She took three steps across the sidewalk and threw herself into his arms. Comfort and a distinct sense of homecoming flowed over her as his arms closed around her body.

"Damn, it's good to see you, Lissandra." He pushed her back and his ice-blue eyes crinkled at the corners. "I've missed you so much."

"I've missed you, too." She tilted her head. "What happened to your glasses?"

He shrugged with a smirk. "That was just to get the ladies interested. Now that I'm with my True Bonded mate, I don't need the accessories."

"I think you look fine without them and yeah, you definitely don't need the accessories for the ladies." She grinned. "So what the hell happened to your truck?"

He released her and shook his head. "I dunno. I guess it couldn't handle this place. It gave up on the other side of the pass."

"We should definitely talk to the local towing company and see about getting it to Cloudburst." She shook her head but couldn't stop looking at him.

Time and events had weathered him a bit, but he'd changed in other ways.

"You're different."

He raised an eyebrow. "I hope so. It's been a long three months and I got a lot done."

"Oh yeah? Tell me about it as we head over to the towing place. How's Suri doing?" She led him to her truck and they climbed in.

"She's doing pretty good." His smile became relaxed. "She's back at school this week and gearin' up for classes in environmental toxicology, like she wanted. I actually got her to do short flights with me this summer so we can both heal from the demon's influence."

"Yeah." She shot another look at him as she pulled into traffic. "How's that going?" She didn't want to ask and she didn't dare hope, but she forced herself to listen.

He rumbled a seductive chuckle. "That's going excellent. But I'll show you later when there aren't as many people around."

She snorted. "I wasn't talking about sex, Denarrion."

"Neither was I." He winked. "You were right about needing the time to figure myself out. There were a lot of things I was ignoring, and being a dragon was only one of them. Suri, too. We became closer as a family, especially when we razed the house and had the *Morukai* do a cleansing on the land. She said she'd like to come visit for the holidays." He stopped and grimaced. "At least if I'm still in Colorado then."

Lissandra bit her lip. "Don't you want to stay in Colorado?" Was he having second thoughts?

"Yeah. Hell yeah. But I wanted to make sure you're okay with it, right?" He gave her a hesitant smile. "'Cause you're the whole reason I'm the dragon I am. And if you don't want me here—"

"I want you here, Denarrion. I've missed you and Skype just isn't the same." She pulled her truck into the local towing place and parked. "I want you to be here, to stay here, and to work on our relationship for real this time. Without ulterior motives."

"Yeah, I'd like to do that. How 'bout we get my truck back first?"

"You know, if they can't tow it for a while, we can always go pick it up tonight when no one's around." She winked and grinned.

He laughed. "Yeah, right. *No* one's gonna be on the highway on a summer night when two dragons show up to pick up a vehicle." His voice dripped sarcasm. "Shit, I bet they'd swear Godzilla had stepped out to get them."

"Heh, or aliens."

He snorted and got out of the truck. Lissandra enjoyed listening to him explain the problem in his Brooklyn accent to the guys at the Cloudburst Towing & Trailers shop. Fortunately, they could go get his truck and they'd bring it back to Cloudburst that evening.

"You want me to come with you to get it?" She waved toward the mountains rising against the horizon.

Denarrion shook his head. "Nah, you don't have to. Once they bring it into town, I'll call you for a ride."

"Are you sure?" She didn't really want to let him go.

"Yeah, it's all good. I'll see you in few."

Lissandra nodded and watched them head back out of town. What the hell was she going to do for a few hours?

CHAPTER TWENTY-FIVE

The answer to Lissandra's question turned out to be, "Clean the house and convince her mother to take the kids somewhere for the night." Solenarra had raised an eyebrow but suggested they go for a camping trip for a couple of days in the San Juan Mountains. Lucenarra and Kressendra cheered and ran to pack their things as Sole pulled Lissandra aside.

"Are you sure this is a good idea?"

Lissandra raised her eyebrows. "What? Being alone with Denarrion?"

"Yes. I'm concerned about the demon's influence in him."

Lissandra snorted. "You're concerned about that *now*? Look, you set me up with him when he was definitely influenced by the demon. I know what he's like when he's tainted, but he's not tainted now."

Sole crossed her arms over her chest. "Are you sure?"

"Yes, I'm sure. He's my True Bonded mate and I have Sight. I can tell." Lissandra raised her gaze. "I wouldn't bring him here if I didn't know he was clear of the demon. *I* wouldn't endanger my children."

Solenarra scowled. "That's not fair, Lissandra. You're

a warrior who's tracked and killed demons many times. You weren't in any extra danger."

"I tracked and killed them when I knew what I was getting into. I never went in blind. Until this year." Lissandra shook her head. "Maybe I should consider finding a new place to live so you can have peace and quiet in your home."

"What?" Sole's scowl lightened into surprise. "You're planning to move out?"

Lissandra shrugged. "I have a mate now, and the girls are getting older. They'll be into finding partners and friends in a few decades. Neither of them has the Sight. Maybe we need to give you the space to train new warriors for demon hunting."

The idea had merit. Moving into her own space would give her and Denarrion the chance to start fresh together, and would allow Solenarra to either train someone else or start her own romance. Lissandra filed it away to consider more fully with Denarrion's input.

"You can't be serious. You'd take my grandchildren away from me?" Sole's eyes widened in horror.

Lissandra snorted and shook her head. "Mom, you deserve your own space to do as you wish. And if the girls, my mate, and I are always here, you'd never get any peace to do what you want to do, whether that's training new Seers or finding your own connection with someone."

"Don't be ridiculous, Lissandra." Solenarra shook her head with a frown. "I've had my mate and my offspring. Now I want to enjoy my grandchildren."

"You will, just not in your personal space." The idea of moving made sense the more she thought about it. "Look, Mom, take the girls camping in the San Juan Mountains for a couple of days. By the time you get back, I'll have a plan of action that'll be mutually beneficial for all of us. We'll talk about it then, okay?"

Sole opened her mouth to say more when the girls

came bustling in, their things haphazardly packed into bulging duffle bags. Lissandra laughed at their determination to take pretty much everything in their rooms and she and her mother helped get them a little more organized for the trip. Sole sent her baleful looks from time to time, but the kids didn't let her resume the conversation, for which Lissandra was very grateful.

It's my life, and I'm going to make it with my True Bonded mate. She didn't want to move far from Solenarra. Her kids benefited too much from having her mother around. But she needed a place that belonged to her and her mate, where they could nurture their relationship, and allow Solenarra to find her own connection.

Maybe with Lt. Henry Fitzroy.

She'd seen her mother take time and effort with her appearance each time they went into town, just on the off chance they'd see the police lieutenant. She liked the man and his interactions with her family. Solenarra always made sure to smile and flirt with him. He reminded Lissandra of Wise Heart from Redfield, with his wisdom and humor.

Sweet glory, he's a Morukai.

"All right, girls. Let's get going." Solenarra marshalled the troops toward the door.

"Aren't you coming with us, Mom?" Kressendra paused at the door of the kitchen.

"Not this time. I'm going to wait for Denarrion to get here."

"Denarrion?" Kress's eyes widened. "He's coming here? Oh, I wanna meet him when he comes."

"You will." Lissandra nodded as she ushered her daughter down the hall. "He'll be here when you get back from your fun adventure. Think of all the stories you'll have to tell him."

"I have stories now." Kress raised her chin and narrowed her eyes.

"I know, but I need to make sure our connection is

solid before I introduce him to you in person." She crouched in front of Kress and Lucenarra, meeting their gazes. "You both are very important to me. My relationship with Denarrion will never change my love for you."

"I know, Mom." Luce gave her wise smile. "It's gonna work out okay. I can feel it." Warmth and vitality flowed over her from her daughter.

That kid's gonna be a fantastic Healer.

"Thanks, Luce." Lissandra hugged her older daughter. "Have a good time with grandma."

"We will." Luce grabbed her repacked bag and trotted out the door. "Come on, Kress. We'll see Denarrion when we get back and Mom will be a lot happier."

"How do you know that?" Kress frowned at her sister as she grabbed her own bag.

"I just do. Come on."

"We'll stay two nights so you can be sure about Denarrion." Solenarra threw a backpack of gear over her shoulder. "Then we'll discuss the idea of moving out more."

Lissandra nodded, though she'd already made up her mind. "Have a good time. And thanks."

Solenarra smiled. "See you in couple of days."

Lissandra closed the door behind them and sighed. Her mother wouldn't like her decision, but the rightness settled into her gut as she looked around the house she'd lived in for the last thirty years. It had been meant as a place for her mother to train new Seers, but after Lissandra's loss, it had only been used for their family.

It's time for a new change. For all of them. But first, she needed to reconnect with Denarrion. *Maybe we'll shop for a new place when he comes.*

She busied herself with straightening up the house and changing the sheets on her bed, but she couldn't push away the anxiousness until Denarrion called with a need for a ride again. When the call finally came, she shot out the door into the late afternoon sunlight and headed for town. Excitement and anticipation thundered through her along with the sense of a new beginning.

****

Denarrion tried not to fidget as he waited for Lissandra in front of the mechanic's shop but the need to see his mate and spend more than a few minutes with her fired his blood. He wanted to start his new life, a life his truck had derailed for a few hours. *Yeah, a hole in the radiator will do that.* It would be a costly repair, but he didn't care if it meant he'd be able to stay with Lissandra.

A blond guy with a leather jacket sporting a gargoyle on a bike with flaming tires wheeled his Harley out of the mechanic's shop and paused on the sidewalk. Denarrion eyed him curiously, the sense of "other" hitting him square between the eyes. The biker glanced up at him and raised his eyebrows, a smirk curling his lips.

"What's up?" His voice was surprisingly smooth.

Denarrion blinked. "Oh, uh, nothin'. Nice bike."

"Thanks. You ride?"

Denarrion shook his head. "Nah, I never got into that. What's your club? I don't recognize the logo."

"Concrete Angels. Local club out of Fort Collins." The guy straddled his bike and settled his helmet on his head.

"Isn't that on the other side of the mountains from here?"

The biker nodded. "Yeah. I'm headed home from Vegas after a contract job. Glad to be in cooler places."

Denarrion nodded, his eyebrows up. "Yeah, I bet. How hot does it get there?"

"Hundred and ten Fahrenheit."

Denarrion whistled. "Definitely better here, I'd say."

"Yeah, I prefer the mountains over the desert." The biker turned the ignition of his bike and the thing rumbled to life with the patented Harley sound. "You here for the long haul or just visiting?"

Denarrion frowned. "Why do you ask?"

"I dunno. You look like a guy who's huntin' for a new home and the bag at your feet is kinda a giveaway." The biker shrugged. "If that's the case, this town is a pretty good place for the Elder Races. You know, if you're looking for a spot to settle down." He winked and rolled away, a grin curling his lips.

Denarrion barked a laugh and shook his head. The guy was cocky as hell, but he definitely had his secrets. Denarrion pulled out his phone to check the time before he glanced around, hoping to see Lissandra. Glory, he missed her.

"Hey, handsome, need a lift?" She pulled up beside him on the street and grinned through her open window.

"Hell yeah." He grinned as he leaned against the passenger door. "Can you help me get my stuff out of my truck? I don't want to leave it in the hands of the mechanics."

She grimaced. "Yeah, it might not be there when you get the truck back." She threw her vehicle into park and got out.

It took them a good twenty minutes to schlep his remaining possessions from his truck to hers, but overall he hadn't kept much from his life in Redfield. He'd brought his woodworking tools, his clothes, and a few momentos, including the bracelet she'd bought for him from the *Morukai*'s booth at the Redfield Craft Fair. He wore it all the time to remind him of his mate.

"All right, is that everything?" Lissandra closed the back of her Forerunner.

"Yeah, that's it." He nodded.

"Good. Let's go home."

Home. The word hadn't meant anything to him in a long time. But any place with Lissandra qualified. He climbed into the passenger seat with a new sense of adventure and hope.

The drive up to her place took about twenty minutes, but the colors of the sky through the trees made it magical. The season had shifted into full summer, but it wasn't as hot and sticky as back east. *Hot enough to kill my truck, though.*

They arrived at a modest log cabin high in the mountains that looked over the town to the north and Ponderosa pine forest to the south. Spaces around the cabin had been cleared to allow for dragon flight without snagging tails or wingtips on the trees.

"Wow, this place is nice." He slid out of the truck and stood on the crushed gravel drive.

"Thanks." She stared at the house for a bit before turning back to him. "It's been home for the last thirty years, but I'm thinking of getting my own place now that my mate is here."

Warmth welled in his chest and his lips curled into a smile. "Oh yeah?"

"Yeah. But we don't have to talk about that now." She came around and took his hand. "Right now, I want to welcome you home to Colorado." She paused and looked at him. "This is going to be your home, now, right? Or do you want to shuttle between Cloudburst and Redfield?"

He squeezed her hand. "Nope. I sold my house, got rid of my stuff, and pulled up stakes. Suri is good at Princeton and the house were my mother lived is gone. I'm free of Redfield."

Her smile bloomed into delight. "That's great to hear. Come on, let me show you my mother's house."

"Your mother's? Not yours?" He followed her up the walk to the cabin.

"No, not really mine. After Mikelorrion's death, we retreated here. But now that you've come to Cloudburst, we can start looking for our own place." She pushed open the front door. "I think we need our own place as True Bonded mates. Don't you?"

"Yeah, I do." He kicked the door shut behind him and grabbed her hand, tugging her close to his chest. "But I'll take what I can get in the meantime." He paused. "Are your kids and mother here?"

"Nope. I sent them on a camping trip for a few days." She grinned and his cock hardened with excitement.

"Well, then, show me your bedroom and you're mine tonight." He kissed her neck just below her ear before he licked the mating mark on her shoulder.

She shivered with pleasure. "I like the sound of that. This way."

She led Denarrion down the hall to her bedroom, her eyes sparkling each time she glanced back at him. The scent of her arousal filled his nose with each step she took. His cock hardened again and his desire fired his blood.

"Will I be sleeping in here with you?"

Lissandra laughed as she closed the door behind him. "You better. There's no way you're staying in a separate room while here."

"What about when your mother and kids come home?" He dropped his duffle beside the closet and turned to face her.

"I'm hoping we'll have already found a new place by then and it won't really matter."

He raised his eyebrows as she sauntered to him. "Are you thinkin' of buyin' or renting?"

She gave a one-shouldered shrug. "Buying. I have enough saved up in addition to the settlement from my husband's death. I think we could get our own place."

He grinned as he settled his hands on her hips. "Let's not forget I sold my own place in Redfield. The market is booming and I had lots of equity."

She tilted her head. "Where's your hoard?"

"Safe." He let his lips curl into a smile. "But I'm more

interested in this treasure right here." He held her hips and rubbed his cock through his jeans against her belly. This was his mate and he'd missed her.

Lissandra laughed. "I think you're giving me the treasure." She reached between their bodies and stroked his cock through his jeans. "In fact, I want more."

She pushed him back just enough to crouch in front of him. "I want to suck your cock before we make love."

He stood still, watching her as his heart thundered in his chest and his cock stiffened. He'd waited so long for this, he wasn't sure he'd last when they got down to it. She pulled his t-shirt out of his jeans and drew it over his head. He lifted his arms to make it easier for her, but when he reached out to touch her, she shook her head and stepped back.

"This is my time to play. I've waited long enough."

He grinned as he dropped his hands to his sides. "Play away, dragon lady."

She growled before she sucked on one of his nipples, licking his tiny areole and trailing her fingers over his ribs. He closed his eyes and groaned, reveling in her erotic touches. She grasped the waistband of his jeans and quickly slipped the button from the hole before sliding the zipper downward. His breath sped up as she dropped to her knees, kissing and licking the muscles of his belly.

She pushed his jeans down to pool at his feet, glad he'd worn loose boxers for the trip. She ran her hands up his legs to his inner thighs, brushing the hairs on his scrotum under the cloth.

Sweet glory!

He jerked in surprised pleasure at her light touches, closing his eyes as he dropped his head back. *Oh yeah, this feels awesome.* She followed the crease of his thighs where they met his torso and he moaned, stars flashing behind his closed lids. His cock pushed against the fabric as she rubbed her thumbs through the hair around its base, not quite touching the hot hard flesh. He thrust his hips to bring her closer, but she kept her fingers away.

"Do you like this, Denarrion?" She looked up his body at him.

"Oh, Goddess, Lissandra, you have no idea." He'd thought he remembered how it felt to be touched by her, but his imagination had failed to capture everything.

"Give me an idea." She spread her hands wider and rotated them so she could pull his boxers down off his hips. "Tell me what you're feeling. What you want."

His cock jerked again as his thoughts splintered into bursts of pleasure. The waist band slid down over his shaft and balls, sparking more arousal. He inhaled a shaky breath and tightened his hands into fists to keep from grabbing her.

"More." He groaned. "Glory, I want more."

"More of this?" She trailed her fingers down his legs.

"No. More of this." He grabbed his cock and tried to rub it over her lips. "Suck my cock, Lissa. Make me see stars."

She laughed huskily but shook her head. "It's not time for that, my dear mate. You'll have to be more patient."

He let out an agonized moan and released his cock, closing his eyes. *Damn, the woman's gonna kill me.* He couldn't help the thought that it would be a pleasant way to die.

She returned to torturing him with her fingers, heightening his arousal. Her scent intensified and satisfaction bloomed in his chest. *She's as hot for this as I am.* She slid her fingers between his scrotum and his thighs, cradling his balls to lick them. *Sweet glory.* He grunted and jerked his hips as she dragged her tongue up his shaft. She reached the apex of his cock, the little slit leaking pre-cum, and licked his essence away.

"Holy Goddess, Lissa; you're killing me." He couldn't stop the full body shudder.

"No, Denarrion, I'm pleasuring you." She engulfed the flared head of his cock with her mouth.

Hot, wet pressure stole his breath and his mind. He clenched his teeth and tightened his hands into fists to keep from thrusting hard into her mouth. He didn't want to hurt her, but his control began to slip.

He grasped her head in his hands and thrust in and out of her lips, careful to move slowly. She held his hips to steady herself as she rubbed his hot flesh with the tip of her tongue. She closed her eyes and moaned, the sound vibrating over his taut skin.

"Aw yeah, Lissandra. Your mouth is so fuckin' sweet."

She sucked harder and his orgasm threatened, but she pulled away and he whimpered at the loss of the glorious feeling. She grinned as she stood up and took one of his hands to lead him over to the bed.

"Lie down." She pushed on his chest.

"Lissa—"

She laid a finger on his lips, silencing him. "Lie down. It's my turn to pleasure you."

"But you sucked my cock."

"And I'm not done." She tilted her head. "You wouldn't want to miss out on what I have planned for you, would you?"

His cock flexed with anticipation and he settled on the bed, resting his back against the pillows on the headboard. She gave him a sultry smile as she removed her t-shirt. Her breasts bounced, free from any bra, and he damn near swallowed his tongue. She unbuttoned her jeans and pushed them down, underwear and all, wiggling her hips. *Holy glory, she's more beautiful than I remembered.*

The evening sunlight streaming through her windows bathed her in golden light and he lay stunned. Her beauty warmed him in places he hadn't known were cold. *Thank the Goddess I'm home.* Lissandra represented homecoming, comfort, pleasure, and love, and filled the lonely places in his being. *My True Bonded mate.*

"Did you know that you're beautiful, Denarrion?" She stood beside the bed, her expression full of wonder as she trailed her fingers down his chest and outlined the strong pectoral muscle above his heart.

He shook his head. "No one has ever said that to me before."

She snorted. "Really?"

"No one has ever said it and meant it." He met her gaze with his. "And no one who meant as much to me as you do."

A smile curled her lips as she sat beside him. "I mean it." She slid her hand around his hard cock and rubbed the shaft with her thumb. "I love your beauty and the strength that comes with it. It's erotic."

Pleasure exploded in his chest, but he raised an eyebrow. "Erotic?"

"Oh yeah." She crawled onto the bed, straddling him on her hands and knees. "I need you to do me a favor, Denarrion."

He swallowed hard as the scent of her arousal made his nostrils flare. "What kind of favor?"

"I need you to lick my pussy." She wiggled her hips again and his cock flexed beneath her belly. "I want you to suck on my clit and drink my cream."

Sweet Goddess of all. He managed a dark chuckle as he moved to get up.

"Then on your back, dragon lady—"

She grasped his shoulders and pressed them back into the bed. His cock flexed again at the erotic strength she showed.

"No. Like this."

She crawled up his body until she knelt with her knees on either side of his head and her pussy positioned above him. Looking down between her legs, she gripped the headboard and wiggled her hips again.

"Make me see stars, Denarrion."

"Oh ho ho ho, yeeeaaahhh."

He grinned as he ran his hands up her thighs to her hips, never losing her gaze. "This works for me." He tugged her down to his lips and dug in.

Sweet tangy cream met his tongue as he trailed it over her nether lips up to her clit. She whimpered and her hands tightened on the headboard as he feasted on her sensitive flesh. He dragged his tongue between her folds, stroking the tip along her nether lips to flick her clit. He was rewarded with her aroused moan and twitching hips, but he gripped them tight and held her still.

He growled against her soft flesh and she rocked her hips, whimpering with each breath. Her juices coated his tongue as he slipped a hand between her thighs to push a finger into her warm depths. Tight heat clasped his finger and she gasped at the intrusion, rocking a little harder.

That's it, dragon lady. Fuck my tongue and finger. He hummed against her pussy as he pushed a second into her dripping slit.

"Oh, Goddess, yes." Lissandra rocked harder as he sucked on her clit and pumped his fingers into her. "Harder, Denarrion. Harder!"

He obliged her with a moan of his own, licking and sucking on her lips and clit as he thrust his fingers between her folds. She wailed and ground down on his face, her fingers digging into the headboard. The bed rocked as she rolled her hips to add more friction against his fingers. He added a third finger and rubbed the special spot within her.

"Oh my glory, Denarrion. I'm gonna come!"

He growled as he thrust and sucked hard on her clit. She clamped down on his hand, wailing her pleasure to the ceiling. He drank down her release, satisfaction filling his chest and stiffening his cock. *I did this. I pleasured my mate.* He kept licking and sucking on her quivering flesh and her orgasm continued for minutes.

At last, she rested her head against the top of the headboard, panting and trembling.

"Oh glory, I don't know if I can move."

"Easy, Lissa." He grasped her waist and eased her down his body until they lay chest-to-chest. "Just enjoy. You're fuckin' gorgeous when you come. You know that?"

She shook her head, but her lavender eyes met his with drowsy contentment.

"And eating you out above me was one the sexiest things I've ever done."

"So, you liked it?"

"Oh, hell yeah." He licked his lips. "Anytime you need me to do it again, just ask."

She laughed. "Will do. But now I want one more thing."

"What's that?"

"Your cock, here, now." She gripped his dick hard and pointed at her pussy.

"Wish granted." He pulled her over on top of him and let her impale herself on his cock. "Oh, fuck yeah!"

Hot, tight pleasure spread from his cock to his chest and he groaned as she came to rest on his balls. *This is truly coming home.* He forced himself to keep his eyes open as he watched her bite her bottom lip when he was fully seated inside her. She matched his groan with her own and her pleasure enhanced his through their True Bond.

"Damn, you feel fucking amazing!"

"I'm all yours, Denarrion." She rolled her hips to build up the pleasure and momentum. "I am your mate, your female."

"Damn right, you are," he growled as he thrust his hips and pushed his cock deeper. "Look at me."

She moaned as she tipped her head forward, her lavender eyes glowing with arousal. He met her gaze and growled. She grinned as she angled her pelvis to accept him deeper and slammed down on him.

"So damn tight. So fuckin' perfect." He gripped her hips and thrust faster. "I will never get enough of you."

"Tell me you're mine, Denarrion." She met his thrusts and clenched her sheath around his cock. "Tell me you're my mate, my male."

He bared his teeth and dug his fingers into her hips. "Always and forever, Lissandra."

"Tell me you're mine to fuck and suck for all the days of my life." Her canines elongated with her snarl as she slammed herself onto him.

He bared his teeth to her and his own canines lengthened in response to her goading. She dipped her head down to lick them inside his lips and his arousal spiked, narrowing his attention down to his lavender-eyed goddess. She rode him with her hands on his shoulders, her claws digging into his traps, and her tongue caressing his canines. His arousal threatened to spill over, but he gritted his teeth, holding back.

She pulled back again and thrust hard, squeezing her pussy around his cock. "Tell me you're mine, Denarrion!"

"Oh, Goddess!" His dick slid along her tight walls, sparking more pleasure. "Oh fuck. I'm yours, Lissandra. You have all of me!"

He came in hard, hot jets of cum that flooded her pussy as he thrust in three or four more times. His orgasm burned a path through him, scouring away the last of the darkness caused by the demon, and strengthening the True Bond between them. Her own pleasure launched him higher. She screamed her joy and release at the top of her lungs, clamping down on his cock as she flew with him.

He sat up and pulled her close, sinking his teeth into her shoulder. She shrieked with delight and bowed forward to lock her teeth into him. The world exploded into light and his soul wove tightly to hers, solidifying their bond.

"I love you, Denarrion." She dropped boneless on top of him, her breasts against his heaving chest.

"Goddess, I love you, Lissandra." He wrapped his arms around her and squeezed gently. "I'm so lucky you came out to Redfield for our blind date."

"Me, too."

Humor bubbled up. "Even fighting the demon?"

"Well." She tilted her head. "I could've done without the drama of that, but it worked out in the end."

"But it's not the end, is it?" He ran his hands over her arms. "We have committed to this courtship, right?"

"Yes."

"And the courtship only ends, either with a proposal or a dismissal, right?"

"Right." She tilted her head as he took one of her hands and brought it to his lips to kiss.

"Lissandra Charforest, will you marry me and be my mate for all time?"

A slow smile curled her lips and lit up her eyes. "Yes, I will be your True Bonded mate for all time."

She threw her arms around his neck as he rolled them over until he lay on top of her, brushing her face with his thumbs. This was the woman he wanted and couldn't live without. *Glory, I love her.* He leaned forward and kissed her. As he pulled back, she met his gaze with all her love shining through them.

"I love you, Lissandra." He rocked his hips and his swelling cock against her mound. "I'm yours forever."

"And I'm yours, my dragon mate. Forever."

He smiled at her and eased his cock back into her, moving slowly and gently. He would never stop loving and pleasuring her. He'd courted the dragon widow and found his perfect mate.

THE END

AUTHOR'S NOTE

This was the first story I submitted to the Golden Heart in 2009 and though they only got three chapters, they essentially told me the story sucked. As I've grown as a writer and have published 29 books (this one is actually #30), I've realized they were right. Even I thought it sucked. It's not a good thing when the author thinks to herself, "I'll just skip to the good parts" in her own writing.

In January 2018, I picked the story up again and made a determined effort to rewrite and revise the story. At the time I started it was at 81K, and boring. It took me eight months, from January to August, to rework it into a story I actually liked. It now sits at about 96K and I don't think it's boring at all.

I will say this story started as a dream I had way back when and expanded from there. I've also added a couple of Easter eggs in it if you look carefully, and there are characters some of you have seen before in other tales of mine. I hope you enjoy this story. It's come a long way and it's certainly matured along with me.

Happy reading.

Siobhan

CLOUDBURST COFFEE & SPA
CLOUDBURST COLORADO SERIES, BOOK 5
SNEEK PEEK

*Moira Callahan knows a thing or two about fresh starts.
Second chances are a different story…*

As an empath synced into the energies of spaces around
her, Moira always understood what people needed, and
tried to provide. But after escaping an abusive D/s
relationship, she's ready to make her own rules as the
owner of the Cloudburst Coffee & Spa. Life is good. Until
her first love shows up in town seeking his second chance.

Aiden Westmorland escaped Cloudburst to learn to control
his sexual needs, but he left behind the one woman who
calmed his statistical empathic abilities. Now he has a
chance to rekindle the fire they'd shared as teenagers, with
the flavor of BDSM. But earning the trust of an
emotionally scarred woman after his long radio silence is
easier said than done.

When Moira's past comes to Cloudburst, threatening the
life she's fought to rebuild, Aiden insists she go to the
police. But her former Dom has a past of his own, and he
isn't willing to let go so easily this time....

WILDFIRE'S HEART
ELEMENTAL HEARTS SERIES, BOOK 1
SNEEK PEEK

When you wish upon a wildfire...

Hot Shot Saif al Nar is a natural when it comes to fighting fires. As an Ifrit—a fire djinn—there's no one better. But he doesn't anticipate the local residents being suspicious and afraid of his ethnicity when his crew comes into town from the fire line for some R&R. Add some unexpected backup in the form of a lovely djinn and Saif is ready to set the town on fire.

A djinn might get burned...

Raihana Nejem retired from being a genie in a lamp centuries ago and now works for the U.S. Forest Service. Fires are devastating her field area, but the sexy firefighter djinn might just be more dangerous. Her people believe Ifrits to be evil demons and Raihana can't be sure Saif isn't responsible for the arson fires cropping up in town.

Or they could set the night on fire...

Is Saif behind the arson or is something darker and more dangerous going on? With hearts and lives on the line, Raihana must decide if she can stand the heat that comes with loving a man like Saif.

OTHER BOOKS BY SIOBHAN MUIR

Queen Bitch of the Callowwood Pack
Her Devoted Vampire
Second Chance Succubus
Wildfire's Heart
Darwin's Evolution

Bad Boys of Beta Squad Series
Bronco's Rough Ride
The Navy's Ghost
Rimshot's Hard Target
Bam-Bam's Inked Hart
Deli's Take Out

Cloudburst Colorado Series
A Hell Hound's Fire
The Beltane Witch
Christmas I.C.E. Magic
Cloudburst Ice Magic
Cloudburst Coffee & Spa
Courting the Dragon Widow

Concrete Angels MC Series
My Forever Cocky Biker Encounter
Dude with a Cool Car

Rifts Series
Take the Reins
A Centaur's Solstice Wish

In Death's Shadow

The Ivory Road Serial
A Walk in the Sand
Outback Dreams

Triple Star Ranch Series
Rope a Falling Star
Star Light, Star Bright

Warbler Peninsula Series
Order of the Dragon
The Valkyrie's Sword
Burning Yuletide

Coming Soon
Angel Ink (Concrete Angels MC #3)
Star Spangled Banner (Triple Star Ranch #3)
Loch'd Hearts (Elemental Hearts #2)
January's Viking (Ultimate Recon #2)

ABOUT THE AUTHOR

Siobhan Muir lives in Cheyenne, Wyoming, with her husband, two daughters, and a vegetarian cat she swears is a shape-shifter, though he's never shifted when she can see him. When not writing, she can be found looking down a microscope at fossil fox teeth, pursuing her other love, paleontology. An avid reader of science fiction/fantasy, her husband gave her a paranormal romance for Christmas one year, and she was hooked for good.

In previous lives, Siobhan has been an actor at the Colorado Renaissance Festival, a field geologist in the Aleutian Islands, and restored inter-planetary imagery at the USGS. She's hiked to the top of Mount St. Helens and to the bottom of Meteor Crater.

Siobhan writes kick-ass adventure with hot sex for men and women to enjoy. She believes in happily ever after, redemption, and communication, all of which you will find in her paranormal romance stories.

Connect with Siobhan online at:
https://www.siobhanmuir.com
https://www.siobhanmuir.com/siobhans-blog
https://twitter.com/SiobhanMuir
http://pinterest.com/siobhanmuir.35
https://www.facebook.com/siobhan.muir.35
https://www.siobhanmuir.com/newsletter.html